BIRCH LANE PRESS PRESENTS

American Fiction

BIRCH LANE PRESS PRESENTS

American Fiction

The Best Unpublished Short Stories
by Emerging Writiers

Number 3

Introduction by GUEST JUDGE
Tobias Wolff

Edited by Michael C. White
and Alan R. Davis

A BIRCH LANE PRESS BOOK
Published by Carol Publishing Group

A Birch Lane Press Book
Published by Carol Publishing Group
Birch Lane Press is a registered trademark of Carol Communications, Inc.
Editorial Offices: 600 Madison Avenue, N.Y. 10022
Sales & Distribution Offices: 120 Enterprise Avenue, Secaucus, N.J. 07094
In Canada: Canadian Manda Group, P.O., Box 920, Station U, Toronto,
    Ontario M8Z 5P9

Queries regarding rights and permission should be addressed to Carol
Publishing Group, 600 Madision Avenue, New York, N.Y. 10022

Carol Publishing Group books are available at special discounts for bulk
purchases, for sales promotions, fund raising, or educational purposes.
Special editions can be created to specifications. For details, contact:
Special Sales Department, Carol Publishing Group, 120 Enterprise Avenue,
Secaucus, N.J. 07094

Manufactured in the United States of America
10 9 8 7 6 5 4 3 2 1

Library of Congress Cataloging-in-Publication Data

Birch Lane Press presents American fiction: the best unpublished
    short stories by emerging writers number 3 /introduction
    by guest judge Tobias Wolff; edited by Michael C. White
    and Alan Davis.
        p. cm.
    ISBN: 1-55972-121-9
    1. Short stories, American.   2. American fiction—20th
century. I. White, Michael C.   II. Davis, Alan.   III. Title:
American fiction.
PS648.S5B56   1992
813'.0108054—dc 20
                                            90-1386
                                            CIP

Dedicated to
Cathy and Karen
and to Dorothy and Louis Davis

Contents

Editors' Note

This is the fifth edition of *American Fiction*, the third published by Birch Lane Press. While there are, as Tobias Wolff mentions in his introduction, many—possibly *too* many—story anthologies published annually, few use a national contest to select previously unpublished stories. Such a selection process, though not without its obvious risks, is intended to support and promote the work of newer and emerging writers. The success of this process is evidenced by the fact that many authors published in *AF* have gone on to have their stories included in subsequent collections. Several authors have won prestigious awards (for example, Antonya Nelson's 1988 prize-winning story, "The Expendables," would later be the title story of a collection that won the Flannery O'Connor Award), and a number have had *AF* stories included in published collections of their own (Marcie Hershman's "Sworn Statements: The Map" and Ursula Hegi's "Baby Mansion" and "Saving a Life" first appeared in these pages). Thus, *American Fiction* is bringing to an eager and sophisticated audience deserving stories that may not otherwise have appeared in print.

We are delighted to have as this year's Guest Judge Tobias Wolff, certainly one of a handful of writers in the past decade who helped gain for the short story a wider readership. As he writes in his introduction, "There was a renaissance...a renaissance of readers—close, particular, passionate readers such as were believed to have gone extinct." Mr. Wolff goes on to say, "That's what this book is about." We couldn't agree more that *AF*'s intent is to place worthy short stories before those close, particular, and passionate readers.

Mr. Wolff selected the following stories as this year's *AF* prize-winners: the $1000 First Prize goes to "Breathe Something Nice," by Emily Hammond; the $500 Second Prize to "Between Revolutions: Holiday, 1982," by Laurie Alberts; and the $250 Third Prize to "Bookends," by Valerie Hobbs. We'd like to congratulate the prize-winning authors as well as the fifteen other authors who appear as finalists in this edition of *AF*.

We will close by first thanking Tobias Wolff for serving as this year's Guest Judge, for taking on those difficult duties, and for performing them so admirably. We'd also like to thank our editor at Birch Lane Press, Bruce Shostak, whose careful, patient, and supportive guidance helped us through another edition of *AF*; both Springfield College and Moorhead State University for their financial support and for grants to provide us with the time necessary to complete this work; at Springfield, Irene Graves, Debby Hayward, and Joan Erwin, and at Moorhead, Deb Marquart, for their superb technical assistance; and finally, with sincere humility, our contributors, for entrusting us with their many fine stories, stories which form the basis of *American Fiction*.

MICHAEL C. WHITE, Editor
Springfield College

ALAN R. DAVIS, Associate Editor
Moorhead State University

Introduction

BY TOBIAS WOLFF

The short story has come in for more than its usual share of attention over the past ten years. A "renaissance" was said to be in progress, a flowering of the form to powers unseen since Hemingway's prime—something like that. This renaissance did stout service as a subject for chin-pulling in any number of articles and reviews, and kept more than one writer's panel afloat through a dreary hour.

As a member of this tribe I should probably be grateful for whatever excitement comes our way, and keep my mouth shut. But I can't help thinking: a renaissance doesn't come out of nowhere, a renaissance needs a dark age to precede it, to mark its luminosity. This being so, what exactly was the dark age of the American short story? When did it happen? Why did it happen? Who doused the flame, and who brought it back to life? The truth, of course, is that there was no dark age. I can't think of a time since Poe when the short story in this country has lacked for inspired, original practitioners.

Look at the period following World War II, the time of the story's supposed languishing. My list is necessarily partial and biased, but who could dispute the achievement of John Cheever, or Flannery O'Connor? Paul Bowles published his classic collection *The Delicate Prey* in the mid-fifties. Bernard Malamud's stories began to appear during this time, and

Philip Roth's, and John Updike's, and Grace Paley's. Hubert Selby, Jr., wrote his dark, prophetic hellscape *Last Exit to Brooklyn*. And consider the short fiction of Saul Bellow, J.F. Powers, George P. Elliott, Jean Stafford, Richard Yates, Peter Taylor. This is a dark age?

It's an exercise in fatuity to flog this subject further, but let's do it anyway. Think of the writers whose stories came of age in the sixties and seventies: Andre Dubus, Joyce Carol Oates, Donald Barthelme, Gina Berriault, Richard Brautigan, Cynthia Ozick, John L'Heureux, Barry Hannah, Leonard Michaels, James Alan MacPherson, John Barth, William H. Gass, Stanley Elkin, and the incomparable Raymond Carver.

This isn't to say that the last ten years or so haven't been a rich season for lovers of the form. Raymond Carver and Ann Beattie wrote some of their best stories during this time. Richard Ford wrote *Rock Springs*, Joy Williams *Taking Care*, Norman MacLean *A River Runs Through It*, Jayne Ann Phillips *Black Tickets*, Tim O'Brien *The Things They Carried*, Ron Hansen *Nebraska*, Carol Bly *Backbone*, Richard Bausch *Spirits*, Stephanie Vaughn *Sweet Talk*, Mary Robison *Days*, D.R. MacDonald *Eyestone*, Frank Conroy *Mid-Air*, Howard Frank Mosher *Where the Rivers Flow North*, Louise Erdrich *Love Medicine*, Robert Olmstead *River Dogs*. Again, my list is partial, and pernicious for what it leaves out. I'll be struck with pangs of remembrance as soon as I put the postage on these thoughts. But as good a time as it was, it wasn't a renaissance. The flame never died, or even dimmed.

There was a renaissance, though, at least as remarkable as the one credited to the writers. This was a renaissance of readers—close, particular, passionate readers such as were believed to have gone extinct. It's impossible to say just who they are, or where they came from. One thing is clear; they have found in the short story something essential, a way of seeing life they can't do without. And they've made their presence felt. Only fifteen years ago Raymond Carver couldn't find anyone to publish *Will You Please Be Quiet Please?* until Gordon Lish insisted on it as a condition of taking a job at McGraw-Hill. Carver's experience, I can promise you, was anything but unique. Today that wouldn't happen. It's not easy for young writers to get their first book of stories in print, but I'm convinced that a collection of transcendent quality is almost certain to be recognized and helped along, for the simple reason that there are readers waiting for it.

But how does a reader know what to read? There's a story about Robert Frost visiting a prison in the 1930s and being told by a friend who led poetry workshops there, "We've got five hundred poets in this prison," and Frost saying, "There haven't been five hundred poets in the world since Homer." In addition to the great number of collections published by commercial, university, and quality presses like Ecco and Godine, we now have—or so I'm told; how else would I know?—over a thousand literary journals that publish short stories. At any given time even the most devoted of us are presented with more work than we can read, and more than we can really believe is worth reading. How do we keep up?

We don't. We find ways of letting other people do the work for us. The annual prizes are a good navigational aid. Hundreds of collections—not stories, *collections*—are submitted every year for the Iowa Short Fiction Award. The same is true for Pittsburgh's Drue Heinz Award, and Georgia's Flannery O'Connor Award, and the Associated Writing Programs Award. The books published in these series have been very fine—take a look at last year's Drue Heinz winner, Rick Hillis's *Limbo River.*

I also follow the anthologies. If you keep up with *The O. Henry Prize Stories* and *The Best American Short Stories* and *Pushcart Prize* volumes, you're riding on the shoulders of editors and sub-editors who read thousands of published stories a year in order to come up with about sixty, all told. The system works pretty well over the long haul. But it isn't foolproof. The stories in all three annuals incline somewhat to the conventional, leading me to wonder what would have happened to Kafka, for one. And of course it has no way of accounting for all those stories which were never accepted for publication, some of which must have been good, a few better than good.

That's what this book is about. Now in its fifth year, *American Fiction* is the one anthology that deliberately and exclusively sets out to find the best unpublished stories by "emerging" writers—a loose category meant to encourage submissions by everyone not yet famous enough to enjoy the certainty of publication elsewhere. This year, founding editors Michael C. White and Alan R. Davis read, with the help of their staff, over a thousand stories. From these they selected eighteen which they sent on to me for the pleasant work of reading and the odious work of making comparisons in the form of prizes. Prizes are a necessary evil if you get one, an unnecessary evil if you don't. I have become increasingly aware that I do not read with the eyes of God. I am subject to mood swings as I read. A single word—"relationship," for example—can make me fall off my chair in a coma. Stories I liked two years ago I don't like now. To breathe is to judge, as Camus said, but judgment—as his character Mersault came to understand—is not the same thing as justice. I was relieved to find, in looking through their names, that I didn't know any of these writers personally. My reactions, however wrongheaded, concern the work, not the authors.

The Guest Judge of two years ago, Ann Tyler, ventured to think after reading the selections sent on to her that "Maybe the American short story is returning to its traditions." The American short story has many traditions. If she meant that her writers leaned toward the well-made realistic story with recognizable problems and believable characters and clearly defined beginnings, middles, and endings, I would have to say that the same tendency is in evidence among the writers I've just read. And this approach to the art serves most of them well, calling as it does on the lives they have led and observed, the people they have known, and the things they care about. Valerie Hobbs' "Bookends" is such a story, an account of the way two old people, husband and wife, confront the fact of their mortality. It's a very troubling story, and all the more so for the elegance of its language and the equanimity of its unfolding. These reassuring narrative elements leave the reader disarmed, unprepared for what turns out to be an entirely comfortless apprehension of debility and death.

Laurie Alberts does the same sort of thing in "Between Revolutions: Holiday, 1982." It's a story of Chekhovian form and feeling set, rightly enough, in Leningrad. An unhappily married teacher of English schemes to have an affair with an

American exchange teacher. It's hard to arrange a bed. The squalor to which they are reduced by circumstance disgusts her, as to some extent it must disgust the reader, but then, in a brilliant turn, her revulsion is seen to be an aspect not of any moral superiority or even romantic sensibility but of simple queasiness, the queasiness of the privileged. The writer has used our complacency with the story's form and apparent moral perspective to surprise us into another way of seeing.

Several of the stories in this book show that kind of mastery over the traditional realistic form. Jessica Neely's "Thunderbird" is a fine example. But there are other traditions at work in the history of the American story, fantastic, grotesque, philosophic, mythic, and speculative traditions, and I wish I'd seen more of them represented here. Forms have a way of taking over, as if we owed them something. The conventional realistic story has been particularly urgent in its claims, implying that those who don't get with the program are evasive, dishonest, cute, tricky, and downright irresponsible. Let us agree that this is nonsense. Forms must dance to the writer's tune, not the other way around. We should approach the making of a story with a sense of play, which is not the same thing as frivolity. Isak Dinesen is at play in her stories; so is Flannery O'Connor; so is Stanley Elkin; so is John Cheever. And we love them for so happily refusing the claims of gravity. "It is a night where kings in golden suits ride elephants over the mountains."

I was happy to see that kind of boldness in Catherine Scherer's "Among the Things from Her Childhood She Is Now Ready to Throw Away," a poetically intense composition whose shape is both original and natural, growing from the narrator's increasingly understandable compulsion to leave her childhood behind. And Emily Hammond's "Breathe Something Nice," for which I confess a particular affection, moves according to a rhythm and logic wholly its own. The story of a college girl's involvement with a prisoner who bears the enviable name "John Mace," it keeps leaping the tracks and finding others you didn't know were there. The alternating perspectives deny us the possibility of sentimental identification. The story is very funny without being cruel, pitiless without being cold. It proposes no victim for us to weep over, no righteous wisdom as consolation for losses suffered, for they are real losses. The language is drawn from some private spring: "John. Whenever she said his name aloud it sounded like food to her, a dessert a married couple might share on a small round table, their feet touching." Emily Hammond is a writer in flight, one of those who make us experience fiction as freedom, possibility, promise.

Amen.

Grace is over. Dig in.

BIRCH LANE PRESS PRESENTS

American Fiction

Breathe Something Nice

BY EMILY HAMMOND

WANDA

Pretty hair, the other girls told Wanda, as if it were the only thing about her worth mentioning. And a lie at that. It was like a sheep's, a woolly cap. Every Wednesday morning—though Wanda lied to herself about this—she dressed up to go to the Youth Authority, where she and the other girls fulfilled their college's requirement for community service. Nothing too fancy or obvious, so the other girls wouldn't notice: a skirt and a print blouse, a bit of makeup. To cheer the guys up, she told herself, in case anybody ever asked. Helena in particular, whom she considered her best friend.

Wednesdays, Helena dressed down. Her combat clothes, she called them, baggy jeans, a men's pendleton shirt, work boots—clothes she never wore otherwise. She was truly pretty and every weekend Wanda would wonder what it was like being her, going to a concert or a movie, her long blond hair spilling carelessly over the collar of her coat.

Helena wasn't vain. That was just it; she was so natural, so unconscious of her beauty, so strong and unafraid, tough-talking yet nice.

"You're not nice, are you?" he'd said to Wanda. Such green

1

eyes, they made her own eyes water. "You're maybe like *dirty* inside, right?"

The first time he even talked to her he began saying those things; she could see that. "You know those trees outside?" he said. The winter trees in the distance, outside the Youth Authority, like crooked brooms. "That's how you are, inside. There." He stopped just short of touching her blouse, the place where her heart would be.

His name was Mace, John Mace, but she didn't know his first name was John until long after. All the guys called each other by their last names, Hey Mosely, Hey Swan, so she thought his name was Mace.

She liked that, Mace. The same as the small cannister she carried in her pocket everywhere except here, because she wasn't allowed to bring it in, but she started bringing it anyway because he told her to. "I want to see it," he said. "I want to see *you* posing with *it*."

She saw herself with the mace between her legs, naked, then felt immediately ashamed and confused. That's not what he meant.

She'd had sex before, that wasn't it. She wasn't a virgin. None of the girls she admitted this to could believe it, especially Helena. "You? Wanda?" Helena had slept with only two or three guys (three if you counted everything but); Wanda wouldn't admit exactly how many she'd slept with. The truth was she couldn't remember. It had started when she was fourteen, one afternoon with the guy next door who was nineteen. She hadn't wanted to, not that he'd raped her exactly.

That night she'd sat down to dinner with her father, mother, brother, almost thinking that when they passed her the green beans she'd leave smudged fingerprints on the serving dish.

Little bitch her father said when he found out. She'd told him because ... she still didn't know why. Maybe she thought he'd save her, harm the boy. Tell his parents at least, not yell at her in front of everybody at the dinner table.

From there things just happened, not right away but here and there, mistakes, accidents at first, then more deliberately, like a person on a diet meaning to do an errand and stopping

off for ice cream afterwards, knowing all along she would.
Wanda didn't look the type to sleep with guys, anybody could
see that. She was more the church type, first the Presbyterian
church of her childhood, and now the black Baptist church
right off campus, where they sang and carried on around her,
her in her old Sunday school hat. The place was so forgiving
and peaceful somehow, the room warm as bread, salty,
smelling of people, and although no one touched her—an
oddity, the only white person there—she felt enfolded in their
arms.

The church type, but just last weekend she had let it
happen again. She'd gone to a movie, lonely, and some guy
with longish hair and wire-rimmed glasses (not the kind to
screw around, she remembered thinking, too serious) had
talked to her afterwards, suggesting they go out for coffee, but
they wound up in his room smoking dope and fucking.
Fucking. The inside of her soul once you peeled away the top
layer.

"Hey," he said, "you're good," and she got dressed, never
bothering to learn his name, lying about her own.

She had put on her raincoat, the kind secretaries wear to
jobs at insurance agencies, and walked out the door. He didn't
try to stop her.

HELENA

Marsanne, Natalie, Jan, all of us hated working at the Youth
Authority. Wanda too—or so I thought at first. The drive
itself was enough, five bucks of gas, for which we weren't
reimbursed. "Think of it as a donation," the professor said.
Which is why we had to carpool. So every Wednesday
morning at 8:00, or 8:05 or 8:10, after delaying as long as we
could, we floored it to the Youth Authority, south of town,
south of South Stockton even, where guys eighteen, nineteen,
twenty years old were locked up for all manner of offenses.
Too young for a real jail, or as one of the inmates put it to me
my first day there, "Too good, baby, you know what I mean."

We could've worked at the courthouse, we could've worked
for the Senior Center or Meals on Wheels, had we known. But

the professor had suggested it to each of us individually, how the Youth Authority needed folks—like you, he said earnestly—to tutor the inmates. The kids, he called them.

Remedial reading at the Youth Authority. Except the inmates never did any reading. They played checkers and talked. Made comments. Asked if we had boyfriends, what we did with our boyfriends. What we let our boyfriends do to us.

They talked about what they did to get themselves here. Robbed a store, sold drugs to the wrong guy. Knifed somebody. Lit a kid on a bicycle on fire. "You did not," I said to one of them once. "You just like to talk. You think I'm scared or impressed or something."

"That's right," he said, running his hand up and down the inside of his thigh. Laughing, half his teeth gone.

There was no supervision; an unarmed guard walked the corridors and sometimes poked his head in, nobody to hear what they said to us, or did.

"Look," one of us would say every so often, "so you want to talk about this book?"

There were only five or six books, no other reading materials. "You bring in some magazines, you girls, know what I mean? The kind we don't got. *Then* we'll do some reading," an inmate would say while the others hooted and spit in their hands, his arm around the back of an empty chair as though feeling up a girl at the movies.

WANDA

John Mace wore white T-shirts, only white, Wanda noticed, although they could wear any color they liked, if they could get it.

He had perfectly manicured fingernails, for which he had her bring orange sticks and nail files. He showed her how to do her own nails; she'd never known before. "You push back the cuticles like this," he said. "You try it." She got so nervous with him watching her that she ripped into her own cuticle. "Gently," he said, "hey, gently."

Within two months of going to the Youth Authority she had stopped even the pretense of talking to the other guys; John asked her please not to. "You're mine," he said, skimming the orange stick across the back of her hands, tickling. "Anyway, they're trash, too rotten for you."

She hadn't forgotten what he'd first said to her, about being dirty, the trees.

"That nonsense," he said when she finally got up the courage to ask him. "I was just trying to make you mad. Because I'm here and you're there. Outside."

He wouldn't tell her what he'd done.

"Did you rob a store?"

"No."

"A gas station?"

"No."

"Deal drugs?"

"No."

She took a deep breath. "Did you hurt somebody?"

"Me? No."

He did tell her about his childhood. Father gambled, mother drank. So poor they used bath towels for curtains. One dead baby sister—he wouldn't tell her what she'd died of.

Wanda didn't question him further, though she wondered. He sounded too educated, and the details seemed out of a movie. Still his childhood, real or imagined, made her pity and love him all the more. Sometimes she would pace her room, list the deprivations and weep: the beatings, popcorn for dinner, spoiled Christmases, forgotten birthdays.

He asked her about the house she grew up in, the neighborhood, her friends, school, what she carried in her lunch box. "Did you have a swimming pool?"

"*My* parents? No."

"I thought you were rich." He seemed disappointed.

"Where did you get that idea?"

"Oh," he waved his hand. "We think all you girls are rich."

Helena said she thought it possible that John loved Wanda, although those weren't her exact words. "He loves your goodness," she told Wanda, "you sweetness, your charity."

Her charity. She had nothing but that to give; she couldn't sleep with him. Rather, he couldn't sleep with her. And if he could, what then? He'd just turned nineteen, a year younger than her, and what's more, he wouldn't get out until he was twenty-one. Not that he'd said anything about the future, their future. Yet Wanda actually saw herself—she confessed this much to Helena—as though in a fairy tale illustration: princess in a conical hat, silk or netting foaming out the top, cascading down her back like a ponytail (she used to try for the same effect as a child, a beach towel on her head). Yes, she had just the hair, the face, certainly the lips—tiny sweetheart rose lips. Yes, she and Helena had giggled together one night, high on a joint somebody had given them; yes, there was something tragically romantic about her. About Wanda, they said, as if discussing another girl.

He didn't like her name, that much he admitted. "Is it short for something?"

"No." She hung her head, afraid for a moment she would cry. "I can't help it, John."

John. Whenever she said his name aloud it sounded like food to her, a dessert a married couple might share on a small round table, their feet touching.

HELENA

I tried getting between them, pulling up a chair once. "What are you talking about?" I said. Mace just looked at me, those dead green eyes, and Wanda acted insecure, as though she thought I might steal him away. Then Mace kicked the chair, the chair I was about to sit in. "We're busy, can't you see that?" he said, and Wanda kind of moaned. "I'm sorry, Helena, you know how he is." As if she'd been married to the guy for years and couldn't be held responsible.

So I gave up on that plan and Wednesday mornings I spent just trying to survive. Most of all I hated the laughter. You'd be playing checkers, jumping a king or doing a double jump, and those guys would burst out laughing. For no reason. "What's so funny?" I'd say.

Or else they'd launch into their broken bones-knives-and-guts rap about what somebody's going to do to somebody else when they get out. "I'm gonna get me a baseball bat and slam that sucker, his brains gonna be all over his mother's kitchen wall." That really got them laughing—stories of revenge.

He was different from the others, I'll grant that. He

wouldn't stoop to such gore—it might dirty his T-shirt—and he talked like he'd at least gone to high school, which was more than you could say about the rest of them. But if I had to be stuck in a drain pipe with one of these guys, it'd be any one of them and not him. They're all talk and it's the way he didn't talk that bothered me. He only talked about what he wanted you to know and headed off any questions he didn't want to answer. Such as how he wound up at the Youth Authority. "But don't you think you need to know that?" I told Wanda.

"He won't tell me."

As if that was that. I'd never met anyone as sweet and helpless and naive as Wanda. It used to drive me crazy. I'd try to get her mad, at him, at me, at anyone, anything. "I can't, Helena," she would say. "I guess I'm not a very angry person."

Everybody's angry, I told her.

I tried to get us out of going there. I made Wanda come with me to see the professor who got us into this situation. I had to do all the talking, naturally, since Wanda doesn't like to offend anybody, and besides, she wanted to continue on at the Youth Authority so she could see *him*. She only pretended to hate it. I told the professor all about it, the lack of books, the lack of supervision, the talk we were subjected to. He listened patiently, almost mournfully, as though he understood my feelings perfectly. Then he said, "That's why this is such a vital experience for you, Helena. You too, Wanda. You won't get this kind of education anywhere else in this university." Then he explained to us all about the system—how we're all prisoners of the system, they're just on the inside and we're on the outside, it's all polarities, the same ball of wax, a society built on patriarchal authority. "Helena," he said at last, "don't you know it's impossible for you to drop this course? You'd lose three credits, you'd lose your scholarship, simple as that."

"Right," I said, standing up to leave. I grabbed Wanda's arm and tugged her after me like a rubber duck on a string. "Can you believe that guy?" I said in the hallway.

She blushed and I knew it wasn't the professor she was thinking about.

So it was back to the Youth Authority. The next day, Wednesday, the guys there wanted to know what was the red stuff on my hand. Actually it was all up and down my arm and across my back but I wasn't going to tell them that—they'd ask to see. "Poison oak," I said. "Got it hiking last weekend." Really I'd been fooling around with my boyfriend on a mountainside and now I itched all over.

"I know a way you get rid of that," this guy named Roberto said. He was a big dumb guy, gentler than the others, just got quiet whenever they started their blood and gore talk. "You put a corn plaster on it."

"No, man, that takes too long. You want to get rid of it quick?" This was another guy, Fargo, he was the best at home remedies. "Bleach, man. Clorox Bleach. Dilute it with water and pour it right on there." He snapped his fingers. "Next day, gone. You thank Fargo."

"What's he doing here?" I said, jerking my head in Mace's direction on the other side of the room where he was holding court as always with only Wanda in attendance.

"Waiting to turn twenty-one, same as everybody else," Fargo said.

"I mean, what did he do to get here?"

"You like him?"

"No."

"You like us better." Big smile on Fargo's face, on all their faces.

"Not really," I said.

"Aw, girlie."

They never called us by our names. On the other hand, I'm not sure I wanted them knowing my name. "What did Mace do to get here?"

"Don't know," Fargo said. "Even if I did, I wouldn't tell. That's his business."

"Must be pretty bad," I said. Usually they were more than glad to fill you in, half of it lies maybe, although they never spoke for each other, only for themselves. Inmates' code of conduct, according to the professor. "Did he kill somebody?"

"That ain't true," one of them said. I already knew that—the murderers and rapists were in another building—I was just trying to goad them into telling me.

"Don't talk to her," Fargo said. So they didn't and it was time to go anyway, down the hallway, led by a guard we hardly saw otherwise, out the gate house where this grandmother-type in a print dress always sat behind a desk and wished us a lovely week.

"What'd you talk to lover boy about?" I asked Wanda on the way home. I was getting nasty like that those last few weeks, digging at her with questions and so forth—trying to get her to *see*. "What stories did he tell you this time, Wanda?" It was her turn to drive and my question caused her to swerve. The other girls tittered. She wouldn't answer me and finally I thought I'd done it, gotten her mad. I rubbed my poor blistering back on the car seat like a snake molting off its skin. "Did you find out what he did yet?" I said. "I wonder if the old lady at the front desk knows, I wonder if she'd tell. Or does she subscribe to the inmates' code of conduct?" I imagined her placing a shriveled finger to her lips, Sh-sh-sh.

"Helena," Wanda said at the next stoplight. Clearing her throat a little first. Her soft white hands squirmed on the steering wheel. "Helena? I wish you wouldn't."

That's Wanda losing her temper. As mad as I ever saw her get.

Later I bought a jug of Clorox. It was either that or take a hairbrush to my body. I was getting desperate. I'd gone through a whole bottle of Calomine—it did nothing for the itch. The poison oak seemed to be spreading, too, each time I took a shower; I had it everywhere now. Not bothering to dilute the bleach, I poured it on straight. My roommate screamed when she saw me, "What are you doing, it'll scar you!"

"Don't be ridiculous." I didn't know that for sure, but if there were scars, they would fade. I stepped on a nail once and I can't even find the place anymore. I have that kind of skin.

WANDA

Out in front of the dorms, when she told the other girls she had a doctor's appointment that day and would take her own car to the Youth Authority, she could tell Helena didn't believe her. "Which doctor?" Helena said. "You mean you're going off campus?"

"They referred me, yes."

"They never refer anybody. Afraid somebody will find out

what quacks they are at the med center—as if it's a secret. What's the matter, Wanda? Is it serious?"

"Not really," Wanda said with the cold little smile she'd practiced in the mirror last night.

"Why bother going at all? God, what an opportunity, a perfectly legit excuse. You could've slept in."

"I think we should get going, Helena. We're late."

She took that as an invitation to climb into Wanda's car. "I'd rather you didn't," Wanda said.

"Ride with you?" Helena climbed back out, giving her a queer look, as if searching for evidence of disease. She actually sniffed at Wanda.

"Helena," she said, twisting away. "Don't."

Wanda followed the other girls' car across town and onto 99 south. It had rained last night and was still drizzling, the purplish sky weighing down on the fields like a water color done on wet blotter paper. Underneath her skirt she wore no underwear, as John had instructed, and in her pocket was the cannister of mace that she'd been carrying in and out of the Youth Authority for the past three weeks—nobody had noticed, the old woman at the front desk merely taking their names so she could phone them in to the professor: roll. Wanda brought the mace not only because John told her to but because she wanted to see if she could, if she'd get caught. Of course not. The old woman always nodded at her sweetly, the guard smiling, too, as if about to pat Wanda's curly hair. It was Helena they usually scrutinized, although all of the girls had to empty out their purses for inspection. They wouldn't dare frisk them, much as the professor would probably like that, the girls joked to each other in the car, as a part of their education about the prison system. No doubt he frisked the women he dated, they joked, as a prelude to sex.

HELENA

I was showing Fargo and the other guys the scars on my arm when I glanced over at the lovebirds in their corner. Something about the expressions on their faces. Wanda was sitting on his lap. I quickly looked away. It couldn't be. I almost laughed it was so crazy. We went back to talking about my scars, they were making the usual dumb jokes about let's see the rest of 'em, and I realized we all knew what was going on over there in the corner, the other girls too, but nobody said anything, not even the guys, which made me respect them in an odd way. My face was burnt pink though. I couldn't get over it—Wanda screwing John Mace in front of everybody like this—and it occurred to me I didn't know her at all. Her eyelids were drooping, her mouth slightly open, while Mace stared straight ahead like a dead soldier, the two of them bobbing in their chair ever so slightly.

"How about a game of checkers?" somebody said and everybody got very busy searching for the board and trying to remember who beat who yesterday and who's up next to play. The other girls and I read each other's faces, silently communicating—are you going to tell or will I? Is this it, then, our last day at the Youth Authority? I was about to stand up, what was the sense in staying, let's get out of here already, let's quit, when Mace rose from the chair, Wanda almost tumbling off his lap. He offered her his hand so she could steady herself—a sort of gentlemanly touch—then zipped himself up. She smoothed her skirt. They left. Just opened the door and left. From the windows we watched as they strolled down the corridor arm in arm. The guard approached them, said a few words; they appeared to be chatting. Mace sprayed him in the face with something, the guard bent over. Mace kicked him in the groin then he and Wanda were running.

WANDA

In her car was the shaving cream and razor he'd requested. She'd picked out the most expensive brands—a round, soaplike bar that came with its own mug and brush, and a razor encased in leather—items she'd purchased from a quality men's store rather than a pharmacy or drugstore.

"What's this?" he said when she presented them to him, wrapped in shiny brown paper with yellow ribbon.

"For you, John." She felt herself blushing. "Open it. Maybe you should pull over first." Now she giggled, a gurgling sound to her own ears. Everything sounded that way as they drove further and further across the valley—a churning, underwater sound—the VW's frantic, noisy defroster barely keeping up with all the rain, John's nasal humming out of tune with the radio, the balls of her feet pressed against the rubber mat on the passenger's side, the fear in her rolling down her legs and out her toes like waves. And something else, not just fear. A bubbling feeling. Excitement. Love. She'd been shocked when John sprayed the guard's face, though he'd warned her moments before that he would. She hadn't been expecting the kick to the groin, however. Yet she was glad, strangely relieved to see such violence, including the old woman in the gate house getting sprayed, and the other guard too, and her own leg swinging out from her body to kick him in the butt. John had cursed at her for that—was she supposed to just stand there?—then they were running again and she realized John had somehow gotten a gun, probably the gate house guard's, the only guard who had a gun at the Youth Authority, and then halfway across the parking lot she remembered John's smashing the stapler against the guard's skull, that was before she'd kicked him. John already had her car keys in his hand, he'd asked her to get them from her purse while they made love, and she'd expected him to use them on her somehow, dig them into her skin to heighten things maybe. But no, he'd wanted the keys for her car, which they ran to, John knowing just what car it was from all her descriptions, yes, she'd described her car just as she had the house she'd grown up in, her neighborhood, what was in her lunch box, John being insatiable for the details of her life. She'd known and not known all these weeks he'd been meaning to escape, somehow using her, how would she ever explain this to anyone?

"Aren't you going to pull over, John?"

"What for?"

She shook the present at him. "Right," he said. He was doing sixty now and they were on back roads, muddy but straight roads that met at right angles as if for some purpose, when really they were out in the middle of nowhere. He turned down another road and they skidded to a stop, mud splattering the windshield. "Now what," he said.

"Your present," Wanda said.

He tore it open, ribbon dangling from his knee. "Why didn't you just get me shaving cream like I asked?"

"I got you something special," she said quietly.

"You need water for this."

"I know that, John."

He held up the cup. "Get me some water. Please."

How like him to add the please at the end. "John. Can't you just wait till later?"

He stripped off his shirt. "Get me some water, will you?"

"Where?"

He handed her the mug. "See that slough over there?"

"What about rain water?"

"I want it from the slough."

The water from the slough was dark as coffee, dank, fetid. She slipped in mud and grass and wondered, of course, what she was doing here. Let him take the car, her money, anything; instead, this seemed an inescapable culmination, a love act she had to go on with no matter how it sickened her. "Here's your water," she said on returning, and watched him mix it with the soap into a light brown lather.

"Did you bring the scissors?" he said.

"In the glove compartment." She was more numb by the minute, her life over, college over with, no more friends, family, as if she'd been waiting for this awful time every day since childhood. "What are you doing, John?"

He set the mug on the dashboard and began cutting his hair, crude, ragged hunks of it falling to the floor. "Get those, will you? Throw them out the window."

"What are you doing?"

"You'll see." He laughed and she almost laughed too. If Helena could see her now. She hated herself, how she hated herself; she reached for the scissors when he was through.

"Get away from those," he said.

"Why?"

"Because." Now he was lathering up his scalp, then shaving, glancing in the rearview mirror as though he did this every morning of his life. He cut himself, the blood trickling onto his ear, but Wanda couldn't feel anymore and didn't comment. "Now," he said. "Something to dry off with." She saw him inspecting her blouse.

"No," she said.

He dabbed at his head with his white T-shirt, then tossed it at her. "Give me your shirt. You wear this."

"You want to wear a blouse with flowers on it? Why are you doing this?"

"Just give me the shirt."

His T-shirt felt soft as it met her skin. He hadn't even noticed the lace brassiere she'd worn, though it no longer mattered.

He started up the car.

"Where to now?" she said.

"It's a surprise."

"I bet." She felt in her element, dirty, wet, cold. "You know I'd really like something to drink," she said. "Could we stop at a liquor store?"

"No."

"Where are you taking me? Where are we going?"

"You'll find out, little girl." He gazed at her, his green eyes huge and flaming against his bald head, her flowered blouse buttoned wrong across his chest.

"This is crazy," she said. "Shaving your head, my blouse. If it's to disguise yourself, well, you look so noticeable. Nobody will forget your face, John."

They were coming to a town, no, some houses. Strange, a neighborhood and nothing else, no gas station, no stores. Just a strip of houses on a couple of streets, crummy houses, shacks, trailer homes plopped down at skewed angles, and nobody around, no children, no dogs. The rain had stopped, the sun came out and Wanda felt hopeful again. Either they were going to his parents', or to some friends'. John stopped at a corner—well, anywhere else it would be a corner. Here it was just some weeds and part of an old picket fence.

"What?" Wanda said over the VW's idle, her whole body vibrating in time with the engine. The sun disappeared into a blanket of fog that seemed to almost seep upward from the ground.

"Get out."

"Out?"

"Out."

She opened the door and stood uncertainly. "Take your purse," he said. "And this, and this." He threw things out the door, the mug, the soap, books of hers in the back seat, a sweater. He kept the scissors and razor. The gun, which she'd forgotten about till now, was still in the glove compartment where he'd put it hours ago, wrapped in her scarf. "Now close your eyes," he said.

She did.

"And breathe. Breathe in through your nose and out your mouth. Again. Keep breathing, faster now. Imagine something—something nice."

Nothing came to mind at first. The air around her damp and close, the fog itself a place that was soft and nice, all past deceits and sorrows gone and lost, as lost as she was now. The car door slammed. She could hear it faintly, feel the force of it swirling particles of fog and air toward her as he drove off. She opened her eyes after a moment and from one of the houses a woman emerged, a woman in an apron with wide thick arms, her hair in a bubble atop her head. She headed down the steps toward Wanda who sat down dreamily, watching the shape approach, this shape that seemed to float.

HELENA

They tracked her down finally, after quizzing me and the other girls, and searching her room for clues. She'd taken the bus south to her parents, just told them she'd dropped out, I guess. I don't know what she told them about her car. Right away she got the job at Lucky's; that's where the police found her. She wrote me a letter about it, how after a few days of sitting in the sheriff's office and answering questions, they let her go, didn't arrest her, no probation or anything. She'd gotten on very well with the officers, in fact, making them coffee and answering their phones.

I called her. "Wanda," I said, "you've got to change. Stop being so nice. This experience almost ruined your life."

"Helena." She paused, maybe thinking something over. "Don't say it just happened to me. It happened to you too. Something happened to you because of this."

I felt like a building with its side blown out, both ugly and delirious with possibility, open to the sky. The day before I'd slept with the professor. We were talking about Wanda in his office—I told him the whole story—when he said, leaning forward in his chair which creaked knowingly, "You're confused, aren't you?" Later in bed he traced the faint scars across my arms and back, murmuring as though he understood me now, believing I'd received those scars in childhood. That I was one of the disadvantaged.

I didn't tell him otherwise.

The police never did find Mace, although Wanda's car showed up in some mountain town, parked in front of the five and dime. You'd think somebody would remember seeing a guy with a bald head in a flowered blouse, but no. Maybe he bought a wig. In any case they stopped looking for him, Wanda says. He's not dangerous. He doesn't even know how to use a gun and anyway he left it behind in the glove compartment. She knows all this because she's dating a police officer now and he tells her everything.

Between Revolutions:
Holiday, 1982

BY LAURIE ALBERTS

On the Anniversary of the Great October Socialist Revolution, while children waved flowers under airbrushed Politburo portraits and crowds thronged the Leningrad streets, Grisha paced his apartment, consumed with the problem of arranging a place in which to sleep with the American exchange teacher Kate.

Grisha had promised he'd set something up during the holiday. On Sunday, the last day of vacation, Kate would be waiting for him at the Mayakovsky metro station, filled with romantic expectation. Yet no empty apartment, no vacant room had materialized. Grisha felt as desperate as a man with a fatal illness who has days to find a cure.

Grisha went to the window. It had rained during the night, and the unplanted swaths of dirt between the concrete highrises of their apartment complex had turned to soupy mud. The buildings were constructed five years ago; already the balcony railings were rusted, chunks of cement chipped and fell to the ground, but the yards hadn't been planted and the phones just installed. Grisha knew he should consider himself lucky; if not for his wife's parents, they wouldn't have a flat at all.

17

Although they only lived a metro ride away, Grisha's in-laws had come to spend the night. They planned to babysit their grandson, Vanya, while Grisha and Alla went to a holiday party. Grisha had performed his duty, lugging home extra butter and sausage from the storerooms of the school where he taught English. As expected, Alla had done little to prepare for the holiday. Meanwhile, her mother had come laden with bottles and bags and jars. The kitchen grew steamy with baking *piroshki* and *pecheniye* while Alla slumped morosely in a chair with a book.

Grisha called his own parents in Odessa to wish them health on the holidays. They wanted only to talk of Grisha's promise to visit at New Year's and what sort of meat he'd bring. Although they had plenty of vegetables in the Ukraine, meat was impossible to come by. Grisha shuddered, imagining what Kate would think of that conversation—familial love distorted by a hunger for sausage and ham.

Grisha's father-in-law, Pavel Ivanovich, watched the parade on TV, switching channels to follow the larger Moscow extravaganza with its boring speeches from the viewing stand at Lenin's Tomb. Everyone was interested in how close to death the senile Brezhnev looked. Alla's father slammed his fist into his palm with pride at the sight of the heavy artillery rumbling over the cobbles of Red Square. Grisha tried to calculate how many pounds of meat each tank was worth.

"What would the States think of those big guns, eh?" Pavel Ivanovich exclaimed. "Just let them start with us and they'll see!"

"I imagine the States have just as many, and enough meat too," Grisha muttered.

"So, they're rich in your decadent west," Pavel Ivanovich shrugged. "That doesn't matter. Nobody knows how to sacrifice like us Soviets."

"I'm sure you're right. Nobody knows how to sacrifice like we do because nobody has to."

"Since when have you become so friendly with the capitalists?" Pavel Ivanovich demanded.

"Oh, Papa, forget it," Alla cried, throwing down her book. "Grisha doesn't like anything here anymore, including us!" She ran, sobbing, into the bedroom.

Alla's mother came rushing out of the kitchen wringing her apron, her face red from the stove.

Grisha followed Alla to their room, where she lay, face down on the bed. He went over to kneel by her and touched her heaving back. "Alla, come on, don't ruin it now," he pleaded.

She turned her teary face. "Me? Me ruin it? It's you who're ruining everything. You with your American."

Grisha pushed away panic. Alla couldn't know anything, it was all speculation. Any American visitor at school was newsworthy and Alla had asked questions when Kate first arrived, mostly about her clothes. True, he'd taken Kate on outings not sanctioned by school officials, and discouraged Alla when she asked to come along. He used the excuse that it would be too tiring to translate between them, since Kate's Russian was very weak and Alla didn't speak English at all. Alla hadn't been happy about it, but why should she suspect more? In any case, there was nothing to suspect. He hadn't done anything, not yet, although for days he'd been plotting the possibilities, making calls and running into brick walls.

"Don't be silly," he whispered to Alla. "You're inventing things. Get up now before everyone makes a fuss."

"Leave me alone!" Alla sobbed.

Her mother appeared in the doorway, eyes filled with sympathetic tears. Grisha shrugged as though such female turmoil was a mystery to him, and returned to the living room. Vanya, looking frightened, sat in his grandfather's lap. Pavel Ivanovich stroked the child's blond hair and pointed out the majesty of the Red Army in a shaken, falsely hearty voice.

Grisha had to agree with Alla. He was a louse, ruining everything, and there was nothing he could do to make things right—to feel pride in those tanks, to reassure her, to be worthy of his in-laws' generous help. He despised himself for tyrannizing Alla with his disapproval, yet everything about her had come to grate on him—her jealousy, her slovenly habits, her constant depression. He resented that she wasn't working now that Vanya was old enough for kindergarten, as though it were a willful attempt to point out his inadequacies: the poverty they lived in, his miserable teacher's salary. He knew it couldn't be good for the child, living like this.

There was something unhealthily pallid about Vanya. A green tracing of veins ran across his forehead and temples, visible under the pale skin. And he was turning into a nervous, furtive child. Grisha had noticed that Vanya often stopped in the midst of play and looked around with a frightened, guilty expression that matched his mother's perfectly.

Grisha loved his son, but he did not love his wife. These facts were a seesaw upon which he balanced, alternating up and down: he would leave her/he couldn't leave him. Not that he had anywhere to go.

"I'm going out for some air," Grisha announced to the room.

Vanya cried out, "Papa, can I come?"

"I'll be back in a minute," Grisha mumbled, avoiding his son's frightened eyes, while his father-in-law gripped the child tight in his arms. And as if by script, Grisha, the villain, fled straight for a telephone.

Initially, Grisha was drawn to Kate out of a lust for information. It had nothing to do with her as a woman. She was slight, with pointed fox features and large, anxious green eyes. He generally preferred buxom women, a more standard Soviet version of femininity. But Kate—he wanted to suck every drop of juice from her mysterious foreign life as one sucked the skin of oranges after the pulp was gone. He would squeeze from her all the life that had been denied him.

He never wanted to be a teacher of English though he loved the language. He wanted to translate, to interpret, to travel with foreign delegations, see the world and play some part in it. Every time he applied he was refused. The officials said he couldn't travel for his own safety. They would protect him from anti-Semitism abroad by keeping him behind Soviet borders. International Zionism was, as always, to blame. It was, of course, a matter of the Fifth Question, the space on his domestic passport where he had to list his nationality as "Jew." There was only one time when Number Five could have granted him advantage, and he kicked himself for having been too cowardly to apply for emigration. Now that chance was gone.

All that he had anymore was pride in his command of the English language. Everyone knew he was best in his class at Institute, his accent perfectly British. No one could have such an accent except those who learned a language before the age of twelve, and Grisha had spent half his childhood with his ear pressed against his parent's shortwave radio, listening to the BBC. The English language was an obsession with him, the only thing in his life he had the power to perfect. And it was wasted on eighth, ninth, and tenth formers.

At school they followed the required curriculum—translating the Soviet Constitution into English, preparing students for their final exams. Grisha tried to find solace in his job, tried to amuse his bored students, to excite them out of their torpor. The school was considered liberal; their director's power on the City Soviet gave them some leeway. Yet even she had told him to rein himself in. He'd been teaching Tolkien's *Lord of the Rings*, and every time they came to the description of Gandolph's bushy eyebrows, his class erupted into hysterical laughter. Eyebrows were a code for Brezhnev, a joke the kids couldn't ignore. Marina Vasilievna, the director, came to Grisha and said, "It isn't necessary. Don't risk yourself." And so he made do with the proper texts: excerpts from John Reed's *Ten Days That Shook the World*, and paeons to the advances of Soviet science.

He was sure he'd end up like the head English teacher Ivan Dmitrich, fat, dandruffy, balding, hoarding his treasured gifts from the foreign exchange teachers—Sinatra records, popular novels. He'd swallow all dreams and delude himself by insisting, as Ivan Dmitrich did, that "One can know a country perfectly without ever having seen it."

Then Kate arrived.

For weeks Grisha had studied her like a math problem, measuring angles and tangents. At first she seemed haughty and willful, arguing with Ivan Dmitrich, demanding that she be allowed to teach in a classroom instead of giving auditorium lectures as the head English teacher preferred. But watching her with the children Grisha was stirred by an edge to her honesty that prevailed over caution.

Kate talked openly of American street crime, of homeless

people, and unemployment. She urged the children into
debate—an unknown concept in Soviet schools. She demo-
cratically called on each student, though everyone believed
she was trying to humiliate them collectively by questioning
the dumb ones who were relegated to "Kamchatka," the last
row in the back.

Grisha knew that Kate was dangerous—listening to her,
watching her teach, he felt a deeper sickness in himself, a
growing impatience with his classes, the drivel he had to force
down the throats of his charges, the blathering idiocy of
Komsomol and Union meetings, the constriction around his
own not very Russian soul growing tighter. In the end, the
impulse to confide in her won out.

"What do you think of our Soviet teaching methods?" he
queried Kate a few weeks after her arrival. He sat on his desk,
one leg dangling, while Kate gathered up her texts. Across the
room a poster with cartoon figures invited students to apply
to work in Asphalt Plant Number 198 after graduation.

"They are different from ours," Kate began carefully,
holding her cards to her chest.

"*I* think they are awful," Grisha said, scattering his own
hand to the wind.

Kate glanced over at the half-open door in alarm. Grisha
rose to close it. She was right to be nervous; he could lose his
job, or worse, for such talk.

"You know," he continued, pacing in front of the black-
board, shaping the words in his perfect imitation of Oxford
English, an accent he hoped would impress her. "I find it
painful to watch you teach. It shows me that we teach our
children nothing. We don't allow them to think, we stuff them
full of information like sausages, and they spit it back to please
us. Not even information, so much of it is false. I am filled
with shame when you ask them a question and they cannot
answer."

"They are shy," Kate apologized for them, quoting the other
Soviet teachers. "You Russians..."

"I'm not Russian," Grisha said. "I'm a Jew."

"Oh?" Kate looked perplexed. "I don't get it. In America,
they are Jews and Americans too. It's a religion, not a
nationality."

"Well, here it is different. In any case, it's true, we make our children shy, but that's not the only reason they don't answer your questions. They can't answer anything if they haven't read it in a book."

Kate sighed. "When I got here I didn't like the way you Russians—I mean Soviets—taught. But now I'm beginning to think your way is better suited to your society. What use would it be for your kids to go around asking why?"

Grisha smiled bitterly. "You are quite right. Here it is often better not to think."

"Grisha?"

"Yes?"

"How'd you learn to think for yourself? You must have learned somewhere. Was it at home?"

Grisha shook his head. "My father is a true believer. A real Communist. I learned from him. Some people learn to think for themselves when they see that things are not as they've been told. Most people don't care." He walked to the window. "It's always so stuffy in here. Would you care for some air?"

Kate shrugged. Grisha pushed aside the flimsy pale green curtains and opened the line of double windows. Cool damp air rushed into the room, carrying with it the odor of rotting leaves. Grisha came back and sat across from her. In a near whisper he said, "Tell me what it is like there, where you live."

Beneath dusty portraits of Pushkin and Lenin, Kate described the brightness of advertising and the abundance in New York shop windows. The furred and jeweled costume parade up Madison Avenue sidewalks, subway graffiti, bums eating out of the garbage. Her forlorn refugees at the Center for Immigrant Americans where she taught English as a Second Language. Her parents' clapboard house in Maine, two cars in the driveway, the sailboat they kept on the coast. Superhighways and supermarkets. New York restaurants filled with groups of lonely women making the best of a Friday night. A city full of single occupancy dwellings and little dogs with rhinestone collars and knitted coats.

"I wasn't even that happy there," Kate insisted, as though ashamed to speak of such incomprehensible variety, such skewed wealth and loneliness. But Grisha had heard the thrill in her voice, its homesick rhapsody.

A metal rake scraped on pavement beneath the window. Kids' voices wafted up from the street. Someone knocked on the door. They both jumped up guiltily, as though caught in an illicit act: the crime of friendship. A fifteen-year-old girl in the required brown pinafore, slippers, and wool tights came in with a bucket and mop, glanced at them, and started swabbing the floor.

"Could we speak again?" Grisha asked, leaning close.

"Sure," Kate said. "If you like."

The following day after the students filed out of class, Kate urged Grisha to shut the door. "I have a confession," she said. "But you have to promise you'll keep it secret."

"Certainly." Grisha imagined wildly—maybe she *was* on an insidious assignment as some of the teacher suspected, those who thought all foreign teachers were sent to corrupt Soviet children.

Kate glanced guiltily around as though afraid someone would burst in. "The other day? When you said you weren't Russian, you were a Jew, and I said '*they* are Jews and Americans,' I should have said, 'we.' I'm Jewish too."

Grisha had to smile at such an insignificant confession. "So, you're a little *Zhidovka*." He used the slang for 'Yid' affectionately.

"There's something else you can't tell," Kate continued grimly. "My grandparents came from here. From Odessa. They left before the revolution, because of the pogroms."

"Odessa! But that is my town!" Grisha was delighted by the coincidence. "It's where I grew up. And if they hadn't left we might have been neighbors, schoolmates! It's amazing. But why is it such a big secret?"

Kate lowered her voice. "I think Ivan Dmitrich is an anti-Semite. He's always trying to sneak it out of me."

Grisha laughed. "Don't you know he's Jewish too? It's why he's never been allowed to travel. He'd be interested to know how you live there, as a Jew."

"I live like everyone else. Still, don't tell anyone."

"But what does it matter?"

"Before I came here people told me not to mention it. Especially about my grandparents. They said the KGB watches westerners with relatives here—not that I have any. Anyway, they said I'd be treated better if people didn't know I was Jewish. And I want to learn all about this place and I hear more this way...like in the teachers' lounge yesterday, Yevgenny Pavlich was saying how Jews caused the food deficits."

Grisha waved a dismissive hand. "Pavlich is a fool. He's a gym teacher." He suspected Kate wasn't just hiding her heritage in order to learn more, but that here, where the hatred was so open, so official, she was ashamed. He found the trait oddly endearing. She was no longer just the foreigner with all her exotic freedoms, but reduced in size, more human.

"You know, Grisha mused, "I used to be ashamed too. When I first got my internal passport at sixteen I was stunned when they wrote 'Jew.' My parents never prepared me. I could have been Turk for all it mattered. I cared only about soccer, like other boys. And here was a fact that would shape the rest of my life. I used to hate it, having to show my passport at the post office, wherever, always being sneered at, but now I am proud, actually, because it makes me less like them."

"I'm not ashamed," Kate protested. "I just don't want trouble. Promise you won't tell."

The privilege of bearing Kate's secret, however minor, swelled in Grisha's chest. "Of course," he said. "I'm not one to tell everything I hear."

For weeks they roamed the city together by metro, secretly, after classes. In English, Grisha shouted out a lifetime of frustrations as they were pummeled by the peak hour crowds, and Kate, though hungry for details, tried to shush him, spinning about suspiciously as though every weary traveler might be KGB. They huddled together in cafes, drinking tea, eating sweets, inflamed by the information they traded like high-stakes gamblers. Kate smuggled Grisha a forbidden copy of *Newsweek* from the American Consulate. He presented her with his own copy of a literary journal in which two of his translations of American poetry appeared.

Kate insisted America wasn't the perfect haven Grisha imagined. "We're lonely there," she said. "Here everyone's always in couples or groups. You should see how miserable my girlfriends are in New York. They think they'll never meet anyone. Never get married."

"And you?" he pried.

Kate glanced away. "Me too."

Grisha smiled. He was amazed at how Kate's plainness had changed to beauty in the weeks he'd known her. What had seemed meager before now seemed delicate, her anxiousness transformed to sensitivity. He couldn't believe she was a foreigner. He'd never felt so close to anyone.

On their last outing, the Saturday before the holiday, Grisha escorted Kate to Petrodvoretz, the czar's summer residence. It was nearly thirty kilometers from Leningrad and would mean they could spend an entire day together. In fact, Grisha had no interest in palaces with their chandeliered ballrooms, portrait galleries, and bed chambers where Soviet laboring heroes wove silk for ten years to replace wallpaper destroyed by the occupying Fascists. He felt no elevation in the presence of a glorious pre-revolutionary past nor pride in its dissolution. After all, it wasn't *his* history. In any case, it irked him that The Riches of The People were kept behind velvet ropes, under the glare of finger-waving guardians and The People had to make way for every foreign tour group.

Kate, however, gaped at the sight of the palace, rising giddily before them, its spires golden, its yellow a child's choice, its mass stretching on as far as the eye could see. "I can't believe one family owned all this," she said.

"Don't your Rockefellers have such places in America?"

"Not like this. Now I know why there was a revolution."

The parking lot was speckled with a few red Intourist busses for foreign groups. The fact that there was no line of Soviets wrapped about the palace made Grisha nervous, and when they got to the door his fear was confirmed. A stolid *babushka* blocked their way. She crossed her arms over her breasts emphatically, and gestured with her head toward a cardboard sign in the entrance window—closed. "Come back tomorrow, comrades."

"Tomorrow is impossible. This is a special foreign guest,"

Grisha asserted. "She's travelled a long way and we made special arrangements."

"What do I care about your foreign guests?" she bristled. "I said we're closed."

Grisha's embarrassment at having dragged Kate so far with no palace to deliver made him stubborn. "You know as well as I do who gets preference here. There are Intourist busses in the parking lot. I assume they're allowed inside?"

"Grisha, never mind," Kate appealed.

"Those are groups," the guard answered, pleased with her logic. "Groups are quite a different matter. A Komsomol like you should know such things, comrade."

"I want to speak to your supervisor," he bluffed. "I'll have to write a complaint. This is a very important guest."

"Grisha, forget it," Kate begged, yanking at his arm.

"Just a minute..."

"No, I mean it," Kate insisted. "I don't want to go in."

"Alright then." He was still angry at looking the fool in front of her. As they turned away, he said to the guard, "You've just immortalized the rudeness of the Russian people. You must be proud of yourself."

"Hooligan!" the guard screamed. "What business do you have with a foreigner anyway? Aren't Russian women good enough for you?" She searched and found the perfect insult: "But you aren't even Russian!"

"Whew," Kate exclaimed. "That was pleasant. What did she say?"

"She made the marvelously astute observation that I wasn't a Russian."

"How'd that come up?"

"It usually does, eventually. I suppose it's written all over my face. I'm awfully sorry about the palace."

"Don't worry about it. I don't even like palaces. I'd rather just walk around the park."

"But that's how I feel exactly."

Halfway down the path beside the boarded up fountains, Kate stopped. "Grisha, do you think I look Jewish?"

"Yes, a bit, I suppose, but you could just as easily be

Moldavian or Romanian. And there is something very American about you too."

"American? How can anyone look American, we're so mixed." She began to walk again, and Grisha hurried to catch up.

"I can't explain. Your expression, perhaps. You look freer than we do. You walk differently. We can always spot the westerners, and not just by their clothes."

"It's funny to think of myself looking free. Where I grew up, in Maine, there aren't many Jews. My parents wanted to fit in. My father thinks of himself as a 'white Jew.' He's proud of the fact that in the Navy, no one thought he was a Jew, he was so different from the brash ones from Brooklyn. The people he hates most are Loudmouth-New-York-Jews. But that's one of the things I liked about living in New York. I wasn't a minority. I didn't have to listen to my mother saying, 'Dear, don't you think you should lower your voice?'"

"And here you get to be American instead of a Jew. Do you enjoy it?"

"No." Kate stopped again. "I keep getting reminded. My father has this joke. Loeb—that's this very rich Jewish family, like Guggenheim, Rothschild—anyway, Loeb is out for a stroll and he meets a hunchback heading into a synagogue. Loeb says, 'You know, I used to be a Jew like you.' And the hunchback says, 'Yeah? And I used to be a hunchback.' You get it?"

"I get it," Grisha said, though he couldn't imagine that the hump of her American Jewishness was in any way equivalent to the burdens, the constrictions on his life. Still, he wanted to salvage Kate's mood. "Now, I'll tell you a joke," he offered. "We Soviets are very fond of jokes. Brezhnev is driving in his limousine and passes by an apartment building. He decides he wants to meet The People. He goes to an entry and knocks on the door. A little boy answers. 'Little boy,' says Brezhnev, 'don't you know who I am?' 'No,' says the little boy. Brezhnev is shocked. 'But little boy, if not for me, you wouldn't have this apartment.' Still the little boy doesn't recognize his leader. Brezhnev says, 'If not for me, you wouldn't have the car your daddy drives. If not for me you wouldn't have food on the table, you wouldn't have clothes. Now, don't you know who I am?' The little boy's face lights up and he shouts, 'Mommy, Daddy, come quick. It's Uncle Morris from New York!'"

Kate laughed heartily, then grew quiet. "Is that why they hate them?"

"Them?"

"Us."

"Who knows? They drink it in with their mother's milk."

They continued on, walking the gravel paths through the trees. The leaves were gone, the trees bare, the sculptures boxed up, protected from the winter, the reflecting pools frozen. Wind rushed through the firs and birches. They found a little gazebo in a copse, with spattered dead leaves stuck around its foundation. Kate exclaimed over the graffiti scratched into the plaster: "Sasha loves Masha" and "*Nyet bombi*"—no bombs.

"Like at home," she said, as though there was something exciting and special about an act of childish vandalism.

They took a seat on a wooden bench. Grisha picked up a scrap of *Pravda* blown against the bench leg. "Shall we have a reading lesson, then?"

"You read. I can't read the papers, they're too hard."

Grisha chose a lead article to translate. "At a congress of friendly Arab nations a resolution was passed decrying the recent actions of the bloodthirsty Israeli agressors in which..."

"Stop! Forget it. I don't want to know."

"Here's something more cheery: General Secretary Brezhnev toasted the brotherhood of Socialist nations with Czech and Hungarian party leaders at a reception at the Palace of Congresses..."

"Oh, Jesus. Better toasts than tanks, I guess."

"Tanks first, then toasts. That's our way. I don't suppose you're interested in soccer scores?"

Kate shook her head.

Grisha let the scrap of newspaper flutter to the ground. "You know, Kate, things are very bad with my wife. I find it unpleasant to be in her presence. She complains because often I won't eat with her, I eat dinner in front of the television."

Kate sighed. "Why don't you leave her then?"

"How can I? I love my son."

"Are you sure that's all? Maybe you hang on to her because she makes you feel important. At least *she* needs you."

"I hadn't thought of it like that, but perhaps you are right. You see into me so much it is frightening."

Kate waved away his praise. "It's just psychobabble."

"Psycho-babble?" Grisha shaped the unfamiliar word.

"Standard pop psychology. Don't give me too much credit."

He sensed that Kate didn't like this talk but he couldn't help himself. He needed to have her listen, to know him as no one knew him. "I'm stuck with my wife for the child's sake," Grisha went on. "I'm trapped in the school. There is nothing else I can do. I'll never be allowed to go anywhere, I'll never see anything. It's for this reason I've had affairs with other women. Not that I'm proud."

"Affairs?" Kate glanced up. "With people in school?"

"With Tanya."

"Tanya! But she hates Jews. She invited me over for dinner at her house and that was all she talked of. How Jews are greedy and unpatriotic. How they complain all the time. How can you sleep with someone who hates Jews?"

"The same way you can eat dinner there, I suppose."

"It's not the same!"

How could he explain? Tanya, with her yellow hair and her bountiful breasts, those dimples above her butt, the way she loved his hairy back—Tanya was what every man dreamed of... Yet he'd lost interest in her since Kate's arrival. "Tanya seems so silly to me now. All her talk of her flat, and the western clothes her idiot husband brings her. With you it is different."

"Shhh," Kate warned.

Grisha turned around to see a couple of young soldiers approaching. Nothing, just a couple of kids on a day off. Kate's timidity, her fear, pleased him. "Kate, if I couldn't talk to you like this I'd go insane."

Kate leaned forward, whispered. "Then why didn't you apply to emigrate, when it was possible?"

"I don't know. My parents... my father convinced me that I

would never find a job in America, I'd be unhappy and never able to return. I let him convince me."

"Of course you'd get a job. Your English is perfect, you could teach Russian at a university. You could translate."

"Well, it's too late now, isn't it?"

"There are other ways, I suppose. I mean, if you weren't married, and you really wanted to leave, I could marry you so that you could."

Grisha gaped at her. "For you it means nothing to speak like that, but to me..."

"Well, anyway, you *are* married, so it doesn't really matter, does it?" Kate abruptly stood. "I'm freezing."

Grisha followed her out down the path, dazed. Her words kept tumbling in his head. If he married her...if he *could* marry her...a door yawned open in his mind, a door long shut, its possibilities frightening.

On the train home, a weary middle-aged man with a large tote bag propped at his feet sat across from them. A two-foot-long sausage jutted up between his knees. Kate began to giggle.

"You think that it is humorous that we must always haul food around?" Grisha asked, offended, because he'd been admiring the man's prize. It was no easy thing to find a sausage like that.

"No, not at all. I think it's sad. But just look at that thing between his legs. Haven't you ever heard of a phallic symbol before? God, you Russians are so full of symbolism, but you can be so blind."

Grisha put his lips to her ear. "I'm not Russian, remember?"

"Right."

"In any case," he added, "here, where sausage is of such importance, we prefer to think of phalluses as sausage symbols."

Kate almost fell off her seat laughing. Up and down the row of seats, stern-faced, exhausted passengers narrowed their eyes in uneasy distaste. Grisha pressed his leg against Kate's, flesh muffled by wool, and a rush of desire filled his chest. He'd made her laugh. He loved her.

At Kate's metro stop he got out, intending to walk her

within a block of her hotel as he usually did—it wasn't safe to come closer. They rode silently up the escalator, Grisha standing a step below and facing her so that he could gaze into her eyes. Embarrassed, Kate glanced away at the passengers descending on the opposite escalator.

"Don't bother walking me," she said when they reached the exit. "You've got a long trip home."

"It's no bother. Actually, I can't bear to go home anymore. You know, in a way it's your fault."

"Stop it!" Kate said, turning away. "Don't do this to me."

"Do what?"

"You make me feel guilty when we aren't even having an affair."

"Let's have one then, so you will have a reason to feel guilty."

"Are you joking?" Kate turned to look at him. They were standing just outside the metro entrance, in the midst of the gathering peak hour crowds.

"Yes, and no. All day I've been going crazy feeling you beside me. The way you look at me sometimes, I think you are the most beautiful woman in the world."

Kate looked pained. "What can we do? We can't go to your place and you aren't allowed in my hotel."

"I have a friend. I'll talk to him and work something out."

"But we won't see each other until after the holiday. They've got me all booked up with official plans and ballet and opera tickets."

"I'll arrange something before vacation ends. I'll find a place."

Kate's face puckered.

"Now why do you look so unhappy?" Grisha implored.

"We're talking about logistics, and we've never even kissed," Kate whimpered.

Grisha grabbed her arm and yanked her out of the metro entrance, into an alley between apartment buildings.

"Kate," he said, pulling her head against his leather coat, pressing his lips to her face. "Kate. Sladkaya Katya." Sweet Kate.

"You're speaking Russian," Kate breathed.

"I can't speak English *now*."

Then a door banged open and a babushka emerged to dump a bucket in the alley. Grisha and Kate jumped back from each other like kids caught petting. Kate turned and started walking briskly toward her hotel.

Grisha hurried after her, spun her around by the shoulder. "I'll arrange something for Sunday," he pledged. "I promise."

Three days had passed and still Grisha hadn't found a place for their tryst. He had one more chance to arrange something at the holiday party this evening, although it would be tricky with Alla along. They didn't set out until after Vanya was in bed and Alla's parents ensconced before the television, which was showing a series of revolution-period dramas.

Alla had roused herself and even made an effort to look good for the party, although dinner had been a depressing affair. Obviously, she'd spilled her complaints to her parents while Grisha was out making phone calls. They shot him embarrassed, fearful glances and were inordinately polite throughout the meal. Grisha would have preferred anger, a confrontation, to this meek, wordless supplication: don't leave our daughter, please.

Walking to the trolley Alla stumbled on her party heels and reached for Grisha instinctively, although she'd been mute and sulky all evening. He steadied her, and feeling her elbow through the thin synthetic satin party dress and her rain-coat—too light for this chill but deemed prettier, he supposed, than her worn woolen fall coat—he was swept with contrition.

It was at just such a party that they'd met. She'd been a docile, sweet-tempered girl with lush breasts and a willing smile, a girl who wanted nothing more than normal life: a husband and child, her parents at holidays, a trip to the Black Sea in summertime, a reasonable job where she could gossip with her friends. That first evening they'd circled each other, sharing glances, aroused and drawn by simple heat, until late in the evening when everyone was good and drunk, they'd stumbled upon each other in the darkened corridor, and mindless of the others, clinched in hot embrace. Grisha slid his fingers up under her dress, into her underwear, as forceful and sure as finding his way home. She'd moaned that she adored him, and it turned out to be true.

Alla adored him, filling him with pride at first, the pride of ownership, of belonging by proxy. Her blunt blondness and robin's egg eyes were a slap in the face of every sneering reference to Number Five. And, he supposed, at first he'd loved her, the same way he'd loved the October Revolution, the patriotic songs, the banners and thrill of his own red Pioneer neckerchief as a child. It was only later that her adoration was transformed in his mind to insult, for only a fool could adore what he himself detested: this futility, himself. The fact that Alla's love irritated and bored him wasn't her fault.

"Grisha?" Alla questioned meekly, sensing his shift in mood.

He put his arm around her waist, and pulled her into his shoulder. "I'm sorry," he whispered into her hair.

Alla, no fool, sighed in despair.

At the party Grisha managed to connect with an old language institute friend whose brother, a seaman, had his own apartment. Seamen were rich. They bought foreign goods on their travels and brought them home to sell on the side at handsome profits. Although officially illegal, it wasn't considered the same disgrace as being a blackmarketeer; rather it was a perk of the job. With the brother's number in his pocket—a good chance at arranging a place to sleep with Kate—Grisha drank more than usual, and Alla kept up with him, her eyes following him like a hurt spaniel's. At home, they made drunken fumbling love on top of their matted bedspread while Alla's parents snored on the folded-out divan in the livingroom, and Vanya slept on a pallet on the floor.

"I love you, Grisha," Alla repeated over and over until he spilled his frustration, his lust, his apologies between her familiar thighs.

On Sunday afternoon, Grisha told Alla he had to prime a student tutee for an examination. It made a passable excuse, since he regularly gave private English lessons to the children of wealthy *apparatchiki*—an illegal, but necessary, act of private enterprise, given his teaching salary.

"During vacation?" Alla asked suspiciously.

"What better time?" he argued, already a smooth liar.

The seaman brother had consented to let Grisha use his bed; the brother would meet them at four and disappear for an hour. When Grisha called Sunday morning to reconfirm, the brother was nursing a bad holiday hangover, and sounded irritated. "Bring me something for my head, if you get my meaning," he advised. But the vodka stalls were depleted due to the festivities, and Grisha hadn't even managed a bottle of wine.

Mayakovsky metro station was only a few minutes walk from Kate's hotel and an hour trip for Grisha, but he arrived early. Mayakovsky was the most unpleasant station in the city, a lounging grounds for prostitutes, hooligans, and *fartsovchiki*—the blackmarketeers. He didn't want Kate's mood to be spoiled by waiting there. She probably considered meeting at a metro station sordid but what could he do? He couldn't very well come to call at her KGB-infested hotel unless he wanted to say goodbye to his clean work record, which was required for anyone wishing to travel. Not that he had much chance of traveling.

Although everyone met in the metros, he felt awkward hanging about. The disapproval of the passing old women, the babushki, was palpable: dark like a Georgian, they hissed to themselves, no doubt up to no good. He grew nervous. Perhaps Kate had forgotten? Impossible. But maybe she'd had a change of mind, lost courage?

Then there she was, striding through the glass doors in a rush of cold wind, a ridiculous Russian rabbit cap perched high on her head, her glance anxious as she swept the entry, searching for Grisha in the whirl of passengers. His pulse raced: it was me she was looking for, me! He wanted to prolong the moment, but the *fartsovchiki* spread against the entry walls perked up as she entered. He could almost hear their calculations: mocking her cheap Soviet cap, chalking up the worth of her suede shoes, canvas bag, western overcoat, the odds that she might be willing to sell dollars. A skinny blond boy in need of a haircut shoved off the wall, tossed his half-smoked cigarette into a stunted grey urn and hurried after Kate. Grisha leaped forward to intercept her.

She looked breathless, embarrassed by their mission.

"You make quite a sensation," Grisha said, grabbing Kate's arm to shepherd her past the control booth at the top of the escalators where the uniformed woman checked their monthly passes and waved them on. "The blackmarketeers lust after your clothes."

Kate raised a mocking eyebrow. "And I thought it was me they were after. Am I that recognizably foreign?"

"Absolutely." Grisha scuttled around her to stand a step below so they could face one another, pressing her against the right rail to make room for the impatient ones rushing down the steep escalator steps.

Kate looked down at herself and shook her head. "I'd rather just fit in."

"You mean wear ugly shoes that hurt your feet as we do?" He couldn't help taking pleasure at catching her out. It was one thing to pretend to be Soviet, another to live like one.

"You know what I mean."

"You'll have to hide that hat if we're going to pass you off as Soviet."

"But it's a Russian hat!"

"A hat for a peasant. What fashionable Soviet girl would wear such a thing? Girls with style wear silver fox these days."

Beneath the rabbit fur, Kate's auburn hair looked fluffy, freshly washed. Silver earrings dangled from her ears, and through the open slit of her overcoat—another Americanism; nobody wore coats open in winter, just as nobody went hatless—a creamy silk scarf flashed. She'd prepared for him, Grisha thought with excitement, imagining creams and lotions and expensive foreign underwear.

Grisha took Kate's elbow, brushed her hair with his lips.

"We have an errand first, and then we'll go to the apartment of my friend's brother. The problem is where to find something for him to drink. It's a terrible bother...as usual."

"We could go to the *beriozka*," Kate offered, referring to the hard currency stores found in foreigner's hotels.

"No, I couldn't let you," Grisha demurred, but the idea had already entered his mind. The foreign currency stores were always open, always stocked. For her it would be easy.

"Don't be silly. It'll save time," Kate protested.

"Then I'll pay you back for it in rubles..." he mumbled.

Kate waved his words away. Still, he noticed something, a flash of annoyance clouding her face.

They rode a trolley back to the corner of Brodsky Street. While Kate shopped the *beriozka* at the Hotel Yevropeiskaya, Grisha waited on the Nevsky sidewalk—another hotspot for blackmarket dollar changers—pretending to admire the overpoweringly ugly enormity of the Kazan Cathedral. Kate emerged with two bottles which he discreetly removed from the tell-tale plastic beriozka sack and slipped into his artificial leather shoulder bag.

They took the metro at Gostinii Dvor to Yelizarovskaya Station, pushing together in the crowded train. When a seat opened up Grisha gestured Kate into it.

Yelizarovskaya was a region of old five-story buildings with crumbling balconies and dented cigarette urns tilting by doorways—Krushchev's slums, they called them; in Russian it rhymed. Wilted flowers, rain spattered placards, gobs of spit littered the streets. Grisha had to ask directions as they got closer to the neighborhood, and he saw how the pedestrians eyed Kate's clothes. "Don't speak English," he warned her. "We'll pretend you're from the Baltic, from Latvia. If you don't have to, don't say anything. I'll cover for you."

"But he's a seaman. Won't he recognize my accent?"

"He travels to Cuba and Europe. He won't know."

"This is weird."

Grisha whispered hoarsely, "Kate, this is the best I could do. It's our chance."

He found the seaman's building and entered, punching in the code the brother had given him to unlock the door. They climbed four stories up a wide filthy staircase painted a dismal dark green, graffiti scratched into the plaster.

Oleg, the brother of Grisha's friend, opened at the first knock. He was a lanky twenty-year-old wearing a warm-up suit, an outgrown crew-cut, and a lascivious grin. Grisha introduced Kate as a friend visiting from Riga and handed over the bottles. Kate had done well: a bottle of export Stolichnaya vodka and a flask of coffee liqueur. Oleg whistled appreciatively. "My brother's got friends in the right places."

While they were hanging their coats Oleg opened the bottles and set out glasses. He cut a few slices of bread and placed a dish of pickles on the table. "Drinking is always good as long as you have friends to drink with," Oleg said. "And something good to drink!"

Kate glanced at Grisha questioningly. He touched her knee under the table, willing her to be patient. Oleg raised a toast, and the Stolichnaya disappeared down his hatch. Kate peered about the room.

Oleg noticed and gestured toward a record player/tape deck combination. "Not bad, eh? But I've got something better. Look!" Oleg turned on a contraption on top of his enormous color television set, slid in a cartridge, the screen lit with grunting Japanese sword-wielders while an impassive male dubber translated their dialogue into flat-voiced Russian.

"Vee Cee Arrrr," Oleg pronounced, nodding at his contraption. "Veedeeo. I picked it up in Rome. Pretty good, eh?" He winked at Kate, who sat ramrod straight in her chair. "She's a quiet one. That's the best way with women," Oleg joked.

Grisha caught Kate's pleading glance.

"Oleg, you're very generous, but you see we don't have much time." Grisha nudged him, glancing at his watch.

"Of course. The room's back there. Go on, I'll just watch the film for a while. I got such a hangover I can't face going out. Don't mind me." He winked again.

Grisha led Kate into the bedroom. The bed was double but had no sheets, the dirty mattress exposed. European rock posters hung over the peeling wallpaper. Oleg's clothes lay spread about the floor. Grisha felt Kate stiffen.

"I thought you said he was going to go out," she whispered.

"He said he would, but he's enjoying the bottle now. Don't worry, he can't hear us with that thing blaring."

Kate sat hunched on the edge of the bed, her face turned away. "This is creepy," she said.

Grisha kneeled before her, placing his palms on her knees. "Katya," he whispered, "Katyusha." He stroked upward, over the ribbed softness of her corduroy slacks, resting his hands for a moment in her lap, moving upward over the creamy cashmere sweater under which her heart beat, over her breasts. Kate bit her lip.

"It's okay." Grisha willed himself into patience, although he wanted to push her backwards, to stretch himself across her and grind into her, into the gritty mattress. Kate. Kate. If only for a moment, he would find entry to her life... he would own a piece of it, of her... he kissed her throat, her jaw, until she relaxed, grew willing to forget this ugly room, Oleg's drunken laughter ringing above the gabble of Japanese and Russian, the tinny soundtrack music in the next room.

Kate put her arms around his neck, sighed. He leaned her back on the bed, slipping his hand up under her sweater, feeling the fine lace of her brassiere, and the soft flesh of her breasts. He pushed her sweater upward with one hand, while kissing her abdomen, her ribs. "You too," Kate whispered, reaching into Grisha's shirt to rub the hair on his chest. He pushed her legs apart. Kate arched up to kiss him.

Then new voices rang out in the living room. Kate froze. Oleg turned down the volume of his Vee Cee Aarrr. Grisha held Kate, listening. A garrulous high-pitched *babushka* lambasted Oleg.

"It's Sunday," she shrieked, "and you're still celebrating here in your pigsty."

"Mama," Oleg protested. "Take it easy. It's a holiday."

Kate whispered fearfully, "What are they saying? Who is it?"

"Nobody, just his parents," Grisha whispered back.

"And you, drinking alone?" the *babushka* nagged. "Don't you know that's the first step to being an alcoholic?"

"I'm not alone," Oleg argued. "I've got friends here... they're busy right now... in the bedroom."

"My God," Oleg's mother screeched. "Friends in the bedroom. And who are they? Where did this foreign stuff come from? Borya, tell your son not to take chances with foreigners. All he needs is to lose his visa to sail, and then where will he be? He won't be such a rich bigshot then!"

"It's only Lyova's pal Grisha with some Latvian girl. She must have some kind of connections, don't sweat it."

"Leave him alone," a second male voice grumbled, the father. "Let's have a drink. Enough of your noise, old woman."

"It's okay," Grisha whispered to Kate, "they won't bother us. I know them. I used to visit them with my first wife." He kissed Kate's breast. Kate pushed him away.

"First wife? You didn't tell me there were two."

"What does it matter? I was young, I made a mistake. We don't have your opportunities to live together in apartments without marriage." He reached for her breast again.

"I can't do anything with them sitting out there," Kate hissed.

"Forget them," Grisha urged. He placed her hand on his groin. "Please. Kate, this is our chance to be together. It was difficult enough to arrange."

"I can't. Kate sat up and pulled her sweater down. Grisha could see the outline of her breast where he'd pushed it out of the cup of her brassiere. He sighed and put a hand on her neck, massaging. A tea kettle whistled shrilly in the kitchen.

"Great," Kate said. "They're having tea now."

"Kate," he begged.

"I can't. Not like this. It's humiliating."

"What do you want, to just sit and wait here until they leave?"

She covered her face. "I don't know what I want."

"Yes, you do. You want me." Grisha pulled her close, too hard, desperate now that she'd slip away.

Kate stared into his eyes for a beat too long. He knew she was searching there, and Grisha could feel the instant when she didn't find whatever it was she was looking for. Almost a click, and then her eyes moved away. He felt a hollowing sensation in his chest, an elevator dropping.

"I'm leaving," Kate said. She got up, zipping her fly where he'd loosened it, straightening the silk scarf over her sweater.

"Wait. You don't want to go out there now...it will be awkward. Wait here with me and they'll leave. I promise."

"You already promised. They could sit there for hours. I'd rather get it over with. What do I care what they think? I'll never see them again."

"But I will. You might think of me," Grisha said.

"That's your problem."

"You sound very American right now."

"I *am* American."

"Don't judge me, Kate. Don't you see if you lived here it would be the same for you?"

"But I don't live here. I don't *want to live here.*"

"Lucky you have the choice."

Kate turned away. "Maybe Tanya was right. You complain all the time and you do nothing about it."

"Kate, you blame this on my being a Jew? It's Soviet, don't you see? It's how we live. It is our democracy, the democracy of degradation for all nationalities! You think if you'd found yourself a pure Russian to fuck it would have been better?"

"Stop it. Shut up!"

But he couldn't stop, couldn't shut up. "Ah, you want to be a white Jew too, like your father. But you can't escape, you can only pretend. You'll always be a hunchback, just like me."

Kate started crying.

Immediately, Grisha's anger dissipated. "Kate, I'm sorry, I'm sorry. Is it so terrible to wait here with me? We don't have to make love. I don't know what I'd do without you to talk to. We'll just talk. Don't go," he pleaded, but Kate was already gone. He listened as she fled through the living room, grappling with her coat and the lock on the door. Oleg and his parents erupted into laughter.

Grisha tucked his shirt back into his pants. How had it turned into such a fiasco? Kate's seductive words at Petrodvoretz mocked him: "If you weren't married then I could marry you so you could leave." But he *was* married, and Kate had run off, not out of guilt over sleeping with a married man, but because he hadn't delivered her a proper romance. She'd found him lacking, and at the first disappointment, she'd retreated back into her Americanness—a place he couldn't go.

Grisha put his head in his hands. Unbidden, the Petrodvoretz fountains rose behind his closed lids.

Last summer he'd visited the palace with Alla and Vanya. They hadn't been able to get tickets to tour inside, another failure. Outside, they joined the crowds gathered to watch the turning on of the fountains. Behind the palace, great golden Samson rent the jaws of the lion and the Grand Canal led down to the Gulf in a golden shimmer. Spectators patiently waited for the daily show: old pensioners with their canes, pimpled young soldiers with shaved scalps, gaggles of schoolchildren, out-of-town peasants from villages and collective farms in their shabby padded jackets, their cheap rubber boots. Mingled in between their drabness were the brightly dressed westerners, their pedantic Intourist guides stuffing their ears with accented English, German, French.

At eleven, the first fountains came on. Water shot in jets from the mouths of golden fish. Slowly, more and more of the fountains spurted their water into the sky. It wasn't a magnificent show like fireworks on May Day, but an odd anti-climax. Water, an element, rose through air to fall again. The foreigners grew bored and wandered away, but the Soviet spectators silently stood in their clumps, watching and waiting, as though there'd be more. They'd been promised a show, and they stood staring stubbornly at the gilded statuary, the narrow water jets, the yellow fantasy palace spread against the sky, the red Soviet flag hanging limp, while water shot up and fell, shot and fell. The spectacle was already over and yet went on and on, a sleight of hand as breathtaking and unyielding as their beloved revolution. Their impassive, animal patience in the face of thwarted expectations had galled him: We were promised. We're still waiting.

So he too had waited—for Kate, for this tryst, for the hope of a different future—as though his eagerness for Kate were anything more than an interruption in his boredom, a thrilling show as ultimately meaningless as the rise and fall of fountains, as controlled and preordained.

Red-faced, Grisha got up off Oleg's bed and wandered back into the living room.

"Grisha!" Oleg's mother crowed indulgently. "You should be ashamed. If you never left Darya for Alla you wouldn't be chasing poor Latvian girls who run away like ghosts. Why don't you ever come to see us anymore? Now sit and drink some tea."

Defeated, Grisha collapsed into a chair while Japanese warriors tumbled and rolled across the flickering screen.

Bookends

BY VALERIE HOBBS

Martin takes the first wave, a two footer, on his left thigh, then steadies himself to meet the next, right foot lifted to let the water woosh beneath. It is a trick he has learned from watching the kids with their surfboards, this thing he does on one leg, and he is inordinately proud of himself for having learned it. Couldn't wait that first time to tell Jean, to beg her, like the ten-year old he is in his heart of hearts, to watch as the surf crashed past and he stood steady in it, a seventy-eight year old going on eleven, his wife waving from above, the bright flag of her hand waving. Watch this!

But it isn't pride, not really, not now that he thinks about it. It is more subtle than that, a pleasure of sorts (though bordering on pride), because he, an old dog, could adapt himself so easily, and after so many years of taking the sea as it seemed to demand, head on.

The surf is higher than it had first appeared from above, from his perch, as Jean likes to call the weathered redwood deck nearly the size of the modest house to which it belongs. When he had first gone out to check at a little past seven, the sea was a calm, deep green, unblinking eye. Perfect. But he had waited longer than he should have, waited while Jean had had her—what should he call it?—her little tirade, and in the meantime, the wind had come up.

Also, though he will not often admit to it, his sense of time isn't what it was, so he'd gone about the business of finding his goggles, never where he expects them to be, his one decent pair of trunks, and gotten ready to have his swim, just like every other morning, or nearly. And Jean, come to think of it, had not objected, had not gone to the window to make her daily surf pronouncement. Instead, she'd simply collected her sunhat from the rack by the door, and they'd gone out into the glare of the August morning together. Business as usual. Only this time, with that between them, that little tirade.

At first, he'd thought, ridiculously, to ignore her odd behavior, pretend that he had not been so jolted out of an unusually good night's sleep. Pretend? When had he last done that with her? Ah, yes, *that* time, the time he'd feigned disinterest instead of the alarm he really felt, the time, as they'd said more often than he wished necessary, that his "Willy wouldn't wonk."

He kept nothing from her, nothing. Or there was nothing, after all, to keep.

In his mind's eye, as he balances to take the next wave, Martin looks down from the perch and sees himself against the great expanse of grey-green sea, an old, potato-white man, one stick of a leg raised and wobbling, an emaciated flamingo. He has no secrets from his wife or from anybody else, which is what it came to finally, a blessing in its way.

The sea is cold for late August. Wind waves soak Martin's undershirt, splash at his eyes. He sees nothing then but sun diamonds as he rides the crest behind the fourth wave, goggles clutched tightly in his hand. Remembering, he yanks them on just in time. Then he is ready. In long, smooth strokes from his chest and out through the bone chilling water, Martin pulls himself in a line parallel to the beach, past the markers he had set long before: the wooden seagull in midflight atop the Cavenders' worn roof, the Miller kid's Hobey with the blue and orange sail, then, halfway to the yacht club, that insolent patch of brilliant red bougainvillea that makes him think every time, he cannot help himself, of blood splashed indiscriminately. Farther down, the little beach cafe, what was its name now? Bilgewater. No, that couldn't be it. Breakwater, yes, something like that, or Break*wind*. Now *that* was a good one. He'd remember that for Jean.

Martin feels particularly strong this morning, as if he could swim the length of the city, past the yacht club, the Inn at Santa Barbara with its ridiculous moorish towers, the homeless jungle appended to it like an impoverished relative, all the way down to Summerland where he would emerge, a merman, on some movie star's front lawn.

Instead, as always, when he reaches the yacht club, of which he is not nor ever will be a member, Martin rolls onto his back and begins the long, slow, backward climb home. The sun on his face, on his peeling nose, feels splendid. He will not, no matter how good for him, wear the sunscreen Jean spreads so lavishly on every potentially exposed part of herself before beginning her morning walk.

Well, she is right about that. Right about cutting back on the fats, too, which account for the cadaverous look of what is otherwise, she assures him, a far healthier animal. How strong he feels in the water this morning, how young. Jean will never know this joy, Jean who takes her daily two miles like a soldier, chin up, arms swinging. Landlubber, he scoffs, kicking a high spray with the motor of his feet, hands cupping the water overhead, pulling it down hard and fast past his hipbones.

He cannot understand it still, why Jean had let the girl get to her, when she knew, as they both had known forever it seems, how obtuse Margo could be. Hadn't they decided as early as the girl's fourteenth birthday (the time she made that crack about her mother's "dugs") that they'd have either to fight her to a bloody raw finish or ignore a good portion of what came out of her mouth? She'd not give in. Capitulation was not in her nature, nor, for whatever reason, was compromise. She was clever, and tactless, and rude, and she was their daughter, their only child.

The odd thing was that Jean always seemed, if anything, less susceptible to Margo's offenses than anyone else. And why *that* word, that particular word, "bookends?"

And that is when, pulling himself backward through a cold, August sea, that Martin begins to worry, when he realizes how unlike Jean that action was, that bolting straight up in bed and spitting, *spitting* that single word out into the life of an otherwise calm morning.

"Jean?" he'd said (after the hesitation in which, for just an instant, he'd thought not to be a part of her). And Jean had looked at him then in a way that had squeezed his heart still, had looked at him as if, for that space of time, not long but absolutely chilling, as if she did not know who he was. "Darling?" he'd said and had touched her shoulder, thin beneath the thinning cotton fabric of her nightie and watched a ghost leave her eyes, and then the bright return of anger.

"You heard her," she'd said. "And so did everyone else. Bookends, indeed!" Jean's hair was in a dandelion fluff, as no doubt was his own, and he'd thought to laugh, to remark how apt, after all, Margo's metaphor was. With their thin limbs, their thinning white hair—was *everything* thinning with age?—they *were* rather like a matched set of bookends. But he could see what a lather she'd gotten herself into and had backed off. They'd each turned then to their own sides of the bed, dropped their feet and rummaged around for their slippers. Bookends. Of course.

Well, she should have laughed, was the thing. Should have been the first to chuckle at Margo's gaffe while he, manhood being what it is even in one so nearly past it, clung to the last vestiges of individualism, miffed. Instead, this, this *tirade*. Because, to his utter surprise, it *had* gone on, even as they'd drunk their juice, locked the kitchen door, negotiated the three flights of wooden steps (thinning, too) down to the beach, she'd carried on about how boorish, how embarrassing Margo could be, how it was the last, the positively last time she'd be welcome at a gathering of *their* friends (didn't she have any of her own?), how mortified she, Jean, had been when Margo, out of the absolute blue, had referred to her parents as "bookends."

"Well, she *had* been facing the bookcase," Martin suggested at the first break in which he could wedge a word. "Not being one for the original metaphor, I mean." But Jean had gone on as if, and that was the thing, as if, once again, he weren't *there*. He could not say, even to himself, how frightening that was. It was as if he were, or she were, dead.

Martin dropped his legs, treading water until he got his bearings, the blue and orange sail. He was breathing too fast, pushing too hard. He would do a slow crawl back. He would make himself slow down, though the sudden urge to be with Jean right at that moment, when they were separated by sea and sand and asphalt and all the grass she marched around, had weakened him, had washed an undertow straight into the pit of his stomach.

Something is wrong, he knows that now. It isn't just this morning. There have been other things as well, little things that he'd chosen, in his blindsided ignorance, to ignore: the kettle whistling itself dry, a favorite book she'd claimed never to have read, lost shoes, misplaced keys, beached thoughts. Martin is making no time through the water, blue and orange sail still at two o'clock over his right shoulder. Is it the current then? But no, it is only that in the opposing forces of his haste to rejoin his wife and his caution to conserve his own strength, he seems to be standing, or rather swimming, still. Ten meters ahead, a brown pelican folds its wings and drops straight at the water. Martin, at other times charmed, is momentarily thrown off course. But then there, just ahead, is his own deck, empty as he'd prepared himself to expect, and he touches down, slogging through foam and churned sand to the beach.

"Jean?" he calls, though she cannot possibly hear him, and "Jean?" again when he is on the second landing. He *is* exhausted. He will take the tea she will have made with a grateful heart. But the kitchen door, when he reaches it, is locked. Martin peers through the dusty screen into the familiar tidy darkness of the blue and white kitchen. No fire beneath the blue kettle. She *knows* he has no keys. Where *is* she? Always she has been the one to lock the door behind them, slip the keys into the pocket of her jogging costume as they set off, each on their separate missions. What is she thinking of?

Martin knocks loudly on the door, loud to allow her to come to her senses, but there is no answer. His house has that feel houses get when no one is inside. Martin's pulse knocks against his Adam's apple. Exertion, worry. He roots through the flower pots (third to the left? second from the green one on the right?) for the spare key which, with shaking hand, he fits into the lock. "Jean?" She is always home before him, *always*.

His feet track wet sand onto the clean kitchen floor. He doesn't care. This has got to stop. She knows he doesn't carry housekeys in his trunks. "Jean!" But she is not in the house. Not in the living room where dust swims through late morning light in broken shafts across the braided rug, nor in the bedroom where her Chinese red robe has been flung across the tumbled bed like a clue. Has she been abducted then?

Martin, shaking in his damp towel and trunks, doesn't know what to do next. He can call the police, of course, though he would chance embarrassing Jean should she have gone shopping, say, and forgotten to leave him a note. He could call Margo, but why? And what would he reply to all the questions she would surely ask. He didn't want interrogation, he wanted comfort. He wanted his wife. Well, then, he would find her himself.

The car will not start. It has sat too long, unattended. Nearly as old as Margo, the 56 Chevrolet Belair is worth twice what he'd paid for it new. Or so he's been told. For a long time, too long, he'd kept her up, polished the quality chrome, buffed her aqua and white sides (the original coat) to a dazzle. Now he can't be bothered. Driving seems a cumbersome method of getting around, though having the car handy for times like these, has always seemed wise.

Martin pumps the gas pedal twice, then turns the key again, forgetting this time to depress the clutch, so that when the car starts, it bucks twice and dies again. "Damned thing!" Martin cries. "Damned thing." But the next time he tries, the engine leaps into life, emitting the low eight-cylinder growl he remembers so well.

It is noon or thereabouts, and the entire city has turned out to fill the park, for what occasion Martin doesn't know. Young, stripped down models of the women he once knew are jogging behind elongated baby strollers or riding bicycles, each on the rear tire of the one before, fannies in the air like bumblebees. There is too much color to contend with, too much disparate motion. A dozen kites, brilliant, insouciant, divebomb the grass, children in mismatched shards of neon race hard on the heels of barking dogs. He cannot see for all this, cannot find in the swirl of color and life the one small, white-haired woman in navy jogging suit that is his wife. His hands on the oversized steering wheel are damp and cold. He had completely forgotten about the act of driving a car, and it amazes him now that he can still perform it. Checking his rearview mirror, he sees a half dozen cars behind, nudging him forward as if he were leading a parade or a cortege. Their patience astonishes him. In their place, a younger man, he would have laid on the horn.

Twice he travels the short strip between home and the park, after which, unless you veered left into the city, the street became freeway. Jean's route was always straight ahead and straight back, and always she was at the house before he, teapot steeping under its blue checkered cosy on the kitchen table.

Martin's head has begun to pound. The sun is too bright, there is too much color in the world, he is sick with worry. So when he enters the dark, cool cave of the garage, it is with something like relief that he lays his forehead on his hands, crossed upon the steering wheel. Somewhere, just out of range of conscious thought, his mind has been spelling out the dangers: Margo's mother-in-law, Rita, with the disease that Martin will not name, who wanders into the shopping mall wearing nothing but her house slippers. In the vain hope that she may come back someday from the world into which she has disappeared, her family has taken to pinning labels on everything: *chair, table, stove*. But Rita no longer speaks and who knows if she reads. She seems not to recognize the sound of her own name.

So caught is Martin in the fabricated misery of his thoughts, that when he enters the house and hears the familiar whistle of the kettle, he does not at first register that Jean is at home, in the safety of her kitchen, that his wife of fifty-three years is right where she should be.

He heads straight for the kitchen to assure himself that she is indeed there, that it is she who has caused the dying whistle of the kettle as it is lifted from the flame, and not some wife imposter. But the relief he feels at seeing Jean, his love, pouring boiling water onto the tealeaves in the pot is not reward enough for what he has endured. Or perhaps it is in his relief that he feels the right to vent the steam of all his other emotions, intermingled, irrepressible, that have been building up inside him. "Where have you *been*?" he cries, in the very same tone, military issue, he used all those late nights on the adolescent Margo. "Where the *devil* have you been?"

The lid is placed carefully into the teapot. The hands, familiar as his own, the long, slender fingers, age spotted as are his, rest upon the dome of the pot and Jean looks up, not at him, but through the window at the square of cloudless blue beyond. When she turns at last to him, her eyes are an only slightly less vibrant blue. "I was lost," she says. And then, in the way that she had, self-deprecating, she shrugs and turns away to set the teapot on the table.

"Lost?" He has no control over the pitch of his voice. There is a ring to it he does not recognize.

"Well, I had gone too far, you see..."

"And?" Rita in her houseslippers. His heart has settled into a hollow place beneath his epiglottis where it thumps like the tail of a speared fish.

The blue checkered cosy is fitted over the pot. He notices that his Sambo's nickle coffee mug and her china cup with the chipped saucer have already been laid down. He watches her take her seat. It is an action he has always loved, and just now realizes he loves, the graceful way she sits at table. He scrapes his chair back, settles heavily into it. It could be any morning.

"Well, somehow I found myself in front of Woolworth's," she explains. "Can you imagine? Gazing at my reflection, or some old woman's reflection in the glass, without any idea whatsoever about how I'd gotten there..." His wife's eyes are unusually bright, dazed, with an expression in them he should have recognized from his hunting days. "And I realized I was...lost." She frowns, takes the cosy from the pot, replaces it.

"Of *course* you weren't lost," he says. Shards of glass in his throat make speech difficult. "How could you be lost? You were at Woolworth's, you said so yourself. Half your life you spend at Woolworth's!" It is an old jibe dispensed this time with none of the requisite humor. He can feel himself heating up. He wants an explanation, but not necessarily the one she has. That one might push him, might push them both, into a place he will not allow them to be taken. The sun behind his wife's head makes a halo of her hair, outlines the dome beneath, pink as the damp rims of her eyes. Is she about to cry? Well, then, he will bring it on. "You're exaggerating again. Making a mountain out of a..."

Her fist crashes down upon the formica table with a force that astonishes him. "Do not *tell* me, Martin, do not *tell* me how to interpret my own life. I know when I am lost. Don't you *dare* patronize me." She lifts her hands to her face, making a temple behind which her eyes, wide, gray-blue now as after a storm, dare him to speak. The room seems to echo that astonishing action of her fist. He does not know quite what to say, should she allow him to say anything. Her actions, for him, have lost their predictability, the comfort of their predictability. Will she knife him in his bed? And at once he is ashamed, mortified at the treachery of which his mind is capable, his entirely selfish behavior.

"I was so worried," he says, lamely. "I drove the car, up and back..."

"Of course you were, my dear," she says, his own Jean once again.

They spend the afternoon in separate places, in their separate domains, she in the den-sewing room, he in the garden. He has always loved this way that they lived, side by side, yet not in each other's hair every moment like some couples they knew. In their own domains, with space between them. Bookends. Jean will come around. She will see how the metaphor affirms their existence, really. How in their sameness, they have always been unique and individual.

Perhaps she is bothered by the fact that, over the decades, they have become so like each other, as masters resembled their hounds in time, an unappealing thought. They do look a great deal alike, he and Jean. She is nearly his height, with the same long arms and legs, only she, with her round places looks a bit less the cadaver. It's true they have, well, until recently they have had, the same, even temperament. And they have always thought alike about so many things, possessed a similar, sardonic sense of humor, a droll way of seeing the follies of their fellows. And their own foibles as well, of course. The world, for them, even in times of relative hardship, has always been chock full of the miraculous, for which they have been unstintingly grateful. They do not take a day for granted. Isn't this what's kept them together for so many years, this shared vision?

Coming up too quickly beneath the orange tree, Martin's head hits a branch and discharges a great, swirling cloud of insects. Examining the leaves while his forehead throbs, he sees that they are covered with tiny, white flies. How could so many have appeared in a single day? Wasn't it yesterday that he raked beneath this very tree? He is heartsick. Has he, in his carelessness, killed their cherished orange tree? Martin hurries to the garage for the malathion, then back again, spray bottle in hand. When he has finished his kill, the leaves are wet and dripping, and the flies, all that he can find, have gone belly up. Martin steps back and addresses his tree. He want to apologize, would have done so if he didn't think someone watching might think the old man out of his head. His mood lightens perceptibly. He has gone to battle, defeated the visible enemy. Well, there were some things you could do, others you simply had to accede to.

Take getting lost, for instance. In Jean's place, what he would have done, first, is relax. That's what he does when he can't remember a name he should damned well know, or any one of the numbers he'd committed to memory long before. He simply refused to worry about it, let his mind, like the sea, go where it willed. After a time, the name or the number would come to him, pop into his mind like a gift. Well, that's what he'd have done in her place. But he knows his wife, knows that isn't her way. She'd have... what *did* she do? And how the devil would he know? She told him nothing, really.

Martin drops the spray bottle and stomps back into the house, letting the screen door slam behind him. He finds his wife where he expects her to be, crocheting something lacy out of green and yellow yarn. She looks up over her half-glasses, eyebrows lifted, as he reaches the door. "So what happened then?" he demands.

"What happened when?" Jean slips her glasses off, dropping them onto the pile of green and yellow yarn on her lap.

"You know very well, *when*. When you were lost. In front of

Woolworth's." He has the distinct feeling that mud is caked on the soles of his shoes. Again, the anger has risen in him, like sap in spring, like the sap he is but cannot help being. "Did you call me? No, of course you didn't. There would have been a message." He runs his fingers through the soft down on his head.

"I didn't call," she says.

"No."

"Martin, what is this? I've told you what happened."

There is a buzzing in his head caused, no doubt, by all those marauding flies. And now his wife, with her dissembling. "You forgot the phone number, didn't you? Didn't you, Jean?"

He can see by the barely perceptible tightening of her lower lip that he has hit the mark. But she picks up her glasses, sets them on her nose and resumes her crocheting as if she hasn't heard.

"You forgot it!" He wants to shake her out of her chair, drop her in a pile on the rug. "Ha!" he says, when he can get no response from her. And, then, because he is lost and frightened beyond reason, he drops his face into his hands and begins to sob.

"Martin! Oh, darling..." She is up from her chair to take his face between her dry, cool hands, just as his mother did long ago and looks into his eyes with that same tender combination of humor and shared pain. "What is it? What's wrong?"

"Don't you see?" he says. "Don't you see? You're forgetting everything."

She drops her hands, her voice takes on a hard edge. "I am *not* forgetting everything. I simply lost my bearings. Once. Have you never done that? What do you think, that there's something *wrong* with my *mind*?" There are bright spots of color in her otherwise pale cheeks. He has never thought of her as anything but beautiful, but truly she is an old woman, an old woman.

"I think we should call Dr. Driscoll," he says.

Her eyes widen. She pushes past him out of the room, knocking him off kilter. The deck door slams. He shuffles, a defeated man, into the bathroom to blow his nose, tracking mud behind him down the hallway runner. In the early years of marriage, Jean cried, every month, like clockwork. Now it is he, sometimes for no reason, often simply because he is happy. Well, they're both a little loony. Maybe her forgetfulness is normal, a normal by-product of living beyond the time when one is required for any earthly thing. If only she would admit there's a problem. They could ride it out. They could share it.

He stands at the door to the deck, looking out at the tripod of his wife's stance, the straight back, arms extended, hands braced on the rail. She is stronger than he. In every way, she is stronger, always had been. But never before had he hated her for it, wanted to take her down.

They eat in virtual silence. The chops are dry, chewy. The macaroni, a boxed abomination, has a gummy, artificial aftertaste. Behind his wife's head, stripes of pink and violet cross the sky. Any other time he would have exclaimed, would have coaxed her from her dinner out onto the deck where they'd have stood, he encircling her from behind, while they watched the last of the day's bright sun drop into a purple sea. But now he only chews his chops, pokes through his peas. At last he can stand no more. "I'm sorry," he says with a weary, dogged petulance.

She looks up at him, then down at her plate, no fool she.

He washes up while she disappears who knows where into the far reaches of the house. The square at the window is black now, an ink black square of moonless night. Martin reaches into the cupboard to the top shelf for the Courvoisier, lifts it down, takes a glass, a second glass, pouring each half full. With this offering, he goes in search of his wife whom he finds on the deck bundled to the eyeballs in her down coat. What little light there is comes from her crop of white curls tossed leeward by a sharp evening breeze. He stumbles on the threshold, sloshing the drinks, finds his way through the dark to her side. Carefully, he sets the two crystal glasses on the deck rail.

"There is absolutely nothing wrong with me, Martin," she says.

"I know, darling," he says, for lack of anything wiser, or truer.

Except for pinpoints of light in the far distance outlining the oil rigs, Hilda, Howard, Hazel, which they have hated for years with a shared indignant passion, all is dark, a pool of darkness into which everything familiar has been absorbed, a black hole.

So she will fight it, he thinks. She will rage while he...? If truth be told, he was more than half in love with easeful death he supposed, a Dickenson to her Dylan Thomas. So they were not so alike in the end, not so alike after all. She will not confront the inevitable, will not give in. She will lock down, hard, with the bone of life still in her teeth. Well, that was her right. He intended a far easier going. He will stand it on one leg, take it hard as it comes with equanimity.

Martin stares out into the darkness. At first it is a struggle to define the line between sea and air. He thinks the sea a somewhat darker purplish black, the sky a thinner wash of indigo. Then the reverse seems true. He lets it go finally, lets himself go, floating out into the semi-permeable darkness as if entering a calm, night sea. He does not rush to meet it, does not hold back. He simply lets it take him. He wants to laugh at how easy it is.

"Martin!" Jean's voice pierces the bubble of his consciousness, pulls him back, an errant soul returning. "Martin!" she repeats. "You're squeezing the life out of my hand."

Thunderbird

BY JESSICA NEELY

1.

At first there were lamb chops at the Rascal Cafe. Lamb chops and mint jelly and kiddie cocktails with maraschino cherries. What an odd trio we must have been, my mother and me in formal clothes and Bubby who knew each waiter by name. Grand gestures. It seems we were always calling attention to ourselves. They spoke as though to the restaurant at large, even about intimate topics. Pauses were strategically planned. He lit her cigarettes at the ends of sentences. Their eyes moved around the room while they spoke. We were regulars on Friday nights, always took the big table near the brass chandelier. She wore shades, sometimes indoors. He gave extremely generous tips.

Joshua and Melany—or their nicknames, Bubby and Mel. The very names sounded glamorous when I was ten. As though at any moment the two sides of the room would swing open to reveal a ballroom floor on which they'd dance. He had the green eyes and diamond-cut jawline of a movie star. His suit jackets were made of an iridescent material, like a black opal or the back of a fly. He shimmered in candlelight; she was matte with her hennaed hair and crepe de Chïne pants. Mel always wore flats. She was five foot eleven and carried it like a sphinx. And they were in love. I need to correct one very big error. They were most definitely quite madly in love. Madly, in the way people used to fall in love in old movies. On screen. Behind martini glasses.

Oh yes they were in love. They could not be apart. If they fought sometimes he'd leave her, but not for long. He couldn't stand it. And she couldn't eat or think clearly until they were together again, refusing to let go of one another, like children. Yes they were in love, though theirs was such a public love. Whole days they'd devote to dressing for dinner. Mel had drawers full of gloves and accessories. And though Josh never lived with us, there was a closet shelf of his hats, and hangers upon hangers of his ties.

At least they were ironic, though, the way they'd try on outfits from among the clothes piled high on the bed then look at themselves in the full-length mirror and double over laughing. Above all else they amused themselves. Everyone else was the audience, necessary to the effect but dispensable in other ways. I don't remember one afternoon spent, for example, relaxing in front of the TV. We never went on typical family outings, like to amusement parks or the zoo. For my tenth birthday party I had a live clown act, a champagne fountain with cherubs squirting 7-Up, and an ice swan. That sort of thing. Sometimes, of course, I resented the focus, the absolute self-consciousness of all they did. But Melany Hurley was my mother, and Josh Epstein loved me better than any *real* daddy could. It's just that everyone else took them so seriously, because of him and who he was. And it's just that she drank.

Our last summer together we were always at the track, Batavia Downs, for the daily triple. Mel chose her horses for the originality of their names. Lucky Digit, Gunpowder, Fancy Nun, Scheherazade's Dream, the horse she won the pool on. We'd arrive early enough in the day for Josh to get us settled in the grandstand, then he'd go down to the paddock to look over horses and talk to trainers. At the track, everyone called Josh by his code name, Bubby.

My mother and I would spend that first hour or so seated at our table, not talking. Those were difficult mornings, and I always thought Mel looked like a brilliant leading lady who'd just suffered the worst possible night. Exhausted, frail look-ing, she wore a nylon scarf over her hair and of course her black sun glasses. She drank her coffee and smoked in silence, staring off, it seemed to me, at absolutely nothing. I'd learned not to start conversations that early, so I spent the mornings looking through Josh's field glasses.

You could slip right into that special world, slide up close to anything in view. I loved the crush of flat grass in the center of the track, and to spy on the groups of betters across the grandstand. Sometimes I'd watch the trainers grooming their mares, covering their backs with the wool blankets, all the horse tack. There was such commotion in the air, coming over the loudspeakers as the first races approached.

By noon Josh would return from the mutuel windows with his charts and papers. He'd sit down between Mel and me and lift our picnic basket onto his lap. We had wonderful lunches in those days, big juicy deli sandwiches wrapped in butcher paper, bags of fresh chips and Cokes for me. Then there was the big thermos the two of them shared, Mel two cupfuls to every one of his. And after a while there'd be a transforma-tion: the glasses would come off, then the scarf, and she'd shake her hair around her neck. In a minute she'd be all giggles and good omens. You could see the change in Josh too, in his eyes. He would reach for Mel and pull her close, kiss both her cheeks, touch her hair. *This* was the Melany he loved and adored.

"Monkey Do in the second. I'm telling you," Mel said. "I have a hunch."

Josh squinted at the chart he'd drawn up for the morning races. At the track he wore two pair of glasses—one around his neck, the other for reading pushed up on his head—but he rarely used either. "She's a sprinter," he said. "The second's a mile and an eighth."

"Fine with me. She'll catch up. I'd be willing to place a *fifty* on her. That's how confident I feel." Mel's eyebrows rose, haughty and sharp, but she looked down and began picking up the lunch things. She wouldn't push it yet.

Josh grimaced. "She's six seconds off. Who's got a fifty to toss away like that? Here. Look at the paper, sweetie. Take it."

I passed the folded paper between them, and Mel pulled it by the corner from my hand. "Lady jockey too," she said, tapping her horse's name. "I knew there was something special."

"Not today. I've got a full plate already." Josh took a pack of cigarettes from his shirt pocket and lit one.

Mel glared at him. "Twenty-five dollars for *my* lucky horse. You know I resent this having to ask, ask, ask for money. It'd be nice if I had some of my own once in a while. Did that ever occur to you?" Mel leaned forward. "Did it?"

Josh didn't answer.

"Deena—" Mel put her arm around my shoulder. "You always bring me luck. Kiss this horsey's name. For luck. We'll win you a great big toy, a stuffed giraffe or something."

"Stop it, Mel," Josh said.

"For Mommy. Remember how you won us that pool?" The pool was an above-ground. I wanted one built-in, though it was true I had blown a kiss at the winning horse.

"She doesn't need to kiss the newspaper," Josh said, but I felt the pressure of Mel's hand on the back of my neck, so I kissed it, right above "Monkey Do."

Josh threw his cigarette on the cement and pulled out his wallet. "I'll place twenty-five dollars," he said quietly, "to show." Then he took my hand and we walked down to the windows together, showing off a little, hamming it up, saying hello to all his friends.

"There's no injustice in the world!" Mel screamed out the car window, red hair whipping across her cheeks. "No injustice!" she yelled to the high four winds. "No. Justice. I mean justice!" She flopped back against the seat, laughing. "No poetic justice, or poetic license. I don't know."

Josh drove his Thunderbird fast along the freeway. He put his arm around my mother's shoulders and pulled her against him.

"Let's all wear red tonight," she said. "You want to do that? It's the victory color. So what if we lost, we can all pretend."

Josh winked at me in the rear view mirror and we drove along, speeding all the way home.

On Wednesday through Saturday nights Jimmy Fiori and
the Rascal Quintet played at the Cafe. Jimmy was the owner's
baby brother and a trumpet player. He had a massive crush on
Mel and he made this known, like a gentleman, in front of
Josh. Besides Jimmy, the other band members were dads in
their forties or fifties, adequate musicians but tired-looking
men who, it seemed, would have preferred to play seated. But
Jimmy, who called himself "a man of the moment," required
that the players stand up and sway during certain numbers or
jiggle their shoulders up and down during others. He dressed
them in paisley smoking jackets and pointy-toe white bucks.
Tonight Jimmy was playing "Is You Is Or Is You Ain't My
Baby?" directing the question, quite clearly, to Mel. *"The way
you're acting lately makes me doubt."*
Mel shook her index finger at him, no no no.
That night Mel ordered up a big meal, prime rib with three
side dishes and a second bottle of wine. As promised, she was
stunning in a backless ruby gown. She'd dressed me up in a
Spanish outfit, a red flamenco skirt and black top. Josh, as a
complement, wore a red bow tie. You might have thought it
was my mother's birthday the way she whirled around that
night. She kept asking Jimmy to play special songs, and
begging Josh to dance with her. He wouldn't, though. The
waiter had brought him a folded note and now Josh was
preoccupied. He finished the second bottle of wine in silence,
which irritated my mother so much that when the band was
on break, she made a big point of asking Jimmy for a couple of
dances. She couldn't really have been attracted to the guy.
Compared to Josh he was a jerk with tinted hair. But it made
Mel happiest to be the dead center of everyone's attention.
And she could carry it.
Like me, my mother was an only child, and like me she'd
been spoiled with material things. My grandfather Hurley
had raised her alone, pretty much all her life. Mel's mother
died when she was a baby. Grandpa Hurley had the money, so
he made sure she had nice things, private schools straight
through, her own car, clothes. My mother would tell me she
was a good daughter and that she was smart. At graduation
from high school she won certificates in chemistry and
physics, and a scholarship to study medicine at Cornell. But

her father wasn't sure. Nursing was, in his opinion, suitable work for a woman, but it was also slightly more menial than he preferred, just a few steps up from domestic work. There was a lot of lifting and hand work involved. He never considered alternatives, that his daughter, for example, might have become a surgeon. Sometimes, despite himself or out of concern for me, Grandpa Hurley sent us money. I'd heard that at one point my real father helped out. But for as long as I could remember Josh paid for everything, including our apartment. And it never occurred to me, all the time I was growing up, that this should be unnatural. Men paid for things. Women were beautiful. My mother, in particular, was a star.

I always admired my mother the way you would a screen image, something that came into sharpest focus the farther away I was. I loved her. I'll always love her, but the senses with which I remember her are sight and sound. I can't remember what it felt like to touch her, whether her hands were cold or warm, whether they were smooth. And sometimes now, when I remember those days, it seems she could have been a beam of light projected onto the smoke in the air, insubstantial; you could reach out for her, but your hand would go right through.

Jimmy put some Cuban music over the Rascal's sound system, and now he and Mel were doing the Mambo beneath the dance floods. Josh held a snifter of brandy in his hand and swirled the amber liquid to the rhythm of the dance. On the floor Jimmy dipped and spun my mother, and whenever he bent or bowed I could see the dark roots of his hair. Mel was graceful if a little woozy on her feet. The two of them screamed out "Ariba!"

Josh groaned. "Are you tired, Deena?"

I nodded.

"Come on. I need to speak with Uncle Carlo for a minute. Then we'll get your mother and take you home."

I made a face. "Uncle" Carlo Fiori was Josh's brother-in-law.

"For just one minute," Josh coaxed. I followed him through the emptying restaurant to the back rooms where Carlo's office was. "Tell him happy anniversary when I give the signal," Josh said. He pressed a dollar bill into my hand, a bribe. He knew how much I disliked Carlo. "It's his and Lily's anniversary tomorrow night."

Carlo answered the door on the second knock, first by cracking the door just an inch, then opening wide. "Bubby! Excuse the caution. And Miss Deena!" He took the cigar out of his mouth and scooped me up in a gigantic meaty hug. "You'll be too big to lift up pretty soon," he said. Carlo planted two fat kisses on both my cheeks then set me down. "Look at these legs! Filly legs. She's gonna be a tall one like Mel there. And just as luscious."

It was hard to believe that Carlo and Jimmy were brothers. While Jimmy was all angles and wiry as a rubber band, Carlo was big and round and formal and imposing. He always wore a three-piece suit, no matter the heat or the time of day. And he smoked cheap cigars with plastic tips which he chewed on while he talked. Together the Fioris were an unappetizing pair, and it seems now that if they hadn't been family in the remote way of marriage, there'd be no way Josh would have worked with Carlo. Lilian was Josh's older sister. Tomorrow would be the third anniversary of her wedding to Uncle Carlo.

"Have a seat. Have a seat." Carlo waved us into his office, a dark tight-feeling room with wood paneling, wall-to-wall carpet and no windows. Carlo had been working. Papers and open ledgers covered the top of his big cherry desk. Beside his ashtray sat the room's only source of light, a Tiffany lamp with an emerald green shade which cast every object in a pale lime tint. Carlo offered Josh and me the two plush parlor chairs positioned in front of his desk.

"How are things?" he asked, negotiating the corner of his oversized desk in the near darkness.

"Well," Josh answered. "Things are well. I got your message about the new jockey, Lormeaux. Lou doesn't like him?"

Carlo smiled generously. "How could Mr. Lou dislike anybody? He doesn't know this man. He's simply unimpressed with the jockey."

There were no arms to the parlor chairs and this put Carlo's visitors at a distinct disadvantage. What was someone supposed to do with his hands? I squeezed my new dollar bill. Josh crossed his arms.

"I'm sorry Lou's not impressed," Josh said. "I followed the guy all spring down at Aqueduct. He's as solid as they come."

"Which is exactly our point. Why then is he riding up here on a second-rate track?" Carlo sighed and opened his hands. "I'm just sensing some boredom in this corner. Mr. Lou is not impressed. I don't know. Maybe it's the sport. He's always been a basketball man. You did a real good job for him this season."

"Your father plays a few dollars here and there. Forgive me if I cannot be overly concerned. I'm under a lot of pressure from considerably bigger sources."

Carlo removed his cigar and touched his lip with his thumb. "Lou feels you give Leonard all the plums. He's angry, as you can understand. He sees this as competing interests and he doesn't like it. Especially given the size of the loan."

"What loan?"

"The three thousand he gave Melany."

"When?"

"Last week. You didn't know?"

"Of course not. What for?"

"Lou didn't ask." Carlo shrugged. "Is Mel in some kind of trouble?"

Josh pulled out his cigarettes and lit one. He turned and stared at me while he smoked, but he wasn't really seeing me. I was just something to focus on as he thought. He was clearly stunned.

"You want to send Deena up front?" Carlo asked.

Josh shook his head. I could see such anger taking shape in his face. His heart beat against the skin of his throat. His eyes were dark. It was a bad idea for Carlo to pull this self-satisfied gangster act. I hated it when Josh got angry. He stood.

"If this happens again you tell *me* first."

"It was between Melany and my father."

"Now it's between you and me."

"What are you telling me, Josh? Are you threatening me?"

I stood too. "Happy Anniversary, Uncle Carlo!" I pulled at the dollar bill to unwrinkle it, then set it on Carlo's desk. "Tell Aunt Lilian too."

"Come on baby." Josh took my hand and we left the office.

We remained at the Rascal for four, possibly five minutes longer. Josh shouldn't have left my mother alone for so long, knowing the state she was in. Her behavior must have been familiar by now. She hated being left; she hated feeling abandoned. If you did that to her, she would punish you back. But she'd never gone quite this far before.

She was all over Jimmy. The band never played its third set, apparently. The two of them had gone from Mambo to Samba and were now the only ones dancing, dancing far too close and far too slowly. On our table were the tall drinks they'd ordered, big fruity concoctions in glasses the shape of a woman's hips. My mother couldn't mix. She had no tolerance for hard alcohol. I'd seen her get violent after only two glasses of champagne. Right now she was out of control, hanging off Jimmy's neck, her thigh pressed against his groin. He put an open hand at the center of her naked spine, then gently arched her back. And there was Mel, eyes closed, mouth open, one strap halfway down her arm.

Josh couldn't stand it. He grabbed my mother, meant to swing her upright, but she tripped against him and wilted to the floor. Jimmy bent down to help her, but Josh punched him squarely in the jaw. Then Carlo was behind him, holding Josh back. "Don't you touch my brother. You hear me? You hear me, Joshua! Let it go."

I ran to my mother. We had to get out of there. I pulled her hand, tried to drag her. Josh was straining against Carlo's grip. "Get up!" I yelled. "Let's get out of here. You're drunk!"

My mother's face tilted up towards me. Her mouth was puffy, unusually red; she could not focus her eyes. "Young lady," she said thickly, "don't you *ever* use that tone of voice with me." And then I felt her heavy open slap crack across my cheek, and heard Josh cry as Melany passed out.

The few remaining patrons in the restaurant called for waiters to bring their checks. Jimmy brushed off his jacket and walked out the back. Someone, maybe Jimmy, had the sense to turn off the music, but the dance light was left on to sweep the floor in irregular patterns. I sat on the floor not knowing what to do. The gears in the head of the light clicked as it rotated. Carlo helped Josh carry my mother to the car. Then Josh came back for me and we went home.

It would happen this way for a weekend or a few days. It had happened just like this before. When she awoke she wouldn't remember anything, or if she remembered, she wouldn't want to know the details. So we would bring her soothing things, aspirin and ice, and open a window for a breeze. And we'd tell her how much we loved her. Sometimes I'd sit at the foot of the bed, sometimes Josh would read, propped up next to her. Ginger ale, warm. Saltines on the second day. She was always so sorry, so repentant. She would cry into the blankets or against the back of my neck. Sometimes she said she wanted to die; but no, we'd say, you'll be feeling well. Pretty soon you'll be okay. And then when she was finally well there would be the jokes, wicked and dark. She and Josh would compete for the funniest rendition, which of them could turn the awful event into the wittiest tale. The best lie was the most far-fetched. And by the time she was up, had a shower, was ready for a meal, we were all quite willing to believe in the glossy comic version. It made things acceptable. Nothing was broken or irreparably harmed.

That last night at the Rascal, though, was when things changed. To begin with, my mother had never hit me before, and second, she wanted to be left alone. Mel didn't want our help that weekend. She didn't know when she'd call. My mother was in misery, purely that, and it was better all around for us to leave.

I stayed with Josh Saturday, Sunday, half of Monday. Josh's condo was a palace to me. It was small but elegant, the only home I'd ever seen that was decorated by an interior designer. The pull-out sofabed on which I slept was done in crushed velvet, forest green, with a matching ottoman. There were twin pictures of matadors on the walls, a brass sword, a smoky glass mirror hung above the dining room table. One of the complex extras was a cleaning service that came regularly. So the apartment was always spotless, as I remember it, pillows lined symmetrically on the backrest of the couch, each brandy snifter clean though never used. The only room Josh really lived in was the back bedroom which doubled as his office. There, at a round Formica table in front of the window, Bubby put on his thick reading glasses and calculated and tabulated and talked on the phone, and spent all the hours he wasn't with us.

I loved being there with him. I loved the opulence of his

furniture, the free rein I had of the place. I could eat all the candy and gum I wanted. There was a big lap pool with lounge chairs in the complex, and I spent the afternoons swimming or sunning, pretending this was Rio or the Caribbean and that I was, of course, someone very famous. In the evenings Josh took me out to Carrols for burgers and chocolate shakes. Then we went to see movies, one night a Katherine Hepburn film, the other *That Darn Cat* with Dean Jones and Hayley Mills.

It was always fun with him. I always felt secure. In fact, the best feelings of my life would be those late afternoons when I'd come in from the pool and have showered, then put on clean clothes. I'd sit on Josh's terrace and sip a soft drink, my skin still hot from the sun, the soda cool and fizzy. I could hear a lawn mower humming in the distance, and smell the freshly cut grass. Everything seemed to move in slow motion in the orange light with gentleness.

By mid-afternoon on Sunday my shoulders were beginning to burn and I went inside to get a shirt. I unlocked the apartment door and opened it carefully, as I always did, so that I would not disturb Josh's work. He was talking to someone, probably Leonard.

Leonard was a voice on the phone, Josh's boss, the man for whom he organized big bets. When Josh talked to Leonard it was always about business, in a quiet voice, in short conversations. So it surprised me, standing just inside the apartment that Sunday, to recognize the tone in Josh's voice.

"She's buying a car," he said loudly. "She wants a brand new car to drive to Florida, and she's paying off all—I don't know! She wants to be with her father. It's ah, it's all become a problem. And she blames me—" Josh's voice cracked. He coughed. "But I'm in love with this woman, Leonard. I can take care of her." And then his voice broke altogether. "She's going to take Deena."

On Monday afternoon Josh drove me home. He didn't argue with my mother when he saw she'd begun packing, that the living room was clogged with boxes and that there were piles of our clothes in the hall, summer, winter, things to give away. Mel kissed me and asked me to go to my room for a minute. I turned to go, but Josh said, "No. Please don't do this, Melany."

There were dark spots under Mel's eyes. I noticed then that the curtains were drawn. She must have been working through the night, not conscious of the time. She looked too thin, she looked unwell, but her hair was freshly washed and combed. She had put on lipstick. There was an almost ethereal elegance to her. "Please understand," she told Josh calmly, as though he were a stranger.

"Understand what?" He stared at her eyes, waiting for the first sign of a joke, a flash of humor—it had been only a couple of days, after all—but her eyes were blank. There was nothing there. "How long have you been planning this, Mel? Why didn't you talk to me, tell me?"

"I need to do this," she said simply. It frightened me the way she gazed ahead like a statue. I moved toward the doorway, toward Josh.

"Look," he said, "you are in no condition to go anyplace right now. Why don't you lie down, Mel." Josh reached for her shoulder, but she took a step back.

"I have to take care of myself. Please leave, now."

"You can't take Deena. I won't let you." Josh put his arms around me and pulled me against his chest.

"You have no say in the matter, Joshua."

"You can't *do* this!"

Mel looked straight at the two of us. "She's my daughter."

I felt Josh let go of me then. He turned away, didn't kiss me goodbye or try one more tactic. Josh walked quietly out the front door, got into his Thunderbird and drove away. I did not see him again for almost five months, until after my mother had died.

2.

Pompano Beach was hot and windy and foreign. My grandfather lived in the center of it, on Northeast 10th Avenue in a high pale building with dozens of floors and dozens of balconies and perfectly tended flower boxes all alike. This building was called "The Towers," because my grandfather had originally planned on there being two of them. But money ran thin somewhere before the plumbing went into the first, and Grandpa Hurley, being a man who knew to cut his losses early, decided one high-rise would be suitable. But there remained the problem of the name. "The Tower" seemed pompous in his estimation, as though this were *the* only complex with thirty-seven floors west of US 1. "The Towers," on the other hand, had a generous tenor. So my grandfather kept the name.

If he had asked for help, I could have thought up better names, like "The Birth of Venus Building" or "The Big Sand Castle." The high-rise was washed-out pink, the exact color of local beaches, with embedded pink crystals which sparkled and winked at certain times of day. It looked as though the building had sprung up spontaneously from the ocean floor, and as though the beaches themselves had been created by rub-off from the building's granite wings. The world was so out of proportion at The Towers. Everything was high up. Trees were just brown stalks from my perspective. You had to peer twenty feet into the air to see the tops of anything. The sun was far too bright, it made me feel floaty and insubstantial, and no matter how hard I listened, I could never hear any music. Instead, in the evenings I'd be kept awake by the crisp racket of palm leaves rustling against one another in the wind, like thick pieces of paper. Who knows why my grandfather chose Pompano Beach to build his retirement palace. He'd lived there ever since I was born.

Warren Hurley was a fearsome man in my eyes, someone who loved us enormously but who disapproved in a silent censuring way of almost everything Mel did—including having me, I occasionally thought. He acknowledged birthdays and the major holidays, but he had visited only a handful of times, and each visit ended with his stomping off in a torrential fury. So I saw him rarely. Instead, he sent me post cards and packages from around the world. My grandfather travelled at least once a year. He was drawn to rugged places with mystique and lore, like Anchorage or Oaxaca, Mexico. His presents would arrive half-squashed, the brown paper torn and plastered with exotic stamps and ink markings. Inside were the most wonderful gifts. An Eskimo doll with a real fur parka or a keychain from someplace in Australia with a genuine crocodile tooth attached. Grandpa was so large and powerful, I would have made a living myth of the man had it not been for the horrible fights.

I later understood that Josh was the real source of animosity between Mel and my grandfather. Grandpa hated Josh, or the idea of Josh, or the fact that he supported us. Mel told me that although she had been with Josh since I was a baby, Grandfather hadn't bothered to meet him more than once. But in Mel's versions of things, her father had never approved of *anything* she'd done, or *any* man she'd loved, including my real father, who she referred to rarely but always as "a mistake." The point was, Grandfather had never approved. And the point was, my mother longed for his approval all her life.

Yet I knew there was another side to my grandfather. Years ago when my mother was growing up, Grandpa had been regarded as a highly ingenious man. He made his money in the automotive industry, designing heating and cooling systems for Chrysler-Plymouth, then Chevrolet. He was quick, he had a mechanical intelligence and understood the internal workings of machines. When I was very young I had watched him replace cords on old vacuums or coils in space heaters which Mel had earmarked for the dump. It was as though he respected the spirit of an appliance—but then, I was four at the time and the whole world with all its objects seemed animated to me. Still, he had been gentle.

I never met my grandmother, whose death, Mel told me, Grandpa Hurley hardly mourned. He invested in Florida real estate shortly after she died. It seems she'd been the only reason they remained in Upstate New York for as many years as they had. His investments grew.

My grandfather was a big man, six feet three inches tall. He drove big cars with fins and hood ornaments long after such things were popular. He didn't trust small cars. "If you're hit, the entire front end will rumple like a tin can," he'd told Melany the year she wanted the first of the Volkswagon lot. So instead, on discount, he bought her a Chevy Impala, mud green and long as half a city block. "You could be in the center of an earthquake in this vehicle," he told Mel, "and perhaps you'd think you had a flat." Mel always had trouble parking that car. She'd bump against things, other cars, the sides of houses; she'd scratch off the finish on garage doors or in bushes. She didn't care. The car was ugly and she hated it. But it wouldn't die. She could deny it water on ninety degree days or leave the lights on overnight in sub-zero weather. The Impala had its own willpower.

Until it disappeared. One afternoon when we were with Josh, she'd left the car parked on the street with the keys in the ignition. Someone must have stolen it.

So we were without a car for a long time until my mother borrowed money from Uncle Carlo's father and bought herself a Fiat to drive down the Atlantic Coast. The car was not only small, it wasn't American, and she had it painted her favorite color, orange, for the trip. The Fiat was so tiny all we could fit inside was an overnight bag. The rest of our things we shipped UPS. Mel touched up her hair with a new henna rinse and had it cut short with Cleopatra bangs. She drove straight down the coast for nearly three days, flirting with motel owners and gas boys all the way. At her side, wedged between our bucket seats, she kept her thermos filled daily. Mel never drank to the point of drunkenness; she just kept the edge. And she was exuberant, pulling in, running up the lawn of The Towers to meet her father. Naturally Grandfather saw the car as an affront to common sense and evidence of Mel's desperation. "You're in bad shape," he said as he took away her keys. "You can't make your own decisions now, Melly. I'm going to have to make them for you." My mother did not disagree. The following afternoon she checked into a clinic in Lauderdale for alcohol rehabilitation, and she stayed there full-time for two months.

It was the first week in September. Soon I would begin at my new school. Mel came home for weekends now, though she wasn't feeling very sociable. Grandfather said it would be good for her to get some air and light, she had no tan. This was part of his new enthusiastic regimen—exercise and outside air. The best Mel would do, though, is sit up in a lawn chair on his eighth-floor balcony, wrapped in a white blanket, and stare down at the two of us.

We were at the pool. It was early, seven in the morning. I was in my bathing suit, listening to Grandpa talk while he cleaned the filter and poured chemicals into the water, waited to test the pH. Soon the sun would creep forward, warming up the grass, then the cement patio and finally the water. But at seven A.M. the pavement beneath my beach towel was cold. I had goosebumps on my arms and shoulders.

This morning he was giving me a sermon on gambling. He told me he had never been to the dog tracks or to see the jai alai games, though plenty of his friends did. Around there people would bet on anything, shuffle board, lawn bowling, TV sports, any subject. But none of this could disguise the fact that gambling was a disease, he said.

Grandpa had a funny way of clenching his cigarette between his teeth while he talked, as though it were the stem of a pipe. The smoke drifted upward in a straight thick line, and as a result, he had to close one eye to keep it from tearing up.

"Now I've got something for you Deena." He reached into his pocket and came out with a palmful of half dollars which he tossed into the deep end of the pool. "You can have all of these—there's five dollars in that water—but you have to dive for me."

He smiled. This was to be a game, but I had no desire to dive into that freezing water so early in the morning. "Go on. Don't be a crybaby."

"I'm not," I said, "it's just cold."

"Oh go on. It's good practice." He grinned.

I stood with my toes gripping the gritty edge of the pool and took deep breaths. The breeze sent a slight ripple across the surface which made the coins, magnified by the twelve feet of water, seem to undulate in their depths. I was a good swimmer, but I'd never touched the bottom of his pool.

"Go on." Grandpa flicked his half-smoked cigarette into the grass. "You can spend them any way you like."

I looked up at the high distant figure of my mother, staring over the balcony railing, wrapped up like a skeleton.

"Five, four, three, Deena, two—"

I dove—it was like being slapped in the face. The momentum of my jump carried me far, but not deep enough to reach even one of those half dollars. I pushed the water from my face. My eardrums were squeezed by the pressure. I pushed farther down. I could see one coin, but there was not enough sunlight to make out its face. Was it heads or tails? And then quite suddenly I had to have air, but I had no sense of how far down I'd made it. I pulled myself upright, felt for the bottom with my foot. My toe touched it! And I plowed up, gasping for air.

"You're not getting the most out of your dive, Deena." Grandpa leaned over the edge of the pool, his big face two inches from mine, and shook his head. "you need to put your hands together to make a point that'll slice the water. Like this." He lined up his fingers as though he were praying and held his hands over his head.

I got out of the pool, dripping, and shook the water from my ears.

"It's a skill," he said. He put his hand on the back of my neck and massaged it. His hand was large and warm. "Catch your breath then try again."

I dove in the position he'd shown me, and this time I came up with a coin. I was ecstatic and dizzy, and I had no confidence that I could get the other nine.

My grandfather applauded. "Very good," he said. "The truth is that after a while a gambler becomes powerless against his vice. It's an illness just like drinking."

The morning wore on this way, me practicing dives in between feeling dizzy and determined, Grandpa pontificating about the evils of organized gambling. I knew that indirectly he was lecturing me about Josh, but I didn't want to hear about that, so I just let him talk and focused on the silver half dollars and what I would buy with ten of them. Occasionally I'd look up at Mel and wave my arms or call to her, but she just stared off into space and didn't respond. Soon others from the building would come outside with their cups of coffee and morning newspapers. There were four coins left when my grandfather said, "You know I hold that fellow responsible, don't you?"

I looked up at Grandfather but didn't say anything.

"Every man has an inalienable right to make trouble for himself. If he craves disaster, he'll find it." Grandfather touched my chin. "But you are here with me now, both of you. I'm going to take care of you, Deena. I promise. This time I will. And you will no longer be influenced by that—that—Jew."

By late autumn my mother said she was fully rehabilitated and that she didn't even need the meetings anymore. She started staying away, going for long drives, she said, up and down the coast to familiarize herself with the area and get used to our new home. I didn't know, of course, where my mother really went in her car all day and often into the nights. She was well and quiet; I was in fifth grade in a new school making new friends. I didn't want much to do with her, and she seemed happy to leave me to my grandfather. What I did hate, though, were their fights, particularly because they broke out so late at night. He'd wait up for her; he didn't approve of Mel staying out so late. She was supposed to be getting back on her feet. My mother would yell right back at him. She was thirty-four years old; she would do with her life as she liked. They fought on like this until one of them stormed off and slammed a door. And then none of us would fall asleep, I'm sure, for hours. Weeks later I found out that Josh had been in Florida for a good month.

He had rented a basement apartment somewhere in Oakland Park and was seeing my mother daily. They'd split the week between Hallandale where he'd work the flats at Gulf Stream track, and Pompano Beach for the trotters at night. I don't know what they talked about or where they ate at night. I was no longer a part of things. I do know now that on several occasions Josh asked to see me, but Mel thought it was better that way, for me to stay with Grandpa and go to school and have my new life. She may have worried that if Grandfather found out he would have told Mel to move out. And that would have been too much. Perhaps it was simply that Mel loved me. She must have known she was losing control, and she didn't want to drag me in. Josh never meant to hurt my mother. And he never meant to bring her to places where she would hurt herself. It's just that he loved her so much he could not say no.

Coming home one night, just before Thanksgiving, my

mother's Fiat swerved into oncoming traffic. It was very late, after two. She'd been out with Josh, drinking. The driver in the other car broke his jaw and one arm. My mother was instantly killed.

I never held Josh responsible, though clearly my grandfather did. He was in anguish and spiteful. He needed a culprit. I remember how Josh looked, walking into the church where my mother's funeral service was held. He was like three dimensions and color inside a black and white place. He was too beautiful. His suit was too fine and his shoes and tie were too ornate. My grandfather stood up and shouted "Get out! Get that man out of here!"

Later, in the living room, my mother's father sat in his comfortable chair and drank straight bourbon and cried. I sat at his feet, too afraid to go anywhere, as though at any moment places in the floor would crack open and I'd fall right through.

Very late in the night when the sky was becoming a lighter blue, Grandpa turned to me. His hands were flat against his cheeks, as though he were trying to hold them in place. "You were *happy* to see that man today, weren't you?"

I shrugged. I didn't know what to say.

He put his face in his hands and shook his head no. "I can't blame you," he cried again. "That man's your father, your blood father. Did Melany ever tell you that?"

At another time, on any other day I would have been elated. Finally. Of course I had wondered. Always I had wanted to know. But there was such anger, such hatred in my grandfather's eyes. So I was blank and mute and I did not cry, while my grandfather drank and openly grieved.

3.

I stayed in Pompano Beach until I was eighteen. I went to middle school and high school there. Then I went to college and to medical school, and I remained in Florida after Grandpa Hurley passed away. I am a pediatrician now with a medical group in Fort Lauderdale. I have a house on the beach and a golden retriever named Shiloh. I have friends. I love my work.

For the first year after my mother's death I would see Josh
often, but I never talked to him. He did not come to the
apartment or call. Instead he'd pull alongside me while I
walked to school, follow me going about three miles an hour in
his black Thunderbird. He'd lean out the window and call,
"Deena, talk to me. Don't you love me, baby?"

I didn't want to look at him. His face was suddenly older,
the skin pulled taut, and his eyes were red. Everything about
him looked frayed and ratty, even his car. I came to so hate that
car. Its shape seemed ominous to me, and he, Josh, pathetic
and embarrassing—maybe even dangerous. I didn't want
anyone to see us or hear him pleading: "How's school going?
Just tell me how you are!"

Sometimes I'd answer, "I'm not supposed to talk to you."
But usually I just walked on. I would think, my mother sat on
that very passenger seat once. I used to fit lying down in the
back. But this just made the whole thing more horrible. I
could not love him. I had a new life, and there was simply too
much at stake.

Sixteen years passed. I was a first-year resident at Las Olas
General when I heard from Josh again. The telephone call was
oddly commonplace, as though we'd spoken only months ago.
Josh had moved back to Rochester. His sister was well, though
Carlo was having heart trouble. I took down Josh's number
and told him it was okay to call me again. Over the next few
years we spoke frequently, and when he retired, Josh came
down here to be with me. He has Parkinson's disease now and
cannot walk or take care of himself, so he lives in the Beth El
home in Coconut Creek, one of the best in the state. His old
boss, Leonard, pays the bills.

Josh is always desperate to move, so we spend the hours of
my visits in transit, moving his wheel chair through the halls
and the wings. I often bring him candy or different small
gifts, frames for his photographs, a vase of chrysanthemums,
his favorite flower. Yesterday I gave Josh two heart-shaped
boxes of Valentine's chocolates, one for him, the other to pass
around. When I arrived he was leaning over the sports pages
on his bed, looking at the scores through a magnifying glass.
A basketball game played on TV.

"Don't tell me they're recycled," Josh said, when he saw the boxes of candy.

"They're brand new. I just bought them at the drug store." I helped Josh to his wheel chair.

"I had hoped there was a romance story involved."

"Sorry, no story. I hate to disappoint you." I unwrapped the cellophane from one box. "You sound good today, very clear."

Josh ignored me. "Here we are: You have two boyfriends, Bob and Ben. Bob is rich and good looking but very . . . proper, very blah. Ben is poor, but he has a great deal of passion. You didn't know which one to choose, so you decided you'd wager on the Valentine's presents. As fate would have it, however, they both gave you the exact same box of drug store candy."

"Sounds made for TV." I handed him the chocolates.

"Good. In that case it's required to have a happy ending." Two points. He smiled.

"I'm not lonely, you know, just cautious. Anyway, what's the point of the story? What's the moral?"

"The moral?" Josh turned away. "You are such a cynic, Deena."

And perhaps I am. Perhaps the truly virtuous stories end well, with affirmations and marriages, in soft focus. Or perhaps I would be a happier woman for believing this. But the story of my father's life would end differently, regardless of what I believed. In fact, it would have two endings. The first ending would be Mel's death. And the second, that one morning when I was in fifth grade, when my father followed in his car as I walked to school, I reported him to the police. I ran to the principal's office and asked to use the phone. The officer wanted information. I said someone had followed me, harassed me, I was afraid. But then I froze. I realized Josh would be so easy to catch. He did not know how to hide. The officer was impatient for a description. What color was his hair? Had I seen the license plate? And so I said he was a strange man whose face I couldn't recall, and that I didn't know the make of the car.

The Blooding

BY RAY DEAN MIZE

My father always said there were only two ways to raise a coon hound—gentle him or blood him. Gentling could take weeks, or even months. But blooding took just a day. And while a gentled dog might be better mannered, a blooded dog was all most of the county could afford.

Calhoun County had been coon country forever, wedged as it was between the Illinois and Mississippi rivers. It was rough and broken land—razor-back ridges and briar swamps, limestone bluffs and black-mud river bottom.

By day, the coons hid deep in the overgrown hollows, nesting in the oaks that grew along the creeks. By night, they raided the hardscrabble farms on the hilltops for sweetcorn and melons. No scent or noise could keep them out, not sprinkled ash nor sweat-stained shirts, not staked-out dogs nor transistor radios wailing country heartbreak into the dark.

Come winter, a heavy coon might bring forty dollars a hide. A good hound sold for ten times that, sometimes more. And most folks said my father raised the best hounds in the county.

The day I turned nine, I was startled awake by something licking my face. A black-and-tan pup scrambled back and forth on my bedcovers, eager for another go.

Unsmiling, my father stood by my bed. His work pants

77

hung shapeless to his cracked leather shoes. He rested his left hand, thick with scars and callus, on the bedpost.

"His name's Cain," he said. "I expect you to raise him to be a first-class hound."

"Yes sir," I answered.

"Do it right," he said. He turned to leave but paused at the door. "And I promise you this. It'll make you a man."

The morning of the blooding, my father ran his traps early and came back from the creek without my seeing him. I had Cain on his back in the yard, wrestling him down in the dirt and tickling his belly, pink mottled with brown. He yelped, rolled his eyes back until the whites bulged, and nipped at my hands.

Cain was large for three months but still moved as if his bones were two sizes too big. He already had the mournful eyes and slack jaw of a full-grown hound. He had the proper markings too, a black saddle on a tan body.

My father's voice came from behind me. "You'll ruin that dog."

I jumped to my feet, my face burning.

"If you want to play, you got toys in the house."

"I'm sorry," I said softly.

Over one shoulder of his heavy wool shirt, my father carried a canvas bag that bulged at the bottom. The bag thrashed, hung for a few moments, then thrashed again.

On the back of my father's right hand was a long red scratch and drying blood.

"You should be watering the dogs," he said.

"I already finished."

"Then get your dog chained up."

Cain sniffed toward the bag. I whistled him back and headed down the path to the chicken house. Cain tagged along easy but my heart galloped. I was excited, happy, and scared all at the same time.

I dragged open the weathered door of the chicken house. Inside it had already begun to heat up. Dust hung in the air where shafts of sunlight cut between the boards.

The tumble-down shack had held our chickens until black snakes got to the eggs and a pair of foxes went on a killing spree. My father tracked and shot them both. Then he covered the dirt floor with straw and moved in a couple of hounds.

I ran my hand to the end of Cain's chain and snapped the swivel to his collar. Still excited, Cain jumped up on me. I held my face against his muzzle. His nose was cool and unmarked, virgin black.

By the time I ran back up to the house, the bottom of the bag had already been anchored, its canvas pulled taut between six-inch gutter spikes.

My father began staking out the sides. He flattened the bag as he worked, forcing the animal inside toward the closed drawstring. Then he pulled on his heavy gloves. The leather palms shone like dark metal.

"Listen," he said. "When I tell you to, undo the slide on that drawstring. Then get the hell back."

He looked around. "Get up on the porch. You can watch from there."

I nodded, scarcely daring to breathe.

He knelt on the bag, spread both hands above the bulge, and grabbed. The bulge squirmed and hissed but my father bore down until it was still. He planted his knees on either side and squeezed.

"Now," said my father.

The animal's bulk pressed hard against the drawstring but I worked the slide free. I snatched my hand away and scrambled for the porch.

With his right glove, my father took a firmer grip on the bulge. With his left, he jerked back the top of the bag. Hissing and spitting, the coon twisted into the light. He fought like a thing possessed but my father pulled sharply on the draw-string, cinching the bag tight behind the coon's front legs.

My father shoved the coon's head into the ground. With his free hand, he tugged twice more on the drawstring and then held it taut.

"Get on down here," he said. "Come up behind me, so he can't see you, and close that slide good and tight."

I hurried around behind my father. I bent over his damp back and fumbled with the slide. I had never been so close to a live coon.

He was an old boar gone gray around the whiskers. One ear was half-missing, ripped off by dogs or a rival coon. His forelegs, free of the bag, showed the cuts of my father's traps.

The coon clawed the dirt deep and hard.

"He's too big," I said.

"No, he's just right," he said. "It takes an old coon to wise up a hound."

My father sent me down for a dog while he went in the house for rubbing alcohol and salve.

Of the eight dogs to be blooded that day, Ringo was my least favorite. I took him up first.

My father snapped a leash on Ringo and led him to the coon. Puzzled, Ringo sniffed at the mysterious creature—half head and forelegs, half canvas bag.

"Coon," said my father. "C'mon boy, get that coon."

Ringo edged closer. The coon lay still, watching and waiting. Ringo sniffed again. Like a shot, the coon slashed out. Ringo yelped and jumped back but my father urged him on—"Get 'em, boy"—until Ringo's nose and bottom lip were scratched and torn. My father pulled him off and clipped him to the porch.

"Where's the next one?" he said. Then he saw my face. "They have to get chewed on. That's what makes them remember."

One by one, I pulled up the next six dogs. The cut dogs tied to the porch bellowed and flung themselves against their leashes. Each new dog shrank, terrified by the noise and the smell of blood and fear. But once hurt, each dog attacked furiously, driven to a frenzy by my father and the other dogs.

The coon, too, had been hurt. His good ear had been bitten off and one paw dragged. But he still ruled his worn strip of dirt. And with each dog, he'd grown wiser.

"Grab your dog," said my father, "and let's get this over with."

So I brought up Cain. He hung back against me while my father clipped on the leash.

"You want me to do this, or you want to do it yourself?"

"I'll do it," I said.

He handed me the leash. "Just keep him far enough back so the coon can't get to his eyes."

I took a firm grip on the leather. Cain nosed toward the coon, easing out the slack. But my hand shook and Cain hesitated. The dogs tied to the porch roared their fury and frustration. Down at the barn, the older hounds joined in.

"Come on," I said uncertainly. "Get that coon."

Cain looked back at me.

My voice cracked. "Get 'em."

Cain stretched his neck and snuffled. From behind his dark mask, the coon stared with the dead eyes of a timber rattler. Cain started to take a step. His weight shifted forward.

The coon struck.

I jerked Cain back and wrapped my arms around him. Through blurred eyes, I watched the scratch on his nose fill with blood. A thin thread of red marred the black.

"Christ," said my father. He shoved me away from Cain and grabbed the leash.

"Sic that coon!" he yelled. "Tear him up!"

By the time my father finished, Cain was cut worse than any of the other dogs. Trails of blood marked his throat and legs. Bubbles formed on his lips and nostrils.

My father uprooted the bag and dragged it, coon and all, down the hill and across the field. He swung the coon off the ground for a few yards, then dragged him again. After a quarter mile more of cutbacks and twists, he let him go.

Back at the house, my father pulled up Banjo and Star, his two best hounds. He quieted the young dogs and untied them. For a few moments it was silent except for the harsh panting of the dogs.

"Coon," my father said. "Get me a coon!"

Banjo and Star cast and circled, their noses to the ground. The younger dogs crowded close behind. Banjo hit the drag scent, stiffened his legs, and bawled.

They ran in a pack, the younger dogs imitating Banjo and Star. They lost the trail, milled around, and found it again. The dogs, young and old, bellowed the cry of trailing hounds.

When they treed the coon, the cry changed to short barks. My father took his rifle and walked to where the dogs, Cain among them, leaped furiously against the trunk of a lone oak. As though hunting fur, my father shot the coon through one eye.

A few days later, my father gave me a small glass medicine bottle. "Every time your dog chases trash, put some of that on his nose," he said.

That afternoon, Cain scared up a squirrel and ran him up a hickory. I whistled him back and unscrewed the bottle. Soldered to the lid was a blue-stained brush. I held Cain's collar while I swabbed the remedy on his scabbed nose. Cain jerked his head and sneezed. When I let him go, he frantically rubbed his nose in the dirt.

Over the next month, I dosed him a few more times but I could see how much he hated it. So gradually, I quit.

One night, my father took me hunting with a couple of his buddies, Ed and Roy. Each of them brought two or three dogs. My father let me bring Cain.

We sat on a fallen tree near the top of Meyer's Hill, listening for the hounds. By the yellow light of my father's Coleman lantern, the men swapped old hunting stories and passed a fifth of Wild Turkey.

One dog boomed out.

"Somebody's hot on a coon," said Ed.

The barking became more frantic.

"He sees him now!" said Roy. He stood up and looked toward the distant sound.

My father said nothing. None of the other dogs joined in.

"Whose dog is that?" asked Roy.

Nobody answered.

Roy looked at me and broke out in a grin. He reached over and pulled my hat down over my eyes. "Well boy," he said, "looks like you got yourself one hell of a rabbit hound."

A week later, I was shaken out of my sleep. My father stood over me, already dressed.

"Come on," he said. "We're going hunting."

The house lay dark and silent as I groped on the floor for

my clothes and shoes. I got my wool jacket and cap from the closet.

"Aren't you bringing your lantern?" I asked.

"Won't need it."

Outside, the night was clear and still. The faint bark of a dog came from a farm far beyond the bluffs. The yard's icy ruts cast sharp shadows and crunched beneath my shoes. My nostrils froze together.

I stamped to keep warm. "What dogs do you want?"

"Just yours," he said. "That'll be all for tonight."

Surprised, I ran all the way to the chicken house. Cain was already up and moving. In the dim light that filtered between the boards, I felt for his chain and roughed his ears. "Show him what you can do," I said.

But when I brought Cain up to the house, my father grabbed him by the collar and jerked him into the air. Cain gave a yelp. His back legs stretched stiff to the ground. His eyes bulged and he breathed hard.

"Look at his nose," my father said. The long pink scars stood out in the moonlight. "You understand why we do that, don't you?"

"Yes sir," I said.

"A pup ain't worth nothing until it's been gentled or blooded."

"Yes sir."

Cain struggled against his collar. "What we do, we do for the dog's own good. You understand that?"

I nodded.

He studied me for a long while and then dropped Cain. The dog came to me but I didn't dare touch him.

"You can go back in if you want," said my father.

"I want to stay."

"Then let's do it."

"Coon," I told Cain. "C'mon boy. Find me a coon."

Cain moved off at an easy trot, his nose a few inches off the frozen ground. His collar jangled as he crossed the first field and began to cast about. He circled twice, snuffled, and then broke into a deep bay. In the moonlight, he hit his stride cleanly and boomed the cry of a trailing hound.

My father threw his rifle to his shoulder.

I reached for the rifle, "no" on my lips. But I stopped short, trembling. Suddenly I knew that it had to be. It wasn't what I wanted but I recognized its rightness. For the first time in my life, I felt within me the ancient scars that bind all men.

That night the world became a smaller, sadder place. A world of duty and not of dreams.

My father pulled the trigger.

Slice of Life

BY CAROLE L. GLICKFELD

"In her line of work, a heart is a handicap, *nu?* So, my daughter does very well," my mother says to Feigele. Feigele is related to my mother through my dead grandmother's niece, also dead. We call her Cousin.

Twenty-three years ago, when Cousin Feigele ran off with a married man to Arizona, the family was scandalized. Not on account of the married man (there is a long tradition of *meshuge* for love) but because a Jew from the Northeast goes to the Southwest only to see the Grand Canyon. Feigele must have realized her mistake, although she tried to convince herself otherwise, writing us letters about the beauty of sand without beach towels and umbrellas, without the smell of egg salad sandwiches wrapped in waxed paper. So much for the wonders of the desert. During my teen years, she sent only greeting cards and only at Rosh Hashanah. We knew something was up this summer when she mailed a postcard from the Ukraine: "All my life I wanted to make this trip. XXXOOO, Your Cousin Feigele." Today she arrives on my mother's doorstep, saying she's come to visit all her living relatives before we turn to dust.

Feigele turns to me now, her pinkish cheek lifting toward her pea green pupil in suspicion. "So, what is it with your job?" she asks; "if I'm not being nosey."

"I book talent for a TV program," I tell her.

My mother interrupts. "You don't remember I wrote you? She's an executive producer. At the end of the show, her name rolls around the television screen with the credits."

I tell Feigele about "Slice of Life," slotted in before the national network's morning show. For what my boss Franco calls "newsy entertainment," we book everything from politicians to bonsai growers. Authors in town for a booksigning. Performing artists for the What's Happening segment.

"So, what's so heartless?" Feigele asks.

"Mostly she doesn't book," my mother rushes to say. She slaps at a pillow between them on the sofa.

Feigele's massive chest heaves, cutting into the square neckline of a shiny purple dress. "Excuse me, a Nazi your daughter isn't, choosing this one he should live or that one, he shouldn't—"

"It seems like it to them," I say, thinking of Jimmie Santucci, a.k.a. Mr. Tough, who was seen crying into his ham scramble in The Iron Skillet, his toucan Mitzi on his shoulder. Later that night Jimmie totaled out his Continental, coincidentally wrapping it around the leg of a billboard advertising "Slice of Life." Although he escaped in one piece, not so Selina Delmundo, a coloratura who tried to hang herself with the belt of a peignoir. When the belt gave, she broke her collar bone.

"Listen," my boss said at the time, "death and disfigurement are downers." Franco stuffed a bouquet of phlox into my hands, and for a moment I thought he was sending me to my funeral. I remember he ran his index finger across his protruding Adam's apple as though cutting his throat—or mine. "Bad, bad publicity," he said.

"Okay," I told him. "You want top ratings? I can do that. You want someone who keeps people alive? Get yourself a goddamn medic."

Franco yanked the bouquet out of my hand, threw it on the floor and ground his heel into the magenta blossoms. "Look at her," he said; "she shows more emotion about flowers—"

"You want me to be kind to everyone, Franco? All right—"

"Wait a minute. You don't have to book the entire world. Just ease the losers out, got it?"

Easing out comes to mind now when my mother, looking at Feigele, asks if I'll make the celeriac salad with my special Dijon dressing for Thanksgiving.

"I'll be out of town," I say, not knowing how to ease her into this notion. Something you learn in my business is not to waste time.

My mother waves her hand at Cousin Feigele. "Heartless! What did I tell you?"

I stand up. "The *chutzpah* of wanting four days to myself," I say. "Without a beeper. Without call forwarding. Without hearing from Franco." I give her a look to remind her that last year, Franco's two dozen tea roses persuaded her to reveal that I was in a chalet on Crystal Mountain, a ski slope in the state of Washington. Further away in the continental United States I couldn't get, yet he tracked me down. "Such a nice man," she says now; "why wouldn't you want to talk to him?" This Thanksgiving not even my mother will know where I am.

"All I beg you is to think about it," my mother says, following me out to the driveway.

"I'll give you the recipe," I say, and then I get into my car.

As I drive to the station a blue Volvo follows me, the driver wanting nothing more sinister, I suppose, than to audition. The worst that's ever happened as a result of my being followed was an assault on my ears, as when Tootles McCree blocked my turn into Main Street with his Dodge van, slid his three-hundred-fifty pound frame out in sections like a seal and, tenor sax in hand, lumbered over to my car. He knelt so that the bell of his instrument beamed at my window, which was stuck half open because the handle didn't work. Behind us cars piled up and honked while he blasted out the "South Rampart Street Parade," not even noticing my fingers pressed against my eardrums. Done, Tootles slipped an eight-by-ten glossy, head shot with horn, into my lap. Being an orderly person, I kept the photo on file.

Recently, when "Slice of Life" had a cancellation an hour before air time, I called Tootles. At five-fifteen A.M. he was sitting on two stools in the makeup room, exercising his lips. He gets double stars in my book: one for filling in on short notice; the other for bringing our dull-witted co-anchors to life when he blasted the blues into their northern ramparts.

In my rear view mirror I see the woman driving the Volvo does not have a glamorous hairdo or a stylized haircut. This means she is the wife, friend, lover or mother of someone she thinks has talent. With Franco's caution in mind, I don't try to give her the slip, although my new Corvette is perfectly capable.

She pulls into the WRAK parking lot, stops near the entrance so that I have to walk past her car. Through the windshield I see her mouth moving. Next to her is a midget and, clambering on the dash, a monkey. No sooner am I inside the station than the Volvo rolls past, which I take for a loss of nerve, not uncommon at the front door of WRAK.

"Paging Mr. Franco," the receptionist breathes into the mouthpiece of her headphone, as she holds out messages between two lethally long fingernails, the exact chocolate color of the carpet. Across my topmost message Tiffany has drawn a skull and crossbones: Stilton Cancelled.

She nods. I put my hand over my heart, feigning an infarction. But only partially. I feel suddenly short on oxygen. "Cancelled" is the big "C" word around here, the most dreaded. Stilton happens to be the most famous public official ever to come to this town voluntarily, even if only to fish Connecticut's south shore. All week I've researched the State Department, compiling questions that would put me on the White House hit list. In lieu of our most important guest ever is one vast hole. Dead space. Which I cannot fill with a no-name. The show is rife with no-names: a local psychic, a pediatrician, and twins playing twin pianos.

Franco bounces into my cubbyhole, stroking the slicked back sides of his dark hair with multiply ringed fingers. Even standing still he looks like he's moving to a reggae beat. (He came here by way of Miami.) "Whatchagotwhatchagot?" he says, all one word.

"In reserve? Howard Oberfest. You know, the baritone?"

Franco looks blank.

"Darling of the housewives. He was drying out last time he was supposed to appear—"

"Oh lady-o," Franco says. "Not opposite Susee Traye."

Susee Traye, the much loved and effervescent star of a soap, is slated for "Mornings with Mitch" tomorrow. How Spike

Lady, my counterpart over at WCKS, ever bagged her not even our spies have determined.

"Sligh Jenkins?" I offer. "The interview Trish did with him in L.A. at the book fair, we've got it in the can."

"Computer Brain, gay detective novels don't sell in—"

"Who knows he's gay?" I argue. "Those cat-gray eyes, the tanned chest. Trish said he unbuttoned his shirt when they began taping. The way he delivers, 'There is nothing more addictive than the mystery of love,' even I could be fooled."

"You!" Franco says, stomping his boot heels in a mock Flamenco, his hands clasped above his head. Looking back at me over his shoulder, he says, "Get the gov."

"Good thinking!" I say, thinking, not on your life. The gov's been seeking a forum to explain why he wants to reinstitute capital punishment. Perhaps we could retitle the show, "Slice of Death." Franco waits while I dial my home number and talk to my machine, pretending it's the governor's office. "How long is he going to be out of town?" I say. Franco slaps the side of his head, and is gone.

"Why didn't *we* do that?" Franco asked me when the gov judged a fathers' diapering contest on Mitch's show. At the Broadcasters' Banquet, Franco even complimented Spike Lady on it. She laughed so hard her purple spikes flopped over onto her pencilled eyebrows. Well, maybe that's a slight exaggeration. Anyway, a gov or anyone else who never says no to an invite is not someone I want as a featured guest.

I close my eyes and pretend to be a typical "Slice of Life" viewer, a married woman between twenty and thirty-four who has one and a half children and works part-time. Whom would she prefer to Susee Traye? What Franco calls my computer brain prints out two words: forget it. I think about Feigele who isn't even on the VALS chart. My mother will wake her in the morning to watch. What is it Feigele would like to see?

Tiffany buzzes on the intercom. "Your mother is on the line," she says, all puffs of air and pauses.

"My life is on the line," I parrot. "Tell her I'm in crisis."

"I did. She wants to know if she should invite Morty and his family for tonight."

"Tell her, not if she wants me in the same house."

A moment later, Tiffany buzzes again. "What if the children don't come your mother wants to know?"

What my mother doesn't want to know is that when my brother's brats came to a Fourth of July barbecue at my place, they got into my Seconal and Dalmane and tried to deny it, but I knew exactly how many I had left. They dumped out all the Maalox, which I discovered belatedly one night when my ulcer almost ate through my midriff. I ended up in Emergency. These are things I cannot tell my mother. "Tell my mother ab-solutely pos-itively NO!" I say to Tiffany.

I ignore the next two buzzes. Perhaps Tiffany appreciates my remembrance at Christmas because she leaves her station, for which she could be fired, and runs in to tell me to pick up the line.

A resonant voice says softly, "This is Senator Tom Tompkins. Is this Marilyn Schwimmer?"

"*The* Senator Tom Tompkins?"

He doesn't miss a beat. "*The* Marilyn Schwimmer?"

I make some strange murmuring sound. At the same time I conjure a composite image of him from the newspapers, magazines, television: a freckled, toothy man in his early forties who looks like an ex-hockey player. I remember that one of his oft-noted charms is his inclination to call people directly, without the usual buffer of Congressional aides.

"Marilyn, I realize your schedule must be hectic, but I'm hoping we could have a cup of coffee or a drink together. Later today?" His inflection barely rises.

"You're in town?"

"Flying up shortly. Say, four o'clock?"

My computer responds: "And when are you flying back?"

"Well, that depends—"

We dance around the subject, innuendos and all, and finally I say, "Senator! You want to be on tomorrow's program, don't you!"

He pauses. "Tomorrow *is* an option," he says.

"Let's talk when you get here," I say, wondering why I'm trying to sound doubtful. I'm still wondering after I've hung up.

A moment later he calls back. "I just wanted to hear your sexy voice again."

"I was just about to call and say the same thing," I tell him, amused by the long silence. A stunned silence, I think, and then I hear him talking to someone in his office. My witty moment is lost. As Franco says, "Timing is everything."

I'm sitting at my desk hugging myself when Franco returns, asking if I've tracked down the gov yet.

"Haven't had time," I say. Pause. "I've been in the process of nailing Tom Tompkins." Pause. "So to speak."

Franco's body convulses as he lifts his arm and snaps his fingers. "Yi-yi-yi. You shittin' me?" When I shake my head he says, "What's he want?"

"All right, all right, I'll find out," I say, because it's station policy.

"Pull this off and you can ask for a raise," Franco says.

"I already have. Asked for a raise. After the last ratings, Franco—"

He covers his ears.

I shout. "You know, ratings? Those numbers you say mean life and death—" I'm about to add, the ones that have soared since I joined WRAK but he taps an intricate rhythm with his rings on the doorjamb, sways his hips, and dances backwards. He collides with my new assistant, who crawls into my office gathering up carnations, a gift for me from The Amazing Amundson.

"This seals his fate," I say. "I loathe carnations."

Kristal giggles enthusiastically, a sure sign of ambition. "Who is he, anyhow?" she asks.

"Does a corny magic act. Pulls ears of corn out of his sleeves."

Kristal looks at my face trying to decide whether she's supposed to laugh. "Your mother would like the flowers," she says. After only a week even Kristal knows my mother.

"Sweetie, they may keep gifts over at WCKS," I tell her, "we do not. Send these to the Children's Home, along with these worry dolls." I point to a shelf I've labelled BRIBERY EXHIBITS. Spike Lady thought the shelf was "cute." "No one can buy *me*," she said, "for less than a Bentley. So I keep it all. Everything."

"Funny," I told her, "the few times I've seen your show I'd've sworn you were under the influence." Spike Lady just laughed.

Senator Tom Tompkins is about to autograph a cocktail napkin when I appear at his table in the Oyster Bar. He excuses himself to the woman who is waiting, and pulls out a chair for me, scrawls on the napkin, hands it to the woman and says, "Please, if there's anything we can do to help—" The woman's eyes roll around as though she's been struck on the head. Her mouth is open but no words come out. She walks away slowly, her head still turned toward the senator, until her hip hits the corner of a nearby table. Glasses shatter.

He looks at me, then back at her, as if wanting to rush forward. "I hope she's all right," he says.

"Senator," I say, suppressing a laugh, "she's fine."

"Thank you," he says. "That's thoughtful." His smile is almost shy. Is he for real? And he's shorter than I thought, exactly my height, which is five seven.

After we order drinks, he props his bony chin on his hands, his elbows resting on the table, and looks into my eyes, something men tend not to do unless they're Latin or black. Unnerved, I babble about the state of the Oyster Bar, how it's changed or hasn't since I was last here.

"Tell me," he says suddenly, "what you do all day. What did you do today?"

No man has ever asked, even to be polite. I tell him about the woman who followed me with the midget and monkey.

"Enchanting," he says. "Tell me more." Almost without taking his blue eyes off me he buys a rose from Gypsy Rose who is making her usual rounds with her antiqued wheelbarrow. He doesn't see Gypsy Rose glare at me. She tried to get on "Slice of Life" but I told her she didn't have an act, a book or a joke. She took it personally. "Tell me," I say to the senator, "about life in the U.S. Senate."

"Oh that," he says; "I'd rather be skiing. I'll be at Squaw Valley next weekend. Care to go?"

Fending off a melt-down, I ask what brings him to our little city.

He adjusts his navy tie, as if it's airtime. "As you may know," he says, "I'm sponsoring a bill for hospice care for AIDS victims and we're looking for public support—"

Reluctantly I get out the pad and pen. "Why here? Why now?"

"Here because we can generate a post-program survey with little lead time. Second, the market is ideal, a balance of political views, good age distribution—" He rubs his eyes. "Sorry, I've been on the go since four this morning."

"I heard you were indefatigable," I joke.

He seems startled. A premature ejaculator? My smart-ass remark has somehow offended him; he flashes a phony smile that exposes his crooked uppers, and meets my practiced cool gaze. The melt-down is in progress. I'm already imagining Thanksgiving with him....

"Well, how about some oysters then?" he says.

Oysters Rockefeller and Côte-Rote it turns out to be and then I put my hand on his jacket sleeve, across the creases. "It's just that I don't believe in mixing business with—" I start to explain.

"One thing at a time," he says. "I agree. Anyhow I'd appreciate having twenty minutes tomorrow to make my case."

"Are you serious? We book months in advance." I'm thinking he and I are made for each other: we each manage to sound so cavalier in the face of our desperation.

"Well, if that's your excuse—" he says.

"Two segments plus," I parry. "You must think I'm drunk."

He leans forward. "Must be drunk myself, thinking thoughts I had no business—" He lifts my hand gently to his mouth and then snorts, pretends to bite my thumb. He slides his jaw down the side of my hand, snort-snort, and starts biting his own thumb. It is then I remember he has small children. I disengage my hand.

"Five of the most gripping moments you've ever aired," he says, as he reaches into his briefcase to give me a cassette.

"We're not about death and dying, Senator."

"Cut the 'Senator' crap. Call me Tom." He cocks his head as if to say, How about it? I'm wondering what I could ask the man to do for me when he adds, "I would really hate to have to go with 'Mornings with Mitch.'" He lets this sink in and then says, "It's such a sappy show."

"Sappy?" I say. "You think our competition's sappy? Okay, that's it, you're on."

"Don't look so unhappy," he says.

I don't tell him it's my ulcer, reacting to something, the wine probably, or the thought of Franco complaining to the station manager that I let my political views get the best of my judgment. "Upbeat, we gotta have upbeat," Franco always says. I warn the senator, "The questions will be tough. I plan to write some of them myself," I say, wondering when. In the morning maybe, while he's in the shower.

"It wouldn't be a fair test otherwise," he says. He looks over my shoulder, tilts his head back. The next thing I know a swarthy man is standing next to us. Tom rises, grasps my hand, leans down to kiss my cheek. "What time should I be in the studio?"

"Five," I say, forcing a smile.

He motions to the waiter, hands him a hundred dollar bill and says to keep the change. Before I can protest, he is gone, the waiter's "Thank *you*" echoing in the air.

In a semi-fog I hear myself being paged. Franco is on the line. "I got the skinny," he says. "Get this, the obstacles to the Tompkins' bill are none other than the two senators from this state."

"Yeah, so?" I say.

"He's probably trying to get a letter-writing campaign going to these guys—"

"Yeah, so?"

"Computer Brain, are you drunk?"

"Yeah, so?"

"Jesus, we can't let this senator—"

"Bullshit, Franco. Who doesn't have an agenda? You? Why should Tommy be different?"

"Tommy? Yi-yi-yi."

"Franco, do us a favor. Go tape a promo. Use a still of him.

We'll slay Mitch. Spike Lady will dive head first into the WCKS parking lot. She'll look like a bent mace."

"Enjoy dinner with Mama," he says, in a slightly sinister lilt. "Your last supper, Lady-O."

I weave my way to the Oyster Bar's parking lot. When I see the police cars I know somehow they are flashing for me. After all, my business depends on intuition. I see the blue Volvo. The monkey is on a leash held by the midget and is scampering in and around the four police officers and the woman who is pointing to my Corvette. An officer tells me he has just rescued the monkey that was trapped in my car, after it climbed in the half-open window.

"Ma'am, it's not a good idea to keep car windows open," he says as though reciting from a manual.

My glance is withering. "You have a lot of monkeys climbing into cars around here?"

"No, Ma'am, but when they do—" He points to the inside of my car, holds his ruddy nose with his thumb and index finger and says, "Whew."

"Nooo—"

The officer clicks on his flashlight, aims it at the red upholstery which now contains splotches of ochre.

The midget moves noiselessly behind me, and I almost trample him. In a voice that sounds as if it's coming through helium he says, "An open window is an 'attractive nuisance.' Don't even think of suing."

What I think about is the definition of vandalism in my insurance policy. Does it apply to monkeys? Is what this monkey did a "natural act" or an "act of God"? The phrase, "holy shit," comes to mind.

Eons pass while the woman, police and I exchange information. Around the monkey running circles around the midget is a gathering and curious crowd. Before getting into her Volvo, the woman says, "I don't suppose you would audition Mighty Mike and his trained—" The word stops us both. She gets in the car and I wait for a taxi.

"Thanks to you the chicken is killed," my mother says when I arrive at her place. "Dead. Without a flavor." Before I can apologize, my beeper goes off.

She rejoins Feigele at the table. Four eyes are beamed at me
as I call from my mother's only telephone, a rotary dial with a
short cord.

"How can you do this to me?" yells Trish, one of our co-
anchors. "I read a whole book preparing for this guy
Stenton."

"Stilton," I correct.

"And now you've got this senator I know nothing about—"

"I promise, Trish, he'll make it easy for you. I'm assembling
a list of questions for you to ask, this very minute."

The click tells me she's hung up. At the table, my mother
and Feigele look hungry, not necessarily for dinner. Because I
forgot to stop for wine, I'm forced to drink the only alcohol
my mother owns besides the rubbing kind: Manischewitz
cream white concord.

I chew the chicken. I keep chewing, feeling that the ache of
my jaw is fit punishment. Out of nowhere Feigele says,
"Darling, he must be very handsome, no?" She bunches her
fingers on her pursed lips and flings a kiss at me. She knows a
fool for love when she sees one.

"It was business. Tom Tompkins is going to be on our show
in the morning."

"Mr. Hockey Player?" she asks.

"Himself."

"He's married," my mother says.

"There are rumors of their splitting up," I say.

"You're not going away with him Thanksgiving?" my
mother says.

"I knew you'd find a way to bring that subject up." I reach
for more sweet wine.

She persists. "Feigele will be coming back then and we
thought—"

I look at Feigele, who shrugs her shoulders.

"Ma, I'm sorry but—"

"The whole family for once—"

"Ma!"

My mother claps her hands together, holds them as if she's
praying. "To young people today family means nothing. It's a
fact of life, *nu*?" she says, looking at Feigele. Feigele looks
down at her lap.

To change the subject I tell them what happened in the parking lot, even though I won't hear the end of it. For delicacy's sake I say, "The monkey defecated."

Feigele inhales, coughs furiously. She expels a cud of chicken, then shakes her head. "The monkey—how you say it—it went apeshit!" She starts to hiccough, only she's not hiccoughing; she's laughing in staccato bursts, which makes me laugh. Soon she and I have tears running down our cheeks. My mother tries to smile but obviously is thinking about the darker side of this comedy, the damage to my new Corvette. "Ma, it's okay. What's funnier than a monkey and a —" My mirth ends suddenly when I remember that I've failed to cancel out the no-names.

By now it's ten-thirty. After explaining to my mother and Feigele what I have to do, I drain the last of the Manischewitz.

My mother points at me, looks triumphantly at Feigele. She says, "Didn't I tell you!"

The psychic cries when I inform her she's not going to be on. "You didn't see it in the cards?" I say, cucumber cool.

"I don't tell my own fortunes," she shoots right back.

"I promise, another day."

She offers a free consultation, which I decline, even when she throws in a complete astrological chart.

The pediatrician's wife says, "You have some nerve at this late hour—" She isn't mollified when I tell her how impressed I am that her husband is on a house call.

"What did you say your name was?" she asks.

"Marilyn Schwimmer."

"You didn't phone my husband earlier by any chance?"

"The schedule just changed—"

"I see. Thank you ve-ry much," she says, articulating the syllables.

Just thinking of the twins sharpens the pain in my gut. Occasionally I have nightmares of rejected musicians lying in wait. They spring from under my bedcovers or the bathroom hamper. One hid in the cabinet under the kitchen sink and tried to push me into the trash compactor before I awakened.

Finding neither twin at home, I chew a Maalox tablet before calling a cab to deliver the twins' postponement notices buried in carnations from the Midnite MiniMart. These twins are

delicate souls, more like Jimmie Santucci or Selina Delmundo, less likely to kill, more apt to commit suicide. But
that's tomorrow's biz. At midnight, two hours after my usual
bedtime, I feel satisfied that today we will demolish "Mornings with Mitch."

I sprawl on the carpet at the foot of Feigele, who is
recounting the time her cousin Shulemith delayed a pogrom
against the Jews by singing to the Cossacks somewhere near
the Russian border. My beeper sounds.

"Major bad news," my mother says, for once getting the
words right. For a long time she used to say, "Bad major
news."

A male voice, prissy to the extreme, says he is calling for
Senator Tompkins who regrets he cannot call personally to
cancel his appearance on "Slice of Life." I think it must be
Franco joking, but the voice continues: "He said you would
understand inasmuch as he was offered a two-part series on
'Mornings with Mitch.' Let me look at my notes—"

I have a flash of myself beating down a door; with only five
hotels in the city I know I can find Tommy. Then I see the
police carrying me away....

The voice continues. "Yes, well, he has gone to bed. We
understand that their marketing area covers more of the
state—"

"Susee Traye cancelled?" I ask. "Do you know?"

"Pardon?" the voice says.

"Never mind. Tell the senator to fuck himself."

Words that Selina Delmundo sang at her audition pop to
mind: *Never have I once looked back to sigh over the romance behind
me....Many a new day will dawn before I do.* That was before
she went home to hang herself. I dial the psychic, waking her
from an obviously drugged sleep. As a favor to me she will
come on the show, providing I serve as her 4 A.M. wake-up
call; it's either me or the paramedics. When I call one of the
twins, she hangs up. The physician threatens to complain to
the FCC. I envision Franco dancing, dancing, complaint in
hand. As the physician rants, I calculate. The psychic is good
for four minutes. I have a twenty-one minute hole. The tape of
Sligh Jenkins is eight minutes. Thirteen minutes to fill. The
pediatrician promises to sue. My on-the-air suicide would take

five seconds. I reject the notion, although it would definitely increase the next day's ratings.

"Sonofabitch!" I rail out loud. "How could he do this to me!"

"Sit!" Feigele says. "You're limp like a dishrag."

When I collapse, she rises, fluffs her thinning hair, dyed jet black. She struts to the opposite side of the room, faces me, her large chest thrust forward, her back to the credenza. She extends her arms. "Di-rect from Tem-pe, Ari-zona," she announces, "the fa-bu-lous Miss Feigele." Grateful for this crazy distraction, I join my mother in applauding. *Tommy, Tommy, Tommy,* I'm thinking.

Cousin Feigele inserts two fingers from one hand, one finger from the other, into her mouth. Her left cheek protrudes as though her tooth were infected. Out comes a strange piercing sound, SEEYOUSEEYOUSEEYOU, that she explains afterwards is the song of the rare rose-throated Becard, first seen last century in the Huachura mountains. "And when it builds a home," she says, emitting a chattering sound, her mouth opening and closing as if she's chewing my mother's chicken. "Yes, darlings, virtually a castle it builds in the air."

She curtseys, steps to one side, curtseys, steps to the other, then back to credenza center. Now her jaw repeatedly drops as she utters a "Chawchawchaw" sound. "The cactus wren, as you may not know it," she says, "is the state bird of Arizona."

When she is done, my mother stares. A serious look. "This I never knew," she says to Feigele.

"If only you had a piano here—" Feigele sighs. "Ziegfeld himself told me I had the voice of an angel—"

"Yes," my mother concurs. "That I remember."

"You weren't there," Feigele says.

"I heard."

Feigele ignores her, turns to me. "My father, may he rest in peace, said Ziegfeld wanted me for my legs and what's between, but I swear, as you-know-who is my witness, it was for my angel's voice—"

"That time we played hookey—" my mother says, her glance avoiding mine. "*Oy,* those costumes were so sheer we see their breasts from the back of the theater."

Feigele pinches my mother's ear. "Did I try to drag you

backstage with me? You said nice girls don't belong in show business."

"Ma, is that true?"

"Who can remember?" She turns to Feigele. "I think that was Shulemith you were talking. Not me. We never went together downtown."

"Excuse me, this is Alzheimer's talking—" Feigele holds up her hand as if to say, Enough.

When my mother goes to the bathroom, Feigele sits on the arm of my chair, takes my hand, which she rubs with both of hers in her warm lap. "It would be the highlight of my years," she says.

"What would be?"

"Getting on the television. It would make up for everything, my whole life—"

"Cousin Feigele—" I start to tell her it's impossible, but she's up again, this time standing a yard in front of me.

"Aba, daba, daba, daba, daba, daba, dabs—" she belts out, her arms flailing in the air, like a wind-tossed seagull with broken wings. Prancing side to side, she shakes her body and sways. Here and there her gamy voice cracks, notes miss their destination, yet her pizzazz is oddly affecting. Her entire face looks rouged. The verses go on and on. When she gets to the end of "Said the monkey to the chimp" for what I'm sure is the third time, I grab her wrist and give a light tug.

She moves so close I feel the heat from her breast, which is heaving. "What you don't know, Marilyn, I should tell you. But not for the ears of your mother." She takes a deep breath. "I have... you know—"

"What?"

"The word I can't say, the terrible thing—"

"Cancer?"

"Shhh," she says, putting her finger over my lips. "That. My days are numbered."

The computer processes: everything. What Franco would say. The bird calls. How long her act would take. How devastating an effect on the next day's ratings. The whole shmear. I look straight in Feigele's pea green pupils. I even process whether she might be lying and decide she isn't.

There is the sound of flushing, and my mother comes into the living room as I get up and Feigele sits in my place. I give Feigele my best sorrowful look, thinking I'll have to make it up to her, maybe by being here for Thanksgiving, the Thursday at least. And in the morning I'll send her long-stemmed roses. As I reach into my purse, I stab my finger with the sharp edge of the plastic case holding Tom Tompkin's videotape. All I have to show for a day's frenzy. I get out my black book, and go to the phone. It'll give me some small pleasure to get the governor out of bed.

Among the Things from Her Childhood She Is Now Ready to Throw Away

BY CATHERINE SCHERER

The two cedar-lined keepsake boxes, hers with the single red rose on the lid and her brother's, the one she coveted as a child, with the foxhunting scene on the lid, men in red coats and horses at the gallop glittering chestnut and black, and white hounds with patches of rust on their flanks as if they were bleeding; the boxes with the cedar smell like freshly dug earth and her brother's box with the broken lid where it had to be forced open because the key was lost after her brother was lost and no secrets inside it, after all.

The Jesus nightlight with the eyes that moved to follow her as she moved; the belief that the people on TV could see her from their side of the screen as well as she could see them, and the agony of always have to be on her "best behavior" in front of the TV and in front of Jesus and not knowing what "best behavior" meant except it meant sitting perfectly still.

The clear plastic, like glass, statue of Jesus that folded into the palm of her hand, that perhaps her father bought her, perhaps when she started first grade, the one that performed a miracle for her once when her brother was going to hit her and she thrust Jesus at him and said, "You can't hit me, Jesus won't let you" and her brother didn't hit her but he ordered her to go to bed, which he had no right to do not being her parent, but she went and she always believed in the protective power of that statue but she never asked it to perform another miracle.

The nun saying during Holy Week, "Christ hung on the cross three hours, but none of you would be able to endure standing with arms outstretched for even three minutes," and when they got home her brother insisted she compete with him to see which of them could stand that way longer and she gave up first but only because he kicked her because for some reason it became urgent for him to win.

* * *

The legend of her mother making ketchup and the possibility that some day she might make it again.

The three black-crusted skillets in nesting sizes, that belonged in some special way to her father, who always said to her mother, "I'll wash the skillet when I get home from work, you'll just ruin it by washing it with soap," and in the largest, deepest of the skillets, that her mother called a "Dutch oven" because it had a glass lid so heavy she and her brother were forbidden to try to lift it, her father made oyster stew with milk and a half-stick of butter, and at least once every autumn oxtail stew with barley.

The thirst in her eyes for the color RED, even though she insisted that her favorite color was blue because her father's favorite color was blue.
Her brother's full set of colored pencils that he was always checking with his thumb, to test the sharpness or bluntness of the points trying to catch her using his property, and her satisfaction in being able to draw dogs better than her brother, who could do everything else better than she.

Dogs.

Her desire for the companionship of dogs, her pleasure in feeding and walking and racing with and rumpling the fur of dogs, and being licked by the wet tongues of dogs and pillowing her ear against their ribs to listen to the secret of their hearts' beating, and the pleasure of her tongue in saying the names of dogs, Buster and Jason and Samantha, their public names always giving place to the same pet name for all their pet dogs, BooBoo, because her father heard in all their barking the same sound "boobooboo," and the flowering again of the simple name Boo into J. C. Booshnaki and Boobooella and Boolukas and dozens of other spur-of-the-moment, quickly forgotten silly endearments, and her urgent desire to command the first place in the hearts of dogs usurped by her brother who always called them "my dog" and excluded her.

The death of dogs.

*   *   *

The belief that by patient accumulation bit by bit as if stone by stone she could build a wall of knowledge in her mind, everything known and worth knowing—the names of all the breeds of dogs and all the baseball teams in the American and the National Leagues, and the answers to all the questions in the Baltimore Catechism, and the singsong of the multiplying tables from 2-times-2 to 12-times-12, and all the rules of spelling, *i before e,* and the exceptions that didn't rhyme to all the rules that did, and the names of all the Presidents of the United States and all the wars the United States had fought and all the heresies against the true church and all the feast days of the saints and what each saint is "good for," St. Lucy for the curing of the eyes and St. Anthony for the finding of lost objects and St. Jude for the granting of impossible wishes, and all the words to the Gettysburg Address, and the Latin words of the *Confiteor* and the *Gloria in excelsis Deo,* and the Latin responses to the Mass prayers that her brother had to learn to become an altar boy and she knew them just as well as he but could never stop being a girl even during the sacred moments of the Mass, and the words to all the Mother Goose rhymes her mother knew, and the German words to the bits of song her father remembered from his boyhood, *Mein Hut er hat drei ecke* and *Hopp hopp hopp Herr Reiter*, and all the things that came in lists, the ten commandments, fourteen stations of the cross, fifteen mysteries of the Rosary...

All her attempts to order the accumulation of knowledge and reduce ignorance to manageable dimensions—the eight narrow-ruled notebooks divided into alphabetical sections by colored tabs and within sections into subjects by clear tabs, *agriculture, art, ballet, baseball*, through the alphabet to *zoology*, as if writing her own encyclopedia, the eight notebooks full of mostly blank pages; and the card index her father helped her start, 3 × 5 cards alphabetized with the titles and authors of all the books she read—all her attempts, that is, before she lost confidence in her child's belief that everything which could be known was known by someone and could be known by her, as if driving out confusion, as if presenting possibilities of rescue, as if breaking the fall so she would never have to cry "I don't know, I just don't know."

* * *

The ability to read a book while walking along the sidewalk avoiding all obstacles by peripheral vision, except that one time she walked into a parking meter hard enough to make her nose bleed.

Any remembered reason why the Little Golden Book, *The Pokey Little Puppy*, always made her cry.

The Little Golden Uncle Wiggly books, which were her brother's favorites and *The Wind in the Willows*, which was her brother's next favorite, that he insisted their mother read over and over; and her mother's voice singing "The bear went over the mountain," singing it over and over because it was her brother's favorite; her brother's loud, off-key voice singing "He installed a bar in the back of his car and he's driving himself to drink," and her mother singing out of her childhood, "Red, white, and blue, your mother was a Jew, your father is a Dutchman, just like you," and singing, "Today is the day they give babies away with a half a pound of tea."

Marjorie Kinnan Rawlings's, *The Yearling*, the first real book, not a story book, their mother read to them, she and her brother sitting on the sofa on either side of her mother reading, when her brother was already in second grade and she was just about to start school behind him and anxious to catch up, and she cried, even her brother cried, at the end of the book when the deer died and then her mother pretended to read about Jody getting a puppy *and* a kitten to make up for the hurt but she knew it was a lie, something made up by her mother, because her mother's voice was no longer a reading voice.

The anger in her mother's voice when she told them "Your father didn't want children, he wanted me to adopt my babies out, no real mother would agree to that," and her mother's false voice, trying to remedy, telling her, "Your father was so pleased when you were born, he told all the nurses you were so beautiful, you looked just like him."

* * *

The accumulation of blessed objects that couldn't just be thrown away because anything blessed must be either burned or buried—years of rosettes worked from blessed palm; scapulars with their squares of felt cloth faded by perspiration; Miraculous Medals, Our Lady of Perpetual Help medals, Sacred Heart of Jesus medals, and faucet washers, all on the same chain that turned her neck green when she wore it in hot weather; her first rosary, with the tarnished metal beads that folded in a little metal case with a raised cross on the lid, that her father gave her and on which he taught her to pray *"Hail Mary, full of grace"* before she went to kindergarden; the rosary with the black beads shaped like seeds that her mother gave her when she made her First Communion but it never felt right between her fingers; her father's rosary that had been his mother's, with crystal beads in triangle shapes that she sometimes borrowed to pray on during Lent because the beads, pressed hard between the fingers, cut little crescent lines like moons into the skin as an extra penance, but her father was always defensive about this rosary, excusing how he had stolen it out of his father's drawer when he decided to leave home at sixteen because he wanted a remembrance of his mother who had died when he was eleven and because his mother had meant him, as her eldest son, to have it, and it was this rosary that should have been buried with her father but the undertaker was aghast because the cross might be gold and she didn't have the courage to insist.

The envelope with the torn scraps of dollar bills and fives and tens and a twenty that her brother took out of their mother's purse, but he never took anything from the "house money" that their father put every week in a frayed black wallet on the bottom shelf in the closet because it was somehow more sacred and neither she nor her brother ever touched it, but once her brother took a whole week's pay out of their mother's purse and he tore the money up and stuffed a handful in his mouth and ate it and flushed more of it down the toilet and some of the scraps fell on the rug and her mother asked her "Please, pick it up for me," and her brother warned her "You'd better not," but she did it anyway, and her mother cried because all her "hard earned money" was being thrown away.

The tack hammer with the gold-colored head that her brother stole from the hardware store, the only thing her brother ever stole that she knew of except money from their mother's purse, and he dared her to steal something too, but he slipped the hammer inside his shirt and snugged it in the band of his shorts and she couldn't do that without lifting her dress which she knew girls mustn't do, and later she told her mother about her brother stealing the hammer but her mother denied it and said, "No, I paid for that hammer," but she was sure her mother was lying.

The ox blood that her father drank because he had low blood pressure, a dark thick tonic that he drank down in one long swallow so he wouldn't taste it and then he put the bottle, with its plain white label with a steer's head on it, on the highest shelf in the darkest corner of the pantry because it couldn't stand the light, and at the beginning of every new school year she insisted her new school shoes be of the same near-maroon color called "oxblood."

Her father's box of emergency shoelaces, labeled BANKER'S CHOICE: CIGAR OF QUALITY, *Made in Florida*, with six pairs of black shoelaces and eleven pairs of brown, and two pairs of "Woodsman's Waterproofed Laces" in yellow, kept in her father's top drawer along with *his* sewing kit, with only spools of black or of white thread, and packets of silver-and-gold needles, which he used to sew on tighter the buttons of new shirts before he wore them, the only sewing he ever did, always insisting on doing it himself because "If you want something done right," he said, and he always ran the end of the thread across the bathroom bar of wet soap and pinched it tight between his fingers to make it thread the needle easier, he said, and her father always said, "A stitch in time," and he always said, "You must grab the bull by the horns" but her mother always said, "You'll have to eat a peck of dirt before you die, you might as well get it over with."

The long shirtcardboards that came back from the laundry with her father's shirts for work folded around them, the cardboards he kept in his shirt drawer but her brother stole them to mount his cigar bands, which both she and her brother collected, but her father would give her the band first if she asked him and he always knew to buy different brands of cigars, once even those strong, pudgy Italian stogies, so they could have the bands, which she kept in her keepsake box with the red rose on the lid and took out to wear on her fingers like proper rings but her brother killed them, pulling the bands apart and mounting them flat on cardboard, and sometimes her brother went in her box and took bands he wanted for his collection, saying "I'm taking this one, OK," but it's not really asking if you don't dare to say "no."

* * *

Her fear of bugs, and all the nights she lay in bed feeling as if bugs were crawling up and down her legs, while she made herself "for the sake of the poor souls in Purgatory" count to ten before allowing herself to scratch.

The comic book her brother dared her to read in which a man had ants inside his body and the tips of his fingers burst open and streams of black ants like black blood gushed out and streams of ants bled out of his nose.

The ice weasels that she knew lived behind the lighted marquee of the Tiffin movie theatre, although she never saw them, perhaps only a glimpse, but they had flesh of ice, and their needling sharp teeth crunched out the bulbs of the marquee with a popping noise, sending down showers of glass.

Her desire to say, whenever they asked her what her childhood had been like, her desire to exaggerate and to say, "It was always cold in my childhood because we lived across from the ice factory and children were always locking themselves inside discarded refrigerators to suffocate and we had a snowball bush in the backyard under which my father buried one of the dogs and my mother always accused my father of being cold as if he were carved out of ice." She remembered her mother saying that and always she wanted to explain, "That's why I can't remember ever sitting on my father's lap, not because he didn't want me to but because he knew ice is hurtful next to the skin," because hadn't her father always warned her and her brother about ice, when every other evening Mrs. Block, who lived upstairs, paid Junior a nickel to accompany her with his wagon, out the back gate and across the alley and past the loading docks and the silent parked trucks of the Jefferson Ice Company that they called simply "the ice house," where Mrs. Block bought a quarter chunk of ice to put in her wooden icebox because she didn't have an electric refrigerator like they did, and Junior would haul the ice, wrapped in burlap sacking, home in his wagon, and she always went along in spite of how the ice house windows at night shone with an eerie blue fluorescence that seemed to breathe out cold, and in spite of the fact that her brother never shared the nickel with her, and in spite of his trying to frighten her with stories of dead people frozen inside the hugh blocks of ice which, during the day, they saw the men load on the trucks, grappling the blocks with sharp tongs and the blocks of ice were taller and broader and thicker than the men were, and constantly their father was warning them about the acid power of ice to rasp the skin off their fingers if they touched it, and her brother always tempted her to press her lips against Mrs. Block's quarter chunk, "Kiss it," he'd whisper when Mrs. Block fell behind, "Kiss it, see if your lips freeze to it, they'll have to cut your lips off."

* * *

The pink baby blanket with the white satin applique bunnies made by Great Aunt Carrie, for whom she should have been named "Carolyn" except that her mother, who was named Carolyn, hated that name.

"Bunny sandwiches," bread and butter and sugar, named after her brother, whose name when they played together was Bunny just as her name was Pursey but she never had a sandwich named after her, not the sandwiches of bread and mustard and green onions and not the sandwiches of buttered bread spread thick with ketchup that were her favorite.

The mystery and the confusion of names, that there are home names, not the play names that she and her brother had together, Pursey and Bunny, which she always knew were private between them not even known to be spoken by their parents, but the home names their parents always called them, Dolly and Junior, until she thought those were their names, her's and her brother's, until she started school and the nun insisted that her new name was Katherine and she dared that first day to insist to the nun that no, it wasn't, and at home her mother told her that her name had always been Katherine and her mother had to show her her birth certificate with the name "Katherine" on it and told her, to reconcile her to that name, that she had been named after her father's mother, but many years later she learned that his mother's name had been Emma and it was her mother's mother who had been named Katherine, and adult though she was, she felt disappointed but knew that if she had known this on her first day of school she would have refused to ever answer to the name "Katherine" but now it was too late; and when her brother, whose school name was Walter after his father but still Junior at home, was choosing his confirmation name, Sylvester, their mother told them the story of how their father, as a boy, chose for his confirmation name "Aloysius" because he wanted his initials to spell a word, W.A.S., and she kept this secret knowledge about her father in her mind so that later when her father had his first heart attack and she had to give the nurse the information for the hospital forms, she told them her father's middle initial was A., and for ten years, until his final heart attack, her father was still trying to convince Medicare and Blue Cross that he had no middle initial, and more than once he wondered angrily, "How the hell did they ever get that idea in the first place?" and she never had the courage to own up it was her; and after the death of her brother, when she was twenty-three, it felt a little bit worse in her mind that she had no adult name to give him, because they had never called him Walter or Walt or Wally, while to still call him "Junior" seemed to take something away that should have been his, but then, after her mother's first fury of grief, her mother never spoke of her son, and she and her father were afraid to speak of him in front of her mother, and finally even to each other, until her mother began to talk as if she had had only one child, a daughter, so that it became unnecessary to struggle to find a name for her brother but that does not mean that she has forgotten him.

Her brother's bronzed baby shoes that her father had kept locked in one of his desk drawers, but after her brother's death, her mother insisted on having them to put under her pillow although she "never expected to sleep again."

Her school name plate with her name Katherine spelled with a "K," printed on ruled construction paper covered with red cellophane, and made by the nun in kindergarten so "Dolly" could keep it on her desk and never forget her name again, but when (in which grade?) did she begin to spell her name Catherine with a "C" because with a "K" seemed too German?

Her favorite song from kindergarten, "John Jacob Jingleheimer Schmidt, that's my name too; Whenever I go out, people always shout, HEY, JOHN JACOB JIN-GLEHEIMER SCHMIDT, that's my name too, ... " the type of song her brother called "around" and had to explain to her again and again that if it got on her tongue and in her mind it might just go around and around and someday she would never be able to stop singing it, but at first she didn't understand what he meant and later, when she did, she pretended she didn't.

* * *

The last felt scrap, the red felt tongue of her most precious toy, Pursey the purse dog, with the zipper pocket in his back, patched and restuffed so many times by her mother it was as if she had always had him, as if he had been born with her, and she carried him everywhere, sitting on him so she wouldn't forget him on the streetcar, and when she played with her brother her name was Pursey just as her brother's name was Bunny after the yellow rattle shaped like a rabbit wearing blue trousers that was his special toy, and often her brother scripted her lines for her, insisting she "Make Pursey say..." and "Now make Pursey say..." and she repeated what her brother told her to say, but she knew what Pursey really said because Pursey spoke her mind for her and she whispered the truth in his ear and he spoke it out of his red tongue but too softly for anyone else to hear, and one day her brother tied a rope around Pursey's neck and hung him from a branch of the tree in the backyard and hit him with the handle of a broom, and he hit Pursey until all of Pursey's cotton stuffing came out and all the stitches came out and she could only rescue a few bits because her brother tried to stop her and they fought but he was three years older and she didn't cry or scream because her throat had locked shut and hurt as if her voice had been torn out, and long after, even after her brother died, she said to herself, "I will never forgive him," and she regretted that when they were children she had never taken his Bunny and smashed it, she had been too much a coward.

The dream of her brother turning into a black dog on the other side of the bedroom door and she could hear through the door his rubber teeth snapping open and closed with a suction sound that made her stomach queasy, and she felt his hot breath through the wood, and she tried to pound on the door to frighten the dog away, but the wood was soft and sticky as honey and caught her hands so she couldn't run, she couldn't scream, she couldn't force the words out of her locked throat, but inside her head she was screaming, *Kill him, kill him, please kill him*.

The power of ejaculations and of sacred names that made her head bow when they were spoken; the power of whispered, "Jesus, Mary, Joseph," to drive the bad thoughts out of her head.

* * *

The image from the TV of Jimmy Durante, in overcoat and slouch hat, at the end of his show saying goodnight, moving out of one spot of light through darkness into the next, getting smaller, further away, turning, saying, "Goodnight, folks," finally turning and saying the very last thing, "Goodnight, Mrs. Calabash, wherever you are," and then being gone and the sadness she felt for him and how she always waved her father off to work like that, from the porch or the front window, watching him walking away and at every other step, he turned to wave goodbye to her and she waved goodbye back at him, until he turned the corner and was gone, it was a ritual, like her picking the tie he should wear to work that day, they always did it even after she was grown up, she waved goodbye to him the day he had his fatal heart attack only she was going away and he was standing at the window waving and she was in a hurry but she could have turned around and waved to him one last time.

The "books full of times" that her father corrected twice a year and she helped him, and he carried them to work as a thick bulge in his inside coat pocket so he could consult them and schedule the mail for the Post Office, which was a very important place to work but hard on his feet because he walked around all day supervising (he wore Junior's pedometer to work once and when he came home it read 22 miles that he had walked) and one of the things she was supposed to remember for him was that he must put arch supports in his shoes before going to work, but working at the Post Office was hard on his ears too because handling mail by the sackful was noisy and he said all he wanted when he came home was a little peace and quiet, and twice a year, when time changed, she had no idea why but so her father wouldn't think she was dumb she pretended she understood, her father asked her, never her brother, to help him make his Time Books, and she sat beside him at the dining room table and read from a blue binder the names of train cities and arrival and departure times, while her father typed them on strips of paper, and then they switched and he read out of the binder and she checked the strips to make sure they matched, and then he bound the strips of paper between a double thickness of brown cardboard so the books flipped open at one end, and sometimes it took many hours over several weekends to make his books and he would ask her, "Do you want to stop, I can work by myself?" but always she said, "No."

All her memories of her father on Sundays when she walked with him to church and on the way he smoked a cigar, and when they were out of sight of the house, he let her have two or three puffs even though her mother disapproved, and when they reached the railroad underpass a block before the church, he extinguished the lighted end of his cigar and, while she stood lookout, he hid it up high in the crevice-like-a-shelf that the cement buttress made when it dogged into the embankment, and those times when she was allowed to sit with her father instead of having to sit with her class under the guardian eye of the nun, she felt apprehensive because her father sucked peppermints during the sermon and if the nun had caught him, she would have scolded, and then on the way home from church her father retrieved his cigar and it was always where he had left it, no one ever stole it, and he relit it to finish on the walk home and those Sundays when he was in a particularly good mood, when they turned off North Avenue into their side street, he put her Sunday hat on his head and mimicked being a girl and they both laughed.

*   *   *

The practicing of her religion that created the rhythms of her day—her mumbled Act of Consecration while she brushed her teeth or dressed or hurried so she wouldn't be late for the eight o'clock Mass that began every school day, and going into church with a flourish of her fingers like a fanfare as she signed herself broadly with the sign of the cross, and dipping and rising as she genuflected deeply enough so her bent knee thumped the cold floor, and during Mass, the kneeling and standing and sitting in unison, and the rhythms of the prayers, even if she didn't know the exact meaning of the Latin words, and repeating the same acts every school day, glancing at the crucifix and the clock above the nun's desk, standing for prayers at the beginning and at the end of the school day, and sitting crowded over on the left side of her seat to make room on the right for her guardian angel to sit beside her, and writing the first thing at the top of every homework paper "J.M.J." to sanctify it, and every day during May, processioning around the classroom, singing Marian hymns until everyone got a turn to be the one to place the crown of artificial flowers on the Mary statue, and the marking of the liturgical seasons, when the color of the Mass vestments the priest wore changed, purple for the long seasons of penance, Advent and Lent,

and the idea of penance and her confidence in the penance of little things, like making herself eat the crust on her piece of pie, or even better, making herself eat hers and her brother's crust, in the hope that these things would make things right again, and the mystery of self-inflicted pain "for Jesus' sake" or for the sake of the souls suffering, for all the people in pain, for the community of shared pain into which they were privileged to be initiated,

and her collection of holy cards with gilt edges reminding her to pray for the souls of the dead, people whose funeral Masses her class attended because otherwise the priest would have had to say Mass to a nearly empty church and the nun said it was a "work of mercy" to pray for the neglected dead and they didn't mind because they got out of lessons, and the dark secret penances of her brother, who went to church at 5:30 in the morning, when their mother left the house to go to work, and he heard all the Masses, 6, 7, 7:30, and the schoolkids' Mass at 8, and some women who attended the first Mass told Fr. Long that they had seen Junior, waiting outside for the church to open, beating his head against the brick wall and when they looked there were traces of blood on the bricks, and it was something so awesome her parents talked about it to each other in whispers because she wasn't supposed to know,

and her belief in the power of the Act of Contrition said while lying in bed every night just in case anyone died during the night, and her never, until much later, having to understand the injunction to "pray for a happy death."

*   *   *

The pocket notebook in which her brother kept his account of indulgences, the notebook with the wire binding, with the sharp thorn of wire and the pages bearing blood traces of her brother's fingerprints, every page filled with his left-handed writing with its sharp, pointy letters, even the vowels, and listing the number of days of indulgence he earned, which meant so many days less he would have to suffer in Purgatory after his death, *300 days, 300 days, 100 days*, earned for bursts of prayer, "All for thee, O most Sacred Heart of Jesus," or for walking back and forth to school mumbling over and over "Jesus, Mary, Joseph", and dotted through the book the pardoning words *Plenary Indulgence* underscored, which would have remitted the whole of his punishment if he never committed another sin after, the plenary indulgences earned by such things as visiting seven churches on Holy Thursday or reciting the rosary for 54 days without missing a day (but he considered it just as good if she recited the rosary for him *if* he made her).

The sight in the memory of her eyes of her brother beating his breast hard enough to make a thumping sound, *mea culpa, mea culpa*," and the sound in the memory of her ears of her brother's voice saying the novena prayers louder than anyone else so that people turned to look at him, and the sympathetic ache in her knees from watching her brother crawling up the church aisle on his knees to kiss the relics after novena or to adore the Cross on Good Friday, the sort of thing that her father dismissed as the excessive piety of the old women dressed in black, with black babushkas knotted into batwings under their chins, the ones her father and mother called "DPs" because of the Second World War.

The photo album with stiff black pages in which her brother mounted the black and white pictures he took of churches and underneath each in her brother's handwriting, in white manicure pencil or in gold ink, the name of the church, "Maternity of the Blessed Virgin Mary," "St. Cyril and Methodius," and the date, "May 12, 1954," "January 6, 1955," during the time (when he was in sixth, seventh, and eighth grades) when he was determined to make a pilgrimage to every Catholic church in Chicago (all 246 listed in the phone book) and he made their mother go with him after school, and her father said, "Your mother acts as if she's roped to your brother," and she heard her father complain to her mother, "You shouldn't leave that younger child at home alone all the time."

* * *

Her father's cautions about not identifying them as "Catholic" because he would be punished for it where he worked and he always said to her, "You don't have to lie," but he always said, "Just don't say anything, when people ask just don't say anything, it's no one's business what religion we are," and he was especially anxious that his dentist friend from before he was married not know they were Catholic but every time she had to go to him, the dentist asked her "What school do you go to?" and she gave the answer her father told her to give, "Oh, just one in the neighborhood," but once when she said this, the dentist dropped the drill and hit her on the head, as if he were angry, but she knew it was God who was really punishing her for denying her faith, which the nuns said was worse than a mortal sin, but she was only trying to protect her father.

The knowledge that her father meant to compliment her when he said to her mother, "I can be in the same room with Dolly for hours without either of us ever having to say a word."

The blue high-heeled shoes, her first pair, that her mother insisted should be dyed by Maling's Shoes to match the blue of her evening gown, the one with the rhinestone straps over bare shoulders, that she should have worn for the first time when a boy asked her to the school dance and she got dressed early and waited and a half hour past the time, he called and said he'd sprained his ankle and couldn't take her to the dance and her mother said, to comfort her, "He's probably just saying that because he found some other girl he wants to take," and she took off her dress and hung it in the closet and she put her shoes back in the brown paper bag and put them in the freezer section of the refrigerator, until a long time after, her father said one day rummaging, "Do these need to be in here?" and she took the bag of shoes and put it in the dark at the back of the closet.

The blue plastic clogs she had to wear for swimming class once a week as part of gym, but she never learned how to swim, just barely how to float if she stopped every few feet to reassure herself by letting down her toes and touching the tiled bottom of the pool, and one day the bell rang for the end of the period and everyone got out of the pool except her, she was alone and determined to complete her float across the width of the pool but still in the middle she drifted into deep water and couldn't touch bottom, and she panicked and she swallowed water that tasted like scrubwater and burned her nose and her throat so she couldn't call for help, but she flailed her arms and kicked and finally reached the safety of the pool curb, and she clung to it a long time just breathing, and she never told anyone about nearly drowning, only afterwards she said to herself, See, it isn't so easy to die, it isn't so easy to make yourself die.

*   *   *

The dream she had after her father died and in it, her father was engulfed in flames but standing calmly, watering the lawn while she stood on the sidewalk, and he sprayed her with the hose and she thought the liquid on her hands smelled like gasoline but the odor was so faint it might be water, she couldn't be sure.

The phrase, "You'll understand when you get older," her father always said, her mother always said, "You'll understand when you get older," and she believed it just as she believed that if she did her eye exercises faithfully she would someday not have to wear glasses, but she still wore glasses and the day was coming soon when there wouldn't be much older to get.

Turning Colder

BY MARY TROY

Marcy leaned down into Baby Jonathan's crib, put her face up against his, and said, "Baby, baby, baby, baby. Such a cute, cute, coot liddle baby." Baby Jonathan smiled and blew a bubble of spit, and Marcy poked him gently in his soft tummy, tickling him she thought, wanting to keep touching him. She knew that Baby Jonathan would grow up to be just plain Jonathan or Jon, a dirty little boy like her seven-year-old half brother, Red, who threw cicada shells at her, who sat across the dinner table from her and stuck out his tongue but was never caught and punished. "Don't expect me to solve your problems," was what her mother said when Marcy told on Red. But before Baby Jonathan grew, he was a soft, squirmy thing, and Marcy was glad his mother, Helen Pease, wanted Marcy's help each weekday morning during the summer.

Ray and Helen Pease lived in a yellow brick ranch house across the street and down one from the white brick split level of Marcy's parents, Sissy and Jake Manning. The Peases had a child older than Baby Jonathan, a girl named Belinda whom Marcy's mother and Marcy, too, called ruined, though Helen Pease called her just different. At the age of four, Belinda could not yet sit without pillows stuffed behind her. She had to be strapped into her stroller, and even though she was the

120

size of the average four-year-old, her physical growth right on target, she had to be carried everywhere. And she still wore diapers and had to be fed. She was the reason Helen Pease asked Sissy Manning if Marcy could come over five mornings a week: Belinda demanded as much time as five-month-old Baby Jonathan.

So Sissy Manning was able to save the money she would have spent on summer camp for Marcy, and Marcy was freed from having to spend each day with Red in the seven-to-ten-year-old group where she would have watched him eat his glue in craft class and would have screamed as he splattered paint on her. And because Sissy worked nine to five in the billing department of Rubicon Furniture Company, Marcy spent each afternoon playing with her most recent very best friend Susan, who lived less than a block from the Peases and whose mother was a second grade teacher and so was home anyway.

"He's quite bright, isn't he?" Helen said of Baby Jonathan as Marcy played with him. "See how he follows you with his eyes." And later, after Helen fed him and she and Marcy sang about clapping hands, she said, "See how he turns his head, looks toward sound."

Marcy nodded as usual, said she could see how bright he was, because though she did not know how brightness in babies was measured, she wanted to agree with Helen in all things. Thin, blue-eyed, delicate-looking Helen, who seemed refined even in her usual jeans and T-shirts, was more wonderful than any movie star. When Marcy and Susan played grown-up, they fought over who got to be Mrs. Pease, and sometimes they would cross their fingers, close their eyes, and hold their breaths as long as possible, willing their brown hair to turn blond. Of course, Marcy was the lucky one, and they both knew why. Helen sent Marcy on her way each afternoon with a kiss on the forehead and a quick but firm hug.

What Marcy liked best, though, was Helen's happiness. It was quieter than the whooping-it-up, jitterbugging-across-the-kitchen kind of happiness of Jake and Sissy Manning: it was one you thought could last a while, one you could count on. "Helen and Ray just don't know how to have fun," Sissy Manning said often to Jake or to Marcy and Red. Sissy started saying it after one of her New Year's Eve parties, the one two years ago when the Peases had been invited because they were new to the neighborhood and probably lonely, but then Ray had refused to play "pass the orange," and both Helen and Ray turned down the extra-potent garbage can punch.

But the Peases did not suffer the way the Mannings did, either. It was not unusual for Sissy or Jake to throw the words *liar, fool,* and *cheat* at each other, not unusual for toy trucks, lamps, and dishes to sail through the air as well, smash against doors and walls. Though Marcy and Red were not as adept at suffering as Jake and Sissy, not yet, he had bitten her hard enough to leave a mark, and she had cried as loudly and as long as she could, stopping hours after the pain was gone. And Marcy was certain the Peases never threw each other out of the house, never flushed each other's car keys down the toilet.

The main disturbance in the Pease household was caused by Belinda, who would suddenly bang and slam herself against the back of her chair, croak like a bullfrog, and flail her arms. Her fits were unpredictable and irregular. An entire day or two could pass without one, and not even the doctors were sure what set them off. When one occurred, Helen or Ray, or Marcy if she was helping out, would stroke Belinda's head, pat her cheek, even squeeze her feet, touch her somewhere, somehow. Touch finally would calm her. Helen said it was Belinda's way of checking to see if she were loved. Marcy, of course, did not want to touch Belinda and did so only because Helen expected it. In fact, Marcy and Susan decided the Peases would be so much better off without Belinda, who looked like a monster with her cold, bluish skin, her red and crusty eyes, her lower lip that sagged from the weight of her drool.

"It took us a while to want another one," Helen said once to Marcy after one of Belinda's spells. "Even though we love her, we didn't want to try again for more than two years." Marcy nodded to keep Helen talking in her soft lullaby voice, but though Susan's mother had told both Susan and Marcy about reproduction—baby production they said to each other— trying had not been mentioned. "He's worth all our fears," Helen said. "He's perfect. Perfect Baby Jonathan."

Marcy's jobs at the Pease house were small. Other than

touching Belinda, she sometimes fed her, pushing spoonfuls of mashed or pureed something into the dripping mouth. And as she fed Belinda, she talked to her, talked to her as Helen asked her to, told Belinda she was having carrots or lamb, told her it was yummy. More often, though, Helen fed Belinda and Marcy's job was to keep Baby Jonathan happy throughout. She would sit in the big armchair on the edge of the living room closest to the dining area, and Helen would place Baby Jonathan in Marcy's lap. Marcy would talk to him then, and sing the clapping song and the one about monkeys jumping on a bed. She would move as little as possible, afraid always he would roll off. Baby Jonathan was wiggly, more so than most five-month-olds, Helen said, but added she knew Marcy could hold him if she were careful.

It was a Tuesday morning in July, the week after the Fourth of July party the Mannings had thrown for selected neighbors—the Peases had not been invited to this one—and after playing with Baby Jonathan, Marcy was now "keeping an eye" on Belinda while Helen gave Baby Jonathan a bath in the kitchen sink.

"What all went on at the party?" Helen asked as she lowered Baby Jonathan into the water.

"First we just played stuff," Marcy said, meaning herself and three other girls, Susan included, whose parents had been there. "But then Red and another jerk kept trying to steal our dolls and put firecrackers in them. They said they wanted to kill our kids. Mom didn't do anything about it, either. All the grown-ups just sat around and told jokes."

"You know," Helen said as she soaped Baby Jonathan's front, "if you didn't scream so much when Red tormented you, he'd get tired and quit. You make it fun for him."

"Mrs. Pease," Marcy said. "You don't *like* Red, do you?"

"I don't know him well, not like I know you, but I suspect he's a fine fellow, a trial only to his big sister."

"Half," Marcy said. "Half sister. My real father died when his motorcycle hit a car. Mom says he was burned to a crisp." Marcy planned to continue the story, to tell all she knew about what happened when she was just two months old, but instead Belinda started one of her croaking and thrashing attacks.

"Pat her head," Helen said.

Marcy touched Belinda's head with the tip of her right middle finger, touched Belinda's head twice, but so gingerly the touching had no effect. Marcy wished Belinda would settle back down on her own—after all, she had started up on her own, hadn't she—and do it soon. Otherwise Marcy would have to pat one of the puffy cheeks, come close to the drooling lip.

But Belinda grew louder, so loud Helen had to shout her next instructions.

"I'll have to do it. Tell her I'm coming." But before Marcy had a chance to tell Belinda anything, as if Belinda would have understood, Helen lifted Baby Jonathan from the water and asked Marcy to run to the nursery for a towel she had forgotten. "Hurry," she said above Belinda's noises.

As Marcy ran through the living room, she heard the front door buzzer, but ignored it. She was on a mission for Mrs. Pease and, having picked up speed in the dining area, was now running so fast she imagined herself in a cartoon, taking the corners on a slant while puffs of smoke trailed behind. The buzzer sounded twice as she reached up to the shelf above Baby Jonathan's changing table, and once more as she left the nursery, towel in hand. Whoever it was was as demanding as Belinda, so on her way back, in spite of the cries from the kitchen, in spite of Baby Jonathan dripping dry above the sink, and knowing she shouldn't, Marcy opened the door on two women carrying books and dressed in dark suits, not the business kind, but ones that even to a nine-year-old looked homemade.

The two seemed official, though, so when the one whose short hair was almost entirely gray asked, Marcy told the truth. Her mother was not home, and this was not her mother's home anyway. This was the home of Mrs. Pease, who was in the kitchen. The women said Mrs. Pease was the one they wanted to see, so Marcy told them to come in and then finished her run.

"Two ladies want to see you," she said as Helen placed Baby Jonathan in the towel Marcy held out.

"It better be important," Helen said and turned to Belinda, bent down and hugged her, made cooing sounds above what were now sobs.

"It's the only importance," the gray-haired woman said. She stood in the kitchen doorway, the younger one behind her, looking over her shoulder. "It's about life and death."

"About life everlasting," the younger one corrected. "About how to live forever."

Helen rolled her eyes at Marcy, who saw but did not understand. She was too busy anyway with Baby Jonathan. He was wiggling in her arms, and she had never held him while standing. She wanted to take a chance and move into the dining area, at least go as far as one of the straight-backed chairs, which would not be as good as a living room chair, but would be better than nothing, but the ladies blocked her way. She knew she could ask them to move, or ask them to take Baby Jonathan even though that would mean turning her job over to strangers, but she could also slide down and sit on the floor, which would be easier. She took two steps backwards toward the refrigerator behind her. She would lean against it to slide down.

"Have you noticed," the gray-haired lady said, "that there is more evil now than ever before? Do you realize the Evil One is among us?"

Belinda's cries were quieter and Helen's sounds of comfort were easy to hear. She said, "Pretty Belinda, sweet Belinda." Marcy took one more step back, and Baby Jonathan began to slip down her front. "Mrs. Pease," she said, starting to ask for help.

"Many people are lost, don't know where to turn," the younger women said, still speaking over the gray-haired one's shoulder.

Marcy tightened her grip on Baby Jonathan, wrapped her arms around his legs and bottom, lifted him higher on her, but he flipped backwards and landed head first on the kitchen floor. Marcy heard the crack, and felt it in her own head.

In the confusion that followed, Helen looked up once at Marcy, looked up from her position above Baby Jonathan, for a fraction of a second looked into Marcy's eyes. Marcy did not know who called the ambulance, who stayed with Belinda, who held Helen as she screamed louder than Sissy Manning had done even at the height of any of her sufferings. Marcy could not remember later how long she had stood and watched the floor, but she did remember the thin line of blood from one of Baby Jonathan's ears. She left by the Peases' back door, cut through the back neighbor's kitchen garden, and ran to Susan's, then stopped and sat in the dirt along the shady side of the house to catch her breath before knocking.

"You're early today," Susan's mother said, sounding put upon. "I guess you'll have to have lunch with us."

"Okay," Marcy said.

And later, after cheddar cheese sandwiches and shoestring potatoes, Susan's mother gave in and took them to the mall cinema to see *Bambi*, which Susan and Marcy had seen four times already that summer, crying louder each time. Marcy did not cry this time. When Susan's mother dropped Marcy off at home it was four o'clock, a little earlier than usual, and for more than an hour Marcy sat alone and through the living room sheers watched the yellow house across the street. Except for the shades being drawn and Mr. Pease's car in the drive, it seemed the same as always. Marcy could almost believe the morning had been a dream, almost believe there had been no trickle of blood. When Sissy Manning arrived home with Red and a friend of his from camp who was going to spend the night, Marcy waited for the question.

"How was *your* day?"

"Okay," Marcy said.

"That's a hell of a lot better than mine then," Sissy said. "We had all the crazy customers today. Try explaining credit and interest to some of the ignoramuses who are out walking around. And I think Jake is about to lose his job. He gets written up for coming in late, and acts like it's my fault. I wake him up. At least I try." She plopped down on the couch as usual, kicked off her shoes. "Oh life," she said. "How wonderful. You boys better not be jumping on the bed," she yelled in the direction of the hall. "I mean he's a grown man. He should be able to get himself off to work. But no. It's all up to me. Everything is up to me."

"I saw *Bambi* today," Marcy said, sitting on the couch beside her mother, wanting without real hope to be hugged or kissed hello, something Sissy did only for Jake and only if she were not mad at him.

"Again?" Sissy looked at Marcy and frowned, but patted

her thigh. Marcy smiled. It was as close to a hug as she would get. "You'll outgrow that cornball stuff pretty soon, I guess."

"And Baby Jonathan died."

By the time Jake arrived home a half hour later, Sissy had the whole story, and not just from Marcy. Some of the other neighbors had seen the ambulance and had talked to the Bible ladies for details. "Those people are cursed," Sissy said to Jake. "The poor things." And to Susan's mother, who had not heard any of it until Sissy called, she said, "It makes you grateful for what you do have. I mean it's easier to put up with Jake and all the rest when you hear something like that." And as Marcy sat in the living room before the dinner that was later than usual because of the phone calls, she listened to her mother's conversation, heard Sissy say, "No. I don't think she blames herself. After all, it was an accident. The Bible ladies saw it," followed by a pause, and then, "Maybe you're right. Kids aren't logical," and finally, "I will talk to her. I'll let you know how it goes."

"You know it's not your fault, don't you?" Sissy said that evening during dinner, and as Marcy made dams and rivers with her mashed potatoes and gravy, Jake echoed Sissy. "Accidents are just that," he said in the voice that always sounded too high to come from such a broad-chested man, the voice that Marcy imitated sometimes to make Susan laugh. "They're things that are nobody's fault. When you drop a dish or a glass," he said, "we don't punish you much because we know it was an accident."

"That's a pretty poor example, Jake," Sissy said.

"It's a comparison," Jake said. "And it *is* the same thing."

"It's stupid," Sissy said. "And let me handle this anyway. She's my daughter."

"I hear that all the time," he said, and pointed at Marcy. "And I'm tired of hearing how much you know about her just because you gave birth. I'm tired of being told how little I know about her, or about anything."

"I know it wasn't my fault," Marcy said loudly.

"Good," Sissy said.

"Good," Jake said and smiled at Sissy across the table.

"Good," Red said and smiled at his friend.

Later when Sissy did the dishes, Jake snuck up behind her and bit her neck, making her squeal.

Before Marcy went to bed that evening, as she sat in the living room and pretended to watch television with Jake but instead pictured the cold blue sorrow of Helen Pease's eyes, she heard her mother talk to Susan's mother again. Sissy said yes, she agreed. If it had to have been one of them, it should have been the girl. She said, "The poor things," for probably the tenth time. Then Marcy heard herself discussed again. "She says she doesn't feel guilty... Yes, I know it will take more time. You're right. Saying's not everything... Well, no. She didn't say why she went to the movie, why she waited to tell someone... Yes, I would have expected her to tell Susan." The last thing Marcy heard was, "Yes, you're right again. I better have another talk with her." Marcy looked up and saw Jake watching her instead of his television police show. His balding head was tilted to one side, and his already tiny black eyes were narrowed. Marcy looked at the floor, at the brown and yellow braided rug, then stood as quietly as she could, and almost tiptoed down the hallway to her room. Red and his friend were playing in it, using it as the prison for their game of Break Out, but they left when she entered. She had not had to say a word.

She undressed and crawled into bed, pulling the sheet up to her bottom lip, tucking it in around her ears. She closed her eyes, but her mother was suddenly there, sitting on the edge of the bed. "Wake up," Sissy said, her eyes narrowed as Jake's had been. "I have to ask you a few questions."

Marcy looked at the familiar round face, at the make-up line that used to separate the face so decisively from the neck, but now, at least from below, there was another chin and the separation was no so clear. Marcy tried to remember her mother kissing her goodnight. She must have done so when Marcy was a baby, when she was Baby Jonathan's age or before that when her father was still alive.

"Why did you go to the movie?"

Marcy looked at her mother and said nothing. It was a question she could not answer.

"There must be a reason," Sissy said. "Were you afraid?"

"No." Marcy turned to the wall. There was no comfort or relief in her mother's face.

"You did like Baby Jonathan, didn't you?"

Marcy remained quiet. How can you like a baby, she thought. She liked Susan. She liked Mrs. Pease. She did not like Red. She wanted to answer well because her mother and Jake and Susan's mother were concerned. She did like touching Baby Jonathan, and she liked seeing him smile. She liked the quiet, loving way Mrs. Pease talked about Baby Jonathan. Maybe that was enough. "I guess so," she said, but Sissy had waited too long for the answer and was already in the doorway, was on her way to call Susan's mother.

The following morning, Sissy stayed home from work so she would be there when the police talked to Marcy. A policeman and a policewoman told Marcy that no one was in trouble, least of all her. They explained that when babies died, there was always a routine investigation. They asked how Baby Jonathan fell, what kind of mother Mrs. Pease was, whether Mr. or Mrs. Pease ever hit their children, whether Marcy was ever afraid at their house, and if Marcy had ever wanted to hurt Baby Jonathan. Marcy answered their questions, telling how Baby Jonathan wiggled from her arms, saying he was cute and smart, saying Mrs. Pease was the best mother in the world, which made the policewoman look at Sissy and laugh as if Marcy had embarrassed them all.

The policeman asked her what she did after Baby Jonathan fell, and then he too asked what she could not answer. "Why?"

"Were you afraid?" he asked as Sissy had.

"No."

"Were you sad?"

She shrugged. she had not been anything that could be said with a word, but she wanted to say what would make them stop asking.

"Why didn't you tell Susan's mother?" the policewoman asked.

Marcy thought for a moment, and finally smiled. She had figured out the answer that would make her seem smart, the one they probably wanted. "It wouldn't have made any difference. She couldn't help."

They left Marcy sitting on the couch when it was over, and talked to Sissy at the front door. "It seems so cold," the policewoman said. "Maybe too much." The policeman agreed. "I'm not saying there's anything wrong," he said. "Not now anyway, but a normal child wouldn't behave like that. Has she cried?"

"No," Sissy said. "No, she has not."

On the Friday morning of the week following the Fourth of July, when the mourners clustered around the tiny grave on a hillside in Calvary Cemetery, the Peases cried quietly, just as Marcy had known they would, and Susan's mother and Sissy wiped away a few tears of their own. Susan cried louder than anyone, though, and Marcy was jealous, especially when Susan ended up with the hiccups. Marcy knew her mother was jealous, too, so she tried to cry. She thought of her mother, of how she would feel if her mother died, of her father dying in flames nine years ago. She pretended Susan was dead. She even remembered the saddest part when Bambi's mother died. Nothing worked. The policeman had called her not normal. She looked around and saw the Bible ladies standing off from the crowd, under an elm tree. One of them had reported her behavior as strange and had told the police that Marcy refused to call the ambulance. The other one—the police did not tell which one said what—said Marcy looked almost happy as she turned and ran. Marcy had heard it all as her mother told Susan's mother what the police said the Bible ladies said. They had called her a strange little girl.

When Marcy looked back to the center of the pale yellow tent stretched over the grave, she saw Mrs. Pease slump against Mr. Pease, saw him make the others who sat in the front row move so he could stretch her out across the folding chairs. Had Mrs. Pease been told Marcy saw *Bambi* after Baby Jonathan died? Either way, Marcy knew she would never be able to talk to the Peases again, and knowing that almost did it, almost produced the tears that would have proved her normal. But even then the tears stung her eyes from behind, filled up the folds of her eyelids, but did not fall, would not. If she felt just one, she would turn to her mother, show her. But maybe they were right, all of them. She could no longer cry.

It was more than a week later as she lay in bed, unable as

usual to sleep until just before it was time to get up and dress for summer camp, that she heard them fight about her.

"Something *is* wrong with her," Jake said. "Red says she doesn't play with the other kids at camp."

"Red may not see everything," Sissy said.

"Stop pretending and face facts," Jake said. "She doesn't even seem to miss Susan, call her after camp. It's not natural. We should have seen it even before when she wanted to help Helen instead of playing."

"Well, if you think something's wrong, do something besides talk. I can't take care of everything all by myself."

"You don't have to act so burdened. I'm trying to help."

"Then talk to *her.*"

"She won't talk to me. She follows your lead in that."

"Oh, so now there's something wrong with me, too? The truth is I talk more than you listen."

Marcy left her bed and stood in the open doorway. These fights used to make her hide under the sheet, used to make her pray for an end, pray that the Peases wouldn't hear. Now, she wanted to listen. It was further proof of how cold she was.

Soon they were talking about Marcy's father. Sissy always mentioned him when the fight got going good, and Jake invariably said something about how he, too, wished the S.O.B. were still alive and Sissy would be driving *him* crazy. Sissy would say at least he would have had a good job, he was so talented, and Jake would say Sissy could have her freedom anytime. As Marcy listened, she anticipated the crash which always came, though its cause varied, and which signaled the end of the fight. Soon after the crash, one of them would leave, and that someone was most often Jake, who was better at it, who could make his car roar as he backed it down the drive and spun around on the street, could make his car sound mad, too. Sometimes the crash was Sissy throwing her silver-backed hand mirror at Jake, and once she threw the bedside lamp at the wall. Jake threw one of his boots so hard the last time they had a real fight, threw it at the wall above the bed and not at Sissy, that it made a hole in the drywall that Sissy wanted to cover with a picture. Jake said leave it as it was, though, to remind him of his own temper and keep him humble.

When the crash came, Marcy held her breath and flattened herself against the wall, waiting to see who would leave. It was Jake, and he rushed past her, slammed the front door on his way out, and made his tires squeal all the way to the end of the block. Sissy's sobs, as usual, filled the house. But this time, instead of crying quietly herself, Marcy knocked on her mother's bedroom door, and entered as Sissy choked out, "Go away."

"I'm sorry I'm not natural," Marcy said. "I try to be better."

"Can't I have a little privacy in my own house?" Sissy said. "Go to bed."

"I don't know why I went to the movie," Marcy said, inching closer to the bed, wanting to climb in and touch her mother.

"I know, I know. You can't help being what you are." Sissy rolled over, turned face down on the bed. "It must be easier not to feel as much." She cried into Jake's pillow. Marcy stood listening until the muffled sobs turned to snores, and then went back to her room. It was still dark when she heard Jake return, and when she finally fell asleep, she dreamed she was stuck in the mud up to her knees and monsters who looked like Belinda were attacking her.

A month later, Sissy Manning took another day off work to meet with the principal of Marcy's school and with Marcy's soon-to-be fourth grade teacher. As she explained it to Susan's mother over the phone that evening, "I wanted them to know Marcy is a little, you know, strange. Like everyone said. I thought it would be easier if they knew beforehand."

Marcy sat in the living room as she listened, dry-eyed, to her mother's conversation. She stared at the yellow house across the street and down one, the house where Helen's hugs and Baby Jonathan's smiles had created a happiness that proved fragile after all. And she pictured the inside of her as empty, her body as hollow and cold. And turning colder.

Fairie

BY JOHN ALSPAUGH

"Trolls are only macho elves," I explain to my niece, who is sitting in the upturned palm of my hand. Stellie suffers from an acute form of ultra-dwarfism. Although she is seven and soon to be eight, she weighs only twenty-three pounds. She is almost two feet tall, but squatting the way she is now—hunkered down on my palm—she seems much smaller.

I am reading *The Three Billy-Goats Gruff* out loud to her for the third time since my arrival. Stellie goes wide-eyed when I speak the voice of the troll. She interrupts me frequently with urgent questions about the nature of trolls. Her voice sounds like a chipmunk's, and every time she says something, I'm equally amazed. We are sitting in amber lamplight, on a sandy, big-cushioned sofa. The salt-smell of the sea and the muffled sound of breaking waves roll in through the open windows. My sister Susan and her husband, Zed, have gone out for a walk, alone for a change, along the dark beach.

"Why does the troll want to eat the most-little billy-goat?" Stellie's voice is high and nasal.

"Oh, he doesn't really want to eat him—he's just trying to scare him for fun."

"What do trolls eat for breakfast?"

"On Saturdays, your average troll will eat a bowl of dirty, balled-up socks."

Stellie looks at me with her lips parted, like a parakeet expecting a bit of cracker. Then she smiles, realizing that I am making this up.

"Uncle John?" she asks. Her voice seems squeezed, as if out of a balloon. "What does the troll eat on Sunday?"

"Oh, he doesn't eat anything on Sundays. That's why he's only fooling the three Billy-Goats Gruff—just for fun."

Stellie looks up at me from my palm and says, "Cause today's *Sunday?*"

"Of course. The troll isn't about to eat anything today. He's fasting."

"'Fasting'? Not even a bite of air?"

"No. Not even a bite of air. It's against his religion."

Earlier that afternoon—under the shade of a big, blue umbrella—we had watched someone's Labrador Retriever chomping in the surf. Squatting atop a yellow Dixie Cup packed with sand, Stellie asked, "Why does he bite the air?"

I told her he was fasting.

In her tiny brain, even small beasts loom to devour her. A rampaging sand crab could easily knock her over. A starfish might even smother her. From her perspective, the world is truly immense.

* * *

The following morning, playing with Stellie in a tidal pool, I sprawl out on my stomach in about half a foot of sun-warmed water. Stellie and I study a few trapped minnows that are swimming around us. When an incoming wave rushes across us in a thick white blanket of foam, I lunge and snag Stellie by her leg before she's sucked seaward in the backwash. She rolls up sputtering, crying from the sting of seawater. Susan and Zed come running.

Back at the umbrella, where it is safe and the sand is dry, Stellie spends the next twenty minutes angrily spanking the beach with a doll-house spatula. I lie face-up to the searing sun on a dry towel. I can see the orange-red glare through my shut eyelids, where squiggles drift across, as if on a microscopic slide.

To the rhythm of the waves, I hear Stellie's wee voice chant:

Jesus loves me, yes I know
For the Bible tells me so
Little worms to him belong
They are weak, but he is strong...

For the last seven years, since Stellie was born, my sister and her husband have waded deeper and deeper into Christianity. As far as I can tell, they are in way over their heads, and it seems that I have more in common with Stellie than I do with either Susan or Zed.

After my nap in the sun, I wake up hungry. Earlier, Susan made cream cheese-and-olive sandwiches that she individually wrapped in Baggies. They are packed in a red and white cooler, stacked on top of an assortment of soft drinks which, in turn, are nestled firmly in crushed ice. I wolf down half a sandwich before I realize that Zed, Susan, and Stellie have their heads bowed in a silent prayer. I immediately stop chewing and stare down at a minuscule insect with delicate electric blue wings. It has landed on my sandwich. With one eye slightly opened, I examine the tiny creature as it quivers in the wind. It is firmly anchored to the spongy surface of my bread. After our sandwiches have been properly blessed, I flick it into oblivion.

I am amazed that little Stellie eats as much as we do. She has the metabolism of a hummingbird. After lunch—on my hands and knees—I start digging a hole for her to play in. Within fifteen minutes, having worked like a dog, I have created a virtual pit. Stellie smiles up from the hole, dwarfed, as I would be, if I were to stand in a newly dug swimming pool.

The hole is big enough to accommodate both of us—but, sitting, I'm capable of seeing out, my head just above the rumpled horizon of sand. I pack a Dixie Cup with deeper, darker sand, turn it upside-down beside Stellie, and lift off the cup. She smacks her little spatula on the mold of sand. It seems quite firm. Then she says, "Uncle John, I'm going to sit on my bucket." When she plops down on it, it collapses and she falls down laughing. We go through this procedure maybe a dozen times before she decides that I should build her a full-fledged castle. She wants to be a princess. She has plans for me to save her.

By now, I have dug down to the water line. I dribble sandcastles around the top rim of sand, making our hole seem deeper still. Whenever Stellie wants me to construct a new addition to her castle, I say, "Yes, Your Heinie," and Stellie's staccato laughter machine-guns me to the quick. We cannot help our outbursts. Now and again, I will glance at Susan, who looks up affectionately from her paperback. Zed also faces our hole, his back to the lure of the ocean and the strolling, bikini-clad women. He is wearing dark glasses, a baseball cap, and a long-sleeved white shirt with the cuffs buttoned. A yellow towel is laid out over his legs. Underneath all of this, he is lathered with suntan lotion that my over-protective sister periodically applies.

* * *

It has only been during the last year that Susan and I have renewed—mostly through letters and phone calls—the bond we once had as children. I am four years older than Susan. It's funny, now that I think about it, but I have *always* been four years older than Susan. Yet, when we were small, that gap seemed greater.

One day, when I was eleven and Susan was seven, our parents left me to look after her. But they were nearby, at the neighborhood cookout staged strictly for the adults on the block. It was summertime—a humid August evening. The drone of insects and the flicker of bats against the twilighted sky had inspired me and Mark—the kid from next door—to make a human sacrifice of Susie's favorite doll.

Susie had named her doll "Star" because of the twinkly effect given off by her realistic glass eyes—the irises were a crystal blue. Susie didn't seem to mind at first, when we tied Star to the back fence with the broken-off pull-cord from a lawnmower's crankcase. But when she realized that Mark and I were setting ourselves up as the firing squad and that we had plans to execute her precious baby-doll—using over-ripe cherry tomatoes as ammo—Susie started to cry. Her crying was soft and resigned, knowing at this point she could not possibly save Star. Things had gone too far, especially after Mark blindfolded Susie's doll with a strip of rag that supported one of the tomato shoots. When he wedged one of Father's crushed out cigarette butts between Star's putty lips, Susie knew that her pleas were futile. She stumbled, bleary with tears, to the swing set, where she sat crying, twisting herself around and around, then spinning and crying louder as she unwound. She kept her head averted as we laughed and pummeled Star's body.

This was not typical behavior on my part. All it took was one well-directed tomato from me, and the orange smear that leaked down over Star's white dress made me want to quit. But Mark—as I remember—thrived on destruction. He was the better marksman, knocking the cigarette out of Star's lips on his third throw. Still, that wasn't enough for Mark. I'm not sure now whose B-B rifle it was—maybe we both had our own at that point—but our firing squad had suddenly become too real. I had Susie's doll in my sights, taking aim down the barrel of the rifle.

When Mom and Dad came home an hour or so later to discover Susie still crying in the backyard swing, I ran to the bathroom and locked the door. I cowered there, waiting for my father's footsteps. When they finally materialized and he knocked on the door, I blurted, "I'm sorry!" Then I started crying—not to save myself, but because I was afraid to look at the inhuman thing I had done to Susie's baby.

"Open up," my father had said softly.

So I did.

He stood there in the threshold, cradling the doll in one arm as if it were a real baby. In his other hand, he held a shovel. His grief was real. Star's eyes were missing, shot out, wholly vacant—and what had been a white dress was now caked with ugly stains and coagulated gobs of tiny seeds. Father tried to hand her to me, but I wouldn't touch her. So he handed me the shovel, and dragged me out the back door.

Burying Susie's doll in the far corner of the dark backyard—digging a grave for her as if she had once been alive—still recurs in my dreams. I know that Susan must have

138   AMERICAN FICTION

similar nightmares. I only pray that Stellie is not somehow
superimposed. Knowing Susan, I am sure that she still thinks
about that. I just hope that she has forgiven me.

* * *

Dinner is on Zed tonight. We have gone out for fresh
seafood to Neptune's Corner. Although Stellie doesn't seem to
mind the car ride over in her baby's seat, she has voiced her
displeasure about having to sit in a highchair when dining out.
She doesn't like eating in public. She is at that age where her
uniqueness has begun to make her self-conscious.

The waitress—a well-endowed bleached blonde—smiles at
me when I enter carrying Stellie. Clutching menus to her
breast, she leads us to a dockside booth. As we sit down,
Susan requests a highchair for Stellie who I have been
carrying—by her own wishes—in one arm as if she were an
infant. And to many, I'm sure this must be the impression—
that I am carrying a small baby. But when I set Stellie down in
the booth, she stands up on the blue vinyl cushion and
informs the waitress, "I really don't want one."

The waitress goes wide-eyed and takes a wobbly step
backward. Not many people have encountered such an articu-
late infant. The waitress composes herself and smiles weakly,
still trying to comprehend Stellie's command of the language.
Her hand trembles when she hands out three menus to Susan,
to Zed, then to me. She has a fourth menu which she
reluctantly hands over to Stellie. Stellie says, "Thank you
very much, but I can't read menus. Only little kids' books."

At that, the waitress laughs nervously, pivots on a squeaking
white shoe, then begins to jostle water into our empty water
glasses. "Would anyone care for a cocktail?"

"Sure," I say, skimming over the menu, thinking that an ice
cold beer would be great. Then I remember that Zed and
Susan are non-drinkers. "Do you mind if I order a beer?"

"Of course not," Zed says coolly, studying his menu, with
his glasses riding low on the bridge of his nose.

* * *

Susan has always been big on fried foods. I prefer broiled.
So that's what I go for—broiled swordfish. When the food

arrives, we all hold hands and say grace. I'm getting accustomed to this.

Susan, Zed, and Stellie are also fond of bread. The third hush puppy that Stellie digs into is left unfinished, resting like a Dutch wooden shoe on the scuffed aluminum tray of her highchair.

Immediately after dessert—Key Lime pie, all the way around—Stellie places me in charge of rinsing off her silverware. This is usually done by Susan, but Stellie enjoys having me attend her like a footservant.

I have to go to the bathroom anyway, I tell Susan when she scolds Stellie for asking too much of me.

The bathrooms are labelled "Buoys" and "Gulls." It makes me think twice before deciding which one is for me. I have Stellie's dollhouse utensils in the palm of my hand. She is very demanding, meticulous when it comes to the care of her little fork, knife, and spoon.

A father and his son, I assume, linger to watch me rinse off the tiny instruments. This man and boy had been sitting two tables away with a woman and a little girl, casting sidelong glances at Stellie throughout dinner.

I go about my business.

"Excuse me," the man says. "I don't mean to be nosey, but your daughter...she's...uh, so *small*."

I wrap the silverware in a wad of Klennex and tuck it into the side of my blazer.

"She's my niece. She's a fairie," I say, directing my statement toward the boy. They both smile, somehow satisfied with what I have told them, and they walk out hand-in-hand—the little boy craning his neck up at his father, perhaps curious to know if his father really believes in fairies.

*   *   *

I am carrying Stellie on our way out because she wants me to. I am almost embarrassed by Stellie's focus on me. But I am not embarrassed by Stellie. Our shoes clomp on the weathered planks as we walk around the outside of the restaurant to get a better view of the inlet here. Seagulls are now swooping in to roost on the upright pylons which look like big bundles of Cuban cigars. I really want a cigar, but I continuously have to check my hedonistic desires, being in the presence of the pious Susan and Zed.

The dock is roped off on either side with sagging cables of hemp, as thick as electrical lines. When we walk out on the dock, Stellie takes my sunburned cheeks between her tiny hands and whispers. "Watch out for the troll!"

I immediately stop in my tracks and cast a worried look down onto the oily water. When I growl, Stellie squeals and clings tight. I lightly drum my fingers on her tiny back and she burps, then giggles.

*   *   *

Susan and I are sitting on the deck of the beach house. A large yellow candle gutters on the glass-topped table between us. Zed went to bed early, shortly after I reappeared—having read Stellie to sleep.

Staring out at the ocean's dark horizon, I focus off to the left at the distant rotating beam of faint light emitted from a far-off lighthouse. I let Susan do most of the talking.

I am amazed when Susan tells me that Stellie—considering her condition—is actually big for her age. Susan says that there are others—mostly little girls, odd as it seems—born with this syndrome who are much smaller than Stellie. It boggles my mind.

"How much smaller?" I want to know.

"Well, Stellie has a special friend who we met through Little People of America—out in California. Remember us going out there about a year or so back?"

I nod.

"Anyway, we went out specifically to meet the Doswells and their little girl, Martha. We were put in touch with them through the Church maybe two or three years ago, and we corresponded, you know, sending pictures and that sort of thing. Little Martha is ten. But she's about the same size as Stellie. Actually she doesn't weigh quite as much."

I wonder if that's a bad sign—an indication that Stellie has done all the growing she possibly can.

"Every day I thank God that Stellie is as healthy and as happy as she is."

Again, I nod.

Susan asks me about my new teaching position and about my love life and about my ex-wife, Kay, and if we still communicate. That sort of thing. She asks me how I think— "I mean honestly"—about how Dad's doing since Mother passed away—as if Mother were newly gone.

"Susie, Mom's been dead for four years now. Dad seems to be doing fine. He misses her—sure, but...he's managing. I only hope I live so long...so gracefully."

"But that *home* smells so. Like urine." There are tears flickering in Susan's eyes. "I just hate what we've done to him, Johnny. Putting him there." Her voice wavers. "What would Mother think?" The candle dies out.

Mother still lives in Susan's mind. When Stellie was born, our mother had suggested that Susan place her in an institution. Of course, Susan's doctor was wrong about Stellie being retarded. Stellie is as bright—if not brighter—than any seven-year-old I've ever taught. Although it's been years since I have taught on that level. Nearly a decade since I received my doctorate.

While Mother seemed proud enough of me and my choices in life, she had always wanted me to make more money. She would often joke when we'd get together with relatives and friends: "Ph.D.? What do you suppose that means—'Phony Doctor'?"

I never let her know how much that hurt me, but I am *not* one of those who dwells on such—whereas Susan tends to remember little things, done or said, and her capacity to hold a grudge is deep. When Susan refused to institutionalize Stellie, Mother called Susan a fool—not only to close ties, but to Susan's face. Susan would never consider the possibility of putting Stellie up for adoption or into a home, so she contrived a protective distance from all of us, and it was Susan's love for her daughter that had—until recently—kept us apart.

* * *

Tonight, Susan seems older than I'll ever be. Deep down— moving unseen in the depths of Susan's mind—our mother lives, mysteriously feeding on Susan's insecurities. Death has made Mother that much larger. After pouring off the warm liquid wax over the rail of the deck, I re-light the candle. Susan looks tired, although her new tan makes her look healthier than I've seen her in years.

"I think I'll go for a walk. Want to come with me?" I say.

"No, you go on ahead. I'm bushed."

I lean down and give her a kiss on the forehead. "Thanks for inviting me. I really am enjoying myself. It's so good to get to know Stellie. She's such a doll." I think twice about what I've said. I wonder if the same monstrous memory lingers in Susan's mind, just below the surface.

But she smiles up at me and takes my hand. "Remember when we'd go to the beach with Mother and Dad when we were little?"

"Yeah. Sure do," I smile back at her. "I used to pretend like I was a shark and I'd swim up under your raft and make you squeal."

"Mother used to, too. You and Mother would always gang up on me."

"Did we?" I really can't remember.

*   *   *

After I bid goodnight to Susan, I check my back pocket for my wallet before heading out to the beach. I am thinking about walking all the way to the nearest convenience store to buy a beer or two and maybe a cigar—depending on what is available.

I haven't let Susan know, but my plans are to head back home sometime tomorrow. It's a five-hour drive. I know that Stellie will be disappointed, but there's so much for me to put in order before school starts up again. In fact, I still have a few late papers to grade, and here it is the middle of August.

I have walked only a mile or so when I notice the distant flicker of lightning—now miles out at sea—but I know how fast an offshore storm can blow up, so I decide to turn around and head back to the cottage. I am mesmerized by the breaking waves. What with the electrical storm coming on, I notice, in each rising swell, the green luminescence of plankton, lit up randomly inside the waves.

Jagged spurts of lighting web the sky now, and the rumble of distant thunder comes quicker, more intense. Presently, I am sitting on the beach directly in front of the dark cottage. When two teenagers—who I assume are brother and sister by what they have to say to each other—walk around me, one on either side. They ignore me entirely, as if I were a deposit of driftwood. I watch their dark shapes fade away with distance. There go Susan and I, I think, realizing our past lives rarely surface.

I am suddenly pelted with the fresh splatter of rain.

* * *

The following morning, I slowly open my eyes. What I see is a billowy white plume, coming up from the side of the bed as though it were a sign of surrender. Someone is trying to wake me by tickling me with an enormous feather. The way the quill bobs and wavers back and forth reminds me of some kind of puppet show. Stellie laughs when I say in a gruff manner, "WHO'S THAT HIDING UNDER MY BRIDGE?" I quickly reach down and grab her.

"It's time to get up and play," she announces, curling up on my stomach like a kitten, waving her huge feather in the air.

I glance over at the clock. It's only 8:45, but I'm glad to be up. It will be easier to leave if I get an early start. I decide to tell her. "You know what, Princess Stellie?"

She crawls up close to my face and says, "What?" Her tiny voice buzzes in my ear like a trapped fly.

"I have to go home to where I live sometime soon."

"Why?" she asks, touching the new beard growth on my cheek. She draws back her hand as if she'd been stung. She momentarily forgets what we were talking about, and she tells me, "You're dirty shaven."

I growl and make like I'm going to swallow her whole arm.

We drop our conversation about me having to leave.

* * *

For breakfast, Stellie and I split a fresh cantaloupe. Susan heaps frozen vanilla yogurt into its spooned-out center. Because Susan and Zed have already eaten, I take the initiative and bless the food with my own little prayer. After we eat, Stellie follows me into the bathroom and I stand her on top of the toilet lid so she can watch me shave.

We are out on the beach by nine-thirty. Although the sky is overcast this morning, it seems to be clearing up after last night's storm. The beautiful sandcastle we built yesterday has been obliterated. What remains after last night's high tide is a smoothed-over, spireless crater that Stellie just stares at with a frown. "We'll build another one, okay?" I say.

Several hundred yards down the beach, a dozen or so people are gathered around a large object that has washed up during the night. Stellie, curious to know what everyone is looking at, wants me to take her down there. Susan and Zed tell us to go ahead. Zed is just now pitching the umbrella, and Susan is trying to spread out the quilt, unwittingly stinging Stellie and me with windblown sand in the process. Stellie looks like she's about to cry, so I pick her up and turn around, hunched over to protect her. We head off down the beach.

Halfway there, Stellie wants me to put her down. When I do, she stares squarely at my kneecap. For every step I take, Stellie takes eight or nine. So I figure for every mile I walk, to Stellie, it is more like eight or nine. To my tiny niece, the small sandpipers that look like wind-up toys, running back and forth on the slick sand, chased by small waves, are as big as storks.

A young woman in a black one-piece suit with white polka dots is walking toward us. Now, only several paces away, she smiles and says, "Good morning. Not a pretty sight up there."

"What is it?" I ask. Stellie and I both stop in our tracks.

"A dolphin. It looks like a shark attacked it."

The woman glances down at Stellie. She smiles again, then keeps walking.

Stellie looks up at me and says, "I want a bathing suit with freckles." Meaning polka dots.

As we near the crowd, the angry sound of flies fills the air. The blued skin of the dolphin is dull looking—not glistening the way one would think. I pick Stellie up so she can get a better look. And as I step closer, I am sorry that I have.

The dolphin's stomach has been torn away. Leaking out from the gash in its rubbery skin are coils of intestine and other raw organs. Although it is too fresh to have acquired a stench, I am almost on the verge of vomiting. I turn away and carry my tiny niece back to where Susan and Zed are waiting. I let Stellie tell them what we saw.

"It was very disgusting," she explains. "It was exploded and unhappy."

I nod in agreement, but Susan and Zed have to go see for themselves. After they walk off, Stellie wants me to bury her in the sand. While I dig out a shallow grave, she asks me questions about sharks. Her questions about sharks are almost identical to her questions about trolls. I answer her as best I can, but my answers—this time—do not seem to amuse her. When Susan and Zed return, Stellie's tiny head is all that shows. I am not really thinking about covering Stellie with warm white sand. I just do it. It's not morbid in the least. But Susan over-reacts. She screams when she sees what I have done. Immediately, I pull Stellie up and brush her off. Stellie, looking like an oversized sugar cookie, walks stiffly over and plops down in her mother's lap, then she says, "Do dolphins go to heaven?"

I look out at the ocean, realizing that I have been here for three days yet I have not been in for a swim. Susan says, "Yes, of course they do, honey."

"Do sharks go to heaven, too?" This really seems to worry Stellie. I can see what she's getting at.

I just can't stand here and wait for Susan to come up with a Christian answer. I tear off towards the water, as fast as I can, and when it starts to suck at my legs, trying to drag me down, I fling myself headlong, diving into the face of a rising wave. I swim long and hard under the pound of water. With my eyes clenched, I pull with all my strength to get beyond the break line, straight out, until my ears start ringing. When I finally burst up for air, I am out over my head. I blink wetly towards the shore, where Susan and Zed are standing. The saltwater stings my eyes, but I notice that Susan is waving as I drift farther and farther out. I am so far out now, Stellie is an indistiguishable speck, sitting on the beach, in the shadow of the blue umbrella.

Alone out here, I am vulnerable, filled with the terror of the unknown—my arms and legs moving freely in the deep, murky water. In Susan's stead, I see a younger version of our mother. It makes me waver for a moment, questioning the existence of whatever lurks beneath the surface, wondering: Is Susan's eyeless doll still buried in our old backyard? And: How long will our father manage to hang on?

The smallest creature that touches me—such as now—assumes enormous proportions. "Do sharks go to heaven, too?" Stellie's wee voice replays itself in my head, when something underwater grazes the side of my foot.

I work my arms and legs frantically in the thick, dark currents, trying to keep my head above water, buoyed by the gentle swells, pulled diagonally out and away from Susan and Zed and Stellie, while my doubt circles me, preys on me.

"Is one's faith ever justified?" I silently ask myself, recalling the face of the little boy in the restaurant when I told him that Stellie was a fairie. I can picture his upturned expression as he looked to his father for confirmation.

I arch my back and float, closing my eyes to the clear morning sun. And the longer I dare to stay here, the stronger my faith becomes.

Across the Line

BY JUDITH TEMPLE

Mrs. Rose Kellerman heard the three sharp knocks that meant Mr. Marcus was waiting. She set her tea cup carefully on its blue patterned saucer and placed her hands on the edge of the table as if about to rise. She sighed. Everything seemed so complicated since her husband Lou had died. For a moment she considered not answering, but then she pictured Mr. Marcus standing on the other side of the door, awkward and expectant. She got up and walked slowly across the beige carpet. She undid the bolts on the door and opened it. "Good morning, Mr. Marcus," she said.

Mr. Samuel Marcus, her next door neighbor in the condominium, had been courting her for the last six months. Although she considered him to be a gentleman, and liked him, Mrs. Kellerman found his attentions confusing and somehow not entirely respectable. She wanted to tell him, "I'm a married woman," and thus dismiss him, but of course she was a widow now.

Two years after her husband had died, Mrs. Kellerman had not yet adjusted to his absence. Nearly fifty years of marriage had left her with as clear a sense of her husband's existence as her own, and his death seemed to have called her own life into question. She felt she had to think about herself as she had not needed to when she was married, as though a sort of insulation had been stripped from her. She remembered how her husband's hands, doing some small repair, had peeled the black covering from a piece of electrical wire, and she had watched the vivid copper emerge. Afterward she had thought of all those wires in every house and that hidden brightness. But she did not feel that clearly defined. She was alone, but she still had her husband's name, and on her hand she wore her marriage ring; it would have to be cut to slide it off her age-thickened finger. She imagined its gold circle becoming thinner and thinner, until one day all that would be left would be the pale indentation on her finger where the ring had left its mark. This she felt even though she knew the gold would outlast her, like the mummy she and Lou had seen once in a museum, its thin bones still stylishly decorated with gold bracelets and rings and a necklace set with green stones.

For the first year after Lou died, every day she had recited the mourner's prayer, the Kaddish, intoning in Hebrew: "When we are alone, we remember that we are also what has gone before." Properly, this was a man's ritual, but she had performed it anyway, hoping for some ease, some miracle of acceptance. She was familiar with the rituals of her religion from childhood, but to be Jewish for her was a matter of identity more than spiritual conviction. She was of that generation which involved itself in the new world, not the old, where religion had been intrinsic to everyday existence. She had never looked to her religion for solace.

Still, two weeks ago, at sunset she had lit the second anniversary candle for her husband's death. At first she had sat, staring into the steady flame which was supposed to burn for twenty-four hours. The next day, as she busied herself with chores, she was aware of the candle burning lower, her eyes returning to it and then looking away as she made tea or dusted the furniture which always seemed to carry a fine layer of the dry ground outside, even though the windows were closed for the air conditioning. If she would simply feel at peace when the flame died, that would be very good, she thought, but after the candle had finally burned itself out, nothing seemed changed. So she had cleaned out the glass the Yahrzeit candle had come in, and put it next to last year's glass on a shelf in her kitchen cabinet near the cups and saucers.

Her grandmother had a whole collection of these glasses—so many deaths accumulated over her lifetime—and had used them as everyday drinking glasses. Mrs. Kellerman had thought nothing of it as a girl, but now that seemed strange to her, like drinking from Lou's skull.

Mrs. Kellerman could not forget she was a widow; it was like tasting a sore on the inside of her cheek. Even in sleep, she was aware of Lou's absence. It was not so much her memory of Lou as a dislocation, as if the world had been moved over while she was not looking. When she went to do anything— sit in a chair, find her hairbrush, her keys—nothing was exactly where she thought it was. Thinking that perhaps it was a mistake to try to keep anything the same, recently she had taken to sleeping on the sofa in the living room instead of in the carved oak double bed she and Lou had shipped to Arizona when they came here to retire five years ago. She had liked having her own furniture with her in the unaccustomed desert landscape, but since Lou had died, even the familiar bed and chairs and tables seemed strange to her. She would bring in a pillow and an afghan from the bedroom and let herself fall asleep on the sofa with the television on. At one or two in the morning, she would wake to the persistent buzzing of the empty screen, switch it off, and hope that she would fall asleep again before daylight.

She was reminded of being a young girl, when every night she would go to bed and dream and wonder what her life was and what it would be like. Fifty years later, again her sleep was full of people she could not name, speaking words in a language both familiar and incomprehensible. She had grown up in New York, the daughter of steerage immigrants from Russia, and she could still remember the confusion of lan- guages—Yiddish at home, English, Turkish, Greek, German and more on the street, until enough English sifted into her awareness to make sense. She had that same feeling now in her sleep of understanding just beyond her grasp. She would awake thinking she had just missed the answer to a question, something crucial, but she could not state to herself what the question was. She no longer dreamed of a husband and children; she had had those. And she did not dream of Mr. Samuel Marcus.

When Mrs. Kellerman tried to imagine living with Mr. Marcus, her mind seemed to stop. She could picture herself sitting in the dinette drinking tea with him while he read the morning paper, but then the morning paper suggested that there had been a night before, and Mrs. Kellerman could not picture herself in her flannel nightgown lying in the double bed next to Mr. Marcus. How could she let a man see her aging body as it was now? She used to complain to Lou that she was getting old, that she could not recognize her own body with its wrinkles and gray hair. She had hardly noticed Lou's aging. He had turned gray, of course, and his flesh had shifted, bony where the muscles used to move firmly under the skin. But it wasn't so important for a man, she thought. Lou would tell her that to him she was still the young girl he had fallen in love with. She didn't quite believe him, but when he deserted her by dying, that image of herself as a girl disappeared with him. Now she seemed to have been born at the age of sixty-nine with no childhood and no memories that anyone else could understand. If she were to say to Mr. Marcus, "I was once young, and some men found me beautiful," that would mean nothing to him. And if he would tell her that he too had once been young and handsome, she would think, "Yes, but you are neither anymore."

Her children had met Mr. Marcus and liked him. They told her she was old fashioned to be so hesitant to establish a relationship. "It would be good for you," they told her, as if they thought it was something simple, like a diet, or taking vitamin C. They didn't understand that there was less of her now—barely enough to maintain her own existence, much less share herself with someone else, to launch into an unknown future when she felt as though the earth had gone flat and she was sailing along the edge peering into nothing.

She wouldn't have thought of any of this, she said to herself, if Mr. Marcus had not begun pursuing her. Now he was standing in her living room asking her if she would like to drive with him to Nogales, across the border in Mexico, and look around the shops and eat lunch there. Mrs. Kellerman had found that she enjoyed this border city only thirty-five miles away; its newness to her demanded nothing of her memories. At most she sometimes was faintly reminded of certain neighborhoods she had known as a girl in New York, where the women sat out on the stoops on summer evenings while their children played on the sidewalks and in the streets. In the retirement community south of Tucson where she and Lou had bought a condominium, one rarely saw children. Living there, it seemed as if the world had been born old. At times she would almost forget that she herself had once given birth to three children who seemed like strangers now, adults who called her "Mother." Her two prosperous sons, so careful, concerned with the secure details of their lives, malpractice insurance, a new house. Her daughters-in-law, polite but distant, like the grandchildren she saw at intervals. And her daughter, twice divorced, always dashing from one enthusiasm to another—yoga, tree-planting. Sometimes she couldn't believe she had once been so close to them she had known what they would say before they opened their mouths.

A drive to Mexico seemed a welcome distraction today, so she told Mr. Marcus yes, she would enjoy a trip to Nogales—across the line, as people around here said: I'm going across the line to buy liquor, or shop, or eat shrimp.

They spoke little during the drive. She remembered what Lou used to say about thinking without words. It's the best way, he would tell her. Early in their marriage, she had felt this as a rebuke. But that had faded, until often she had felt closest to him in silence, watching his always busy hands as he repaired a lamp or a leaky faucet, or what he most liked to do—shaping a block of wood into a bird or some other small creature, patiently carving the layered feathers or fur. Afterwards, Lou would discard the carving, interested only in the process. But she would gather them up from their careless perches in Lou's workshop to dust them and stroke their smooth surfaces. Now they crouched on her shelves, sleek little animals with their hard wooden stares.

Mrs. Kellerman looked out the car window at the highway median strip, which bloomed with yellow and orange poppies.

"Do you think they planted those?" she asked Mr. Marcus. In this southwestern climate she had not yet become accustomed to the seasons and changes in vegetation. Spring began almost in February; summer lasted through October.

She surprised herself by liking the sparse desert landscape, but it remained foreign to her. She watched the clear outlines of the Santa Rita mountains through the window when she sat down to drink her morning cup of tea, although on some days pollution from nearby copper smelters shortened distances until the mountains became only smudges. She would realize then how much she missed them.

"Those are wildflowers, Mrs. Kellerman," Mr. Marcus was saying to her. She had almost forgotten her question. Then he was pulling the big Chrysler off the road at a rest stop. "So we can look at the flowers, Mrs. Kellerman," he said.

She looked at him to see if he were laughing at her, but his face was serious, his white moustache drooping slightly over his upper lip. They drove past the lines of motor homes and campers to an empty parking space. Here too most of the people were elderly, retired and with the leisure to go anywhere, any time, respectable gypsies. They saw spring in the southwest, summer in the mountains, winter in California or Florida or even Mexico, no longer living as they used to, tied to one familiar house and a job.

Mr. Marcus bent to pick a few flowers, then handed them gallantly to Mrs. Kellerman. "Such flowers don't grow in New York," he said to her in Yiddish. Without thinking, she responded in the same language, "No, one does not find such flowers there." It was the first time they had spoken Yiddish with each other. She and Lou had often spoken Yiddish at home, although in public they always spoke English. For her, Yiddish was the language of intimacy. As if he were aware of her thought, Mr. Marcus reverted to English, asking if she were ready to continue their drive. Maybe he had spoken Yiddish with his wife, too, Mrs. Kellerman thought.

She settled herself in the car again. The air conditioning blew unnecessarily at her face on this early spring day. "Perhaps we could open the windows," she said to Mr. Marcus.

"Sure," he said, "why not?" and pushed the button which automatically rolled down both their windows. "How's that?" he asked.

"Fine, Mr. Marcus, just fine," she said. Even on the freeway at sixty miles an hour, the air felt soft, carrying into the car the smells of earth and new vegetation. Mrs. Kellerman looked down at the flowers she still held in her left hand. The poppies were gold in color, shading to a deep orange in the center where the stamens and pistils emerged. She held onto the flowers until they reached Nogales and Mr. Marcus had parked the car on the American side of the border. Then she laid the flowers carefully on the seat although she knew they would be wilted by the time they returned.

"We'll park here and walk across the border," Mr. Marcus said. "It's simpler than driving."

"That's fine," said Mrs. Kellerman. "I like to walk." She and Lou had done the same thing, walking the few blocks to the wire fence that marked the border. When her daughter had visited her, they too had walked past the last supermarket on the American side with its shelves full of American canned goods and cereal and hard frozen American dinners, past the always crowded McDonald's to the border entry that proclaimed ENTRADA A MEXICO.

Mr. Marcus had parked the car in front of an old gray stone building. Above the door there was a cross and an inscription carved into the stone. Mrs. Kellerman recognized the word *Deus* from her high school Latin, but she couldn't make out the rest of the words. To the right were four mailboxes. In the yard to the side of the building a tree was covered with pink blossoms, so thick the branches were hardly visible.

"I think it's a peach tree," said Mr. Marcus .

"I wonder how they decide who gets the peaches," Mrs. Kellerman said. She hadn't quite meant to speak aloud.

"Probably the landlord," said Mr. Marcus and laughed. She smiled politely.

They walked with other tourists across the border. Now there were crowds of people, boys selling ice cream, watches, darting into the traffic with a handful of jewelry. Men stood in idle groups looking at the entering tourists. Mr. Marcus gave a quarter to an Indian woman sitting wrapped in a blanket, her body so hidden she seemed to be without legs. A silent baby lay on her lap. The woman had stretched out her arm as they walked past.

"I don't give to all of them," Mr. Marcus said to Mrs. Kellerman, "but I have to give to some."

"That's fine, Mr. Marcus," she said. "You don't have to apologize for being kind."

She hadn't been here since last fall with her daughter, during the Mexican Day of the Dead celebration *El dia de los muertos*. Then the children on the streets sold grinning sugar skulls. She had wanted to buy one; she had the urge to bite into the glistening white. She wondered if it would have a taste, or just a stale sweetness, like cake decorations. But her daughter had been repelled by the rows of tiny skulls on trays and the dangling toy skeletons the children played with. So Mrs. Kellerman had not bought anything but a bunch of the marigolds vendors had been selling to decorate the graves. The golden flowers were mounded over the newly white-washed gravestones, and the smells of meat and corn and spices from the vendors' carts that were supposed to reach the spirits of the dead reached her too. She wondered at this celebration of the dead that was so different from her solitary recital of the Kaddish. It was like the difference between the simple white Yahrzeit candle she had to go all the way to Tucson to find and the gaudy red and green glass of the votive candles, decorated with pictures of saints, that she would see in the grocery stores in the same aisle with the batteries and work gloves and brooms.

Today there were no sugar skulls or plastic skeletons, only the usual tourist merchandise. She and Mr. Marcus turned to the right and started walking up a street lined with small shops filled with serapes, embroidered blouses, leather hand-bags hanging from the ceiling, rows of clay pots against the walls. Men stood in the open doorways urging the tourists to come in. Whenever Mrs. Kellerman lingered over a shawl or a carved chess set, someone would come over to her and she would shake her head no. She was just looking, she told Mr. Marcus, she didn't need anything. Mr. Marcus bought a wooden toy, a ball and cup connected with a piece of string. "For my grandson," he explained to her. She had grand-children too, but she did not feel like shopping for them. Maybe on the way back she would get them something, she thought, but now she just wanted to smell the strong scent of the leather shops and to think of the small houses someplace deep in Mexico where people sat painting the garishly colored pots in red and blue and yellow, or others, more beautiful, in brown and rust, with odd creatures and birds perched among branches and flowers.

Then in one store, at the back, past the pottery piggy banks and onyx boxes and tall stacks of straw sombreros that smelled like wet hay, she found a table covered with a jumble of out of season merchandise: stamped tin Christmas ornaments— trees and stiff looking angels, miniature statues of soulful, bearded saints lying in plexiglass coffins decorated with painted flowers, and finally, half a dozen of the tiny plastic skeletons she had seen the children playing with at the Day of the Dead celebration while their families whitewashed the gravestones and picnicked among them.

She picked one up; it was very light. The ivory colored bones were carefully articulated, the skull smooth to the touch of her fingers. Without showing it to Mr. Marcus, she walked to the front of the store and held it out to the cashier, who looked at the odd little skeleton lying in the palm of Mrs. Kellerman's hand, and said, "One dollar." Mrs. Kellerman was sure she had just invented the price, but it was cheap enough. She paid and slipped the skeleton into her purse. As she turned to rejoin Mr. Marcus, she though she could hear the muted rattling of the plastic bones.

As they stepped out onto the sidewalk again, Mr. Marcus asked her if she were tired and would she like to sit down and eat something. She realized that yes, she was tired and was surprised that Mr. Marcus had perceived it before she had. All she had felt was that suddenly there were too many colors in front of her, but she saw that she must be tired of walking and looking at objects which, it now struck her, had nothing to do with the rest of her life.

They sat in a small restaurant where the menu was printed half in Spanish and half in English. The prices also were given in both Mexican and American currencies.

"Have a beer, Mrs. Kellerman," said Mr. Marcus expansively. She consented, although she drank very seldom.

"I guess a beer wouldn't hurt," she said. She looked around the restaurant. The table tops were formica, and the seats in the booths were covered in vinyl, like kitchen chairs. Artificial flowers were placed at regular intervals along the walls.

The effect was almost that of an American fast food restaurant, but the flowers were too bright and the waitresses of course spoke Spanish. Mrs. Kellerman kept feeling she could almost understand what was said, like the language spoken in her dreams.

After eating most of a combination plate, she felt better. She was a little drunk from the Tecate, which the waitress served with a slice of lime on the top of the can. Mr. Marcus had urged her to finish her drink. "With Mexican food, you need Mexican beer," he said. He insisted on paying the check although Mrs. Kellerman offered to pay her share.

"Don't worry about it," he told her. "You can be a liberated woman. I don't mind. But I'll pay the check."

Outside, she wanted to continue walking, but was weary of the shops and sidewalk vendors, so they turned and began walking toward the houses that straggled up the steep hills of the town. The sidewalk turned to stone steps.

"Like San Francisco," said Mr. Marcus. Mrs. Kellerman nodded although she had never been in San Francisco. They climbed slowly. A few of the houses looked substantial, built of blocks of stone, but most were ramshackle, the stucco falling from the adobe walls. Mrs. Kellerman glanced into one open doorway and saw an unmade bed on the floor and crumpled clothes tossed around the room. She felt embarrassed, as if she had been caught doing something improper and afterwards made a point of not looking toward the doors or windows of the houses they passed. A brown and white dog barked frantically at them from the flat roof of a house as they walked past. Mrs. Kellerman was afraid he would fall off the edge, and increased her pace. Children played in the street and between the houses in yards hung with laundry. A boy about eleven years old was hitting a younger child with a belt.

"Look at that," said Mrs. Kellerman. The little boy was crying, his nose running. Mr. Marcus called to the boy with the belt, "You there, stop that." The boy looked at them, and raised his hand again. The little boy screamed although he had not been hit. A few houses up the street, a woman with long hair falling forward over her shoulders leaned out a window and shouted to the boys. Mrs. Kellerman had the uncomfortable sensation that she and Mr. Marcus were being talked about, perhaps laughed at. The children they walked past looked at them as if they wanted to know what these *turistas* were doing on their street, away from the shops. When Mrs. Kellerman glanced back, the older boy had stopped hitting the younger one, but still held the belt in his hand. They were looking up the street to where Mrs. Kellerman and Mr. Marcus were again slowly climbing. She felt out of breath when they stopped at the top.

The pavement had ended. Below them lay a dry wash, and beyond the wash, on top of another hill stood a small blue painted church outlined against the sky. Mrs. Kellerman could see figures of women walking toward it, but the street on which the church stood did not intersect the one she and Mr. Marcus had followed. She felt disappointed that the church was so difficult to get to. Looking down into the wash, she saw two stray dogs and an old man with a boy making their way through it. She looked again at the point where the cracked cement of the sidewalk stopped; a rough descent of sand and rocks led steeply down into the wash. As she and Mr. Marcus turned and began walking back down the stone steps, she carried with her the image of the church, blue and unattainable, and she felt an envy of the black-clothed women making their way toward it. How foolish, she thought, it wasn't even her religion. Yet she could not rid herself of the feeling that she had missed something important, like the dreams she could not remember in daylight. How much else had she missed, she wondered. While she had lived her life one way, she had let so much else go past her—secrets of faith, entire continents she had never set foot on.

Mr. Marcus put his hand under her elbow as they walked past the spot where they had seen the two boys, as if something had been understood between them. Mrs. Kellerman felt too weary to protest. When they reached the bottom of the steps, she said apologetically that she needed to rest for a minute again. When she looked toward the shops, the thought of walking past the men in the doorways who would ask her to come in and look at the leather purses and embroidered blouses made her feel almost ill. She sat down, and for a moment, she felt like the earth was tilting, ready to slide out from under her. She put her hands out to touch the stone of the steps she was sitting on to anchor herself.

A small girl wearing a red dress that was too big for her walked toward them. As Mrs. Kellerman focused on her, the ground leveled and resumed its usual position. The girl's face had a sharpness to it, shaped by the wanting of things she would never have. She was carrying a tattered, heart-shaped candy box. She opened it to show them photographs of herself smiling in various poses, in the same red dress she was wearing now. Mr. Marcus smiled and pulled a quarter from his pocket. The girl shook her head and said, "*Mas, mas.*" She did not smile. Mr. Marcus added another quarter, but the girl still shook her head. Now Mr. Marcus shook his head and said, "No." The girl shrugged, closed the box and from a pocket in her dress pulled a picture which she held out of a nude woman whose pubic hair had been shaved. For a moment Mrs. Kellerman thought it was another picture of the girl magically older before she realized what it was. She stared at the picture; there was something perversely innocent about the woman so stripped. Then she was standing, shouting at the girl in Yiddish to take her filthy picture and go away.

Mr. Marcus was apologizing as they continued walking, but Mrs. Kellerman shrugged, much as the girl had, and told him it didn't matter. They walked now without saying anything. She let him take her arm again, although she did not feel weak anymore. They walked past the stores, past the donkey painted in black and white stripes like a zebra, with two blond children wearing ornate sombreros perched on top of him while an old man took their picture with a Polaroid camera, telling them to "smile, smile."

The whole way, Mrs. Kellerman could hear the plastic bones of the little skeleton clacking frivolously in her purse, muffled, but present, like the nakedness of the girl's picture carried one level deeper. They walked past the Indian women crouched on the sidewalk holding out their hands, their eyes flat and unapproachable. Mr. Marcus pulled change from his pocket and handed it awkwardly to them, as if he were afraid that they too would refuse his offering.

Mrs. Kellerman said to him, almost impatiently, "Don't worry, Mr. Marcus. It isn't your fault." Then, abruptly as if someone had pulled a switch in her, like one of Lou's fix-up projects that suddenly worked, a broken lamp flooding a room with light, came an image of the girl with the candy box and the too-long dress and the hunger in her face that Mrs. Kellerman recognized: It wasn't her fault either. No one's. Not the woman's in the photograph, vulnerable, naked. Not Lou's fault. Not Mr. Marcus's. Not hers. This was a realization clear and unshakable. The conclusion of the Kaddish which she had recited so many times came to her now as a gift: "May God who causes peace to reign in the high heavens, let peace descend on us." Finally here, walking through these foreign streets, she had no words—neither complaint nor question—only wonder.

The small boys importuning them to buy candy and gum seemed edged with light. Even the men clumped in idle groups were burnished with dignity. And the brown eyes of the Indian women had such depth, they were doors she could step through into unmapped countries. There was no distance between herself and whatever she looked at. She studied Mr. Marcus's profile as they walked. She felt like she could see beneath the features of his face.

They were both silent all the way to the border checkpoint where the customs official asked if they had anything to declare. She had nothing to declare, said Mrs. Kellerman, smiling at the woman in the green uniform as she walked past, certain that the tiny plastic skeleton in her purse was of no interest to customs. Mr. Marcus showed the toy he had bought and was waved through. She and Mr. Marcus walked slowly through the nearly empty streets, so different just a block from the border fence. The feeling of illumination was leaving her; objects looked ordinary again, or nearly so. As they reached the car, a cloud of small birds rose noisily from the peach tree in the yard, then settled back onto the branches. While she waited for Mr. Marcus to unlock her door, she gazed at the stone inscription, which she still could not read, and at the blooming peach tree in the yard before her.

The poppies lay wilted on the front seat, the blooms

flattened, but when she picked them up, their color was still vivid, reflecting a faint orange glow onto the palm of her hand. It looked as if her hand itself were giving off light, the veins bright as copper wire, the bones beneath glowing.

How strange, she thought, to live for sixty-nine years and to see the world in its intricacy as if for the first time.

In the car, she laid the poppies on her lap and smiled at Mr. Marcus. But she was watching the scenery unroll itself like a great scroll on which she had finally found her name inscribed.

Fires

BY CHRISTINA ADAM

For over twenty years this memory stayed with me: An afternoon when I was nineteen, lying on my cot at the ranch, a breeze pushing through a window with no screen, no glass— only the flat blue sky and the warm, baked smell of sagebrush. Outside on the line, clean bed sheets filled with white light, and snapped in the wind. I drifted in and out of sleep in a long, empty peace I thought would last forever.

I lived alone up on the Latham homestead for two summers after I left home, washing laundry. By then the Lathams ran a lodge across the valley, but they sent the laundry to the old place for the water.

The last time I came, I worked as a laundry girl again and studied for a test to graduate from high school. In the fall, I started college, just a city college in L.A. But I always wondered what would have happened if, instead, I'd gone with Joe.

It was the summer of the fires. Fires burned in the mountains. By August, the valley disappeared in a thick, brown haze, and overhead, heavy bombers, gleaming like fish in murky water, carried load after load of lake water and chemicals. The town on the other side of the pass filled with fire fighters, and a tent city sprang up to the north. I picked

Joe up on the highway, hitchhiking into town on a three-day break.

I didn't know until the next day his hair was blond. He'd cooled off under a spigot at the fire camp and his hair was flat and dark. He needed a place to stay, and I let him sleep in an empty line shack. In the morning, I drove him across the valley to the lodge and waited in the truck while he asked if he could rent the cabin. But the Lathams left it up to me.

I was used to stopping on the road for hay crews and fire fighters. But Joe was different. He had hair the color that comes later to children who have been very blond—dark underneath and gold streaked in the sun. His eyes were blue, and on the day I picked him up beside the road, his wide, flat cheekbones were smudged black from the fires. He was tall and broad across the shoulders, but something about the way he moved, not a limp, but an unevenness, made him seem more slight.

He was quiet. In those first days after he moved into the line shack, I passed his open door, glancing in to see him sleeping on his cot, or reading. Sometimes I caught the heavy smell of marijuana.

In the mornings, the girls from the lodge drove into the yard with baskets of dirty laundry and traded them for clean. I loaded two tubs with hot water, let the white linens soak, and guided them through a wringer into a galvanized sink. On most days, I could have it all hung out by lunch time. I remember the heavy wetness of the sheets and the taste in my mouth of wooden pins. In only a few hours, the dry sheets floated, horizontal in the wind, and I gathered them in against my body, filled with the smell of heat and sage.

Joe's crew worked without breaks, but the fire boss gave him time to rest his leg, four days on and three days off. When he was at the ranch, I sat cross-legged on my cot, the door open, working through the test book, learning geometry by a sheer act of will. But an excitement, a high fluttering energy, took the taste of food away. I could hardly eat.

That was more than twenty years ago. I didn't know exactly why I needed to come back. I'd sometimes gone for years without a thought of Joe. But in the last few months, the memories had been coming, clear and frightening, like dreams.

Only an hour before, I'd driven over the pass and dropped down in the valley. I had called the lodge from town, but a nervousness kept rising. Would the ranch still be there? Would it be the same?

When I finally found it, the place seemed bigger and more desolate, the tired buildings so much smaller and too far apart. The homestead cabin listed sideways, like a house of cards pushed slightly over, the gray shingles on the roof curled up and peeling. Behind it, the old wash shed had caved in, and purple thistles bloomed up through the floor. At the edge of the yard, the leaves of a single cottonwood twirled silver in the breeze.

After so much time, I couldn't bring myself to leave the car. I stared out through the dusty windshield, the quiet buzzing in my ears. Across the irrigation ditch, three line shacks stood in an uneven row. The pale logs had dried and pulled apart, and clumps of sod, the grass parched thin and white, hung from the eaves.

But the car was hot, and I could taste dust from the drive. I climbed out and crossed over on a splintered board. The door to the cabin where I had lived stood open. Inside, the small room had the sweet damp smell of mice and of rot where the pink gray linoleum, blistered and nearly black with age, peeled up from the corners.

I walked slowly down the line to Joe's cabin, the silence like a stranger watching. A fencing spike had been wedged into the rusty clasp, but I worked the nail out and let the door swing in. The wood plank floor had been swept clean and the cot pushed square into the corner. It was made up with a gray army blanket, spotted with grease, but neat. Somebody lived here.

I turned around and crossed back over the ditch. I didn't know what I should do. Standing in the yard, the sun burning hot on my arms, all I wanted was to climb in the car and drive back to the airport. But the car was packed with camping gear, a week of groceries. I broke a path through the dry thistles, the needles catching in my jeans and prickling my ankles through my socks, and sat down on the steps of the homestead. The rough gray boards were warm.

Below me, hay fields, blooming faintly blue and lavender, carved at the dry hills like a shoreline. On both sides of the valley, the gray sagebrush hills sloped up to knuckled canyons, dark with trees, and beyond them, granite peaks.

High, white clouds stacked up in thunderheads and moved over the pass, casting huge, gunship shadows on the valley floor. I had forgotten how the place could change so fast, be quiet at one moment and dangerous the next. Each summer I had come, climbers had been trapped by sudden storms in the mountains, and twice a man had died.

I knew who had made up the bed in Joe's cabin. It had to be the cowboy, hired by the ranchers to watch the cattle on their grazing permits in the mountains. My chest felt hollow with disappointment. Always when I pictured the ranch, I came back by myself. I didn't want to meet up with the cowboy. And if he was an old man like the ones I'd known, he wouldn't want to find me here.

The clouds drifted over the sun in the west and the air turned sharp with cold. I gathered up twigs and stumps of sagebrush and built a fire out near the cottonwood. When the coals flaked white, I roasted a potato and ate it sitting on a rock beside the fire. Afterward, I filled a saucepan at the ditch, boiled the grounds in the water, and drank the thick, grainy coffee with canned milk. The sun disappeared behind the mountains, and shafts of light, falling long across the valley through the canyons, turned the air dusky gold, then blue.

A red pickup truck and two-horse trailer crawled down the highway. In the thin mountain air, I could hear the engine and the sticky whirl of tires on heated pavement, the sound too loud for so much distance. As I watched, the truck turned off the blacktop, and a cloud of dust came toward the ranch.

I had a quick, child-like urge to jump up and drive the car out of sight. Then I tried to will the truck to drive on past. But it rattled into the yard and came to a stop at the ditch. I stood and pulled my jacket on.

The hinges on the pickup door pried open and closed, and a

big man, his hat tipped low over his eyes, appeared beside the trailer. He looked in my direction for some time before he started across the yard, walking like an old man. He held his back upright, but bent slightly forward, his white shirt gleaming phosphorescent in the dusk. He stopped a few feet from the fire.

"How'r you?" He spoke in a slow, easy voice, but he didn't look at me.

"Good," I said.

His hat was dove colored and new. It gave him the handsome, angled look all cowboys have at first glance. He stared out past me into the sagebrush. His jaw was square, but his face was long, his gray eyes, almost triangular, sloping slightly downward at the outside corners. I wondered why his shirt and jeans had both been ironed, the creases sharp.

"You can't camp here," he said, his lips hardly moving.

"I called the lodge from town." I kept my voice low and steady. "They said I could."

"Well, I guess you can then." He squinted, looking at me for the first time. Then he held out his hand. "Hessie Baker," he said.

"Susan," I said. "Susan Gerton." I shook his hand, startled by how dry it was, and waited for him to say something else, but he only looked down at my fire, then over to the small white car I'd rented at the airport.

"Would it be all right," I asked him, "if I move my things into a cabin?"

He shifted his weight. "Don't ask me," he said. "You're the one that's got authority."

For no reason, I felt the pinch of tears coming. Why? I thought. Why are these men, old ranchers and cowboys, always out to show you what a fool you are?

He looked over at the old shacks. "Take your pick," he said. "I got horses to feed."

He walked across the yard and backed two horses from the trailer, turning them out in a pole corral beside his shack. I watched him pitch hay in quick, neat strokes, his arms and shoulders hardly moving. He finished and disappeared into his cabin. After a while, a lantern glowed inside.

I sat on my heels down close to the fire. The night when it

came was black, the white stars touching the horizon. It was very cold. The cowboy always kept a camp up Carmichael Canyon, behind the ranch, and that's where Hessie Baker should have been. With any luck, I thought, he'll be gone in the morning. I dumped my coffee on the coals, and went to the car. I carried a flashlight and sleeping bag to the middle shack and went to bed myself. I hadn't thought to bring a lantern.

In the morning, Hessie baker's truck stood in the yard, brick colored under a film of dust, but both horses were gone. The air was damp and cool, but almost as soon as it came up over the mountains, the sun was high. I tugged a towel from my bag and walked up the dry creek bed toward the flume.

I watched the sandy earth at my feet where small tracks skittered under the sagebrush. I followed a larger, dragging track, a badger I thought, and came to a smooth hole dug under a stump of sage. If it was a badger, I didn't want to be the one to wake him up, but I tapped inside the hole with a stick and rolled out the tiny skull of a mouse. I held it for a long time, weightless in my palm, so fragile the sunlight shone through the bones, before I put it back. It pleased me to know I could still follow a trail and find bones like that.

At the flume, I worked off my shoes and socks, and dangled a leg in the water. Submerged, my skin seemed very white, almost blue, the skin drawn tight in a network of shiny wrinkles. The deep spring-fed water, dammed up by head-gates, was so cold it burned like snow. I looked up toward the north.

That summer when the fires had first started, no one paid any attention. The Forest Service brought in fire fighters and trucks, but they said the fires were under control. Early in July, I'd seen one plume of black smoke rising straight up from the shoulder of a mountain to the north. Then another fire broke out, and another.

Joe had moved all his gear into the end shack. I went on with the laundry, but I felt his presence, even when he wasn't there. I cooked meals in the homestead cabin, food I couldn't eat. I made stew and soup, biscuits, things I thought Joe would like, but I never asked him to eat with me. We watched each other, but we hardly spoke.

Then one night Joe came to my door and asked me to a movie in town. And afterward, we walked up here, to the flume. The night was warm, but so dark we stumbled over rocks and sage. Joe went in swimming, and later, sat just close enough, I could feel heat radiating from his shoulder. He dropped smooth stones from one palm to another. We talked only a little, the moon rising round over the mountains, and Joe told me he had been in Vietnam.

His friends had gone to college, but he'd been drafted—and his father made him go. I could hear a twist in his voice. He didn't want to hate his father, but he did.

In the darkness, his words were careful and distinct, as if he'd never said these things out loud before. "I thought I was dead. Everything was black. But I woke up in a hospital, in Hawaii." He let the stones drop in the water. "I cried," he said. "When they told me I didn't have to go back, I cried."

A land mine had broken his leg in three places, torn up his back with shrapnel. When they finally shipped him home, he stayed in San Francisco, in an old house in the Mission with his buddies. They'd played music and smoked dope, sleeping late and picking up odd jobs. But something had happened between them, some fight, and Joe started hitching cross country. When he ran out of money, he volunteered for fire crew. He talked about a town on the coast of New England, a big family, but he didn't want to go home.

That night, at the door to my cabin, Joe tipped my face up, and kissed me. He smiled, with something like regret. "I wish," he said, "I could have courted you a long time."

Hessie Baker didn't come back, and I had the ranch, the long, slow walks through the sagebrush, to myself. Late in the afternoon, I hiked up the dirt track toward the mouth of Carmichael Canyon, thinking I might look at where the fires had burned, but I turned back. My tongue was dry and cottony with thirst, and I wasn't sure I wanted to see how the canyon looked now.

The morning Hessie finally walked out to my campfire, I

hadn't even heard him riding in, or noticed the horses were back. He stood above me, watching the sage stumps burn, and I waited for him to make some remark—how I'd built the fire wrong, or what kind of a fool would want to camp out in the first place.

"Got any extra coffee?" he said. He raised an eyebrow and rolled over another rock without waiting for an answer. He lowered himself down, his long legs stretched out to the fire, and let me pour the coffee. He blew on it and took a shallow sip. "Hell," he said. "You could float a horseshoe in that coffee." He shot me a quick glance. "But not bad."

I wanted to laugh, but wouldn't give him the satisfaction. After what seemed like a long time, he asked if I was going into town.

"I could," I said.

"I've got a letter needs mailed," he said. "To my wife." He looked at me. "You married?"

"Not anymore."

"Sorry," he said. I wasn't sure if he was sorry he asked, or sorry for me.

It turned out he only cowboyed in the summer, just to get away. He owned a big place in Colorado—and Nebraska. He and his wife had split up years ago, but they couldn't divorce. If they divided the land, neither one would make a living.

I promised to take the letter, and wondered why I hadn't told him I was a widow. It would have made things easier, but I couldn't say it. I never thought of myself as a widow. Richard had died in our bed, at home. We hadn't split up or divorced, but we should have.

And my name wasn't Susan. It was Suzy. My father had named me for a gold mine. As a little girl, I pictured the mine shaft, the mountain, the gold in round coins. But after he left, they told me the Suzy had only existed on paper. When I went to college, they wanted my "real name," and so I gave them one.

Hessie stood up, poured the last of his coffee on the edge of the fire and watched it sizzle and steam in the coals.

When the sound stopped, the air was suddenly too quiet. It surprised me, but I didn't want him to go.

"Do you think," I asked him, "I could ride out with you one day? Up the canyon?"

He seemed to consider for a long time, and I wished I hadn't asked. I couldn't tell if he was thinking how to say no, or just thinking. Finally he nodded.

"Don't see any reason why not," he said.

"Do you have another saddle?"

"I guess I could find one someplace," he said.

At dawn, Hessie loaded the horses and we drove up into the canyon. I grabbed onto the edge of the open window, braced against the impact of the jolting truck. Hessie drove with his chin tucked in, his hat low over his eyes. He steered with the heel of one hand, keeping the wheels of both outfits riding high over the deep ruts in the washed out track.

We crossed Clear Creek and pulled over at the cow camp. Where I expected to see a house trailer and a tack shed, there was only a pole corral, one corner built out into the creek. Three horses whinnied at us, and Hessie slipped in through the gate, caught one, and asked me to hold her head while he fitted on panniers and loaded blocks of salt. The pack horse stood nearly asleep, but she made me uneasy. I hadn't been around a horse in so long.

Hessie backed a short, stocky horse from the trailer, and nodded for me to get on. He leveled the stirrup, cupped a hand under my knee, and helped me into the saddle. I felt his touch on my leg, the warm pressure of his hand, for a long time afterward. I couldn't remember when a man had done a thing like that for me.

He rode a tall, black horse and led the pack mare up the canyon into the trees, my horse trotting to keep up. He stopped to lean down and open the drift fence, explaining how it ran for miles along the foothills to keep the cows from drifting home too early in the fall. I knew what a drift fence was, but it was good to hear him talking to me. Beyond the wire, the dry mountain grass was speckled gold and rust, dotted with tiny blue and yellow flowers.

We crossed the first ridge, but I saw no signs of fire. I kicked my horse up next to Hessie.

"The fire," I said, "where was the fire?"

"Which one?"

"The big one," I said.

Hessie reined his horse up. He glanced at me, then pointed all around us. I followed his gaze. Everywhere the trees grew close together in a canopy. For a moment, I couldn't understand it. Then I saw. The lodgepole pines were all exactly the same height.

"Look here," Hessie said. He turned off into the trees and jumped both horses over a fallen log. I found a way around and came to a small meadow where the lush grass had been cropped short. All across the clearing, fragments of bone, shards of ribs and pelvis blades, were scattered, the bones chalky white against the green. It had a strange effect—as if the grass were wet, the bones too dry. They seemed somehow like ancient, human bones. Hessie leaned over his saddle horn.

"Hundred head of cattle died here," he said. "Bunched up in the smoke."

"When?" I asked.

"Not the fire you recall," he said. "Must have been two, three years ago. Coyotes dragged the worst of it away. In a year or two, you won't see anything at all." He kicked his horse up.

In the next draw, Hessie unloaded the salt, and we started back. My knees and back began to ache. I kept quiet, but Hessie must have noticed. He turned off at the drift fence, riding up along the wire to a stand of young aspens. On the ground, nearly hidden by tall grass, a tiny pool of water reflected the sky.

"Best water you ever tasted," Hessie said. He dismounted and lowered himself on both knees, lifting a jar from behind the spring. With one hand, he cleared the surface, then dipped the jar full. He stood and carried it to me. When I looked down at his face, his eyes were sharp and blue, not gray.

On the ride back, it began to rain, a light rain but with drops as big as dimes. They splashed hard on our faces and left round pock marks in the dust. The air filled with the smell of wet sage, clean and cooling, like a sudden drop in temperature.

It was after dark before we drove back in the yard. I sat on the cot in Hessie's cabin and watched him fry steaks in a skillet on his hot plate. He had the room fixed up with a small table and chair, a trailer-sized refrigerator and an extension cord strung over to the wash shed. Everything was neat and clean.

Without his hat, his gray hair damp with sweat and flattened down, Hessie looked old. His broad forehead was smooth, nearly translucent, his cheeks red with broken veins. He'd ridden all day, but his shirt was white, the long sleeves buttoned at the wrist and holding a sharp crease. I looked at the curve of his thumb, dark against the line of his cuff. Outside, I heard dull thunder in the canyon, rolling like a detonation underground.

Hessie lifted my steak onto a yellow plastic plate and handed it to me. His fingernails were broad, flattened at the ends, and a threading scar ran down between the first finger and his thumb. Hessie caught me looking at it.

"Only bayonet charge in the whole damn war."

Hessie cleaned his pocket knife and set about cutting his steak into small pieces. For a minute I thought he was going to reach over and cut up my steak, too. But he handed me the knife and started eating. He wiped his chin with a dishtowel. "101st," he said. "Dropped us in on D-Day."

Because of the movies, D-Day was almost the only battle I knew anything about from World War II. It seemed amazing he had been there.

"It was spring," Hessie said, as if the fact was still a mystery to him. Still a surprise.

I thought he might say more, but he finished his meal and stirred up two cups of instant coffee. He poured canned milk into mine without asking.

"If I'd known you could cook," I said, "I would have let you make the coffee."

He grinned and took my plate. "You learn," he said, "to make do for yourself."

After I'd gone back to my cabin and stretched out in the sleeping bag, the rain stopped and I listened to the coyotes drifting along the ridges, circling the valley. My legs and back ached from the long ride and my hair smelled of dust and horses.

I was exhausted, but suddenly filled with sadness and desire. If things had been as they used to be, I would have gone back to Hessie's warm cabin and climbed in bed with him. When I was young, things were easy that way. Sex was a simple move from talk to bed. But I knew better. Women in Hessie's world didn't do that.

I thought back to the night Joe and I went to bed, in this narrow cot. How it felt, the first time, to lie down against his body. To open my shirt and feel the shock, the cool surprise of his skin on my breasts. We made love hard, then slowly for a long time, our skin so alive we couldn't sleep. I remembered Joe's hands, his square wrists and swollen knuckles, the place where his smooth arm curved up into muscle. Holding him, I traced the shrapnel scars above shoulder blades, diamond shaped and raised like thick embroidery.

We stayed awake all night, our skin just touching, sometimes sitting up to smoke a cigarette. "I can't get used to how it feels," Joe said, "to light a cigarette and smoke it in the dark."

After that, Joe worked the fires and came back, washed in the flume, and slept around the clock. I passed his door every hour, but I never woke him. When he did get up, I made something for him to eat, and we went to bed. I had never been in love this way, never felt so always wanted. I couldn't keep from smiling at the laundry girls. But I hardly slept at all, even when Joe was gone. I couldn't eat. And I was afraid. I couldn't study for the tests anymore. I sat down on the steps with the books while Joe was sleeping, but I couldn't think.

The tests mattered. It mattered to me to take them and pass. I had already, in so short a time, failed so much. I'd hitchhiked to San Francisco and Chicago, and lived in the slums of New York. I'd left a dozen jobs, and as many friends and lovers. My best friend, Elaine, was a whore, a prostitute. I'd stayed with her in Reno, sleeping on the floor, and watched her come home with black eyes, red swollen bruises on her cheekbones. Elaine, who wore narrow, knit suits from the thrift store, was always elegant. She had long, light brown hair, swept up in a bun. It fascinated me to watch her pin it up that way, without a mirror. I'd left home when I was sixteen and I'd seen the sixties, but I didn't want to see them anymore.

The next morning I found Hessie leaning up against the cottonwood drinking coffee.

"Help yourself," he said, and nodded toward the campfire.

I laughed and bent down to pour myself a cup.

"I didn't mean it," I said. "I can make the coffee."

"If we want it for lunch."

"Oh, I'm sorry—what time..."

"Forget it," Hessie said, "I'm doggin' it today. Thought I might take a ride into town—tell the government they got a fire."

"What?" I said. He pointed south, to a ridge in the mountains behind us, where a line of smoke rose thin and black until it blew sideways, like smoke from a train, and disappeared.

"Lightning," he said.

I couldn't understand why he wasn't gone already. "Don't you think you better go?" I said.

"No hurry. They might have seen it already—and they might just let it burn."

"I'll go. You want me to go?"

Hessie lowered his cup and gave me a long look. "Come along if you want," he said. He emptied his cup on the ground and started toward the truck.

"No," I said. "I'd better stay here."

"Suit yourself."

I watched him drive out of the yard. I needed to leave that day. I'd meant to tell Hessie, but I hadn't quite told myself. I sat down, facing south. The valley seemed suddenly vast and quiet. I could hear the tick of locusts in the dry grass. On the ridge to the south, I thought I saw a lick of red flame. I couldn't take my eyes away.

During the summer of the fires, there were days when the brown smoke hung so thick in the valley, I burned a lantern in the cabin in the daytime. The sun was a dirty bronze glow. It had the feel of something terrible, like the bruised yellow sky before a tornado. I couldn't hang the wash. In the night, dry winds blew ash against the door, and in the morning I found it in perfect, charcoal drifts. When Joe came home, his clothes and hair smelled like wet, burning wool. We hung blankets over the windows and made love in the dark.

Once I tried to pull myself away, spend an hour working through the practice tests. Joe went to his own cabin, but every few minutes I found an excuse to knock on his door—to find a pen, ask him a question. Each time I put my arms around him, sank into a kiss, and had to pull myself away. Finally he looked up and grinned, "You make me feel," he said, "like a sea anemone, waiting for the tide."

I remember nearly every word Joe said, but we hardly talked at all. I never told him where I'd been, where I grew up, what it meant to me to pass the test. In bed, I tried to hold and comfort him, but I never asked him about the war. Joe stopped eating meat, and I thought it had something to do with the war. But it strikes me as strange now that I never asked.

Even when he told me he was leaving, we didn't talk. One day he walked down from the flume, his hair hanging wet and his shirt dark in places where he'd used it for a towel. He sat next to me on the cot and told me he wanted to go home. He hated the heat and the smoke. He wanted to see the ocean.

I couldn't protest, or beg him to stay, because if he stayed I would fail the test. He asked me to go with him, but I didn't believe he meant it. Still, only a year before, I would have gone. In the end he said, "What if it's only sex?" And I didn't know what to say. It hurt me so much I couldn't answer.

I drove him to the interstate, a drive that took all day, and let him off beside a concrete overpass. I didn't look back. In town they told me the fire had jumped a draw and trapped a fire crew. Twenty-two men had died. They talked of calling in the National Guard.

But the fires kept burning. People thought they might as well give up. Only the snow in the fall was going to put them out.

Black rain clouds churned over the foothills to the south. The rain might put the fires out, I thought, but ozone buzzed in the air. The lightning could start new ones. I looked to the north, half expecting to see the smoke from the old fires rise again. Then, turning back, I saw the fire in Carmichael Canyon.

I searched the highway for Hessie's truck, but I knew he was gone. I didn't know where the fire was exactly. Or what to do. It could be close enough to trap the cattle or the horses. But I didn't know.

I took three running steps toward the car and stopped. My low car wouldn't make it up the canyon. I ran to the corral. When they saw me, the horses spun away to the far rail. I tried to calm down, move slowly. But every time I got close, the horse I'd ridden threw up his head and shied away. "Damn you." I gritted the words out between my teeth. "Damn it, stand still!"

It took a long time, but finally I had the bridle on, the cinch strap buckled down and wrapped. I climbed up on the rail and lowered myself into the saddle. Out of the corral, the brown horse picked his way through the sage. I waited for the trembling in my arms and hands to stop.

Near the mouth of the canyon, I saw the cattle moving down from the hills. Three white-faced cows were drifting slowly, stopping to eat, but they were moving away from the fire. I looked, but I couldn't see their calves. Maybe they were hidden in the tall sage, but I pushed the horse harder. We climbed up into the canyon, following the fist of black smoke in the sky. I had to get to the pack horses first, then open the drift fence.

The horse lunged uphill, but after the first mile, he began to breathe hard, and his neck glistened black with sweat. I was afraid to keep on. I pulled up and reined him off the trail where the canyon widened into a stand of tall cedars. At the creek, he jerked the reins from my hands and lowered his head to drink.

It seemed so peaceful there, no sign of fire. I stretched my legs in the stirrups, the bones in my knees cracking. A cloud passed over the sun and the skin on my arms prickled with cold. I hadn't stopped for a jacket. I heard the wind shift in the branches overhead and saw the smoke. It twisted dark gray, coming low through the trees. The horse threw his head up and danced in place. I took a grip on the saddle horn and tried to turn him, to get back to the trail, but I felt his back arch under me. Smoke burned in my eyes, and I started to cough. I lost a stirrup. I remember thinking, I would just swing out of the saddle and land on my feet. I would just step off.

I thought at first I had climbed off the horse and stretched out on the ground. But a dull, hard ache circled my skull from back to front—and an ocean of noise, a high, stinging buzz, roared in my ears. I was on my back in the creek, and the horse was gone.

The water dragged on my jeans, colder than the flume. I tried to stand, but the sound screamed in my ears—like a siren going off, insistent, in the trees, and a needle of pain shot up through my leg. I lay back down. The water felt warmer then. But I knew I had to get out. Already, my breath came hard and my arms and legs were numb. Slowly I inched my way up on the bank.

My fingers and toes burned hot with pain, and my body began to shake. I tried to sink inside, find one warm place, calm down. But I couldn't stop the shivering. My teeth chattered so hard, I thought they might break. I tried to reach my shirt buttons, pull my wet clothes off, but it was as if my arms and hands were baffled in thick padding. I wanted more than anything to crawl back in the creek, where it was warm.

After a long time, the shivering stopped, and it began to rain. The rain struck my face and my arms, white with snow and bits of ice, but I couldn't feel it. It was as if I had no body—as if the rain were pounding on cold earth.

No one knew where I was. I was going to die here—but it didn't matter. I drifted in and out of consciousness. I thought about the day I drove Joe to the interstate. I came back to the ranch and stood in his cabin, looking at the wooden floor, the bare ticking on his mattress, searching for something. A book or a pencil. A wrapper from a razor blade. I found myself kneeling down in the kitchen, going through the trash. But there wasn't anything.

When I came to, the rain had stopped and it was night. I had dreamed my husband's sister called me on the telephone, saying he was coming to see us, coming to her house in

Mexico. Even in the dream, I knew she had no house in Mexico. But I felt lifted, floating in a sea of warmth, a sweet euphoria. And I was weeping, "Oh, I thought he was dead. I thought Richard was dead."

I fell asleep again, and dreamed. I dreamed that everybody was alive.

Then I was choking, my heart pounding wildly. Smoke came drifting in the dark, burning in my throat, but I couldn't see it. A deep, animal fear hit like an electric shock. All I wanted was to stay alive. But I couldn't move.

I woke up naked on the ground. I saw myself from up above, exposed, like some hurt dog left lying in the road. But Hessie was there, naked, rolling us in blankets. Slowly, I felt the warmth of his skin seep into mine. I tried to talk, to ask him, where are the horses? Are the animals all right? But Hessie couldn't understand.

It seemed much later when he shifted to get up.

"Need to get more wood," he said.

"No," I said. I was so warm now, I couldn't bear for anyone to move.

When I woke up again, a campfire burned low close to my face, and the moon was white above the trees. Hessie's fingers pinched into my shoulder, shaking me.

"Look." Hessie whispered close against my ear.

A doe elk stepped slowly toward the creek, her ears pricked wide, and lowered her head to drink. She was so close, I could hear her draw up water and swallow. I hardly breathed. The elk raised her head, listening into the dark. Then she backed away. I thought I heard her for a long time, moving through the trees. But I wasn't sure if I had dreamed or seen her.

I heard Hessie's voice and opened my eyes. The campfire was hot, the sky black overhead.

"Talk," he said. "Where do you come from? Who are your people?"

The light from the fire caught in his eyes. He had been awake all night, shaking me and watching.

I was alive. I took a deep breath, the night air sharp in my lungs. And I was awake. Suddenly aware of another body, my face resting on the ridge of Hessie's collar bone, his arm heavy across my shoulder. A hardness pressed on my leg. My whole body tensed up in alarm.

Hessie rolled over on his back. "Don't worry," he said, his voice low and rough with laughter. "The old dog's only barkin'." It made me laugh, too. But it hurt. It hurt my head to laugh.

He got up and threw more branches on the fire. While he was gone, I tucked a blanket around me, but I didn't need to. He came back wearing long white underwear.

"How's your head?" he asked me.

"Hurts."

"Be good if you could keep awake," he said. "Talk to me."

The sky was black above the trees, but the black seemed softer than it had before.

"You never did say what you're doing in this country in the first place," Hessie said.

I started to tell him about Joe. But I couldn't explain why Joe was still with me, after all this time. "Tell me about the war," I said. "Were you afraid?"

Smoke burned again in my nostrils, coming in the darkness. I couldn't see, or move. I fought the urge to thrash out of the blankets, stand up. But Hessie didn't answer. I closed my hand around his forearm, just above the wrist. As if to make a contact there could keep us both from being scared. But his muscles had no give. His arm was hard as stone.

"We almost made it to the last," he said. "There was me, and one of my brothers, Will. You wouldn't think we'd end up in the same outfit—but it was all a mess." Hessie's voice caught in his throat. "He got blown apart. Standing just right next to me. No different from a deer...

"It's not a thing you tell about," he said. "Nobody knows."

"I know."

I wasn't even sure I said the words. But Hessie stopped. "My husband died," I said, "at Christmas. I sat up with him in the dark, listening to him drowning in his own breath. The sound of it. The rotting, sick-sweet smell."

My hand went weak, and slipped off Hessie's arm. "For a long time after Richard died, my own breath smelled like his."

Tears welled up behind my eyes. I didn't want this to happen. I wanted to grab onto Hessie, to hold and comfort him. I saw him as a boy in France. With Will. But he circled his arms around me. I buried my face in the wet collar of Hessie's shirt, my mouth wide open, my teeth striking bone. What had I done to be so unwanted? How could I have loved them all so much, Richard and Joe, even my father, and be so alone? I couldn't make the crying stop.

But Hessie held on, his arms hard as wood. He rocked back and forth, his chin pressed sharp on the crown of my head. I gasped for air against his neck.

I was like a baby crying, an engine you think will never stop. But finally, my body gave up. I lifted my head to breathe. It hurt to open my eyes, see the white of Hessie's shirt, the wet bark on the trees around us. After a long time, he reached out and pulled the blankets tight.

That's when I told him about Joe. I thought it wouldn't matter now. But it was hard to say the words to Hessie, to talk about sex and marijuana. Out loud, the story made us seem so young and unimportant. Telling it, I heard the truth. Joe hadn't loved me. Not enough. It should have made me sad, but what I felt was shame. A hot rush of shame burned in my chest and on my face. The lie of hanging on so long to a boy I hardly knew.

But Hessie seemed to think it all made sense. When I finished, he shifted up on his elbow and looked at me. I wanted to hide my swollen face, to look away. But he said something I never expected.

"It's good," he said, "to feel love for people. It's not a thing you give away. It's a thing you have."

He lay back down and pulled my head onto his chest, his broad hand on my hair. I felt him draw in a breath and let it go.

"You could have gone with the boy," he said. "You would have been all right."

The sun was hot, but Hessie didn't move. A mist seeped up from the wet ground, glowing iridescent, as if lighted from within. I closed my eyes, curving my cheek into the hollow of

Hessie's neck, my arms loose around him. My fingers touched the smooth, raised muscles along his spine, under the steaming blankets, and the damp wool smelled of gasoline and sweat.

I dreamed again, not quite sleeping or awake. In the warmth and sunlight, everybody was close by.

Dinosaurs

BY JOANNA HIGGINS

"You're *kidding*," Anita said.

"No, I swear to God," Tommy V. told her. "The guy just needed to make his car payments."

"How big did you say?"

"Twenty *acres*."

"*Un*-believable. I was thinking maybe a miniature golf-type place, or something."

"No! Acres! The guy must be nuts. Why don't you come up there with me, you and Billy?"

"To see it?"

"Sure, see it. Stay, if you want. I bet we could make a go of it, you and me."

Her hand curved around his beer glass, the fingernails little red hearts. Then she whisked it away, black skirt, white blouse, all business.

He couldn't believe he said that—*make a go of it, you and me.* The dumb way it sounded, and how she'd probably take it the wrong way. Would she bring the refill or ignore him? Ignore, he figured. Keep away, waiting for him to leave. But the thing was, they *could* make a go of the place, maybe. She was a hard worker, and he had the property, and the property had lots of potential. And he'd always believed you got out of life what you put into it—a fact that usually depressed him when he thought about it because the other side of the coin was, you had to put your energy and will power into the *right* thing. And this is where he always screwed up. Royally. He'd known guys who went to school on the G.I. Bill, learned meat-cutting or TV repairing or what have you, and then started their own businesses and now were sitting pretty. Nice big houses. Families. Grandkids. No money worries. As for him, he'd fallen into and out of hourly-wage jobs, never his own boss, never the right thing; into and out of a marriage and nothing to show for it except regret, bad feelings, and two sons living near their mother in Texas. Then a little too much drinking over the years, an accident in a fork-lift factory, and now his bum hip pinned together, early retirement and peanuts pension. Retirement. Sometimes this struck him as funny, other times as grounds for suicide. What got him was how you're young for a hell of a long time and it seems there's always something ahead of you somewhere, something you'll find or will find you, but then one day you know, you just *know* you're old and the whole shooting match is over. You don't even have to look at the bunchy, old-man skin, the color leaking away, you just wake up one day and it's there, inside you, *Hey, Tommy!* and you wind up carrying that around with you too, bad as those pins in your hip.

But now the pins were drumming a crazy new message. *Anita.* Even though she liked to kid around at the bar, saying she was over the hill too, she wasn't. Not in his book. She was only in her early fifties, whereas he was pushing sixty-five. On her good days, she looked maybe thirty-five, with her figure and hair and pep. The pep was the main thing. When her only son and daughter-in-law were killed by a drunk driver, she took in her grandson, an infant, and people who didn't know the story assumed Billy was her own child. "You can't let it get to you, kiddo," she liked to say, "or you're dead in the water." Recently, when the boy's junior high became caught up in a gang thing—kids beating up on other kids and stealing lunch money—she gave a speech at a P.T.A. meeting and was quoted in the newspaper. Reporters now stopped at the bar and wrote her words down in notebooks and called her Anita. She laughed with them, flirting. She had sunken half-circles under her eyes, but the rest of her skin was shiny and moist—a lot of make-up, but so what? It looked good. Her short blond hair sprang away from the terrycloth headbands she wore, and he didn't mind the black roots at times. Then her hair reminded him of some bright shrub flaring up from strong dark stems. He'd never gotten up the courage to ask her out. He figured seeing her here, at the bar, was all the out a guy in his position could reasonably expect, and be glad for the laughs and small-talk, the friendly routine of it. So why the heck did he have to blow it with his madman *make a go of it, you and me*.

"Were you serious, Tommy?"

There was his refill, and the little hearts. "Sure."

"You think it could fly?"

The pins throbbed. "I don't see why not. I keep hearing there's nothing like it up there. Except, maybe, for this place that's got the World's Largest Cross."

"Where's that? Close by?"

"Thirty miles or so, but no big deal. Could be a tie-in, I'm thinking. You know. A tour bus, or even tourists in cars, could stop there and then at the Dinosaur Gardens, or *vice-versa*."

She kept her head down. "I don't believe this."

He didn't, either.

"Tommy, I don't have any money to sink into it. I mean big bucks."

"That's okay. It's paid for. I can swing the rest."

"Also, I'm talking a business thing. I mean strictly. You know?" Her brown eyes flicked away and back, then away again.

"Sure," he said.

"The thing is, all the drugs here, in the schools and everywhere—I'm sick of it."

"Yeah, right. Hard to raise kids."

"So," she said, giving him the benefit of those brown eyes, "I'm thinking, what the hell. Let's."

"Oh God," Anita said, getting out of the car after their day-long drive north from Detroit. "I'm too old for this!" Her Celebrity rode low on its springs, burdened on top by ladders and, inside, with all their luggage and supplies. Tommy couldn't walk at first and had to stand there on the weedy gravel, hunched forward a little and pretending to size up the scene—two log cabins, their white chinking and the white circles at the corners alone defining them against dark woods. Billy kept close to Anita. Tommy felt sorry for him and liked him well enough but wished, now, that things were a little different. The cabins looked small as hell. The pins in his hip were sending out all kinds of angry and scared messages which he interpreted mainly as Dumb! Stupid! Look at this place. There wasn't even a sign saying Dinosaur Gardens. He did not believe, then, there were any dinosaurs here. The pins were telling him what he already knew. The guy had pulled a fast one, and he, Tommy V., was an A-number-one jerk for getting sucked in. Again.

She was too polite to say anything, he sensed, so he had to. "Well," he said. "This is it. Custer's last stand."

"The thing is," Anita would say, "we just have to keep our spirits up. Not *defeat* ourselves right off the bat." And she had kept their spirits up, right from that first night, fixing up a little party for them of pop and beer and salami sandwiches and the "home-made" brownies they'd bought at a gas station and convenience store just off the interstate. But the cottage was damp, and Tommy's hip ached hard that first night. The lightbulb in the ceiling fixture might have been a floodlight, and held within it, Anita looked her age. Worse. He couldn't shake fear, not even the next morning when they all stepped outside to a wet, green world so lush and sweet-smelling it seemed edible—a world of pine and cedar and fern and wet sandy soil, a world disturbed only by the enthusiasm of many birds and a few cars zinging by on the two-lane highway.

Everywhere they looked, though, was work. Big-project work. The other cabin proved to be a wreck of a snackbar and souvenir shop, now a cluttered storeroom of damp cardboard boxes and long shelves messy with scattered key chains, post cards, educational items, and tiny plastic dinosaurs strewn everywhere. But they gave Tommy hope. If these, then somewhere, maybe, the big ones, the real thing.

And then they found them—back in the cedar swamp. Massive concrete shapes lurking just off overgrown, muddy paths. Paint flaking off. Teeth hanging loose. Eyes runny with fading paint. Armored plates broken off. Tails. Blood spots turning pink. Several appeared to be sinking in some tropical rainforest. One, a great bird-like creature, was stuck in a clump of low cedar growth, flopped there all askew and gazing at them with an outraged eye.

"That's a pterodactyl," Billy said.

"A what?" Tommy turned to the boy. "How d'you know that?"

"He knows them all!" Anita said. "I meant to tell you. Kids are *into* dinosaurs today."

Flushed with praise, Billy ran ahead of them on the path, jumping streamlets of boggy water where footbridges had rotted and fallen apart. In a pond all black water and chartreuse algae, an elephant-like creature made its own last stand against three life-sized human figures in loincloths who aimed long poles, their sharpened tips pink with faded paint.

"*Un*-believable!"

Anita repeated the word when they came upon a giant concrete snake, erect and appearing to watch them at eye level. "Most women," she said, "would be outta here by now. Hi, sweetheart! How ya doin?" She patted the snake's chipped, black head. "Benches, we need. Also, to fix those bridges. And—" She raised a wet blackened sneaker. "Something for the paths, sawdust or something. So people don't get all mucky. Darn it, we need a notebook."

And Tommy was saying to himself, benches, bridges, paths. This I can do. I can *do* this.

A rickety wrought-iron stairway led to a doorway in the last display, a dinosaur whose tree-like legs lifted him high up into the cedar and poplar and balsam. His long neck curved away into the swamp. So did his tail. They all wanted to see what was inside and decided to go one at a time, Tommy first, in case—as Anita said—"there might be something not nice, if you know what I mean."

But inside the dinosaur's belly was a plain room with a small window showing tree branches, and another smaller window set into a partition across the dinosaur's chest area. Through it a tiny room was just visible, empty except for a picture of Christ with a damp-warped sign underneath. *The Greatest Heart in the World.*

"That's got to go!" Anita said, clumping down the stairs. "Now *that* is creepy."

Tommy thought it was interesting in some oddball way, and something they might be able to tie-in with the Greatest Cross thing, but Anita wanted nothing to do with the idea. It was "freaky," they'd be called religious freakos, and people would stay away in droves. Besides, the steps were too dangerous, and they couldn't afford high insurance premiums. Deciding to leave well enough alone, Tommy pulled away the stairs so no one would be tempted.

"Listen," she said, reading his bleak look. "Everybody starts small. *Every*body has to overcome obstacles in the beginning. You can't let it get to you!"

Other words had gotten into his head, though, and wouldn't leave. *Sixty-four, another door! Sixty-four, another door!*

"Let's shoot for the Fourth of July," she said. "A grand opening."

That was only a few weeks away. The pins were pulsing in protest. "There's a heck of a lot of work."

"So? We just knuckle down and *do* it."

But while he and Billy got to work, first cleaning the cabins, then painting, then clearing spaces around the dinosaurs, Anita fooled around—that's how Tommy put it to himself though he was careful not to say anything. He figured she needed to scout around, check out the territory, meaning the town fourteen miles away. She called this her public relations campaign—talking the place up, making contacts, sending out the word. Probably a good idea, he thought, but the place was too quiet without her. Just a watery wind in the cedars and poplars, the streams burbling away, and every now and then a mosquito honing in on its target. Once in a while there'd be a car or a semi in the distance, and then the arcing roar as it sped by, and then just leaves and wind again. When she returned around five with food, treats, and stories about finding a good beauty shop or grocery or running into "this neat guy" from the Chamber of Commerce or the Kiwanis, it was party time again, and he'd tell himself that he worried too much. Brooded. Always. And it had to stop. He remembered the words of an athlete he'd read about in a newspaper article—"Give up on yourself and the door closes."

"So what did *you* guys do today?" Anita would ask finally, winding down. Tommy would look at Billy and Billy would get his vague, scared look, so Tommy would start it off. Fixed this footbridge. Hauled woodchips and shredded bark up to this or that point. Painted Sam or Jake or Verna—his names for the dinosaurs whose real names were, he felt, totally beyond him.

"And how about you, honey?" she'd say to Billy.

"Helped."

"He's a darn good worker, too," Tommy might add, not wanting the silence.

"You miss your friends?"

"They weren't my friends."

"You miss home, then?"

"It's okay here."

And Tommy, exhaling, would turn his attention to Anita's newly-colored and set jumble of hair, thinking, Oh Christ, let it be. Just this one time, let it *be*, okay?

Their cottage had two bedrooms, each with a flowered drape for a door. The daybed in the main room, near a squat cast iron stove, was Billy's, and Tommy made bookshelves for him and drove in a few nails for clothing. In each bedroom was a chipped iron bedstead with a sagging mattress on buoyant, noisy springs, and a mirrored dresser whose drawers, when opened, emitted a musty, pungent odor. Each night the musical springs in Anita's bedroom sang to his imagination, his hopes—all crazy and impossible, he knew. In the cabin, anyway, where the racket alone might bring down the mossy roof. He counted himself lucky, each morning, when he couldn't remember his dreams.

One afternoon, Anita returned early from town and, holding back the drape to Tommy's bedroom, found him sitting on the edge of his bed. He'd been lying down and hadn't been able to stand quickly enough when he heard her car.

"You okay?"

"Sure," he said. "Just tired."

"It's cold in here. You should be outside in the sun. Where's Billy?"

"In the snackbar. Making signs, or maybe hanging posters."

"I have a terrific *surprise* for you!"

He opened the grocery bag, hoping for strawberry short-cake, or better yet, a six-pack, but pulled out something that turned out to be—though he didn't say so out loud—a Jungle Jim suit. Khaki jacket with big square pockets. Buttons all over hell and back. And those goofy straps or whatever on the shoulders. And pants with big pockets. An outfit he wouldn't be caught living or dead in.

"Look at those creases!" she said. "It's never been worn."

"I wonder why."

"That's what I wondered too! I found it at this neat thrift shop."

"Do they give refunds?"

"You don't like it?"

"It might be okay—for somebody."

"Try it on."

"It won't fit."

"How do you know! I bet it will. I held it up."

"I don't want to wear this, Anita. It's a gimmick."

Her displeasure pushed into the room. "That's exactly what we'll need! A gimmick! People love gimmicks. Everybody wants some kind of fantasy. You can be the safari *guide*! They'll love it."

"This is a dinosaur place, not some big game park."

"Same difference. Tommy? You have a pretty good build, you know that? You could look nice."

"What do I look like now?"

"Now? Most of the time—like a slob-ola."

She let the drape fall back. Her bedsprings screeched at him. So did the pins holding his hip together.

He put on the outfit without looking into the mirror, then gave her a tour of all they'd done that day. New woodchips spread along the paths glowed in the early evening light. The air was fragrant with damp cedar bark.

"Un-believable! Oh, this is going to *work*. I have a good feeling about it! And look at *you*." Words zinging through him, and gold flecks everywhere—on the path, in her hair, on eyelids, arms, chin. "Let's *see*," she said, laughing as she unbuttoned the safari jacket. "Let's just see that nice build of yours!" Desire, then, and panic—Where was the boy!—as she led him, safari jacket flapping in the warm wind, toward a dry couch of woodchips. *This is it, Tommy!* the pins sang afterward.

And it seemed to be, even after a drizzly Fourth of July weekend that drew only a few people—parents propelling their children back to heated cars and campers that sped them somewhere else. Tommy, dressed in his safari outfit, offered his services as guide to a group that'd come in a vacation vehicle as large, it seemed, as one of the cabins. "This one here," he told them, "and you can read his name right there, on that sign—this big fellow could only eat grass and water weeds and such, so you figure it was easy for the other guys to gang up on him. Just like today." At the mammoth under attack, he said, "And here we have man at work, doing what we do, pretty much." At the big snake, "Watch out for this guy! He means business." And at the last footbridge, "My wife over in the snackbar over there is waiting for us with some nice free hot coffee and some pop for the kids. We can go over there right now, if you want." But they took off for their snazzy vehicle, as Tommy later put it, like bats.

Soon after this, Anita got the idea of making Billy the guide, since he was so good with the names. Besides, it would draw him out, and possibly help him, later, in school. "People," she observed, "are noticing your *limp*. And when people feel sorry for somebody, they just want to get away." But she made him wear the outfit anyway. "It looks official. People naturally *respect* uniforms."

Lying on the woodchips and looking up at the canopy of woods—his trees!—he thought how he'd never done such a thing before—lying on the ground, looking up at the sky— except maybe when he was a kid. And now here he was. Earth and sky, sky and earth.

"What're you thinking?" Anita said. "You look pretty darn happy."

"I was thinking I can't believe I *own* this."

"That's true," she said, sitting up and getting into her red jogging outfit. "That is true."

And he knew he'd blown it.

A few days later, while they were washing dishes in the snackbar where they had their meals, he asked her to marry him. Share the wealth.

"Are you serious?"

She was offering him a way out, he sensed. Everything warned him to make a joke of it, but he said, "Sure, I am."

She covered his hand with her soapy rubber glove and said she needed to think about it. It was a pretty big step for someone like her.

Was it? Why? He thought of his limp and how she'd fired him from being guide because he couldn't say the dinosaurs' real names. He took Billy into town with him one afternoon and came back with a new haircut, a dictionary from the thrift shop, and a notebook from Woolworth's. Nights, the two of them worked on names, while Anita did her nails or tried to watch the snowy TV.

"Wait," he said. "Don't tell me. I know it! The pinhead one."

"They're all pinheads," Anita said, "if you ask me."

"The Stegmeir one!"

"He's thinking of beer," Anita said. "Again."

"A stego-sore ass is what he'd get if he tried to sit down on all them plates."

Billy and Anita regarded him, offended and bored.

"Just a joke! It helps me remember."

In August Anita enrolled Billy in a country school only six miles away, but lost interest in their walks to the woodchip pile. The bad cancelled out the good, in his book, though he resolved to make the best of it. *A business thing, strictly*! As for the other, what had caused that, he couldn't be sure now. And even the Jungle Jim outfit wasn't helping there.

Then Anita found a girlfriend called Red who, with her husband, ran a campground on a branch of the Devil River a few miles south of them. "They're so darn enterprising, those two!" she'd say. "They have so much on the ball, real go-getters, I'm telling you!"

But Tommy didn't want to hear. This new kick, this new high, coming after her slump over the past weeks, scared him. Why couldn't she settle down and do some real work to help the place? It seemed there always had to be some big distraction, some big-deal excitement in order for her to be happy, in high gear. Now it was Red and Kevin.

"It's like with food, you know? People need food," she'd say. "They have to pay for food, no matter what. And they also need a place to stay. It's not a *luxury* item, like dinosaurs!"

A place to stay. These words led to worries about the coming Northern Michigan winter. The Big Test.

"What do they do winters?"

"That's the beauty of it! They go to Florida and operate a campground down there! But you've got to see their place, Tommy. There's a swimming pool, even. A big, fat, indoor, heated swimming pool—for the campers!"

A swimming pool.

And a cute laundrette neat as a pin. And these great bathrooms with big showers, and everything *really* clean."

Jesus, he said to himself. Laundrette. Bathrooms.

"And canoes, and everything so well kept up. That's the thing. All the grounds, the grass. There's this huge cobblestone fireplace in a big gathering room. Knocks you for a loop when you see it. Better than the Holiday Inn! Honest to God."

"They must have the bucks."

"Sure. Or else investors."

Investors. A word as foreign to him as *stegosaurus* had been. He went into the cool mustiness of his bedroom—it always reminded him of walking back into the 1930's—and thought how the place would be great for people who liked the idea of roughing it for a week or so. But for the real thing—*no*, ten times *no*.

When Anita managed to get them all invited to a cook-out at Green Waters, Kevin—and not the cobblestone fireplace— knocked him for a loop. The man, not young, was lean and rugged-looking. His black hair and moustache showed a lot of gray, but it seemed more like silver filings lodged there, glittering. Tommy watched Anita while Red and Kevin gave them a tour and knew Anita was a goner. He was too, nearly. Red was a flame in her yellow sundress, backless except for some flimsy crisscrossing straps. When she talked to him, he imagined solar flares zooming toward him, long fingers of heat. The freckles under her suntan were little embers. When she talked to Anita, she was giggly and confiding. It was quite an act. He was surprised Anita bought it.

They had huge steaks, fancy salads, and bottle after bottle of some imported beer, and then a cold dessert which Anita later told him was chocolate mousse. There'd been too much of everything—food, beer, talk, looking, praising, comparing. Lying in his bed, trying to erase the day, Tommy felt the dead, dragging weight of useless things, impossible hopes, wrong choices. Then Anita was in the room, tipping the bedsprings as she got in beside him.

"I drank too much," she whispered. "My thoughts are racing like crazy."

"Mine, too."

"I'm so depressed I could kill myself."

"Don't say that."

"I know it. You shouldn't let it *get* to you. But I was thinking, why don't we sell? Get your money out, anyway, and maybe we could try something else."

"A campground?"

"Yeah, right."

They were lying in a little well of mattress, each braced against the other on an incline. At long intervals a car or semi passed, a large sound or small, then crickets and other night creatures took over again. He imagined them living out their insect lives in his woods—and being happy enough.

"The thing is, Tommy, I'm scared. There's not much of a future here, you know? I mean, Christ, what're we gonna do over the winter? We'll go nuts."

He thought of their paths and new bridges, the dinosaurs all painted nice. The snackbar, the woods, the good air. And he knew what an allosaurus was. A brachiosaurus and a stegosaurus. He named all the other names he knew, picturing each of them. "I still think we can make a go of this place," he said finally, but she was asleep, and after a while his dinosaurs pulled him into sleep as well.

In the morning he moved the wrought-iron stairs back up to the belly of his brachiosaurus, which in real life, he'd learned, might have weighed as much as fifty tons. Inside, he sat on a stool he'd brought up without Anita knowing and looked out the side window at cedar branches, and then through the inner window at the *Greatest Heart in the World* picture. No ideas came, but Red and Kevin slipped off into the distance and no longer bothered him. In the daylight, he told himself, things didn't seem so bad.

But then Anita was at the top of the stairs saying, "Listen. I just got this great idea!" Her energy and conviction shot out at him like Red's little signal flares. He could see the three of them packing the car and taking off within the hour.

"What?" he said, not wanting to know.

"Development."

"*What?*"

"Development. A mall. Here! People wouldn't have to drive all the way into town. The summer people, the people in little communities. We'll get some brochures printed and interest some investors, and then—"

"But it's—This is a swamp."

"Fill," she said. "We bring in fill."

"Twenty *acres* of fill?"

"Why are you being so damn negative?" She took a cigarette from a pack she always carried in a leather case, along with her lighter. "What're you doing up here? Going goofy on me?"

"Thinking."

"Well, think about *this*. We gotta wake up and do something, kiddo, or go under. We're not gonna make it on your social security. Simple as that. When something doesn't work, you have to change, adapt, for chrissake, do something different or you'll be dead in the water. I could probably get a job in town, but that's nothing. This—this is the *big* time, Tommy. And we've been sitting right on top of it—asleep!"

"You could check it out if you want. See what's what. How much fill costs and so on." He figured the best thing for her would be a project, keeping busy, some kind of plan.

"That's what I like about you." Her tongue flicked out to demolish something on her top lip. "You're a real go-getter."

In the next weeks Anita learned, as she put it, more than she wanted to know about government regulations, environmental impact statements, and above all, about state forest preserves. The Dinosaur Gardens, built in the twenties, had been grandfathered in a state forest tract, where malls and trailer parks, stores, subdivisions, private campgrounds, and all such enterprises were not and never would be allowed. The Dinosaur Gardens could only be what it was—a garden for dinosaurs. "In perpetuity!" she said. "*Un*-believable. Talk about thwarting progress."

"I could have told you that," Kevin said. "We checked all that out before we put down a penny."

"Live and learn!" she joked, her eyes bright with pain and anger.

There were fall color tours in canoes up and down the Devil River, campfires, swims in the heated pool, cook-outs. Anita tried to reciprocate, inviting Red and Kevin for sunset walks at the Gardens, but Red made polite, understandable excuses. One of them always had to be close to the office, the way people were always coming and going, or needing something. Then Tommy felt bad about closing the Gardens for all those hours and so stayed behind, waiting for tourists, while Anita and Billy spent weekend afternoons and evenings at Green Waters. Who could blame her? he asked himself. But it was like carrying somebody around with him on his shoulders, and he was tired all the time. When a carload of tourists happened to stop, or, once, two older ladies carrying handbooks, he said, "Have fun, there's lots to see," and turned away. He began wearing his old flannel shirts again, and the green workpants.

A large basket of chrysanthemum daisies arrived one afternoon with a card saying, *Congratulations on Your New Venture and Best Wishes for the Future!* "Who the heck's Ernie Dinwiddle?" Anita asked, reading the card, but Tommy didn't know either. "Probably some guy I met at the Chamber of Commerce or something," she said, and put the basket on the snackbar, then forgot to water the flowers. The basket, with its withered stems, red bow, and note stuck to a plastic prong, stayed on the counter, becoming as invisible to them as the napkin dispensers, salt and pepper shakers, and plastic menus.

Then on a day of heavy wind, low cloud, and snow flurries, Red and Kevin stopped to say goodbye. There were warm promises to keep in touch, to get together again next spring.

Their promises, not his. It was Anita's turn, then, to grieve. With Red and Kevin just a few miles away, she at least had a little spark. Now seeing them inches apart in bucket seats, their neat trailer in tow, Anita became teary. "I'll miss you guys!" And they said they'd miss her too, and Billy, but Kevin was already glancing toward the empty highway dusted with snow.

Their leaving coincided with the end of Indian summer and the beginning of wet, cold autumn. Anita was restless yet complained of exhaustion. She began going into town again and coming back later and later—"lit," as Tommy put it to himself. He had a few himself, between jobs, little rewards. And there was more than enough work for him—all of it necessary if they were to make it through.

He bought a caulk gun and tubes of caulking for the windows. Sakrete to repair the crumbling chinks between logs. Roof tar. A long-handled brush for cleaning stovepipe. New chains for his chainsaw, with which he added to his log piles. He regarded the squat cast iron stove with an anxiety bordering on despair, then told himself it might be cozy. But to have to go out in a storm to make a meal in the snackbar? The plumbing and toilets worried him even more. He bought pipe wrap and pipe insulation and heat tape, spending money, he told the clerk in a hardware place, hand over fist. He tried telling himself it was better than sitting in a bar someplace, which is what he'd be doing, otherwise.

A freeze hit. Leaves ripping off, gusting, a whirl of them everywhere. Snow squalls. His woods thinned, letting in gray light. His dinosaurs looked goofy to him, oblivious in their poses. They reminded him of a game he'd played as a kid— "statues." You whirled around until dizzy, then fell, freezing in some stupid post that made the other kids laugh. That's how it was, he told himself now. Whirl, whirl, whirl, then some idiotic pose forever. Lonely, with Billy in school and Anita in town, he walked his paths, stopping once in a while to tell Jake or Verna these thoughts. At the mammoth's pond he told the hunters to lay off and give the guy a break. On a milder day in late November, he sat on one of his benches, in thin sunlight, and watched a cloud of insects making their tiny cyclone motions around one another. Night would come and that would be it, he knew, for them. "Sayonara, guys," he said, finally, and went back to split more wood.

The contents of the note didn't surprise him, but the note itself did. He hadn't figured she would pick that way, go without telling him. And she probably told Billy to keep quiet about it, too, which hurt. He found another note on his pillow. *Dear Tommy, I took some of the little dinosaurs from the snackbar. Anita said it would be okay. I'll miss you. Love, Billy.*

The springs swayed under him as he lay back, one leg hanging over the side. Who cared if he could make it up or not. Her car wouldn't be pulling in. Possibilities presented themselves—the main one being The Dry Dock bar in town. But then he remembered he had no car. He got up eventually by rolling onto his side and scrabbling around for a while. He climbed the stairs to the brachiosaurus's belly, shut the door behind him, and sat on his stool. Everything hurt—head, hip, fingertips, eyes, eyebrows, brain. He remembered the insects that morning, and a thought formed: *We are all miniatures.* He could see it on a sign, maybe along one of his paths. People could think what they wanted about it as they walked along. He could make up some others, like the old Burma Shave signs.

The greatest Heart in the World—
Dead as a doornail.
So what gives?
What's the story?

Hope sparked, then died. He opened the door and kicked the stairway to the side—a rattly, tinny crash. A few yellow poplar leaves were twirling in the breeze. Except for the knocked-over stairway, everything was the same.

He could see a coyote creeping in, cautious. Then some racoons. Crows and turkey buzzards hopping closer. Then moles, mice, and ants cleaning up. Flies. Then snow. Then nothing.

Oh Jesus.

Headlines: *Man Falls From Dinosaur.*

He sat down in the doorway, letting his legs dangle. If he didn't do it right, he'd wind up an invalid for who knows how long. But if he'd jumped right away, it might be all over by now. Too darn much thinking! That was his problem, always.

The weak sun fell behind the brachiosaurus, and cloudcover and wind moved in. Tree limbs clattered. He thought he heard a car door slam and listened hard. Nothing.

He stood and, closing his eyes, let go of the doorway. "Sayonara guys," he said, sad to think the swamp would get the dinosaurs again. But the wind seemed to be doing odd things and he grabbed onto the door frame again to listen. *Whoo-oo*, it said. *Whoo-oo!* He opened his eyes. Somebody on the path, coming toward him. Somebody in heavy boots and trousers and puffy jacket. Hope dissolved. This person also wore a squashed-down tan hat and carried a straw bag over one shoulder. Ashamed, he tried to hide.

"Excuse me! Excuse me, sir!"

He had to go to the doorway, surprised to see an older woman in that explorer get-up.

"I didn't think you were here!" she said. "Are you still open for the season?"

"That's a good question." Her thick round eyeglasses reminded him of binoculars. A flush crept up his neck, burning his ears.

"You've gotten yourself in some predicament, sir. I see that now!"

"The wind," he said. "I was up here working. The wind can get real bad."

She looked at the fallen stairs. "It must have been." Before he could think of another lie, she had the stairs up and was climbing them with great agility. "How unique! In the belly of the brachiosaurus, are you?"

"And pretty darn chewed up, too." His laugh sounded like a crazy man's to him. His ears pulsed with heat. The binocular-glasses were taking in everything—windows, the Greatest Heart picture, him. The stems of her glasses were attached to an elastic strap—the kind athletes wore—and he knew why, the way she was tipping her head up, then down, then sideways like some bird trying to see a thing from every angle. A weirdo—in his book. Then she was telling him about the brachiosaurus' leg and pelvic structures, the length of its neck and tail, and how the brachiosaurus probably lived all over North America, possibly in deep pools of water. Behind the glasses her eyes were wide-set, a gray all lighted up—he got an image of little night lights burning back in there, and the machinery always working. The eyes fixed on him as she went on and on, telling him of the latest fossil discoveries in Montana and how older, long-respected theories were now being contested left and right. Warm-blooded, not cold-blooded! Nurturing, gregarious, herd creatures, and not solitaries! Swift-moving, not stupidly slow and clumsy! "So you see—just when we think we know something for sure. Have it all worked out. That's what delights me to no end."

"I see what you mean." It figures, he was thinking. Run a freaky place and what do you get?

She descended the stairs, hardly giving them a thought, it seemed, and that amazed him. She had to be his age or better. At least.

"Ernie Dinwiddle," she said, on the ground, and held out her hand. "Short for Ernestine. And you, sir?"

What could he do but tell her, and then tag along while she gave him a guided tour of his own property, talking not only about the dinosaurs, but also about treebark, stones, moths, and newly-set buds. It was taking forever. The words were one thing and probably would drive a person nuts in no time, he thought, if it weren't for the way she looked at everything. And when she knelt down in leaves that could be hiding anything and began rummaging in the black dirt, his heart started aching worse than his hip. Her splotched and veiny hands looked like brown leaves themselves, cupping the swamp-muck, then showing him something probably important though he didn't know what he was supposed to be looking at.

"Oh, this is such a wonderful place! You know, I came here earlier this summer with a dear friend and we'd hoped to talk to you then. We wanted to congratulate you on all the improvements."

"Yeah," he said, "and it's for sale. Maybe you'd be interested in buying it?" Hope churned.

"For sale? But didn't you just purchase it?"

"I bought it to fix up. An investment."

She turned the binoculars on him and he felt spotted with the lie.

Owning such a place was impossible for her, she told him. As for managing a business, well, that was out of the realm, too. She had other priorities and no time, now, for business.

"You lucked out there." He offered her coffee, and in the snackbar thawed some frozen donuts.

"The last good days," she said, looking out cloudy windows at the woods, "are always so difficult, aren't they? You simply don't want to go in."

When she again turned to him, he was still trying to think of something to say to that. The way she was staring at him, he felt like one of her stones. All dead weight. He wished he were lying down on his mushy springs and mattress. He wished he could close his eyes. With great effort he said, "What do you do winters, up here? Or do you go south?"

"Oh no! I love my little house, Mr. Vieczorek. I stay up here. Hole up."

"How the heck do you manage?"

"Read, for one thing. There's so much to know. No end to it! A person can't know enough."

What for? he wanted to ask. What's the point?

She tapped her forehead. "Soon, this is going to go." She touched her eyeglasses. "And these." She raised her hands. "And these, too. Arthritis, probably. Or Parkinson's. Any number of things. A hundred things can go wrong at any time. The wonder is that they don't—for so long!"

The pins howled. He shifted on the chair to ease his hip.

"Well, I might be here, too," he said. "Maybe holing up."

"Maybe?"

She knows! the pins jeered. She sees right through you! "Yeah. Maybe." The ache inside broke outward, making his voice wobble. "I don't know. What's next, I mean." Glancing around to escape the binoculars, he saw the basket of dead flowers, the bow, the note, the name there. Oh Jesus, he said to himself.

"It hasn't been a good season, then?"

"Not exactly." He laughed to hide the wobble, the weakening. "It was a mistake, if you want to know. This place. People today, they want Star Wars stuff, Disneyland, but that's not it, that's not what—" The pitch of his voice scared him now, the tightening everywhere—throat, heart, blood vessels, it seemed, shrinking to nothing. "The thing is—it's just that a person gets to the point where you, ah, see the end, you know? The end of the line." He took hold of his coffee mug to anchor his hand. All his life he'd lived by the rule that it never paid to show weakness, but what did it matter when you're going to get stomped anyway? "For me," he said, "this is the end."

"The *end*?"

"Yeah. I gotta face it. That's all."

"So."

"As I see it, the only choice I have at this point is—" Oh shut up, he told himself. Stop whining! "You want more coffee?"

"Please. It's my one vice. But I'm hoping you *will* be here. I wanted to ask if I might come and walk a few times a week. I've done that for several winters now. These trails are just right for the exercise one needs."

"Walk?"

"On snowshoes. That way, you see, I can walk all winter."

"Ah." He didn't have snowshoes, he told her, trying to be polite, but it sounded like a pretty good idea.

"It is! It's wonderful. You must *try* it."

That'll be the day, he wanted to say, but humoring her—she meant well, after all—he went into a long story about his hip, the operations, the pins, the trouble, now.

"But it's just walking—on snow. It would be just the thing for you. And I have," she said, "an extra pair of snowshoes."

He saw himself in his safari outfit, his feet strapped to things that resembled tennis rackets. Un-believable! he heard Anita saying.

"Ah—that's okay. Thanks anyway. You go right ahead, though."

"Splendid! And perhaps you'll reconsider."

Splendid. Never had he heard that word spoken—not even on TV. Never could he have imagined it might apply to anything having to do with him. Splen-did.

"I could fix us something nice," she said. "For a winter picnic. You know! A wineskin. Some good cheese, nice crisp bread, cold cuts. I sometimes do that just for myself. Then if anything happened, I could last for a while, anyway. I always carry matches, too. And a good-sized piece of heavy plastic."

"Plastic?"

"It's a marvelous windbreak and keeps you quite warm."

"So you'd have a picnic, then, worse comes to worst."

"Oh no! For a picnic you need one other person, at least."

He looked at his new guide, the flush coming again, and tried to imagine it—a picnic in the snow. Wine, bread, cheese, lunchmeat, his donuts.

"Well," he heard himself saying, "I could maybe bring some beer." Oh stupid, stupid! the pins railed at him. Think of the non-stop talk. Think what you're getting into *now*, you jerk. She's lonely and just pulled a fast one, is what! But he said, "And maybe some donuts." Shifting, he placed one hand on his sore hip, trying to stop the racket there. "Wonderful!" he heard her saying, "but we don't have to wait for winter, you know. Especially if this good weather holds!"

"Oh, by the way," he said at her car, "I want to thank you for those flowers. That was real nice."

"Well, Mr. Vieczorek, *this* is real nice, too. So we're even."

"Tommy," he said. "Call me Tommy, if you want. Everybody does."

"Splendid!"

At sunset it was still too mild to go in and he walked his trails, thinking how he wouldn't have to wear the Jungle Jim suit now and she wouldn't mind—in her squashed hat and baggy trousers and boots. Oh, unbelievable, the things he got himself into! But for the first time in weeks he saw how nice the paths really did look, winding through the swamp and making it all a kind of weird garden of ferns and rocks and streams and a million other things that were somehow all his. Un-believable, Tommy. Splen-did! Passing his dinosaurs, he told them they didn't have to worry, not for a while anyway. He, Tommy V., was still around and kicking. On the way back he sat on the bench near Tony, his triceratops, its three horns angled fiercely toward the darkening woods. Watching shadows grow, he imagined he could see her there, at the edge of the clearing, digging around in the mud and leaves. A few flying insects found him and did their cyclone dance, and from the mammoth's pond came the pulsing of crickets. But he heard something else, too. What? He stiffened, concentrating on the new sound. Someone coming? *Something* coming? A bear? A wolf, maybe? Or a rattler crawling through leaves and woodchips? He looked at Tony, who seemed to know something was up as well. He looked at the woodchips. Nothing— that he could see. He looked toward the woods where it was too dark to see anything at all. *Soon these are going to go*, Ernie told him again, touching her thick glasses, and not being afraid—or so it'd seemed. Well, he wasn't either, he told Tony, and went to the edge of the clearing to listen.

A crackling and crumbling but so faint under the sounds of breeze and crickets and his own breathing and the bumping of his heart. Something like the smallest doors in the world creaking open one after another. Then he was kneeling, his bad hip shooting pain everywhere, swamp water seeping through his workpants, and a boggy smell wafting up. It was crazy as anything, he knew, but the sound seemed to be coming from the leaves, the ground, and could only be what she'd showed him—all those tiny things digging in, now, with little root feet no bigger than hairs and hanging on for all they were worth.

The Tattoo

BY LESLEE BECKER

Jean Calhoun hadn't meant to get the tattoo. She wanted to get out of the house, a house she had rented, sight unseen, two weeks earlier. Dale, her lover, would be gone, she assumed, by the time she returned. When she left that morning, he had been packing to return to California.

She went to a furniture store, but didn't find anything there. She noticed the tattoo parlor as she returned to her car. It was called Permanent Solutions, and its window displayed a huge skull atop vivid red wings. She thought immediately of the time she and Dale had gone to a carnival and heard a young man pleading with a tattooer to replace a girl's name over his heart with another's.

"That kid's going to want another one eventually," Dale had whispered to her. "I can't watch this."

But Jean had insisted that they stay. She saw a girl watching the young man and heard her say, "You don't have to. I know you love me."

"That's my girl," the young man had said to the tattooer. "Kim. That's what I want. Kim."

Jean and Dale had laughed later at the tattoos on display in the tent. She had picked a feather design for Dale for his shoulder, but he, to her disappointment, told her he could think of nothing that would suit her.

Three people were inside Permanent Solutions, a young woman, a man who looked to be in his thirties, and a teenager with long, stringy hair. They were sitting together in a seat that had once belonged in a car, an older model. The teenager was smoking a cigarette and picking at something on his arm. The woman was dressed in a black leather skirt and vest. Rings and bracelets were tattooed on her fingers and wrists. The other man wore jeans and a black T-shirt, his arms and neck covered in a design of a diamond-back rattlesnake. In the center of his throat was the tail, a careful pattern showing each ring of rattles, ending in a sharp tip. Jean looked at the designs on the wall, hundreds of them encased in glass.

"Looking for anything in particular?" the woman said.

"No," Jean answered.

"We've got more," the woman said. "Just go down that hallway there. Take your time."

"Thank you," Jean said and went down a short hallway, both sides filled with designs. There were notebooks too, and she looked through those and at the chairs clients sat in, barber chairs. She saw no instruments but did see blue plastic sheets and photographs showing men and women with tattoos.

"Any questions?" the older man said.

"How long does it take?" Jean said.

"Depends," the man said. "Anywhere from half an hour to a whole day. Depends on the design."

"Most people want to know if it hurts," the woman said.

"It hurts," the teenager said.

"Depends on where you get it," the woman said. "You take your neck area or your breasts. They're different from an arm or a hand."

"You oughta know," the teenager said.

Jean wished another customer would come in, but she continued to look even though she found nothing in the samples she liked. Too many skulls, hearts, flowers, and foolish-looking cartoon characters. And to her surprise, barn-yard figures, chickens, pigs, and cows. In one of the note-books, she saw religious designs, crosses, bleeding hearts, and an entire crucifixion scene, showing the soldiers, the other victims on their crosses, and women in robes, their heads hung low in grief.

"We've got more to worry about than you do," the man said. He had come up behind her and was looking over her shoulder as she looked through the notebook. She smelled something sweet, like rose water. "Our instruments are sterilized, but we don't know about your blood. We could get something from you."

"I bet you have to be careful," Jean said.

"We take precautions. You've got to know what you're getting into," the man said. "It's like buying a car, except this is a permanent decision. You'll have it for the rest of your life."

"I know," Jean said.

"I was sixteen when I got my first one," the teenager said.

"Everyone remembers the first time," the woman said.

"I didn't want to be like everyone else," the boy said. "I came up with my own design." He got up from the chair and showed Jean a blue design on his arm. It could've been a coffin, but he told her it was a car. "I wanted a car," he said.

"It's a wreck, Floyd," the man said. "I'm teaching the boy the trade. He did that on his own, with knife and ink."

The man and the teenager returned to the car seat.

"I can see you with a peacock," the woman said.

"A spider," the boy said.

Jean saw the older man shake his head. "This lady," he said, "wants an original, something no one else has. I don't see a peacock or a panther or a spider."

"What do you see?" Jean said.

"Something delicate, fragile," the man said.

"A spider web," the boy said.

"Shut up, Floyd," the man said. He began looking at a magazine, as if his interest in Jean had passed. The woman got out of the seat, came to where Jean was, and began showing her designs in another notebook. Her hands were pale and thin, the fingers red, as if she suffered a blood disorder.

"Where will you get it?" she said. "The shoulder? The breast? Buttocks? Lots of gals go for private locations."

"Cher's got 'em all over," the teenager said. "How tall do you think she is?"

"I don't know," Jean said. "At least five ten."

"Wrong," the boy said, making a sound like that of the failure horn on quiz shows.

"Five four, tops," the woman said.

"Don't mind them," the man said in a disinterested way. "Sit down, Barb. Leave her alone."

The woman did as told and then she and the teenager began to talk about what they'd get for lunch. The man told them they were free to go, and in a short time the two of them left. Jean wondered if they'd be discussing her, perhaps making assessments of her and bets as to whether or not she'd get a tattoo. She was glad when they left. The man remained in the seat, reading, as if she weren't there. Jean saw him take out a note pad and colored pencils. He began to draw something.

"I guess a lot of people would think twice about getting a tattoo these days," Jean said.

"People should think twice about everything they do," he said.

"I rented a house sight unseen," she said. "I've never done that before. I came out from California."

The man said nothing. He seemed absorbed in what he was drawing, and Jean wondered if it pertained to her.

"I've only been in town two weeks. I was looking for furniture when I saw your shop."

"And something drew you in," he said, not raising his head. "You're looking for something."

"Yes," Jean said. "You mind if I smoke?"

He said nothing, and when she took the cigarettes from her purse, she realized her hands were shaking. "I have a job at the college. Remember that hot spell? That's the week I came. I thought it would be cooler. I thought I'd have a view of the mountains. The house," she said, hesitating, "lacks personality, if you know what I mean. Do you live in town?"

"Nope," he said.

"I might move up into the mountains later," she said, seeing and hearing herself, as if from someone else's view. She realized she sounded foolish. The man didn't care about her, didn't even seem to care if she got a tattoo or not. She put out her cigarette and found herself looking at the designs again but this time trying to imagine one of them on her. She looked at a panther and pictured getting it on her shoulder and knew in an instant that whatever design she chose, it would go where people could see it. Why not? She was forty and had no one to answer to now. The people at the new counseling job might wonder about her, but this was perhaps what she wanted. Something to make people take notice.

"I bet it's pretty here in the winter," she said. "I haven't seen snow for years." The man still showed no interest, and Jean realized she could say anything.

"When the landlord described the house to me on the phone, I said no outright. He told me about the yard, the fireplace, and the location, and I thought, 'Why not?' What's the worst that could happen?" As she spoke, she recalled the day she and Dale arrived in town, the heat so fervent, it made her dizzy in the car. "My house," she remembered telling herself when she saw it. It was unremarkable, so much like the others on the street, she couldn't find it the night she and Dale came back from eating out. But on that first day, Dale had taken her hand, commenting on the handsome rose bush near the door. When they stepped inside, glad to be out of the heat, a battery of moths burst upon them, stirring about the room outrageously, their wings ravishing the air. She would, she knew, blame the house for a long time, make it and not herself responsible for what might happen.

She and Dale had been lovers for two years but had never lived together. He was ten years younger than she, and she had met him at the boys' school where she worked as a counselor and he as a cook. She had taken night courses to earn a higher degree, and Dale had been attending culinary school to become a chef. When she learned she had gotten the job in Colorado, she went out immediately and bought him a set of knives made in Germany, costing nearly four hundred dollars. She felt good knowing she was leaving her job behind. She counseled boys from wealthy families who would come into her office mainly with teacher and roommate complaints. On many occasions, she had wanted to say to them, "So, you think you've got troubles?" What she wanted to describe to them or someone was her frustration with her job and salary, her fear of growing old and anonymous, and her conviction that Dale didn't really love her.

When Dale told her he would help her settle in, then finish out his job, and at summer's end return to Colorado to be with her, she couldn't believe her good fortune. In her office, she'd listen patiently to the students and then urge them to take control of their lives. As she described what control meant, she knew she was talking about her own life, her own happiness.

She recalled waiting for him, the morning the movers arrived, watching the men load her things into a truck that already contained a car and someone else's possessions. The car bore an Alaska license plate and along with it were children's things—tricycles, wagons, a swing set—and a savage-looking bearskin rug, containing in its open jaws a man's boot.

When the movers finished, Jean waved at them, as if saying goodbye to old friends, and when Dale finally appeared at her apartment, she felt anxious to get on the road and angry with him for holding her up. She drove above the speed limit to make up for the lost time and kept looking in her rear-view mirror at his car, wondering what he was thinking.

They arrived in Colorado two days later, during a record-setting hot spell, and as she drove through town, she wondered if Dale was disappointed.

She recalled the sinking sensation in her chest as she turned onto the street where the house was located. The ranch houses looked alike. On both sides of the street the small lawns were brown, many of them containing an assembly of toys, broken-down cars, and forlorn-looking lawn decorations. Somewhere, on another street, a dog barked and yelped.

"It's not what you expected, is it?" Jean had said as they stood outside the house.

"Jean," he had said, "it's got lots of possibilities. I'll bet you can have a garden out back."

For two weeks, although she had hated the way she behaved—finding fault with everything—she couldn't stop herself and remembered looking to Dale for signs of displeasure and regret. Finally, she had said, "You won't be coming back, will you? You don't like it here."

"I don't like what's happened to us," he said.

"Maybe after I get the house in shape, we can relax, go to the mountains or someplace else."

"You know I have to go back, Jean."

"You've already decided," she said.

"He left me," Jean said in a low voice and looked to the tattoo artist to see if he had heard. He did look up at her. Then he got up from the seat, and without saying a word, showed her what he had drawn. Three designs, a butterfly, a wooden match burning, and a face, doleful and long, a sadness so frank it could be, were it not a woman's face, the face of a Byzantine Christ.

Jean said nothing, nor did the man, but she felt a pang in her heart at the sight of the face. "I want," she said, "you to do it. Now."

He led her to the room with two chairs, put a plastic sheet over a chair, then handed her a form, which she signed immediately, without reading.

"The face?" he said.

Jean looked at it again. "No. The match."

"The match," he said. "Where?"

"Here," she said. She pushed up the sleeve of her blouse and put her finger on her forearm. She felt his hand on her arm, his fingers rubbing the spot she had selected. Then he brought a stool up to her chair and a metal cane with a rubber-gripped handle. "You can hold onto this, or me," he said.

"You," she said.

He removed the cane, then excused himself, and went down the corridor. Jean closed her eyes while she waited for him. The face was there, long and brooding, sadder even than the man's picture.

When he returned, he began mixing dyes behind her at the counter. He pushed his stool next to her right side and showed her a piece of transfer paper. He said nothing as he placed the paper on her arm. When he lifted it off, the outline of the match and the flames was there. Then he slid his hand into the needle device. He turned it on, and a small buzzing sound began. Then he turned it off.

"That's" he said, "what it sounds like. What it feels like is up to you."

Jean closed her eyes. Without looking or thinking, she rested her hand on his thigh.

It burned, what he was doing to her, but he stopped just at the moment when she thought she could take it no more. Then he began again. He swallowed and she saw the snake tail move on his throat. She looked down at her arm. The design was outlined in blue. He dabbed at it with a piece of cotton.

"Like it?" he said.

Jean nodded. He looked closely at the dyes, then told her to close her eyes. It didn't seem to hurt as much, but she found herself clenching his thigh.

Then it was over. The colors didn't look distinct, the blue, orange, or the red of the flame.

"In a while," he said, "you'll see a change." He told her how to take care of it and handed her a slip of paper outlining what she must do and not do. Then he rubbed some ointment on and taped a piece of gauze over the spot.

Although she didn't know why, she felt embarrassed giving him money. He placed it on the counter and helped her out of the chair, extending his arm to her in a gentlemanly fashion.

"The others," she said, "may I keep the drawings?"

He nodded.

"Just in case I want more," she said. "I'm glad I decided to do it. Very glad. Thank you."

"You come back, if you're not satisfied." He turned away from her and began cleaning off the counter and folding the plastic sheet.

"Thank you," she said again. She waited a moment. "I went out today for a table and I got a tattoo." She wished he'd say something, and when he didn't, she felt a small sadness.

She saw herself out and realized, as soon as she got into her car, that she had never learned his name. It was bright and warm outside. She put on sun glasses and before she pulled out of the parking lot, she saw the man return to the car seat, putting his arms behind his head and smiling.

She stopped at a cafe and looked at her arm, wondering what Dale would think about what she had done.

"I got a tattoo," she told the waitress. She lifted the bandage, and both of them stared at her arm. "It's a match."

"So that's what it is," the waitress said. "I wouldn't take you for the tattoo type. You ride a bike?"

"Yes," Jean said.

She dreaded returning to the house and felt, once again, a sinking feeling as she turned onto her street. To her surprise, Dale's car was still in the driveway, and behind it was a yellow compact car with a missing fender. She heard voices inside the house, Dale's and that of a man. She felt her heart race.

They were in the living room, Dale on the sofa, and a man and a boy sitting on the floor, vacuum cleaner parts surrounding them. The man had an ebbing hairline and a red mustache and looked to be in his thirties. The boy, around eight, had bone-colored hair.

"I didn't expect to see you here," Jean told Dale.

"I'm supposed to be heading back to California today," Dale told the man.

The man got to his feet and told Jean his name was Scott, but the tag on his shirt said Bob. "This is my boy, Austin," he said. "Your husband says you've just moved to town. Welcome."

Jean looked at Dale. "We have so much to do," Jean said to the man.

"I'll try to make this quick and painless," the man said. "You already got yourselves a fine set of steak knives. Yours for having us come into your home."

"I picked the knives for you," Dale said with a shrug.

"He had a choice of those, a flashlight, or a candy dish," the man said, "but you could pick something else."

"No, the knives are fine," Jean said, wondering if Dale had chosen them because of the ones she had bought for him.

"Your name's going to be entered in our sweepstakes," the man said. "You could win a thousand dollars. Now, my boy and I will show you this wonderful product."

"I already have a vacuum cleaner," Jean said.

"Most people do," the man said.

"I think Jean's trying to say this isn't a good time," Dale said. "Sorry."

"Let's go, Dad," the boy said.

The salesman looked at his son, then at Jean and Dale.

"I need to talk to you. Let's go outside," Jean said to Dale.

"She's the boss," Dale said. He and Jean stepped over the parts on the rug and went out through the kitchen to the back yard.

"I thought you'd be gone," Jean said. "Why did you let them in?"

"I was in the bedroom, and when I heard them, I thought it was you. I decided to stay."

Jean felt something grab in her heart. "For good?"

Dale said nothing.

"This morning when I left the house, I knew what it would be like to be without you," Jean said.

"You knew what that was like even when I was here."

"Dale, I made a mistake. I got so caught up in the move."

"I know, but what happened isn't all your fault. Maybe I wasn't ready for this."

"You never really meant to stay with me, did you?"

"It's what you wanted, isn't it? You've been preparing yourself for this all along."

"Hey," the salesman shouted from the kitchen door. "You folks ready?"

Jean looked back at the salesman. He was smiling at her. "Please," she muttered.

"Nice yard," the man said, then retreated from the door.

"I'll take care of him," Jean said and went into the kitchen. When she glanced back, Dale was looking down, his back to her, as if assessing the yard and considering what he would do with it. He would plant a garden. Things would grow under his care. We could've been happy here, she told herself. She saw her reflection in the window and imagined it as the sad face the tattoo artist must have seen. She rolled up her sleeve to look at her arm.

"Did you hurt yourself?" the salesman said, startling her. The boy was behind him, looking at Jean's arm.

"Yes," she said and rolled her sleeve down. "A burn."

The salesman winced. "They're painful. Did you put ice on it? That's what they say to do now."

"Want me to start timing now, Dad?" the boy said as they returned to the living room.

"Wait till everything's ready," his father said, then told Jean he was working on his demonstration time. "My goal is to complete it under thirty minutes."

"He goes over it," the boy said, "every time." He looked away as his father struggled to fit a hose into the neck of the machine.

"Isn't it a beauty?" the man said, twisting the part. "It's space-age plastic."

The boy giggled.

"I'm sorry," Jean said, "but this isn't a good time for me." She heard the back door, then watched Dale walk into the living room.

"I was just about to give the missus a demo," the salesman said. "Glad you could join us. Sit down, relax."

Dale looked at Jean, took her hand, and sat on the sofa with her.

"It's got at three-speed motor," the man said. "This is the best machine money can buy."

"Tell them how much it costs, Dad," the boy said.

The man paused, then said in a low voice. "Twelve hundred, but we have low monthly installment-paying plans."

"Twelve hundred," Dale exclaimed, "for a vacuum cleaner?"

"It'll last a lifetime," the man said.

"I'm sorry," Jean said, "but we could never pay that much."

"With the move and all," Dale said, putting his hand on Jean's leg, "we've had setbacks."

"We know about those, don't we, Son?" the man said. "But wait till you see what this machine can do."

"Now, Dad?" the boy said, looking at his watch.

"Now," his father said. He put a filter in, turned the machine on, and went over a patch of carpet. Then he turned off the machine, extracted the filter, and showed it to Jean and Dale. It was filled with lint and dirt.

"Amazing," Dale said, "and we cleaned when we moved in, didn't we, Jean?"

"That's all we did, cleaned and tried to get the house in shape," she said.

"Even if you vacuumed day and night," the salesman said, "your machine can't do the job of this one. This baby'll go way down. Watch, I'll show you."

"You better hurry up, Dad," the boy said. He looked embarrassed, and Jean felt sorry for him and for the father. She watched the salesman put in another filter and go over the rug.

"It's got a special attachment for curtains, too," he said. "I'll show you."

"I'm sure it's a wonderful product," Dale said, "but we just can't afford it, and we've got things to take care of today. I've got to get on the road pretty soon."

"He's almost finished, Dale," Jean said.

"You got pets?" the salesman asked, but before she could answer, he said there was an attachment for shampooing pets, for giving them or a loved one a massage too. He turned off the cleaner and showed her the pet attachment. "Actually," he said, "I can't see a pet standing still long enough to run a machine over it."

"We tried it," the boy said, "at home."

"That massager comes in handy," the man said, looking away from Jean. "This company has been in the business for years. They're famous for their vacuum cleaners."

"How long have you been selling them?" Jean asked and was certain she heard Dale sigh.

"This here's my third week," the salesman said. "I was a mason before."

"You're going to run over again," the boy said.

"I hurt my back," the man said, "so I had to take up a new trade. Did you know that most of the houses in Denver are made of brick? See, there was a fire years ago, and after that a city ordinance. All new homes had to be made of brick. I built some of those homes."

"Dad," the boy said.

"Okay," his father said. "Now, I'll show you the three-speed motor and let you take the machine for a little spin yourself."

"We really can't," Dale said, "but we appreciate your effort."

The man turned on the dial and let Jean take the handle. A little light cast a path over the carpet. Jean was surprised at how easily the cleaner moved over the rug, and she continued to push it along while the others watched.

"What do you do for a living?" the salesman asked Dale. "If you don't mind me asking."

"I'm a chef," Dale said.

"I thought you might be a salesman," the man said, "having to be on the road and all today. You got kids?"

"No," Dale said.

"It's just Austin and me. His mother left us," the man said.

Jean turned off the vacuum cleaner and returned to the couch.

"Dad," the boy said. "Come on."

"We're doing just fine without her, too. 'I can't take it anymore.' That's what she said, whatever *it* means. Want to know what I told her?"

The boy groaned and began taking the attachments from the machine.

"I told her a girl all wrapped up in herself makes a mighty small package. I was laid up, too. Imagine that."

"Jesus," Dale said.

"You said it," the man said. "I never felt so awful in my whole life. Had to sell the house. The boy and I live in an apartment complex now. I'm getting back on my feet again, a day at a time. You gotta go on, you know."

"You went way over this time," the boy said and tapped his watch.

"And I haven't even demonstrated the special features," the man said. "Okay, let's pack her up, Austin."

"They've got to fill out the form," the boy said.

"It's for my supervisor. You have to answer some questions about my performance, and you have to say I showed you the works."

"I'd be happy to fill it out," Jean said.

"She's going to have to lie, Dad. You didn't show her everything."

"Austin," his father said, "ease up, will you?"

"Do you sell many of these cleaners?" Jean said, as she filled out the form, giving the man the highest recommendation.

"Not yet," he said. He went over to the fireplace. "They did a good job on this one," he said and ran his hands over the bricks.

"Let's go," the boy insisted.

The salesman thanked Jean and Dale for their time and wished them luck in the sweepstakes. Then he handed her a card. "Just in case you change your mind. You two talk it over."

Jean assured him that she would and that she'd call him if she changed her mind.

"People don't talk things over anymore," the man said. The boy opened the door and went out, carrying the boxes. Jean watched the man run to catch up with the boy and saw him struggling to take a box. Then she saw the man hit the boy on the side of the head. She stood back from the window. "Dale," she said, but got no answer.

She found him in the spare bedroom, a room designed for a child, with wallpaper depicting a procession of cowboys, horses, and chuck wagons. With boxes left to unpack and with Dale's suitcase on a mattress, the room looked sad and pleading.

"I felt sorry for him, didn't you?" Jean said.

"Yeah."

"I didn't know what to think when I saw your car still here and his."

"I couldn't just leave, not without talking to you," Dale said.

"Dale, I did the strangest thing today."

"What could be stranger than the two of us listening to a salesman, today of all days?"

"Look what I did," she said and removed the bandage. The flesh around the tattoo was raised, red and protesting. "It's a match."

"Why?"

She was about to speak when she heard the front door open. She went into the living room and found the boy standing near the door.

"He lies," the boy shouted. "She never left us."

"Austin," she said.

He looked down at her arm. "Lies," he said, then ran across the street and got into the car. Dale came and stood near her, both of them watching the car disappear down the road.

"Did you hear him?" she asked. "Maybe the father made his wife leave."

Dale nodded. "The kid probably doesn't know what to believe."

"Yes," she said, covering her arm. She looked away from Dale and glanced at the patch of rug she and the salesman had gone over. It looked no different, and she wondered if the salesman and the boy were going to another home and if other people would hear the story and know what was true.

"I can stay the night," Dale said, "then shove off in the morning, first thing."

"I'm all right," she insisted. "I'm going to fix things, paint the spare room, work on a garden. You don't need to stay," she said, surprised at how eager she was to see him leave.

She stayed in the living room while he went for his suitcase. She knew Dale had been right about her. She had been preparing herself all along for him to leave her. She realized that the picture she had conjured earlier of an imagined life with Dale had not been true, but, rather a way to make herself feel something.

She went into the spare room, saw him looking out the window, his suitcase in his hand. "I feel lost," he said, and she felt a pang, as if she were watching and hearing herself, but from a great distance.

"I'll miss you, you know," he said.

"Please, Dale."

He held her, and then they walked outside to the car. Without looking at her, he muttered, "I loved you."

He backed out of the driveway, and she waved and waved until her arm hurt. As she turned to go inside, she looked at the rose bush and recalled Dale commenting on it that first day and how he had tried to make her see the possibilities.

At some point, she knew she would write and call him, describing the house, the town, the positive things she might discover. It would hurt her, she knew, to hear him say, "I'm glad you're happy."

She would meet new people at work, and she would tell them about her first weeks in town and the day the salesman and his son came, the day her lover left, the day she got a tattoo.

"You see," she could imagine herself saying, "I was afraid of getting lost."

"That's what love is like," someone might tell her.

She went inside the house and called the tattoo parlor. The teenager answered the phone.

"Is the owner in?" Jean asked.

"It's for the boner," the teenager said.

Jean heard the woman laugh, and then the man came on the phone.

"I was in earlier today," Jean said. "Remember? You drew some designs for me?"

"Yeah?"

"My tattoo doesn't look right. I picked the match."

He said nothing.

"Don't you remember?" she said.

"I remember saying it would take awhile to see the difference."

"I was wondering if I could come back."

"I told you you could come back," he said. "Not now, though. We're fixing to close."

"Yes, but could you tell me how long it takes for the pain to go away?"

"Didn't I give you that sheet that explains everything? Read that over. It's supposed to hurt, lady."

She hung up, and she imagined the three people in the tattoo parlor talking about her and the man knowing she should've picked the face. Perhaps they'd be waiting for her to show up the next day. Even though she knew it would be humiliating to return, she thought of going first thing in the morning to have the artist look at the design, perhaps go over it again so that others would know what it was supposed to mean.

Maybe Eve

BY BRIAN MOONEY

It comes that time like it always comes every few years now, when I know the wind up there is blowing colder, that I start wondering what it's like in the Old Town, and so I start scratching for information about those certain people, but it's like a ragged rooster scratching in the snow for feed that's not to be found, and then this ragged rooster comes to the point where there's no way to get that feed save for up and contacting someone and disregarding all our raising up (whether we were brung up, or in my case, drung up) and modestness and asking outright: who's alive? and likewise, who's not? It's around that time when I give the whole thing up. But I can't forget the Old Town, though it's forgotten me. Cousin Helen, the closest to family I ever had save for Florence my wife, once told me that the thinkers say we men marry in our mother's image. Well, mother's image is like the dusty backside of a cheap hand mirror, and mirrors never meant much to me anyway, and on top of all that who knows where Helen is now? Might as well just forget it all. But try as I can, I can't.

* * *

Today I was in the supermarket. I felt then, and I feel now, bad for what I did last night and for how I might have ruined it for them and for how I treated them. But I couldn't help it. All that spitting out of blood and broken teeth from my past, all that for today in the supermarket.

I do all the shopping because Florence can't stay on her feet too long. Polio. She had it when she was young, before I even ever met her. I say to her when she says she can't go shopping, I say, "Florrie. If I'm not huntin', then you're shoppin'. If you get tired then lean against the cart. Do you good to get out of the house for once." But she says she'd rather not go, so what she does is she plays her piano and writes her poetry. She's had her poetry published, vanity press, but it's something. Nothing big, nothing hardcover, but little things, pamphlets really. I think it's all silly, but I don't tell her that because whether it's silly or not, it's something, more than a lot of people got. And she used to teach piano, too.

*   *   *

I don't hunt anymore, of course. Nothing to hunt here.

*   *   *

I say to Florence, "What's the use in having any talent if you never go out? Where's there to be inspired in the house all day?" And she says back to me, "Frank, don't nag me so. I'm happy here. Creak and pop when I move, and my fingers barely bend, but I'm happy. Comfortable anyway. If I don't play piano and all right now it's not like I have all the tomorrows like I did a few years ago. So you go shopping. And don't forget the gefilte fish."

She's got a think about gefilte fish. She counts them, making sure there are as many in the jar as the label says. Sometimes there aren't. So she writes an angry letter to the gefilte fish company demanding an apology and explanation why there aren't as many gefilte fish as they promised. Once the gefilte fish company sent her an apology and an entire case of gefilte fish, twenty-four jars. She counted the contents of each jar, made sure they were all there and then threw it all out. She hates gefilte fish. But that's not important. What is?

What is it that for all her talents, my wife counts fish for a hobby.

*   *   *

Now what would all the porch swing Catholics back in the Old Town say about that? Down the street in Little Ireland I can hear Mrs. Rooney yelling over to Mrs. Mahoney that "that backwards little orphan went and married a...Jew!", and Mrs. Mahoney whispering to Mrs. Power, "Like the chicken said what swallowed the fishbone, 'It sticks in my craw!'" Well, I showed all them. Come that fateful time on March first, which was a Saturday, at five oh five, while that Fahey's Lumberyard whistle blew, out I come and into this world born, and while many people are of the opinion that when that whistle blew it was to let the workers know the work week was over, there are others who believe that whistle was blowing to notify people, especially the relations and *especially* Father Patrick Murphy standing over my mother and shaking his head and wishing I was dead (and that's no exaggeration because I remember once cutting across the rectory lawn on my way to school late one morning and he caught me and he shook me and scolded me and said I was the "right orphan heir to a blackthorn stick" and that my footprints were never meant to have ever bent back a blade of grass and that I was wearing out a more worthy soul's shoes) that the whistle was moaning that the old ways were gone, that the most important person that town would ever produce was being born.

*   *   *

So I'm leaning on the cart and limping through the grocery. I don't have to limp, mind you, but I like to can't help it anymore. I'm making maybe up for Flo, sympathetic, trying to be like her more, trying to understand. See, Flo's got the steel brace and can't go upstairs and clicks and pops when she walks. Forty years ago it wasn't such a problem. When she walks through our house—it's only a one storey, just like all the others here, and it's not really ours, just like all the others aren't anyone else's—each little kerchunk of that brace is so evenly spaced that I can fit whole thoughts between her steps. Kerchunk...evenings listening to the old Irishmen from the mill, and me sneaking jots of cider when they pretended not to look...kerchunk...them singing and telling how "the little divil," me, descended from two of the ancient warring tribes of Gael, and me so anxious to believe it went around after that being every ancient warrior all rolled up in one nervous and scorned boy...kerchunk...joining the service and all it promised and everyone if anything glad to see me going, see me gone...kerchunk...and how of all the faces ever bidding me well, for what that was worth, how of all of them I saw Helen's clearest because it seemed the saddest and that's always seemed to me the way to send a kid off to war. If he's gonna go, send him off sadly, because that's what war is; it's above all else sad that things come to it.

I've changed so much. But none of that matters now. All that matters is that after I got out I did my share of wandering, kept a promise, and set about the business of trees—putting down roots.

Kerchunk...and then we had a daughter...kerchunk... and then we didn't...kerchunkchunkchunk.

And so on, till I have to stand myself up and go for a walk down the street by myself. I walk by all the houses just like ours. They're good houses, everything in them you'd need. Sure, and they can get boring, but Florence and me worked long and hard to come here, and we're committed to staying, so damned if we don't enjoy it. We've got everything we need here. Bright and airy. Not so dark and squalid as the kitchens I was shuffled to and from; the neighbors here go about their own business without dipping their hands in ours, and the plumbing here is horrible, which is good because it keeps me busy. I was a plumber, still am really. I'm definitely the most important man here. I'm like the retired doctor who still sees patients, only I'm more practical. Without me many of these people would be paying good money for bad plumbing from the outside, but with me around they get the best plumbing you can get for only a few dollars spending money after the check comes, or wherever those dollars come from.

I walk down those straight, fresh paved streets and by all

the houses and one day a while back I realized I was limping as if one of my legs was shorter than the other. I stopped and stared at my feet a minute or two, maybe more, who's counting, my feet aren't gefilte fish for crying out loud, and then I kept right on walking. I felt closer to Florrie than I had in a long, long time. I was out on some sidewalk and she was back inside in front of the TV or something. I don't know, but there it was. I don't do it when I'm around her.

*   *   *

So I was shuffling along through the grocery and I'd already picked the vegetables and the coldcuts and some of those canned soups which I know are bad for us because of the salt but I buy them anyway because I can just open one up and pop it in the microwave whenever I'm hungry, which is pretty regular. Our house came with a microwave. You don't beat that with a stick. Hell, I can remember when it was a big deal if a house came with indoor plumbing. And I was in the aisle looking at cheeses to see if any had gone bad—I'm a careful shopper, and I always check expiration dates—when somebody tapped me on the shoulder. I knew right away who it was because it was the kind of pecking with stiff fingers that you feel right down in your bones, and it's so squinting up annoying. I turned around and there they were, and he said:

"Checkin' out the cheeses, are you, Boss?"

Lord grant me serenity because Lord, I hate this man.

I looked at the hunk of Muenster in my palm and then at him and then at the Muenster and then back at him. He had his left arm around his wife, my daughter, who kept looking at me like I'd not wiped my mouth from lunch, and he was fingering his little brown mustache and I stood up a little straighter to take the weight off my left hip and I glanced back at the cheese, then at his wife, my daughter, who looked away and then I looked at her husband's thin little mousey mustache over his crooked little smile. And I thought, "Cheesey."

*   *   *

It all started three days ago when I came home from picking up some rubber cement to fix up the seam around the refrigerator door, and I'm thinking about how I'm going to unclog the trash compactor of all the gefilte fish pieces, and Florence tells me that we're having company in two days for dinner and to be nice, they seem to be good people. No we don't really know them, she says, but we used to. I started to say I'm not living down here to have company, but before I got many words out she started to mist up so I left it at that. Fine, we have some company over. I know where it'll end up if I push it. It'll end up with her saying she's never forgotten like she says I have, and she'll turn away and that'll be that.

Later on, after I'd fixed the seam and the compactor and was plucking bugs off my avocado tree—it came with the house, too—she asked me even if I was curious who it might be coming to dinner that we didn't know now but knew then and I said yes, I was curious, but I didn't care so long as the food was warm and the sink unclogged. She said, "Frank, you really might like to know," but I said no, if it's faces from the past let me see if I can tell them at the door.

So she didn't tell me. She was mum as anyone when I was toddling and asking "Where's my daddy?"

And then I forgot all about it, just like everything else, until the doorbell rang and Flo scooted off to get it, more excited than I thought she had a right to be, but then I found out why. They were standing there shifting their weight and of course I knew who they were but I let them stand there a little while while I took it all in. It was like the time once when I was throwing rocks down at the river and Joey Bawnson ran up to me to ask if I wanted to play catch with him. He had a new mitt all fresh oiled and he wanted to try it out and see how broke in it was. "Smell," he said, and he held it out. I put it full over my face and inhaled and it was the sweetest smell, that mitt to a boy was like lilacs to a girl. It had the musky, sweaty smell of summer sandlots, and where a lot of oil had sunk in was a dark brown almost black, and where only a little bit of oil had sunk in was rich coffee brown. I'll always remember that smell. It was like pipe tobacco and half used bars of shaving soap, and it was like damp workboots airing out on the front porch. I asked Joey who bought the mitt for him and he said his dad, and I asked him who oiled it for him and he said his dad, and then I threw that beautiful mitt right into the river and I asked him who was gonna get it out for him, his dad? It floated on down stream, right under the Great Bridge, past the lumber yard, down and down stream. Joey couldn't believe it. He stood there and watched it drift away. It didn't sink. I really thought it would sink. He never said a word. Just looked at me, waiting to see what I would do.

There I was, holding my hand to them. Her husband took it and shook it hard in the doorway and I thought he'd break it he pumped it so hard, and I looked into his face. He must have been maybe fifty, but it was that young and strong fifty, and my bones ached for fifty. Then I shook her hand. After all the years I took her hand. It was a younger hand, his wife's, my daughter's, Eve's, and it was hesitant, and she looked at me the same way I looked at him. Deep into the eyes, really penetrating blue eyes, not as piercing as Helen's and not as deep as Flo's, but close, and my bones ached again. Every one of them aching away.

* * *

This might be important or maybe not, but I remember once standing in front of Rexall's Drugs right next to Chief Shea and we were watching the trolley go by. I was around eleven years old at the time. There was a man sitting at the very back of the trolley looking out of it and as his eye passed along the street it rested on me and stuck there like having glue on your fingertips: the more you try to wipe it off the more stuck you get. It was a peculiar look on his face. Chief Shea said to me, "Do you know that man, Frank?" Now, most boys my age were intimidated by Chief Shea, but not me, and I said to him, "Nope, I don't, but he just the same looks familiar," and Chief Shea said to me, "Well, that's your uncle. Your mother's brother." I never knew I had an uncle. I told that to the Chief. "Well," he said, because most things he said started with "well," "Walter's always known he had a nephew. I guess that's enough for him." I watched that trolley clear out of sight, and it was all I could do not to run after it. When it was gone I looked up at Chief Shea who was still standing next to me with his big hands in his pockets, rocking a little on his heels like he'd do, and I said, "What's he do?" Then Chief Shea told me he was a plumber. I didn't quite know

what a plumber was at that point, but I pledged it right there
in front of Rexall's Drugs, a promise I've kept, "I swear it to
God I'm going to be a better plumber than that man." And by
God I am. When you figure in all the technological advances
plumbing has made since then, why, I'm miles better than he
ever was in his prime. I was State Plumbing Inspector for
twenty-one years; I've installed sprinkler systems in some of
the state's finest golf courses and every one of the kids I've
taught in vocational education has gone on to a successful
practice, and dammit, that one glimpse of that man who'd
ignored me so well that I never knew he existed, and once he
knew I knew he always crossed to the other side of the street
when he saw me coming, Hell, those few seconds decided my
life. And I don't regret it a bit, because I kept that damn
promise.

I told that story to the kids I taught, and they learned quick
that plumbing isn't something you take lightly. That's where I
met Florence. Florence was a teacher, too, a piano teacher at
the high school. I earned more than her, and I was wild,
drunken wild and free and she wasn't and that's probably what
brought us together because there was enough of attraction for
each to each since she needed to come up and I needed to come
down, so before you knew it I was taking piano lessons and she
was flushing apples down the toilet so we could see each other
and then Bingo! we were going to have a kid and because I
wasn't going to be like my father—God bless his ragged
resting place, wherever it is—we got married. Easy as that.

This was all up in Massachusetts, long before I retired and
we moved down here.

And then, sixteen, seventeen years later I was county
plumbing inspector and Flo was still a piano teacher only now
she also wrote regretful little rhymes under the name of
poetry. Now, people don't say "Oh, you're a plumber, how
interesting!" though they should if they'd think of the importance of plumbing. No, they say "Oh, you're a *piano* teacher!
And a poet! Tell me about it..." But I earned more than her,
more I bet than any honest worker did in the Old Town.
Bankers and lawyers don't count as honest workers because
they don't sweat, and doctors are a different breed of people,

so they don't count either. So I earned more than her. But I was still wild, too wild and maybe too drunk and definitely not so free.

I guess if anyone's to blame it's got to be me that Eve ran off with him and all his promises, and I know that better than anyone. I'd always tried to teach her, to *instill* in her, all about the proud power of a promise, how a promise is solid and permanent and a kept promise is to be respected; it doesn't matter what it is. I taught her to be faithful to her word and I never figured she'd be faithful to anyone else's words but her own and mine, but I figured wrong. I tried to teach her what I believed, but he got her believing they could both be in movies, his smile, her eyes. But they had to do it together, he said, because she'd never be anything without him, and of course to them the East was drying up so they had to go West. She listened to him. For a long time I blamed the whole thing on him that he took advantage of her, then on Eve because she didn't know what was good for her, and then on Florence because she never took a stand except for in front of the window waiting for them to return. But all that blaming is like when I pitched a rock through old Tanner Slaney's bay window and when I got caught said it wasn't my fault, if he'd never put the window there in the first place then the rock could never have gone through it. Never heard from her again, not even ever a card. She went her way and we went ours. Lived through the years, installed sprinklers, played piano, wore winter coats, wiped sweat off foreheads, slept, ate, and then came down here to the flatter, easier land of warm weather and box houses. Now we're nothing but comfortable. The house came with a piano, if you can believe that. I know a deal when I see one. It's a big white grand in the living room, not one of those rickety old uprights. Just the same though, even in a different house in a different state, Florence kept waiting for her return, or her call, or something. I don't know what. Reminded me of my mother when certain trains came into the station and she'd get dressed up and dress me up and we'd wait on the platform to see if he was working that train, if she could even glimpse him, but she never did. There's not much difference between waiting people: they all age. I'm nine years older than Florence, but she's older than me, if you know what I mean.

* * *

The problem was that nobody had anything to say to anyone. They were the last people I expected to see, and even if I had expected them I still wouldn't know what to say. After the usual how are yous and fines we sat down to eat. Florence made a nice roast, so there we were sitting at the table enjoying at least the meal, and I asked how they found us and Eve said she'd phoned the Forshee's, our old neighbors in Massachusetts, and they'd directed us down here. Eve said she'd phoned here and talked to Mother and didn't I know any of this? I said nope, news to me, and then Florence said she was about to tell me but I'd wanted to be surprised and I said I sure was. After that the conversation went stale, and then he started in on how cute and clean and quaint everything was, the reunion, the house, us. I didn't like it and I wasn't thinking highly of George Forshee for giving out our address. I've never liked that word, cute. Clean I don't mind, because it comes with the occupation, but cute no. Everyone used to call Eve cute and then she started acting cute and got to be almost impossible to keep in line with her wisecracks and crying. So I have this built-in thing against cute. Second off, he kept saying how nice the house was, and Eve would nod, and so I told them every house here is almost exactly the same, the first one might as well be the last one and all the others in between, and it seems to me so stupid to praise one house of all of them. Then they said, and Florence too, that *all* the houses are nice, and I shook my head and sighed and that was the end of that, thank you Lord kindly, and then I got back to eating.

* * *

What I've got revolves around food. I go to bed thinking about breakfast, and when I get up I have a good sized one: toast, cereal, egg, juice. Sometimes I'll have a bagel, and sometimes I'll get those sugar coated blue crunchy things for cereal, and I'll have my egg this way or that, and there's always different juices to choose from. Florence nibbles at a piece of toast, every day. I don't see why she even bothers to wake up at all. In the afternoon I have my drink. I've always been a whiskey straight man and don't see the point in ruining good drink with additives, but lately my stomach gets the knife-twisting hollow whiskey burn, so now I throw a couple ice cubes in. I have my drink and I think about my day so far— what I think about most is little blue crunchy things and what I'm doing to my teeth and how I don't really care because I'll probably get new ones soon anyway. Then I have another drink to get me set for what I'm going to do that afternoon. I drive to town, run an errand or two while Flo diddles with the piano and peeks out the front window through the thick white curtains. And for dinner I have a nice quiet meal Flo makes me up, mostly pasta with red sauce because it's easy, and before bed I have another glass of whiskey to stir up the bees in my head, and a bowl of ice cream to freeze them where they fly, and I go to bed to wake up and do it all over again. We next to never have company.

*   *   *

So we ate and then he broke through the chewing and asked what we do now. I expected Florence to answer since she invited them and all, but she just sat there with her eyes sometimes narrow sometimes plates like she was flipping though an old photo album trying to remember where she was for the photos she wasn't in. It was like she wasn't even in the room. She'd wipe her mouth with her napkin at the appropriate times, but she'd miss the food on her chin. So I told them I go for walks, and I fix up the house when it starts falling apart, which it doesn't do nearly enough, and I do some freelance plumbing for the residents, and I read a bit, and I watch the moody sunsets after the thunderstorms. I told them that Flo here played a little piano still, and she'd taken to writing poetry. Eve perked up at that and said, "Poetry? I didn't know you wrote poetry." (See what I mean?) Flo nodded with her napkin against her mouth and said it was nothing, but Eve was interested. Then I asked them what they did and he said he was in real estate, the acting never panned out for either of them. Cheered me right up to hear that. She said she was an English teacher and a drama teacher at the local middle school and that she really loved working with kids and that her pupils made her feel like she was part of a huge, extended family.

Then there was another lull, and dinner turned into a lot of careful chewing and quick glances across the table and then quick glances back to the food when someone noticed the first quick glance across the table. Everything so usually quiet got loud. Chewing, frigerator humming, Flo's leg against the chair. Quiet so heavy in coming down that, with the wine from dinner helping me, I started thinking maybe someone should start talking to cover up the quiet. I asked Steve what he did on his job. "Lots of things," he said. "Buying, selling. You know." Then I asked if they had kids and they said no they gave up trying and I looked at him and he shrugged and said, "Guess when we go that's the end of the line." As if he was family. I told Florence to pass the salt. She stared into nowhere, and I told her again. Nothing. Then Eve asked to see a poem. Nothing again, just staring off.

It takes a lot to snap her out of it when she gets like that. Usually I don't even bother because it's really only her and me at home, and I like the privacy of her going off in space, but when she does it in company then I get frustrated. It's like she's abandoning me.

She had good lively eyes when I met her; fragile blue but behind them was strength like steel. Everything dims eventually, though. There used to be music in her eyes like it was coming right up from the piano through her fingers and then out her eyes, but now it's like the piano's playing a couple blocks away, and it's almost all gone. But that's not so important. What is is that when Flo didn't respond to mine and Eve's requests I grabbed the salt and said I'd go get a poem and read it to Eve.

That got Florence. At first she blinked, then she tried to protest saying they weren't appropriate poems. I had her now. If she'd only held up her laundry line of the conversation then there wouldn't have been any of this, but there it was. I stood up and walked into the piano room to what we call the library even though it's not much more than a single shelf of books and most of the shelf is bookends to keep in the books—as if they'd jump away if they had a chance. But library or not I found what I wanted, and what I wanted was a tiny paperback pamphlet Flo wrote called "Rain." Now I've never put much stock in the poetry business, and Flo knows that, it all strikes me as swimming uphill, but that's mostly because I know what every one of her poems is about, and I don't see writing poetry changing anything one bit.

* * *

Now, if I could write a poem I wouldn't write what Florence writes, those little lines with little rhymes. I would write a good long one about how the headlights that took Eve away splashed all down the street in the rain and the puddles. We lived on a regular neighborhood street then, and I'd write about the neighbors all peeking out their windows, and how I yelled and waved my hands like an idiot and how I stopped and let her float away, down and down stream. Once she gets past that bridge, who knows or cares anymore if she sinks, swims, or just gets waterlogged? I'd write why I stopped, which was because I gave up. And I'd write that poem and it would cover up all the bruises everywhere, because I hit Eve enough. Didn't mean to, but I'd raised her up like I was, and I couldn't help it sometimes. But I guess I went and did it once or twice too often. I didn't think things worked that way. That I could do that, chase her off. When I was a boy I swear to God I always rathered getting hit than ignored.

And I'd only write one poem, not so many as Florence. And if I did write another it would be about the war, but I don't bother with either one. There's no sense dwelling on what's not there, on what's gone and gone and not coming back. That's, I think, what's important. If I ever told Flo that, though, why, she'd have nothing left through that window to be looking for.

* * *

For me to suddenly want to read must have scared Flo. I don't know, maybe it wasn't such a great idea for me to read it, but at the time I had my reasons, and I hold hard to my reasons. If Florence had stayed in the conversation, well ...there you go. But that's not what happened. What happened was that I sat down and read a little four line, all the same rhyme, little thing about how Eve left in the rain that one night and how his car never came back. I think the rhymes went rain, pain, again, blame. She's a lot better at the piano.

Eve nodded throughout and bit her lower lip. "I like that," she said. I guess then I must have made a sound like a snort—I didn't mean to—and she flipped her hair just like I remember her doing and said, "I do like it." I guess I made that sound again because Flo hid her face in her napkin—she can be so Goddamned too dramatic—and he looked at his empty plate. Then there was another space, dead air, where everyone thought of what to say but didn't say it, and so I said it and stood up—I had to grab the edge of the table cloth to do that, and I spilled some of their coffee, which seemed to me no big deal, but of course there were differing opinions on that—and I said, "I guess it's cute, too," and then I went into the other room to put back the book.

I was standing in that other room, standing right next to the piano with the book in my right hand and my left rubbing those white keys. I don't know how to play. She tried to teach me, but I couldn't get it. Plumber's hands. Eve got it, though, and Flo taught her to play really well, chandalier music. But she ran away before she could have been really good. I'd have liked to hear her play now, see if she still knew how, make sure she hadn't forgotten.

I'd wanted to destroy that old piano we used to have. After Eve left all Flo did was stare at it and rub the damn keys and say we should go find her. It's not important now, though.

I heard them all shuffling about in the kitchen, and I started thinking how it's really something that she should end up an English teacher. My mother used to say my father was a poet. Other people said he was just a hustler and a smoothie, but either way it's words in their Sunday best. If I'd known what he was before I knew Walter was a plumber then you can bet I'd have changed my promise pretty quick. My mother always wanted to teach, but with me around she never got to, and who'd let the likes of her anyway? She wrote stories, though.

That I know. She never showed them to me, but I know she did.

* * *

There's a story I've always wanted to write, but I doubt I ever will. It's about a young man, all lonely and alone, who stares out his bedroom window day after lonely day across the street at a young girl who plays the piano day after day in her own room next to her own window. Late at night all along the street it's only their windows all lit up, nothing else, and she looks over at him sometimes and he dives out of the way because he doesn't want to get caught staring, and he wants so bad to meet her. Then, one day, on the street, paint it sunset, he does. Eve, he does, but it turns that she only pretends to play; her fingers dance just above the keys, and she hums imaginary little tunes. She can't play a damn. But he loves her anyway, even though it isn't what he thought, and she loves him because he watches without hearing. There. That's my damn story. And there I was in the piano room. I don't know how long I was there for. It didn't seem like very long.

* * *

I put the book back and went out to the kitchen. They'd left. I didn't miss them gone, but I didn't mean to miss them going. Florence was sitting stiff staring at the wall. But it wasn't like she was seeing anything. I got scared, I tell you that. I've seen the bodies, it was years ago, but you never forget eyes like that, and I got scared. She wasn't looking at any photos of the past this time, and there's nothing left to see in the future, and the present I can't decide if there is one, so it was like she wasn't seeing anything at all. So I held her hand. Sure, and it was cold. But she smiled. I felt silly. She turned to me slow and said, "Help me. Help me up and let's go for a walk." She flicked a smile and my muscles were aching away. It was a good ache, and that's important. For all I do, she's always there. Damned if I can ever understand it.

* * *

So I was standing with a hunk of Muenster in my hand and I just thought "cheesey." And I didn't mean to say next what I said next; it just happened, like they expected me to say it, them standing there looking at me, taller than me and knowing it, and I said, "What do you want?"

Eve said, "We thought we'd say goodbye." He patted me on the shoulder and said, "Bye old man. Thanks for last night." Then Eve kissed me on the cheek and started to say something but didn't. Then they turned and left. They never even looked back.

At first I felt like throwing that cheese at him. Then, when they didn't turn around, I started to think I was the only person in the store. I thought of running, limping after them to tell them to stay and hear my story, but I didn't. Better to let it go. Like everything else.

*   *   *

When we walked last night I stood straight up and walked with my wife down the street, and all the street light reflections from the brief afternoon rain flashed and lit us beneath and behind, and each kerchunk was like a single note in the dark, and I think ... no. I don't. I don't know. It's not important anymore, whether I know or not. Doesn't change anything down here at all. "Kerchunk." Helen. "Kerchunk," Flo. "Kerchunk." Eve. "Kerchunk." Eve. "Kerchunk." Eve. "Kerchunk."

Gathering

BY PERSIS KNOBBE

I have resisted learning how to make strudel since I was ten.
Now that my mother is in her eighties, I am still putting her
off, not always nicely. She and I are in her kitchen where she is
sprinkling flour on a wide pull-out wooden board especially
designed for baking. The decor of the kitchen is fifties kitsch:
pale green formica, linoleum spattered with coral confetti,
switchplates with asterisk stars, dark cabinets distressed
according to instructions from an antiquing kit.

She stretches the dough high and thin like a mime moving
air. "You think I learned in a snap? Give yourself a chance."
She won't be here forever, she reminds me. Someone has to
learn strudel-making, someone has to take over. It's another
version of my father's Last Guided Tour of the Garden. He
points to the guava bushes and the pomegranates. "They don't
need much water," he says. "Once a week is okay." Then he
gets a twelve-foot-long pole with a net at the end and scoops
red needles of bottle brush from the swimming pool. He
empties the net under a lilac bush and hands over the pole as if
it were his legacy: father to daughter, swimmer to swimmer.
"Keeps you busy." he says, "but you can't let it go."

"Okay, Pop." I never argue on last tours. I don't argue with
my mother. I chop nuts, crumble bread, sprinkle cinnamon,
spread guava jam. She tells me to add a handful of flour. As

well as I know her hand, I don't know how much flour it holds. I watch her when she kneads the dough. "Not too much," she says. How does she know when it's too much?

After she places the strudel in the oven, Mother says, "Whew. I'm stuffed." She wipes her face with a dishtowel that has a burn in one corner, an embroidered teapot in another. She's stuffed? Does she mean she's tired or too warm? It's not the first time she confuses the source of her discomfort but it makes me uneasy.

Her face is blotchy with exhaustion. "My face is a map of the world," she says when she looks in a mirror. Maybe she means it's a map of her life. Her complexion is smooth but not peaches and cream. Ruddier, berries and honey. Her eyes dilate when she studies a problem.

"Would you take this thing off the mixer?" she asks. I am the only one who knows the trouble she has with the new mixer. You shouldn't get people new things after a certain point in their lives. The new mixer, a gift from my cousin Joan, is like the old one except for the way the whip is engaged. There is some small thing you must do, a twist, a pressure. Mother bends her head to study the opening. She likes to puzzle things out, she says.

I bring the whip and bowl to the sink where my father has come in to do the clean-up. He takes one look at the encrusted pan and says Oy, then reaches for the steel wool. He is the one who gives her the biggest order for strudel. He presents it as an honorarium to the nurse in Dr. Haber's office, to the produce man at Petrini's, to anyone who has been kind. He watches with a proprietary expression when they take their first bite. People bite into her strudel slowly, the way they bite into dark chocolate.

"I finally wrote down the recipe," she says, bringing me her recipe book, originally a ledger. "Dunk pages in oil and brown sugar" could have been its first instruction. She turns the curled pages. Some of them have magazine recipes pasted on them along with her pencilled-in comments: "needs more filling" or "let it sit."

"All these years people ask me how to make strudel and now I can give them a recipe." She studies what she has written. "Of course it doesn't go into detail, not every little thing. But it gives the general idea." She looks steadily at me. My mother wants to pass on the art, touch finger to finger. And she wants me to take over now. "Play with the dough," she says when she instructs me. Once in a while I try. I don't have to sign a contract, I tell myself. I lift the dough in the air. Wherever my fingertips touch I leave holes. She patches them. "Sometimes it works and sometimes you make it work," she says.

I was not cut out to make strudel, I tell her. I was not born to make dough thin as paper. And there is something else I was not cut out to do.

"What would you do with him?" Mother asks me. We're putting grocery bags in the car after a shopping trip that included three markets because each one had a special. Usually my father does the driving for these triple ventures since I refuse to go to more than one grocery store in a day. When my father gets into his blue Buick, he's back in business, a man with a plan. He carries a pocketful of coupons, some of them out of date. Once my mother looked them over in transit and groaned, "Good God, Morris, the one for margarine expired three months ago."

"Just give it a try," he urged. "What have you got to lose?"

"Only your self-respect," she said.

I put the bag of canteloupes in the back seat. When the produce man saw my mother today, he went to the storage room and came out with a marked-down bag of canteloupes. She gives him strudel, he gives her bargains. "Why are you getting rid of these?" she asked. "Too ripe," he said. "Are you kidding? Smell," she said, putting the soft spot of the canteloupe to her nose, then to his. "Smells like a canteloupe," he said. "That's when it's time to eat it," she answers.

I sit beside her and put the key in the ignition. She stops me from turning the key. She wants to talk. "What about the ice cream?" I ask.

"It's okay," she says, "it's hard as a rock." She looks out the side window at the lines of cars in the parking lot. "They sure cram in a lot of cars and not an ounce of shade."

What would I do with him? Is she giving him to me? What did my father do now? At first I don't know what she means.

Is she asking me what I would do with him if she weren't around, if she were dead?

"It's something to think about," she says. "I can't live forever. Who wants to? Not when your head is full of pain. Enough is enough."

That's what she said Friday night after reciting the blessing over the candles. Friday nights my cousins and I stand with her, facing the candles. After she lights them she pours a little water at the base and says, "Dear God, give us a good week." Last Friday she changed it to "Dear God, get me out of here. Enough is enough."

She presses her palm to the top of her head where the arthritis lodges. She wears a tan beret almost all the time, even in the house. "It helps the pain," she says. I have an image of the beret absorbing the pain, countering it, pressing it back.

What would I do with him? I had no idea because that wasn't the way it was going to be. He had angina; he would die first. Then she would come to live with us. She didn't need the house and the pool. He did. His way of life depended on the swims, taking care of the garden. He would want us to move in with him.

"I hope we live as long as our marbles hold out," she says. "Then I hope we go fast."

"That's what everyone wants." My voice sounds strange and slow. I don't try to make her laugh, put her off. We watch as a tall blond teenager creates chains of grocery carts, then joins the chains together in a long line he slowly pushes to the store.

"I can't live with the pain," she says as I help her with her seatbelt. "They don't consider people's busts when they strap you in, do they." She pulls her beret to one side. "It's just not worth it to me. The only reason I'm sticking around is for him. To keep him going."

I take a deep breath and get a whiff of the canteloupes from the back seat.

"The minute I'm out of sight he picks up a big shovel and starts turning the earth." She gives the absent Morris a scowl. "What's he farming for? An angina crop? Is he digging my grave?" She presses me. "What will happen to him when I'm not around?"

I look at her, her hands to start with. They are a mess of cuts and bruises. Her fingers still wield the knife that slits the veal for stuffing and occasionally misses. Her worker hands contrast with the watch she wears, an oval shape with two tiny diamonds and a silver mesh watchband. My father bought it in the days before inflation shrank their income.

Damn, I want to say. It's not cancer, not your heart. It's only hardening of the arteries. And the pain of arthritis. Sounds like a commercial for aspirin, not a threat to life. I should think you could stick around with stuff like that. You call yourself a fighter. How about it? Don't give up on me now. Don't leave me with him. Don't leave me. I take her hand. My fingers recognize the recent cuts on hers. Silence. We have never looked more directly at one another.

Finally I say, "You don't have to worry about Pop." She looks away from me with a slow exhale and withdraws her hand. The spell is broken. We negotiated something but I drew back from perpetuity, from binding her finger to my own, God to man, mother to daughter. I look down at my hands on the steering wheel. They are not worker hands like hers but not gorgeous either, not manicured. Nail polish makes me conscious of my hands, as if they belong to someone else.

She does not object when I start the car. On the way home I feel remorse. What do I mean, she doesn't have to worry? Will I take my father unto my lawfully responsible life? Will I give him what he needs to live without her? Will I love him as I love her? I will not be my mother. I will not cut his meat. I will not go on with Friday night dinners. So why did I tell her not to worry about Pop? What are my intentions? Honorable. I will take care of him. Is that what I was saying? I'll take care of him so it's okay to die.

"What will you do with him?" she asks as we pull into her driveway. "Would you move in with him?"

"I don't know." I keep my voice flat. I am stalling. "We'll be together," I say. That's as far as I can go.

I see Joan's car on the driveway when we pull up, the back window almost blinding us with reflected sun. Joan visits often with her little girl. They meet us at the front door. Do other seven-year-olds dress like Sophie? She is wearing several pairs of pants. The layer closest to her body looks like long thermal underwear. Then comes a pair of shiny pink shorts. And ruffling above them is a striped jersey top that matches her ankle bands, both worn on the same ankle. Sophie helps Joan and me put away the groceries while Mother takes a short nap from which Sophie awakens her.

"Auntie makes circles when she wakes up," Sophie demonstrates with her hands. "Circles on her forehead, then her eyes, then her cheeks."

"She's trying to wake herself," Joan says. "Or did you wake her? Hm?" The fist Joan shakes at her daughter has not one ounce of anger in it. "It's hard to wake up when you're older."

"Wake up? You just open your eyes."

Mother takes Sophie for a walk to the weedy lot where they always manage to find a family of quail. Joan and I, holding our mugs of coffee, watch them leave. My mother leads the way, taking big steps. I tell Joan about our talk in the car and my voice lowers in tone and rhythm. It was the same when my friend was dying last year. We spoke slowly and carefully. We couldn't tell any lies. Joan listens well, with small smiles of understanding, fast shakes of her head. Joan's hair is so close-cropped there is never any movement of curls.

Sophie comes back first and goes right to Joan. Mother returns a moment later, her beret filled with acorns that she sets out on the railing of the deck. We follow her there with a second cup of coffee and face our chairs to the sun and the view. The houses between us and Mount Tamalpais are masked by trees: the apricot and pear trees in our own yard and the taller trees in the distance, birches, poplars, even palms. The deck furniture should be replaced but Mother keeps patching. She sews striped towels together to cover the torn chaise mattresses.

Sophie has a dish of ice ream while my mother plays with a red and yellow beachball. "Good exercise," Mother says. Joan smiles at me. Does she remember the workouts she had with my mother? Joan used to come over to spend the night with me and the two of them would do floor exercises in their pajamas. Bend the knee and kick. They wanted me to join them when I put on a few pounds; that was the whole idea, I suspected, to entice me into exercise. But I refused. I thought Joan was obsessed with her flat stomach, never flat enough. Once she asked Mother to sit on her stomach. When my mother lowered herself as if to do so, Joan screamed.

Now Mother bounces the ball high, catching it after each bounce. "Look, even with arthritis. Did you know I played basketball? I was the best short fat player on the team." She is remembering and at the same time she is a child playing with a ball. There is something challenging about the way she looks at Sophie, the way seven-year-olds might look at one another.

"Can you do this?" she asks Sophie. Mother tries to lift her leg over the ball but doesn't make it. "Almost," she says.

Sophie leans against Joan, looking away from Mother. She is less embarrassed than uncertain, afraid.

That night all hell breaks loose. That's what my father says over the phone at two in the morning, his voice sleepy but urgent: "Come over, hell broke loose."

He lets me in and makes a gesture of his finger to his head. He lets out a loud wavering sigh that could be mistaken for a yawn. Mother is in the middle of the living room, her hands punching the air. One last punch when she sees me come towards her. She pulls her hands back, fury giving way to surprise. She sits down on the sofa, exhausted, shows a place for me to sit. I rub her knee with one hand, the wool tweed of the sofa with the other.

"I finally got rid of them," she says. "*He* didn't lift a finger." Her thumb jerks towards my father. "The living room was full of them, men with beards, men with overcoats. You'd think it was freezing out there."

"Men with beards?" I ask. My father's wave tells me there were no men, that it is all nonsense.

"God knows where they came from," Mother says. "They looked like friends of Papa, milling around the room. I couldn't get rid of them. At least he could have called the police." She shakes her fist at my father who is already walking down the hall towards the bedroom, parting his hands in a way that expresses disgust and despair.

"Frightening," I say to Mother, acknowledging my own fear.

Is this how it's going to be for her? For us? Will she be like my friend's mother who wanders the streets in her bathrobe, unable to find her way home?

"Go to work," my father tells me the next day. He assures me that everything is under control. "I'll keep you posted."

"Shouldn't we call Dr. Haber?" I ask.

"It's nothing like last night," my father says. "She's putting in a wash." He's on top of the situation. These past months Mother says he's driving her crazy, watching what she eats and drinks, keeping track of her pills. He sets them out on her dinner plate and she looks at him. She resents "the new boss."

I look at the papers on my office desk. They haven't moved all morning. I don't know why I came to work. My father calls. Everything is normal, he says. He wants us to keep our date for a family party at Joan's house. I hesitate. I call Joan and warn her: it's hard to know how Mother will act. Will Sophie be there? Perhaps I dread seeing her. With a secret smile, she lets me know how much she knows.

Mother does fine. It is a small gathering. Sophie greets us wearing a pink hat painted with black watermelon seeds, the brim green, color of the rind. I relax when I see Sophie take Mother's hand and play with her rings. Mother tells a story at dinner: how her own mother spoke perfect English on her death bed after a lifetime of speaking only Yiddish to her children. "Mama was a realist. She didn't say, 'Love each other'; she just said, 'Talk to each other.'"

After dessert, Mother begins another story, this one about the events of Monday night, working herself slowly into the hallucination. "Do strange men ever come into your living room?" she asks Joan. Before she goes further, we have her out in the car and on the way home.

"Why so fast?" my husband asks. Am I thinking that this is a social occasion and don't want her to embarrass herself? Or is it me? I want to draw the curtain. She isn't wandering the streets in her bathrobe but I don't want anyone to see her like this.

Mother leans forward from the back seat and taps me on the

shoulder. With a smile not unlike Sophie's, she says, "I know. I know why we had to leave. I shouldn't have said anything about the men in the living room, should I?"

"All part of the pattern," Dr. Haber says the following morning when I describe my mother's behavior. "Paranoid hallucinations. They think the nurses are having parties, dancing in the hall. Or someone is stealing from them, invading their lives."

I ask if painkillers could trigger such hallucinations. He says it's hard to say. "Sometimes these things are drug-induced; sometimes they just happen—" He looks at me, sizing me up, before he adds, "when the patient is near death."

I was going to ask if it's possible to discontinue all medication for a time but now I am trying to inhale normally. Exhaling is easy. Exhale, exhale. Dr. Haber sized me up wrong. Mother talking about dying has one dimension. The doctor is giving it three. Is she near death? Yesterday she was bouncing a ball on the deck. She walked up a hill and found a family of quail. There is still last week's batch of strudel in the freezer.

My father asks me to spend the following night at the house. I am awakened at one in the morning by the clang of dishes on the kitchen counter. Mother is making herself breakfast.

"Her sense of timing is completely askew," I tell the neurologist Dr. Haber sends us to see. He is a psychiatrist/neurologist. "Two for the price of one," my father says, "without a coupon."

Mother stands on a pedestal in his examination room answering his questions. Now raise your right hand, move your left foot. She is right about half the time, dilating her eyes, giving me looks that say, "Can you believe these questions?"

Later I sit in the neurologist's private office, surrounded by his wife's weavings. "My mother is ambidextrous," I tell him. "She has never been clear about left and right."

He closes his eyes in compassion, then smooths his neck with the back of his hand, barely touching his beard. "It's you that concerns me," he says, suddenly looking into my eyes. "You look exhausted." Is that how he wins the daughters? Lets them be the martyrs?

He dismisses my questions, especially the one about putting all medications on hold. Instead, he prescribes some heavy sedatives in an effort, he says, to turn night back into night, day into day. "Best thing is to put her in the hospital. They'll see that she takes her pills. She won't get up and fall in the middle of the night and break her hip." I keep my face free of emotion, seeing my mother in a hospital bed with the bars up. "That can happen if you keep her at home. You're not to feel guilty if she falls."

Doctor and priest. I am absolved in advance.

For the time being (that's how we are living), my husband and I take turns staying the nights with Mother. Occasionally Joan takes a night and tells us not to thank her. We watch my father too, even if Dr. Haber says not to worry about him. It's not his angina, just nerves. He reads his newspaper, walks the perimeter of the house, comes back in and reads some more. At least he sleeps through the night. Not Mother. At three in the morning, partially dressed and with a purse under her arm, she comes into the den where I am supposed to be sleeping. She wants to go grocery shopping for Friday night dinner. She pushes on the sofabed to wake me. I can't open my eyes all the way. She is saying that my teacher will be mad at me if I am late for school. "She's mean. You should change schools like I did."

When Mother was ten, she had a teacher who punished her for being absent on a Jewish holiday. Unfair, she said. She would transfer herself to another school, to Starr King. Who would know the difference? Her parents spoke no English. Mother told the principal of Starr King that her family had just moved to the area. And that she was in the fourth grade. She put herself back a year because her teacher had told her she was stupid. Three weeks later she was moved to the fifth grade where she committed to life-long-memory pages of David Copperfield, Hiawatha and Macbeth. "If it were done when 'tis done, then 'twere well It were done quickly." Her recitations were delivered, as in childhood, hand over heart.

My mother puts her hand on my forehead and says, deep concern in her eyes, "You're very tired, aren't you." Her tone is that of visitor to the sickroom.

"Yes," I answer, tired enough to laugh.

She sits on the edge of the sofabed and begins a pantomime of stitching that will continue, on and off, for three days. For hours she pulls invisible threads with an invisible needle. Or she picks up invisible bits of lint from the rug and brings them towards her mouth. I've heard it called gathering or collecting. It's something that people do when they are close to death, a movement of hands towards the upper body. It's sad and graceful and constant. Dr. Haber said he has seen people tear at their bandages in an effort to complete that gesture. He thinks they're collecting bits of their lives.

Each of us sees the gesture differently. I see it as picking up bits of lint. My husband sees it as bringing food to her mouth. He says one night she kept up the pantomime of eating for hours. Tasting, chewing and then pausing before she would chew again. Was she baking? Thinking perhaps she should add a little cinnamon?

"Picking up bits of broken glass," Joan said. Broken glass? How could Joan say that? My mother is picking up pieces of her life, good things, food, thread, sand or water sifting through her fingers. Now Joan sees broken glass? Does she see my mother bringing it to her mouth, cutting herself? No. Mother never let me pick up broken glass with my bare fingers.

And there was so much of it. My mother would drop things and never mourn. She celebrated. Mazeltov, good luck, she would say when she broke something. As if she had made a toast, drained her glass and tossed it into the fire.

One night she never closes her eyes. All night she collects, bakes or shops. "My teeth" is the only coherent thing she says. "The day they pulled my teeth."

I have heard about that day. Her doubts about the dentist. Did he know what he was doing? Weren't there any teeth worth saving? It was her own fault, she said. Too much peanut brittle. She would sit on the couch, read a book and munch on peanut brittle, her idea of a peaceful evening, like my father listening to Beethoven.

"I was forty-two years old," this story went, "and I became an old lady. I worried would I make the clicking sound my mother made when she ate? No more peanut brittle, okay, but what about cashew nuts? Licorice? Steak? It was like my first period, nobody to warn me, nobody with me. That was the worst: I was alone. Why didn't Morris take time off? Why didn't my sister come with me? She could have left Joan with a neighbor. Why didn't I ask my own neighbor? I came out of the dentist's office an old lady, my chin sucked in, and alone." She is amazed in each retelling, raw and angry. "You know how I got home? I took the streetcar up Geary Street, chinless, still tasting blood. And who got on the same streetcar? Your violin teacher. I don't think he knew me. That was the sorriest I ever felt for myself."

I was no help to her. I have no memory of that day but I do remember when she came home with her new teeth, white and perfect and larger, it seemed to me, than before. Even though she had pleaded with the dentist for teeth that looked natural, not all white. I was stunned with a sense of loss when I saw her. When she smiled at me with her big teeth, I thought, You are not my mother. I tried to look away from her mouth when I talked to her.

Again I think, You are not my mother, when she is having her paranoid delusions, imagining that Joan is in her kitchen burning the pots, making them black. ("Joan? You think Joan would burn your pots?") Or that there are two women sitting in my Toyota, parked on the driveway. ("What do they want? Why don't they come in?" Mother asks.) She is so believable that I check to see if the pots are burned or if the two women are waiting in the car.

Now she is convinced that today is Friday and we must get the table ready for dinner.

"Mother, it is not Friday. It may seem like Friday but it's really Wednesday."

"They're going to be here in a few hours and the table isn't even set. I don't even have a challah. See if there's one in the freezer. Can't you give me a hand? Can't you see how much I have to do?"

I try to take her hands; I want to pull her to three o'clock Wednesday afternoon. I want to hold her hands with all the cuts and bruises like blinders over my eyes. When I open them I will see my real mother. Three o'clock, time for her pills. Joan says she has no problem with the pills. "It's easy," she says. "Here they are, Auntie, open your mouth."

It works. Open your mouth. And she does. But I catch it, the look of Caesar to Brutus. A quick look, but a jab. She has a little smile, as if she always expected me to betray her. I will not betray her. I will set the table for Friday night dinner. She watches me from the doorway. I am a child having to do it right while someone is watching. My heart beats the way it does after a near-accident. I drop a knife on the floor.

"That means a man is coming," she says.

Mother never liked it when her sister said things like that. Superstitions, not for Mother. The woman watching me from the doorway is not my mother.

The last time I bring her the pills she refuses to take them. "I want to go home," she says. Her eyes have a green wire of energy behind them. I ponder the source of that energy as I study the pills in my open hand. Then I close my fingers, wishing I could toss the pills, tell her that she's home, I am her home, my father is her home. But we're not, not if home is a place where you feel free. I don't want her to go to that place, not yet, but so what. She says you have to do what you have to do.

We are in her bathroom, steamy after her bath.

"Mother, the doctor says it's important. If you don't take your pills I'll have to call him. He'll put you in the hospital."

"Let him try."

We are standing next to the bathroom sink. "Just open your mouth," I say. Who do I think I'm talking to, my son, my daughter? My hand is under her chin. She pushes my hand down on the sink. It is the only time in our adult lives we have a physical struggle.

"Go to hell," she says, her last words to me. How could that be, my best friend, how could that be? I thought she would leave me with a benediction, and she leaves me with that? But soon I rejoice in her last words, I dwell in them. I tell my husband, I tell Joan: How many people do you know who go out with a bang?

Independence Day

BY NOELLE SICKELS

Claudia Steele lifted up her three-year-old brother so he could reach the top of the vine. When she set him down he ran off holding high a heavy bunch of dusty, dark blue grapes and calling out to the three other little kids gamboling under the sprinkler.

Claudia stayed near the arbor because it gave her a vantage from which to observe the whole scene of her family and the Coreys at their annual Fourth of July picnic, though the sweet smell of the ripe fruit was slightly sickening. She could never bring herself to eat grapes right off the vine. Their flesh warmed by the sun, they seemed too much like living tissue.

The coppery-green iridescence of a fat Japanese beetle eating a grape leaf caught her eye. She gently plucked the insect off the leaf and deposited it on her wrist. While she looked around at everyone, she could feel the beetle's prickly legs walking slowly up her bare arm. She wondered if it would fly off before it reached her shoulder. She tried to keep very still so it would not.

Counting herself, there were eight children scattered around the yard, four from each family. Claudia, twelve, was the oldest. The four adults were loosely grouped in the dappled shade of an apple tree. Louise Corey tended chicken and steaks smoking on a grill. Jim Corey, the Steeles' family doctor, was seated at the picnic table. Stephen Steele rummaged in an ice chest, and Mary Ann Steele, Macy to almost everyone, stood between the men. Claudia could tell by the tilt of her mother's head and the way Jim leaned forward on his elbows that Macy was listening to him.

Claudia like watching grown-ups. There was something closed about them that drew her. She was shy and had only one close friend, Christine, who was away for the summer. Except for her, Claudia was comfortable only with younger children, whom she could boss or pamper, and adults.

Claudia spent a fair amount of time around adults. They rarely shooed her away as they often did the other children. Claudia could be relied upon to be quiet while the grown-ups talked, to fade to the edges of a scene when their laughter grew loud and clannish or when their words became tightly clipped or their voices began to purr at one another. Sometimes she made clever remarks that amused them, and she was never rowdy or squirmy like the younger children, never whiny or insistent. She was a grown-up's kind of child, self-possessed, alert, independent, rather like a cat, only with a greater interest in what her masters were about than cats usually have.

"Claudia," Louise was calling to her. "Get those kids dried off, would you? Food'll be ready soon."

As usual, Claudia moved to obey instantly, even though it meant losing the beetle. Her obedience was not mere cooperation or good-naturedness. She operated like a sure-footed Indian hunting in the forest, advancing with sharpened senses through the tall trees and tangled underbrush as if she were an organic part of it, and her rewards were a hunter's rewards, sustenance and survival.

On the porch Claudia passed her sister Valerie and Dan Corey. They had finished their assignment of shucking corn and were busy counting sparklers and planning how few they could get away with giving the little kids before they'd protest and the grown-ups would interfere.

Claudia took the corn into the house. She put it in the large pot of water her mother had left on the stove and turned on the heat under it. She scooped a thumbful of chocolate icing off the cake and smoothed the spot over with a wet spoon. Macy made great chocolate icing, velvety thick and not too sweet.

"The chocolate must be allowed to be itself and not be overpowered by sugar," Macy had said to Claudia that morning as the girl slowly stirred two melting squares of baker's chocolate in a double boiler. Then Macy reached across her daughter's arm to add two drops of almond extract to the pot.

"My secret ingredient," she said. "Even chocolate can use a little boost, like a drop of expensive perfume on the backs of the knees of a beautiful woman."

Claudia ran her tongue under her thumbnail to retrieve a last smudge of icing. She guessed her mother was probably wearing her Chanel #5 behind her knees today. She looked so beautiful in her white sundress. It showed off her tan. Claudia was embarrassed to note that the dress also showed Macy's unshaven underarms. Claudia had once heard her father say that was European and sexy.

Claudia didn't like it when her father said such things. She preferred him on the periphery of the family. Since he was away all day and worked some evenings and Saturdays, that was his usual position. It wasn't that Claudia disliked her father. She actually gave him little thought one way or another. Claudia believed she owned her mother in a way no one else did or could.

"Oh, Claude, there you are," came her mother's voice behind her as she stood daydreaming by the linen closet. "Where are the band-aids, do you remember? Jim's cut his hand on that new knife. I told your father he had made it too sharp."

Claudia noticed a streak of blood on the bodice of the white dress. Had Macy lifted the injured hand to blow on it as she did when one of the children scraped a knee or elbow? Or had Jim reached out too far to show it to her? Claudia winced as if the wound were Macy's. She supposed the white dress would have to be thrown away now. She knew blood stained.

"I saw a box of gauze under the bathroom sink yesterday," Claudia answered.

Macy entered the bathroom and Claudia opened the closet and pulled out two beach towels. She looked in the bathroom door as she walked by and saw her mother, the box of gauze in her hand, scrutinizing her face in the small medicine chest mirror. She was turning it slowly from side to side, as if searching for a flaw. Claudia was reminded of how Macy would walk round and round a vase while arranging flowers, carefully placing one stalk at a time until she achieved the desired effect.

Outside, Claudia turned off the sprinkler and quickly rubbed down the shivery children. She helped them pull off their wet bathing suits and pull on shorts and T-shirts. They jostled against her as she squatted in their midst and laid their plump hands on her arms and thighs. Their bodies smelled like puppies when they were close like that; they panted like puppies, too, and grapes scented their breath.

An old quilt was spread out for the children on the grass next to the rock garden. Claudia fixed plates for the four little ones and herself and sat down between Dan and Valerie.

"I hope there's lots of fireworks tonight," Valerie said.

"Every year the show seems shorter to me," said Claudia.

"I went down to the river Monday and got some cattails to burn to keep away the mosquitoes," said Dan.

"Oh, that never works," said Valerie.

"There's hair on my corn," wailed four-year-old Melissa.

"It's cornsilk," corrected Dan. "Just eat it."

"It's yucky," declared Melissa.

"Hey, don't spit," Valerie objected.

Melissa heaved the half-eaten corn under a nearby lilac bush.

"I want corn," demanded Melissa.

"You can't," piped in five-year-old Joey.

"Mom" called Melissa toward the table, "Joey says I can't have corn."

"She threw hers away," yelled Joey in the same direction.

"It was too hairy," Melissa explained to him in an almost reasonable tone.

"Your butt's too hairy," giggled Dan. All the little ones except Melissa laughed obligingly. Certain words were guaranteed hits with them.

"Mom, Dan said 'butt,'" yelled Melissa.

"Dan," called his father, "come get Melissa an ear of corn."

Claudia glanced over at the table. Jim had not even turned his head away from his companions when he called out to his son. Jim had intervened in the dispute without ascertaining facts or gauging personalities. His goal, Claudia knew, had not been fairness but merely the removal of an irritation to himself, like picking out a splinter.

The Corey baby woke up and began to cry. Claudia carried him from the playpen to the table. She sat down between the two women and jiggled the baby on her lap. He began reaching out to the littered table. Claudia pushed away a wine glass and a knife and a bowl of peanuts. She left two spoons and a roll within his grasp.

"Hello, baby," crooned Louise, tickling his cheek.

They all called him "baby," as if he had no name, as if he belonged to all of them. Claudia was old enough to recall that each infant was known simply as "baby" until he or she began to talk or was supplanted by a new baby.

"*Desire Under the Elms* is going to be on TV Wednesday night. Why don't you come over and watch it with us?" Macy was saying to the Coreys.

"That's my late night at the hospital," said Jim.

"I thought you were there Thursdays," said Macy.

"Schedule changed a couple of weeks ago."

"That's an O'Neill play, isn't it?" asked Stephen.

"I'll come over if I can get a sitter," said Louise.

"Claudia will sleep at your place and mind the kids. Is that okay, Claudia?" Macy said.

"Sure, I guess so."

"Baby's a little rank, isn't he?" Stephen said.

"Baby, you've just been insulted," laughed Louise. She stood up and took him from Claudia. "I'll take him in and change him" she said, hefting him onto her left hip. "Shall I bring out the cake?"

"Yes, better do," answered Macy with a glance at the sky. At twilight they were to walk to the park for the fireworks display.

"Stephen," she said, "why don't you go in and make some coffee? And bring out those small paper plates and some clean forks."

"Yes, ma'am." He kissed Macy on the top of her head when he passed behind her on his way to the house.

With the departure of Louise, Stephen, and the baby a lull descended upon the table. Jim was looking around the yard.

Every stray movement held his interest briefly: the Steeles' collie circling to settle himself for a nap in the slanting early evening sun; the children playing tag at the far end of the wide lawn; a couple of jays pecking at food scraps on the quilt. Macy, on the other hand, only watched Jim. Of the two of them, she appeared the more animated, despite her stillness.

"How's the hand?" she said.

Jim regarded his palm with mild surprise, as if he had just noticed the strip of gauze wrapped around it.

"Oh, fine," he said. "Probably don't even need this any more." He tugged at the bandage.

"Doctors do make the worst patients, don't they?"

"Depends on the nurse." He grinned, so Claudia knew it was some kind of joke. She didn't get it, but then Macy didn't seem to get it either because she didn't smile.

"Louise said you had a new nurse at the office. What's she like?" Macy said.

"She's all right. Come by for lunch Friday and I'll introduce you."

"I can't Friday."

Jim shrugged and began another reconnaissance of the yard. This time Macy, too, looked around, generally following the path of Jim's stare, except that she kept glancing at the kitchen door and Jim never did.

"Claudia," Macy said. "Stop fiddling with those spoons and go play."

Claudia put down the spoons. She'd been sliding them around on the tablecloth, tracing out the swirling pattern woven into it.

"Go on now," Macy repeated, frowning.

People always said that Claudia and her mother looked most alike when they were frowning. This pleased Claudia because she did not much resemble her mother otherwise.

Once Claudia and Macy had squeezed into one of those little booths that takes four photos in quick succession. Claudia insisted they both frown in every shot, and they had, except for the last one when Macy had burst out laughing. Claudia kept the strip of four small pictures taped to her bedstead. But Claudia did not like her mother's frown when it was directed at her.

She stood up, aware that Jim was watching them with sly amusement. She realized that her expression was mirroring her mother's and that for some reason this entertained Jim. Annoyed at them both, Claudia ran to join the game of tag.

She found herself running faster and tagging harder than was really necessary to the game. The stretch of her arm and leg muscles, the thud of her feet, and the rhythmic swelling of her lungs simultaneously fed her annoyance at Macy and Jim and deliciously released it.

Once she stopped to brush her bangs back from her sweaty forehead. She threw a quick look at the table. Jim had gotten up and moved around the table to stand next to Macy. They were touching glasses in a toast. The screen door slammed as Louise exited the house. Macy stood up and began clearing a space on the table for the cake.

Just then, Dan, who was It, side-swiped Claudia violently, causing her to stumble a few steps forward. Earlier, she had tagged him with such force he had sprawled onto the ground. His rough tag now was clearly fair vengeance, but it angered Claudia anyway.

"You're It," he screamed, still on the run.

Claudia raced after him helter-skelter through the yard, even plummeting through the off-limits vegetable patch. She was intent on only one thing: catching Dan, defeating him. She didn't think. She didn't watch where she was going. She saw only Dan's back, always just out of reach in front of her.

Dan leaped up onto the porch and into the house, pushing the front door shut behind him. But Claudia was right on his heels. She held out her arm to push aside the half-closed door without breaking speed.

Suddenly there was a crash of glass shattering. The noise stopped both children short, one on each side of the doorway. Claudia stood, perplexed, looking down at the shards of glass on the porch floor. It was as if she had just wakened in the thick of a dream and was not yet sure which aspects of her surroundings were real and which were dream residue. Then she saw round drops of red liquid falling onto the floor.

"Gross," Dan was saying, staring at her forearm.

Claudia bent her elbow and looked at her arm. A deep gash was bleeding freely. All at once it began to throb with pain.

"What happened?" Valerie said, coming up on the porch. The glass noise had brought her running, followed by Macy and Louise. The men had already left for the park with baby and the little kids, who were slow walkers.

"Claudia put her hand through the glass door," Dan said.

Macy took Claudia's hand and extended the girl's arm to better inspect the cut. She held her white skirt away from the dripping blood.

"I guess she was going too fast to stop," Dan added on Claudia's behalf. He couldn't tell yet whether they were in trouble or not.

Macy shifted her gaze from the wound to her daughter's face. Claudia felt confused. A part of her wanted to crumple against her mother like a toddler, to hear her mother say everything would be all right, everything could be fixed. But another part of her wanted inexplicably to strike out at her mother, to refuse comfort and stand alone in her distress, and this part was stronger than the other, so that Claudia did not crumple, did not speak or move at all, but only cloaked her face with her mother's frown. Macy let go of Claudia's hand.

"Go put a bandage on it," she said crossly. "I'm not having my holiday ruined because of your recklessness."

Macy turned and left the porch.

"Valerie, Dan, are you coming to the park?" she said at the sidewalk without looking back.

"Sure," Dan said eagerly, glad to escape a possible scolding from his mother.

"See ya," Valerie said quietly to her sister, following Dan off the porch. "We'll save your sparklers."

"Let's go inside and wash that," Louise said efficiently to Claudia.

It was dark when Louise and Claudia arrived at the park. At the crosswalk, Macy was waiting to lead them to where the two families had spread their blankets. She reached out and touched Claudia's hair with her fingertips.

"You okay?" she said.

Claudia nodded.

"I think Jim should have a look at her arm when we go home," Louise said. "She may need stitches."

"I don't want stitches," exclaimed Claudia.

"Don't worry about it now," said Macy.

A loud explosion caused them to look up. A fountain of green sparks surrounded by small golden sprays arched across the sky. The crowd *oohed* and *ahhed*.

"We're just over here," Macy said, walking away in the direction of a large sugar maple.

It was strange being in the doctor's office late at night when no one else was there. Jim walked ahead of Claudia and Macy, briskly flipping on wall switches. Fluorescent lights fluttered awake, revealing an environment of gleaming stainless steel and white formica. The absence of nurses and patients allowed the cold technology of the place to assert itself in an almost sentient way.

Claudia had had stitches once before, in her knee, so she knew it was not that terrible an ordeal. She actually felt a mild thrill at being in the office at this illegitimate hour, as if she and Macy and Jim were partners in a small adventure.

That feeling had begun during the ride here. They'd come in Jim's Alfa Romeo with the top down. It had only two bucket seats, so Claudia had sat in Macy's lap, something she did less often than she used to, now that she was older. The warmth of her mother's body pacified her, and the cool night air blowing on her face was a lovely contrast. In three distinct areas of the moonless sky she saw the distant, noiseless fireworks of neighboring towns.

"All right, Claudia, sit up here and roll up your sleeve." Jim indicated an examining table, then turned to wash his hands in a small sink. Next he began to pull instruments out of drawers and line them up on a metal tray: scissors, syringes, glass vials of clear liquid, cotton balls and gauze pads, three or four curved needles, heavy black thread, a plastic bottle of orange-red Betadine soap, adhesive tape.

Claudia could not take her eyes off his businesslike motions. Her anxiety was returning, a nervous "dentist stomach," as

Joey called it. Macy held Claudia's hand and stroked the uninjured arm.

"You can lie down," Jim said to Claudia. He perched on a stool on the opposite side of the table from Macy and shone a bright lamp on Claudia's arm. She felt its heat on her skin.

"This won't take long," he said and set about his task.

Maybe from a doctor's point of view the suturing didn't take long, but to Claudia it seemed an endless procedure. The tight circle of bleached light in which Jim's hands worked cast the rest of the room into shadow. Claudia felt as if the three of them were huddled together in the one habitable spot in a vast emptiness, like lost travelers round a campfire in a desert. It was the sharp boundary between the light and the dark that implanted the notion, that plus her own hurt condition and Jim's grimace of concentration and her mother's glittering eyes.

"Last one," Jim finally said. "You've got some pretty tough skin. I bent two needles."

"How many stitches?" Claudia asked, reluctant to look.

"Eight."

Claudia sat up and Macy held a gauze pad against the cut while Jim taped it down.

"You were very brave," Macy said to Claudia. She put her arms around the girl's shoulders and kissed her forehead.

For the first time that day, Claudia felt tears in her eyes. She pressed her face against her mother's chest just above the soft swell of her breasts. She was glad that before coming here Macy had changed out of her dress into a sweatshirt and jeans; Claudia would not have wanted to lay her face against the bloodstain. She wished her father had come with them so they could go home now in their own car. Exhausted, she craved the familiar.

"I'll go call Dad and let him know you're all right," Macy said. Apparently she, too, had been thinking of Stephen.

A few moments after Macy left the room, Jim left also. Claudia waited for five minutes or so, wandering around the room and looking disinterestedly into cabinets and drawers. It was once again simply a room in a doctor's office, dimly lit and hushed, but neither grand nor ominous.

Bored, Claudia opened the door and walked down the narrow hallway to the reception area. Her mother stood beside a desk. She must have just hung up the phone because her hand was still on the receiver. Jim stood close behind her. He stepped in even closer and wrapped his arms around her waist. His right hand slid under her sweatshirt. Macy canted her back against him and closed her eyes.

"Mary Ann," he said. "I've missed you."

"She's Macy," said Claudia loudly.

The two adults were startled apart. Jim looked embarrassed, but Macy's expression held fear.

"Claudia," she said, making the name sound like a plea.

"I'll wait in the car," said Jim. "Take your time."

He turned at the door. "You know how to lock up," he said to Macy.

Neither Macy nor Claudia paid attention to his exit.

"Claudia," Macy said again, this time with resignation. She leaned shakily against the desk behind her.

Macy seemed to be waiting for Claudia to say something. But Claudia could not think of even one question. She needed Macy to take charge. Claudia wanted instruction in what would happed next, in what she should do.

"What are you thinking?" Macy finally said.

Claudia did not answer. She bent her head down and watched her big toe wiggle through a hole in her canvas sneaker. She heard Macy move, but she did not look up until her mother was standing directly in front of her.

"Let's sit down," Macy said, gesturing to the waiting room.

Claudia slumped against the back cushions of the leather couch. It gave off a pleasantly bitter aroma, and it creaked when she shifted her position. Macy sat primly on the forward edge of the couch, as if she were a bird alighted only briefly on the tip of a branch, ready to fly from any disturbance.

"You know, you're getting to be more grown up every day,"

Macy began. "But there are still a lot of things about being grown up that you do not understand yet."

Claudia kept her gaze steadfastly on the magazines fanned out on the glass-topped coffee table. She was not sure she wanted to understand all the things being grown up meant.

"What you just saw," Macy continued, "is one of those things."

"Does Jim love you?" Claudia demanded, looking squarely at her mother.

"Oh, darling, it's not as simple as that. It never is."

"Do you still love Dad?"

"Of course I do. Very much. And I hate the thought of hurting him. I think you know enough to know that this would hurt him, don't you?"

"Yes."

Macy looked fixedly across the room as if a movie were being shown on the opposite wall. Claudia realized that her mother was not going to offer any more information. She felt a great weight settle upon her. She suddenly believed herself responsible not only for the restoration of her own sense of peace but also for the safety of her entire family. Though she felt infused with power and importance, her power frightened her and her importance lacked joy.

Macy began to cry. Claudia had only seen her mother cry two or three other times, and it always alarmed her. Macy's crying isolated her from Claudia.

Claudia scrambled forward on the couch. She wrapped her arms around her mother's neck and lay her cheek on top of Macy's head. Macy returned the embrace.

"It's all right," Claudia insisted. "It will be all right."

They stayed like that for several minutes. Then Macy disengaged herself from Claudia and stood up. She reached out to the girl, and hand-in-hand they walked to the bathroom in the inner office, where Macy rinsed her face with cold water.

When they went outside, Jim was reclining against the car smoking a cigarette. He calculated them as he might have done accident victims in triage, but he said nothing.

It seemed to Claudia that Jim drove home more slowly than he had driven to the office, despite lighter traffic. Once when he was shifting gears, his knuckles bumped Claudia's leg. After that, Macy shielded the spot with her hand. Then Claudia felt the little jolts less sharply. But she was still aware of them.

Concerto for Piano, Paperweight, and Change Machine

BY THALIA SELZ

The Old Lady interviewed him. Padgett wasn't expecting this. Though he knew that the immense wealth was primarily hers and that she lived with her son and daughter-in-law, he'd assumed that they—middle aged and still energetic, according to the employment agency—ran the household.

But the motherly-looking maid who opened the front door (the agency had warned him not to arrive via the service elevator) cued him in as she took his coat. "If you want the job, Mr. Padgett"—with a trace of brogue—"you'd best cozy up to Mrs. Goelet. She's the one that runs things up here in the clouds."

She said this because it was a penthouse, but he sensed a vastness that wasn't characteristic of penthouses. The elevator had risen up *into* the apartment, which must occupy the entire top floor of this large Fifth Avenue building. The foyer alone was twice the size of his mother's parlor in Lebanon, Pennsylvania. He wanted the job right then. He knew the racket from the street would never reach him up here; anyhow, he liked to be above things. He thought, I've always wanted my own kingdom.

"Mind the pond!" As she led him around the reflecting pool sunk in the terrazzo floor of the foyer.

He liked the plain moon face of this maid and the rock and tilt of her Irish speech. He could hear a musical phrase in his head: something playful for a soprano, maybe accompanied by trumpet and continuo. The sort of piece most contemporary composers wouldn't think of tackling because of the old-fashioned instruments and the risk of melody. He would make her young in his song, much younger than he wanted *her* to be. He had his own girl, Judy; anyhow, relationships made it hard to concentrate on composing.

The maid led him through a huge double parlor that overlooked Fifth. They passed a Bechstein and he thought, I can play it when they're out. He'd learned that when the rich weren't entertaining they were usually "out."

The Old Lady was waiting in a sitting room that seemed to be part of her private suite at one end of the penthouse. She sat by the windows with one-third of midtown Manhattan floating below her right elbow. Padgett felt this was appropriate, since her family money lay in New York real estate. But he didn't like the challenging way she wagged the chamber music program in his face.

"Do you really compose?"

"Yes, Mrs. Goelet." He had noted on his application both the NEA Consortium Commission and the fact that he composed from five to seven every morning, because he wanted his employers to know what they were getting. Better all around.

"How are you going to do it here? I won't have that modern racket going off on my piano at five A.M."

So she'd read his application. And goodbye to the Bechstein unless he was able to adjust his needs to hers.

"I compose in my head, Mrs. Goelet. A lot of contemporary composers do."—"So did Beethoven," he *didn't* say.

"It certainly doesn't sound as if they use a keyboard. Why do you want to be my butler?"

"I like security, Mrs. Goelet, and a well-run household. Most composers have insecure teaching jobs in colleges that aren't well-run." He wouldn't confess to a horror of wasting his days struggling with students who had lead ears; he was afraid of sounding arrogant.

"Sissy Harriman's caterer sends a poet to tend bar at her parties. But he's a Negro." She pronounced it *Nig-ro* "Seems more fitting." She was toying with a glass paperweight on the tea table beside her; after a moment she looked up at the maid with a nod of dismissal. "Sit down, Padgett. I like your name. Padgett has the right sound for a butler. I suppose you know that. A composer's ear, though I'll bet you do butlering because you want to be close to the rich."

Now that he was on her level, she was examining him with eyes as clear and cold as blue glass. He repressed a shiver. He'd read that an involuntary tremor was the body's way of releasing tension. He could feel those eyes piercing him like glass slivers. He wanted them to soften in admiration, though why should her admiration matter? He was twenty-nine; she must be past seventy.

She said, "I think we'll get on. You're a personable young man, and you worked four and a half years for the Burdens; Charlie and I were third cousins once removed."

He knew from back elevator gossip that before old Burden's death they had shared a Vanderbilt and an Astor in their gene pool. He'd get on with her if his considerate treatment by the Burdens was any indication. "I was wondering, Madame, if I might use the piano when you're out?"

"As long as it's not a nuisance. You'll be directly responsible to me except when I go away; then you'll be responsible to Mr. Harry..."

She meant her middle-aged son; by "go away" she meant trips to the hospital for surgery and then to the Bahamas for recuperation. Maura, the Irish maid, filled Padgett in during the next few days. The Old Lady was trading pieces of her body to the old man with the scythe: a breast for five years, another breast and some underarm nodes for an additional five.

When he told Judy on his day off she shuddered. "I'd rather be dead."

"Because you're young and have gorgeous breasts"—he kissed one—"and need your pectoral muscles to play the cello.

But she's old, and I guess she wants every bit of life she can get no matter what it costs her."

"Doesn't she need her pectoral muscles to play the piano in her parlor?"

"I think she's given it up. I wish she would go away quick so I could try it out." He did an arpeggio on her belly, then executed some grace notes in her pubic hair. "I'm having trouble with a new concerto." He meant composing. If he had an instrument, it was the piano, perhaps the clarinet. The new concerto employed both. But he hated practicing and technique bored him. Composing alone gave you the freedom to explore instruments and invent new ones, like that device in his concerto.

"Get a different kind of job."

"My paycheck bought that joint you're smoking." He didn't add that the joint was a lot better than anything she could afford, waiting tables in a Broadway coffee-house when she couldn't snag a TV commercial or a job with a pickup orchestra. He sighed. Why did love make people feel they had to change you?

"I said 'different *kind*.' You don't have a life of your own."

"Maybe I don't want one."

But of course he did. Only how could he be a composer and afford a life of his own? He had to be in New York to get his pieces performed and published and to hear what the competition was doing. And there was Judy—still at Juilliard—and the undeniable fact that he liked to live well. The young composers and musicians he knew all jobbed around—playing in piano bars, teaching private pupils, even clerking in cheese shops unless they were lucky enough to land work with a musical that might run for a while. They scurried like rats while he had a comfortable room with his own bath and a view across penthouse terraces to the Queensboro Bridge. Bertie, the cook, was first-rate, and the Goelets didn't scrimp on the food bill. There was one thing the Old Lady wasn't generous with, though.

"Padgett, please don't recycle my old *New Yorkers*. I like to read them at my leh-zhure." Unspoken reminder poised, blade down, above his head: *Your salary is more than adequate for a subscription of your own.*

"She keeps her distance," he told Maura.

"No more than you, Mr. Padgett."

"What's that supposed to mean? And please don't call me 'Mr. Padgett.'"

"It's a bit odd your being a butler, is all. Bertie and me, we were raised to service." She faced him, flushing, and he thought she was going to say something revealing of him or of her way of looking at life, but they were in the kitchen, and Bertie trudged in from the back entry with a box of live lobsters packed in ice at the same moment as the buzzer sounded from the sitting room. Padgett picked up his tray. "Well, if she's so class conscious, why did the agency tell me not to use the service elevator when I came for my interview?"

"'Twas before you'd entered service. You were still a free man. Once she pays wages! She's a My-Lady, all right."

He carried the tray with her daiquiri into the sitting room and set it on the tea table next to the glass paperweight. She was reading a magazine (*The Atlantic*). He decided to make her look up. He wasn't a butler who scribbled songs in his spare time. He was a composer who earned an honest living as butler. Beethoven had refused to enter Viennese palaces through the servants' entrance. The paperweight sparkled in the late afternoon sunshine. An overlay of red glass on it was cut to resemble a blown rose, lush and erotic as a blossom by Georgia O'Keeffe. He needed something from this woman, something that had nothing to do with her money but everything to do with who she was. "Anything else, Madam?"

"If there should be, I'll ring." The voice wizened, thin as string.

His contacts with her were full of small slights like this, and because she ran the household he saw her many times each day: delivering her newspaper and cocktail, picking up the mail and going to the post office, doing her personal shopping except for clothes, and waiting on her guests. She had many guests, partly because she disliked going out, so that people had to come to her if they wanted to see her. Finally, though, he got a chance to try the Bechstein, only to discover that it was agonizingly out of tune. When he ventured to suggest a tuning, she said they could discuss it another time. He complained to Judy. "Sometimes she treats me like my piano teacher used to treat her worst pupils."

"You said you've butlered six years. Isn't that part of being a butler?"

"I was at the Burdens' the night after my *Homage to Varèse* premiered at Alice Tully Hall, and they toasted me in champagne. A few of the guests had even gone to the concert. They kidded me about my pots-and-pans music, but they loved having a composer wait on them. It gave them a buzz."

"Did their kidding give you a buzz?"

He spoke coaxingly into her hair. "It's a joke remembering everyone's name and that old Mrs. Warburg drinks rye on the rocks and how that pretty Parkinson is sleeping with her cousin on one side of the family and her uncle on the other. It's a game, Judy."

She drew back on the pillow and examined his face coolly. "You're Siamese twins. One's the prince in disguise, the other's *really* a servant. Where're you going?"

"Home. I'll come back when you're ready to quit analyzing me." He knew he was being petulant, but he was already out of bed; it was too late to back off, though two A.M. was no time to walk alone down West 111th Street without your favorite firearm.

"So I'm not supposed to think, either? You're beginning to believe your own games, and that's dangerous."

"You can think of all you want. Just don't tell me about it." He waited, hoping she would sigh, "Oh, shit," so he could jump back into bed and apologize, but she didn't and finally he went into the bathroom. Then he had to take the lid off the tank to flush the mechanism. "While you're thinking, think how to get your landlord to fix the toilet tank."

"If you were nice you'd fix it."

He slid back into bed. Quickly, before she could change her mind.

"I wish you'd quit butlering. It makes you dependent."

"Who wants me to fix their toilet tank?"

"Have you fixed that concerto you were working on?"

"Which one?"

"Piano, winds, and change machine. You're not serious,

damn it. You get some fantastic piece going, and then you start work on three others and don't finish any of them."

"How come I've had five new pieces performed in the past year?"

"That's the trouble; you're good. You could be a leader, an innovator. But you'll end up another follower. A butler." She threw her arm across his chest, lodged her chin in the hollow of his shoulder. "Quit."

"I'll think about it."

But later he remembered he'd said "home." He was in Harry Goelet's study, accepting a packet for delivery to the family lawyers. Harry G. was a sincere coupon cutter, but he looked like a thug, grunted like a bassoon.

"Ump! Told Ollie Belmont about you. He said music's beautiful but sailing is important." Here he actually chuckled. "He wants to borrow you for a weekend at their place in Newport. Show you off. But Mother won't let us. She never lends staff."

This was home? He was something to be loaned out, or not, as his owners saw fit? Well, why not? This way he never had to deal with other people's emotions, and in the perfect silence that lay under his surface he could listen for sounds. He'd catch a cab down to the lawyers' to deliver the packet, then take the bus back uptown so he could concentrate on the rhythm of the change machine: *da*-dada, *da*-dada. *Concerto for Piano, Winds, and Change Machine* ...

When he came in from the lawyers' he was surprised to hear someone playing Mozart's *Rondo alla turca* haltingly but with verve on the still untuned piano. As he entered the parlor she broke off. "I want you to make an appointment with my tuner."

"In this climate," he blurted, "it should be tuned at least every six months."

"I used to play a great deal." She stood up and headed for the door. "Lately I've had my mind on other matters."

If he hadn't believed she disdained irony as the tool of ineffectual persons, he would have sworn her tone was ironic.

He started finding excuses to hang around her. He wanted to wrest acknowledgment from her that he *was* the prince in disguise though his father was only the manager of a small discount store in Lebanon, Pennsylvania. In bitter moments Padgett thought of himself as one of the store's better products: quality at a discount price. But she didn't notice him unless she needed his services.

"My sable, Padgett; I'm going out."

The sable engulfed her. She looked like a small furry animal going into hibernation, although it was mid-April. She would go down to the park and sit on a green bench with Maura or Padgett in silent attendance while she read one of her magazines. In the sunshine her skin looked like old wax. Sometimes it puckered in the cool air of late afternoon like the surface of the pond where the children sailed toy boats. Then he felt sorry for her.

As the spring gathered, he had a recurring fantasy that he was a servant in disguise. In the mornings he began to enjoy putting on his uniform. It felt supportive, like a brace or a mold. On his days off he pulled on jeans but instead of the ease and relief with which he'd slipped into his other clothes in the past, he felt a wild capering around his heart, followed by a sneaking fear. What if he were recognized for the servant he really was?

He went on trying to compose. From five to seven most mornings he sat at his desk with music paper in front of him and stared at it. Occasionally he would make notations. While the sun gilded the finials of the Queensboro Bridge he pretended to listen to sounds in his head, but what he heard were the scores of other composers or, worse, a sound vacuum that wasn't silence—which before had always filled with sounds as he listened—but a hollow that the sound had been sucked out of. He felt as if he were coming unstrung.

He called up Judy and invited her to a performance at Cooper Union. During intermission as he talked music with their friends she said very little. Her Tartar eyes were green, not a cold blue like the Old Lady's, and her gaze didn't impale him, but he felt fixed by that watchful stare. It provoked him to a foolish claim that the Musical Elements had commissioned him to do a piece for violincello and electronic tape. Her lids flickered in embarrassment for him. He felt humiliated by her pity, and suddenly he heard himself saying that he had just been elected to the Academy of Arts and Letters. His voice hung crazily in the air. His friends drew in their breaths; then came their envious congratulations. Gooseflesh rose on his arms, and he laughed with excitement.

As the buzzer sounded to end intermission, Judy drew him aside. "For God's sake, quit it."

He felt a thrill at being unmasked.

"Why are you saying these crazy things?"

How could he explain his fear that he was only masquerading as a composer? He hung his head and said nothing.

"I'm going home. No, don't come with me."

He tried to hand her cab fare, but she brushed it away and the bill fluttered to the floor between them. His legs felt so weak that he returned to the auditorium and sat down. The next morning when he put on his uniform, he thought he must have lost weight. His shoulders seemed to be shrinking. He pulled at the jacket. The uniform had been tailored to fit, but it was as though *he* had been tailored to fit *it*. The annunciator went off, and he looked up at the electrically controlled signaling apparatus on his wall to see which room was calling him. The Old Lady's suite. It was unusual for her to buzz him before nine-thirty; she got up early but relied on Maura till after breakfast. Now he had only to hear her buzzer to jump like a cat—eager for the sunny windowsill, the dish of cream, the prescribed life that made no emotional demands, leaving his invention free. Yet he wanted her approval, as a cat wants stroking. It made no sense! He missed Judy already, had missed her all the way uptown on the subway, and all night in fitful dreams, missed her now while he opened his door and hurried through the kitchen where Bertie was mixing muffin batter, to the Old Lady's sitting room.

She stood fully dressed, and her overnight case lay open on the settee. Maura was sliding several magazines beneath what he recognized as her favorite robe. Where was she off to?

"Padgett, run out and get me a small tube of toothpaste. The concession never has my brand."

He felt slighted. He hadn't heard even a word about her trip. And what "concession"? Maura was looking at him over her shoulder. Did she know what was up?

"Maura, tell Bertie I won't be having breakfast."

"Yes, Madame."

"And if I'm not back by Memorial Day, remind Mr. Harry to order wreaths for the Goelet plots. Stupid traditions. As if the dead gave a hoot. Padgett: *toothpaste*." As he left the room he heard her instructing Maura, "Give this envelope to Mr. Harry at once; it's got the keys to all the safe deposit vaults—"

Trust her to hang onto them till the last minute! But where was she going? Why hadn't she told him? In the kitchen, as he waited for the service elevator off the back entry, he asked Bertie.

"To the hospital. She don't like it spoke of ahead of time. Makes it less real maybe. Or maybe she thinks cancer's shameful."

He felt a pang. To lose her and drive away Judy in less than twenty-four hours. But it was silly to feel an attachment to this selfish old woman who only cared if he lived or died according to whether he was around to wait on her.

When he returned with the toothpaste, she told him to have the car brought around at ten-fifty. "I don't intend to check in till after eleven." In the foyer she elaborated to Harry and Mrs. Harry: "No point in paying for last night. I give them a yearly contribution."

Padgett wanted to wish her luck, but he stood mute beside the house telephone because his uniform was giving him orders. When the doorman phoned up that the car was waiting, Padgett came forward to escort her down, but she took her son's arm.

He spoke in spite of the uniform. "We look forward to seeing you again soon, Madame."

She stepped into the elevator without a sign that she'd heard him. As she turned to face the closing doors, her eyes looked as flat as two pennies.

He stared down at his image in the reflecting pool. *Personable*. Was that all he was? There was ability in that exceptionally broad forehead. He didn't care about Harry and Mrs. Harry. The Old Lady alone had class; she had married a member of her very own family—distant enough to be safe but keeping the genes in the bank, the millions in her pocket. Even—*especially*—her prejudices were part of that class. He might find the remark about the poet who was "a Nig-ro" annoying or even funny, but it marked her as someone indifferent to fads, including democratic chic.

He wandered back to her sitting room and picked up the paperweight. Relationships were dangerous (look at what had happened with Judy), but women were the receptacles and guardians of power; they bore the heirs and attended to the wreaths on the graves, the safe deposit keys, to everything that had begun with the Old Lady's birth and marriage within that family so long ago. A shaft of noon sunshine stroking in through the window penetrated the magenta whorls of the rose, revealing a bloody glory.

He heard a stir at his back. Maura came around and looked at him; he saw that there was a new solemnity in her face.

"Is she going to die?"

"I heard Mr. Harry tell Missus they fear it's spread through her system, poor thing. For all that she's correct as a countess, I don't wish that on her." She came close to him. Touched his hand. He put down the paperweight. "Now's a good time for you to play the piano. The two of them will be busy with her at the hospital and Bertie and me could use some music to cheer the place up."

"That's nice of you, Maura."

"Can you play *Jesus Christ Superstar*? It's uplifting, don't you think?" She patted him on the arm. It was the second time in a few moments that she'd touched him, and he pulled back automatically, stammering, "I'm sorry," at the same instant as Maura said, "Excuse *me*, Mr. Padgett. I'll be making arrangements to have a novena said for Mrs. Goelet. If you're a religious man, you might be paying a visit to the church of your choice. A prayer never hurt anybody, now, did it?" And she marched out of the room with her chin up.

Padgett felt ashamed of his snobbishness, and that evening when he went around to see Judy he described the scene to her. She eyed him sardonically. "You think you're better than Maura the way you think you're better than me."

"It's not the same at all!"

"You just use me: to fuck and confess to. Your real romance is with that old millionairess."

"Why do women always suspect another woman?"

"Because there's usually another woman to suspect, though in your case it's the symbiosis that's suspect."

"There's no symbiosis."

The voice was mocking, the green eyes sad. "Okay, so it's what they used to call being a social parasite." But he could tell she was glad he'd come by, and he wallowed in that though it made him feel guilty.

Before long the Old Lady was back, clay-faced and gaunt. She wasn't going to the Bahamas this time. The surgeon had taken a look inside, then stitched her up again. He told Harry and Mrs. Harry it was a matter of weeks. She lay in the air-conditioned rooms, gazing out at the sun-blasted city. Or she would move about in a brown study as if she were readying herself for a significant test. He was reminded of the way the people he had worked for looked when they received invitations to visit the White House; then he was ashamed of the comparison.

"May I get you something, Madame?"

"No, thank you, Padgett."

A chime rang in his head. One of the first things he'd learned when he entered service was that the rich tended not to thank their servants unless they'd been around a long time. "If they are thanking us, my dear," a Hungarian butler had told him, "they are saying every minute 'thank you.' My dear, absolutely this is unpractical."

Padgett took a step toward her as if her next move must be a gesture of friendship.

She turned her face toward him. He saw the red circles under the blue eyes, the bloodshot stare. He stepped back, embarrassed that she had been crying. "Madame—"

"What is it, Padgett?"

He answered in almost the same words. "Is anything wrong, Madame?"

For the first time since he'd met her, he heard emotion in

her voice. It was the sound of repressed but violent outrage. "I'm dying, Padgett! Can't you see that? I'm very busy *dying*. Now please go away!"

He stumbled backwards before the wretchedness and pain in her eyes. He saw the horror of her suffering—an old woman's suffering—and felt sick.

She bent forward, as if she were dragging herself out of a corner. One hand tightened on a rolled-up magazine; then her head came up. She held her shoulders erect. "One moment, Padgett." Trying to focus on him. "You see, not everything in the world has to do with you. You're an educated young man. I suppose you know the story of Narcissus?"

"Yes, Madame," he whispered.

She seemed to gather herself into a single knot of energy. When she spoke, her normally thin voice almost thundered. "He drowned!"

Five weeks later she was dead. At the end she went so fast that only her last week was spent in the hospital. After the funeral and the reception in the penthouse for funeral guests, Padgett wandered back to her sitting room. In the face of her concentration, his life seemed weightless. His heart thumped when he remembered how those fierce, bloodshot eyes had fastened on him. The beam of her sight had been narrow but sharp as a laser. Her knowledge of herself and her place in the world had enabled her to see through his smooth surface to the loose parts banging around inside him. Next best to winning her approval had been winning her notice and reproof.

He picked up the paperweight. It felt cool and solid in his grip. Royal orb, memento of a queen. He slipped it into his pocket. He had never stolen anything in his life, but this wasn't stealing. This was taking something to keep her with him. He went back to his room and tucked it under the jockey shorts in one of his drawers. Though pretty, it had no real value, and if it were missed, the household would assume that one of the hundred and fifty funeral guests had taken it. Even Maura said, "There was more than a score of them" she had never seen before. Everyone knew that hangers-on came to these affairs—buzzards circling above wealth or fame.

He was wrong. Mrs. Harry noticed the paperweight's absence as soon as she started to go over the inventory of her mother-in-law's possessions, and sent the staff scurrying in search of it. It *was* valuable. French. Signed "Gallé" and dated 1884 on the bottom. He hadn't examined it because he hadn't wanted it for money. He thought of putting it back or pretending to find it where a thief might have dropped it, but he needed a touchstone of her power. Ever since he'd met her, she'd been concentrating on dying in control, as she had lived. She had been consistent above all, which above all he was not.

The Harrys decided to put the apartment up for sale and move into a smaller penthouse on Park, together with Maura and Bertie. Without Mother there was no longer any need for a butler, but would Padgett consider moving uptown three blocks to Ollie Belmont's?

Padgett knew that with his references he would have no trouble finding a job, but he was grateful to the Harrys for smoothing his path. The next morning he went to pick up the deed to the penthouse at the lawyers' and when he returned, the super and a workman he didn't recognize rode up with him in the service elevator. "Sorry to see you folks leaving," the super said. "God knows what riff-raff will buy the place. Some of those beautiful people I wouldn't let into my kitchen."

He found Harry G. in his study and handed him the envelope containing the deed. Harry Goelet placed it in a square of sunshine on the desk, and reaching into a drawer, lifted out the paperweight and set it on the envelope. It flashed like a beacon in the light, almost blinding Padgett, but he managed not to flinch.

With his forefinger Harry Goelet pushed a sealed envelope toward him. "Severance pay. I want you out of the building in one hour."

Possibly Maura had remembered seeing him with the paperweight in his hand that day. While he threw clothes and scores into his suitcases, he had the sense of her smoldering self-righteously beyond the walls, but what he had to face was so much greater than Maura's disapproval or venom. Now all the wealthy people he had always felt superior to would know about the composer-butler who stole like a common thief.

As he crossed the foyer carrying his two suitcases, the super and the workman, who turned out to be a plumber, were draining the pool. "Good luck," the super called. "Come by someday and I'll treat you to a beer in The Shamrock."

Clearly he didn't know about the theft, though he'd learn soon enough. Padgett nodded and rang the front elevator bell. Damned if he'd ride down in the service elevator, though by tomorrow he'd probably be waiting tables, at least till he could find a job that would leave him time and energy to compose.

Out on Fifth he turned south and began walking aimlessly toward midtown, but the scores made his suitcases heavier each moment. How could he tell Judy he'd been canned for grand larceny? He wouldn't. He would say he'd been let go because with the old woman dead, the Goelets had no more need for his services. It was close enough to the truth to sound convincing.

The sweat had begun to trickle down from his armpits, and he was afraid of ruining his shirt, so he crossed the street and sat on one of the benches on the park side of Fifth Avenue. The bench reminded him of the Old Lady and how she had sat out here—not here exactly, for she always chose a bench inside the park, but close by—and how she had read her magazines cover to cover all through the spring while she waited for the next visit to the hospital. Had she sensed then she had only a short time left?

The sun had cleared the tallest of the buildings facing him and was driving back the shade of the horse chestnut overhanging his bench. He looked to his left and then to his right, but all the shaded benches were occupied, so he continued to crouch under the huge spotlight of the sun.

Where could he go? A cool shower was what he longed for, but he didn't want to spend even a part of his two weeks' severance pay on a hotel room. He had a key to Judy's place, but she would guess the instant she saw him that he'd been fired. People like the Goelets didn't suddenly throw out trusted help. He stank of his shame. He could smell it on himself—a sour stench, ranker than sweat.

Why the hell had he lifted that paperweight? He looked around furiously, as if the old witch were perched on a bench in the shade. She had ruined his life with her monstrous wealth and vicious notions of class. It was her fault he had stolen the paperweight. If he had it in his hand right now, and if she were sitting on the next bench, in the shade of that horse chestnut, he would fling the paperweight at her head, and the solid thud it made as it cracked her skull would find its way into a new concerto, followed by a cluster of all the little splitting sounds of her cranial bones.

He almost choked on his laughter; then he put up his hands to hide his face. He must look like another Manhattan looney. But the sun's blaze turned his fingers translucent in front of his eyes, and the sweat streaming off his forehead made him loathe the touch of his own skin. He was drowning in sweat. She had predicted it. God damned old hag, rotting in her fifty-thousand-dollar mausoleum. *As if the dead gave a hoot.* Well, he would give a hoot that she was going to hear—or since she couldn't, Harry G. and Mrs. Harry and the Belmonts and the other Names That Ran Things. They were going to listen to his noise: loud enough and strange enough and terrifying enough to wake the dead.

I won't have that modern racket.

And he would say without cringing, *You will.*

He stood up, staggering a little. As he bent to grasp the suitcase handles, the suitcase went white before his eyes, like an overexposed film, and he panted for breath. He'd better get out of the sun and lie down. He began trudging uptown, toward the stop for the westbound bus, halting in the shady spots to rest and catch his breath.

He would have to tell Judy the truth. Like lancing an abscess. Maybe she would say that he was using her, and in a way she would be right. That was his curse. But he did not think that she would throw him out.

And Still Champion

BY STEVEN BRYAN BIELER

Randy had never learned how to nap on a bus. He was certain that if he fell asleep, the driver would too. He shifted under the coat he was using as a blanket and checked his watch. They were seventy-eight minutes south of Boston, one minute more than the last time he had checked.

Snow floated through the early evening, smoothing the differences between the small towns, turning to a treacherous slush on Route 138. Unable to escape into dreams, he turned again to the Master in the seat across the darkened aisle. The Master's hands, skin loose and rumpled like a couple of old dogs, moved above the chessboard on his lap, choosing the rook, then the king. At his touch, the pieces sent forth beacons of light that illuminated the position. The Master pushed the Black pawn, the one that had advanced the farthest, another perilous step forward.

"Damn it," Randy said with anger, because he had again fallen for the fool's mate, playing the student to the angry god of chess, but with caution too, because the two teenage girls in the seats ahead of him already thought he was a nut. The bus stopped at an intersection. These old brick buildings with their ranks of deep, inset windows must be Saltmarsh. Soon there would be people and distractions and other things to think about besides the Black pawn, the one that had cost him first place.

The bus turned off the highway and plowed across the low drifts lapping the shore of the Greyhound terminal. The Master thumped the pawn several times against the board, but Randy wanted out, not illumination. He slipped on his heavy leather coat and dragged his suitcase down from the rack.

The last flutter of snow descended. Inside the terminal, the ticket seller handed the driver a mug that exhaled steam. There was no one else inside the cinder-block building, and, shortly, no one outside it; the cars that had been waiting for the bus, engines running to keep patient friends and family warm, had claimed their own and fled. Someone named Leveque, from the Saltmarsh Chess Club, was supposed to meet him here, now. Lena used to meet him at the end of a tournament. They'd stay up late, drink beer and eat pastrami sandwiches in bed, celebrate his victories, mourn his defeats. Randy put his suitcase down by the pay phone and, alive with too much coffee and too little sleep, slogged across the parking lot and the tire-tracked street to the town green.

On the green, now tucked beneath the first blanket of winter, sat the antique cannon and stack of cannon balls that might be needed should the Redcoats ever return. Randy high-stepped through the snow to the base of the flagpole, where the Master stood, touching a match to a cigar fat as a belaying pin. "You're just a footnote," Randy said. "Who cares what you think?" The Master flipped a Black pawn from one large, knobby hand to the other. He had still been staggering around when Randy was a child, pushing chess pieces, chewing cigars he was forbidden to light, drinking grape juice and calling it zinfandel. His last four words to Randy before his death, on a rainy weekday morning twenty-five years ago, were: "No no no. Wrong!"

"Mr. Schiller?" someone called, perhaps for the second time. A woman in a knit cap, dark pleated overcoat, and pointed purple boots stood on the sidewalk. In this crystal air her voice was as distinct as a lesson in diction. "I'm Andrea Leveque, from the *Evening Patriot*. Are you Rudolph Schiller?"

Randy made his way off the green. Snow gathered in the

cuffs of his pants, invaded his shoes. On the sidewalk, under the street light, he could see brown hair curling from under the woman's cap and tears in her eyes from the cold. "Randy," he said. She shook his hand with both of hers, warming him with the soft leather of her driving gloves. "That's *Randy* Schiller."

"Whoops," she said. "Rudolph was the grandfather, Randolph is you. I was playing over some of his games last night—"

"You're late," Randy cut in.

"I'm late? Mr. Schiller, you're the one playing in the snow. The exhibition starts in an hour. You're really cutting this close."

They studied each other. She was about his age, early thirties, and his height, average. A third person would have said he looked okay and she was not bad.

"Call me Randy."

"Andrea," she laughed, shaking his hand again.

"Can we go now?"

"Follow me." She led him to a green Pontiac station wagon. Loops of wire held the rear license plate to the bumper; a sticker in the rear window proclaimed the owner's advocacy of PAWN POWER. Randy's suitcase was already lying across the back seat. The Master had opened a board on it and was setting the chessmen in their ranks.

"I have a million questions for you," Andrea said as she fired up the engine. "My editor is giving me the lead story for the Lifestyle section!"

Randy brought out his Walkman. "We'll have to talk later," he said. "Right now I have to get ready. Mentally, I mean."

Andrea wore thin hoop earrings, wheels within wheels, that provided a tinny soundtrack as she looked right and left and backed the car away from the terminal. "Of course. You must have all kinds of mental exercises to get into fighting trim. I'm going to ask about those, too."

Randy could tell that Andrea was trying to drive and read the label on the cassette through the Walkman's little window. "Haydn," he told her. "Watch where you're going! Horn concerto in D, no. 3."

"Write that down, will you?" She pointed at a pad of paper

taped to the dashboard. Randy grabbed a pen that swung from the rearview mirror, scribbled on the pad, and settled back, earphones in place. He had long ago pasted fake labels on his cassettes. He flicked the start key, closed his eyes, and sank into the familiar chain-saw rip of amplified guitars.

They pulled into the parking lot of the Bay Colony Motel, past a line of tall oaks, foliage furled for the season. Andrea swung through the light that burst from the motel office and parked in the first available space. "You're home!" she sang, repeating herself after Randy switched his music off. "Fifty minutes to curtain. Let's do it!" She jumped from the car and pulled his suitcase from the back seat. "You're in 116. Go open the door," she said, handing him the key and fending off his grab for the suitcase. "No, *I* can carry it. Did it all the time in the Army. Airlift command. Turn left. There."

Randy opened the door, found the light switch and snapped it on. The wallpaper depicted the hardy life of the lobster fisherman. "Anything you need?" Andrea asked.

A full night of sleep in the next fifty minutes, he thought. "A roast beef sandwich on white bread. And a cup of coffee, black. Got it?"

"Affirmative. Be right back!"

When Randy was alone, he emptied his coat pockets onto the yellowing chenille bedspread: his Walkman, three cassettes, a roll of lemon breath mints, and a roll of paper money bound with a rubber band. The band broke when the money hit the bed and a few bills fanned out like props in a gangster movie. The night the tournament ended—only last night!— he had returned to the Swansea Hotel, the elegant stack of white bricks in Copley Square, not to the huge ballroom that served as the tournament hall but to the adjoining room that had been set aside for practice and analysis. There he had held court until dawn, playing against young men, old men, and even a few women, guys in slick sets of clothes and guys who couldn't tell checks from plaids, all of them willing to put down five or ten or twenty dollars for a try at beating the top-ranked player with the famous surname.

"Six-fifty, six-eighty, six-ninety-six," he counted. "Almost seven hundred bucks." But first prize had meant thousands, first prize had meant the real glory, and with all his frantic playing and small-time hustling he hadn't managed to erase from memory the one move he hadn't had the nerve to make.

After his shower, he wiped steam from the mirror and saw in it the Master sitting on the bed, counting the money. "So sue me," Randy said, kicking the bathroom door shut. He lathered his face, ran his blade under the hot water, and peered again into the mirror, seeing the final position of his last-round game with the young Rumanian, Hosnik: Hosnik's rook and knight stalking Randy's king, Randy's pawn running for the last rank and the promotion to queen. The game had turned as cold as this dreary day, the position austere, only a few pieces still afloat on the dark seas sweeping the board.

Someone knocked on the outside door. Randy, wrapped in his bath towel—always startle your opponent—opened the door for Andrea, who marched into the room with a white paper bag held triumphantly aloft. "The power of the press," she said, and stopped, taking in the suitcase split like a clam on the floor, clothes and chess books caught making a break for it, the cash littering the bed, the chess master in the towel and shaving cream. "I didn't think you'd have a tattoo," she said.

"I didn't think an old soldier would blush," Randy said. He nonchalantly brushed the flock of bills into the drawer of the bedside table. "Have a seat. You might as well start asking questions, too. We're in a time crunch." He went back to the bathroom to finish shaving.

Andrea threw her coat over a chair and pulled off her knit cap. She wore navy slacks, a white blouse, and a navy vest with pockets. She followed him to the door of the bathroom. "First question," she said, wielding pad and pen, looking and not looking. "What happened in that last game in Boston?"

"Hosnik needed a draw to clinch first place." Randy slowly scraped the lather from his face. "So he offered one."

"But you needed a win to finish first," Andrea pointed out. "What was it about the position that led you to accept his offer of a draw? Did you see that you had lost the game?"

"The game hinged on my passed pawn versus his mating attack," Randy said, then bent to wash. Was it an error to push the pawn? Was it an error *not* to push it? The Master would have pushed it. The Master would have eaten poison if he'd thought it would do him any good.

Everyone had been watching Randy and this shooting star from Rumania, the kid—they were all starting to look like kids—billed as the next world champion. People were seated just beyond the strand of blue ribbon that separated from the rest of the tournament the table he and Hosnik were playing on; a crowd studied the big display board at the far end of the ballroom, talking quietly and insistently; and Randy could picture his fellow masters in the analysis room next door, jabbing at their chessboards, exploring lines of play he felt too dim to understand. He was convinced he would make the wrong move and be made out a fool. And so he had accepted the draw, finishing in a tie for third with Timman of Holland. Hosnik-Schiller had ended abruptly, in an ambiguous position, but his share of third was worth five hundred dollars.

Hosnik's clear first was worth five thousand.

"To me, the factors cancelled out," Randy told her. "I couldn't win. Neither could he." He brushed past her and pulled some clothes from his suitcase.

"Okay, we'll come back to that when we can sit down at a board somewhere," Andrea said as Randy returned to the bathroom. "Let me ask you a few questions about your grandfather—"

"Uh, if you'll excuse me a moment," Randy said, trying to close the bathroom door. Andrea was still standing in the doorway. She looked up from her notes. "I mean," he said, "unless you'd like to come in here and help."

"That depends," she told him, folding her arms. "You got any more tattoos?"

"Want to find out?"

Randy was almost able to count to five while Andrea studied her watch. "Twenty minutes," she said, and smiled. Her eyes were pale green. "Better get those clothes on."

Been a long year, Randy thought, as he adjusted the conical wooden buttons on his cream-colored sweater. He knew how to dress; the fine, familiar textures made him feel in command. Randy ran a belt through his tan slacks and pulled dark brown loafers from a plastic bag. A year since he and Lena had split up. A year to think, even when he didn't want to.

Randy opened the door on the smell of still-hot roast beef. He tore into the sandwich Andrea handed him. There were tomatoes inside, but he was hungry. Andrea sat on the bed and crossed her left leg over her right. Her left foot began tapping a favorite rhythm, up, down, up-up-down. She had a good way of sitting, as if she could spring up, ready for anything. A thin silver chain emerged from behind her neck, dived over her collar bones, and disappeared beneath the topmost buttoned button of her blouse. He suddenly wanted to tell her of his relief when Hosnik offered the draw.

"Aren't you going to sit down?" she asked.

"Too nervous." He gave her the sandwich, pried the lid off the plastic mug, and gulped the coffee with pleasure. "Are you married?" he asked, handing her the mug and reclaiming his roast beef.

"Me? No, not anymore. Look, I'll ask, you answer...Are *you* married?"

Lena could never tell him straight out that she was upset about something. She would send him a sign instead—like putting slices of tomato in his sandwich. Randy wondered if he could politely ditch them. "Technically. My wife and I separated a year ago." He wolfed down another bite of sandwich. "If only you could play life on sixty-four squares..."

"Yes?"

He laughed. "I don't know. You know what Lasker wrote: 'On the chessboard lies and hypocrisy do not survive long.' Sounds like a better world to me."

"Sounds pretty predictable to me."

"Predictable? I've been playing this game since I was a kid, and I still don't know what's going to happen next."

"Obviously," Andrea said. She checked her watch. "Ten minutes. Eat up."

The first thing Randy saw when he walked into the Saltmarsh VFW hall was Wilhelm Steinitz, the world's first chess champion, talking on the pay phone in the corner. Steinitz, short and built like a top, had claimed before his death in 1900 that he had beaten God at chess; they had played by telephone. Randy had never seen Steinitz before. Steinitz surveyed him with eyes like trapdoors. Randy felt the air leaking away, and as his heart accelerated he wondered if it really was sleep or time off he needed or if he was actually heading around that bend to the place where so many of the great chess masters had gone, the place where you talked to God and howled at the moon.

But then a wide man in a gray suit with leather patches at the elbows grabbed his hand and compressed it hard enough to produce coal. "Joseph E. Petrillo," he boomed, "president of the club! Call me Joe. This is an honor, a real honor. Rudolph Schiller, in our club!"

"Randy," Randy said, struggling to wake in the grip of this giant. Andrea came and took his coat. "That's *Randy* Schiller."

"Folks, we'll be starting in just a few minutes," Joe announced to the room at large, his voice able to get the job done without amplification. The long wooden building, a ranch-style house with the interior walls removed to form a large hall, was probably as full tonight as the fire marshall allowed. People clustered around the coffee machines and the plates of jelly doughnuts and yellow pound cake at the far end of the room; or around the twenty who had paid to take a board against Randy; or milled about, chatting, reading the notices for auctions and bake sales on the bulletin board. "Will the players please take their seats?" To Randy, Joe said, "Randy, yes. Hah! I knew that. This is such an honor, I can't tell you. Now, if you'd just stand over there—thanks. I just can't tell you!"

As he had done a thousand times, in VFW halls and civic auditoriums and church basements all over the country, Randy walked into the long, wide aisle between the two tables set with games. He was home. If the space he stood in had been a robe, it would have been purple, and he would have swung it around his shoulders without hesitation.

"Ladies and gentlemen," Joe began, reading from a stack of blue note cards that he held as if he expected them to fly away. "I am Joseph E. Petrillo, president of the Saltmarsh Chess Club, and I welcome you to an evening with International Master Rudolph—*Randolph* Schiller!"

They applauded. Randy nodded. The Master waved. A man in a dirty trench coat and a badly blocked fedora, a man who had been a cliché of style for so long that he was almost back in style, exploded a flash bulb in front of them.

"Not now, Frank," Andrea said. "We'll need pictures when he's playing, not when he's standing around."

"Mr. Schiller," Joe boomed, shuffling his cards, "finished in a tie for third this past week at the Boston Invitational. He also finished third earlier this year at Barcelona, fourth at Milan two years ago, and he has contended a number of times for the national championship." The spectators applauded. The players watched Randy the way mice watch a cat—or tried not to, fiddling instead with the chessmen, trying to center each one exactly on its square.

"Mr. Schiller is, of course, the grandson of *Rudolph* Schiller, the Austrian-American master who rose to prominence in the last century. Rudolph Schiller is best remembered for his many battles with Steinitz, Zukertort, Blackburne, and the other giants of that era, and for his first-place finish at the legendary Paris Chess Congress of 1888. It's been said that Rudolph Schiller was capable of a good game right to the end—*and* he lived to be 106 years old."

"Cut to the chase, Joe," Andrea whispered.

"Yes, yes," Joe said. "The rules for this evening's exhibition of simultaneous play are simple. Ten of you have White and ten have Black, in alternating sequence. Mr. Schiller will move from board to board and play his move. You can respond while he is at your board or while he is away, but you must move before he returns. If you need more time you can pass; you can pass three times, but then you'd better move something."

"Yeah," someone called from the back of the room, "just start takin' stuff." Everyone not sitting at a chessboard laughed, even Steinitz, who was still on the phone.

"Yes, well," Joe said. "Are you ready, Mr. Schiller?"

"Please."

Joe waved his hand as if to confer a blessing, then took his station at the head of one table, behind a set of Black pieces. Randy began with him, moving the White king pawn ahead two squares. Joe nodded vigorously and began biting a fingernail. Randy moved to the next board, where a young woman with short orange-red hair standing up like a brush had already deployed her king knight. A green Eiffel Tower dangled from her left ear. Randy sent his queen pawn to the center of the board.

His next six opponents were grade-school students, four boys and two girls. Two of the boys were done up in sport coats and ties, two in camouflage shirts and pants; one girl wore a plaid party dress with a white collar and ruffled cuffs, the other black tights and a pink sweater upon which white horses raced. Andrea stood proudly behind them. "They're from the club I run at the grade school," she told him. She put her hands on the shoulders of a serious-looking little boy who kept pulling on the knot of his bright red tie. "This is Ethan. He's mine."

"*Mom*," Ethan said, appalled at his mother's acknowledgment of their relationship.

"Good luck," Randy said to Ethan.

"Go ahead, move," Ethan told him. Randy pushed pawns on all six boards.

Following the children was a man in a high school letter jacket and a flat cap that made him look like a cab driver, and an older man in a brown suit that hung on his frame, a wide gray tie decorated with a flamingo descending from his collar. More routine opening moves.

At the end of the row Randy faced a kid with acne and an attitude of silent, self-assured contempt. He was encased in an enormous white sweatshirt that said MUSCLE BEACH in black letters in a circle over his heart. Slumped in his chair, he was reading page one of *The Scarlet Letter*—the comic-book version. He had the White pieces, and his king pawn was already sitting in the middle of the board. Randy parried on the flank, placing his queen bishop pawn on the fourth rank. The first two moves of the Sicilian Defense—a common beginning. He turned to the other table. Most of the spectators stood behind their friends or relatives who were playing, the way the villagers stood behind their champions in centuries past; but a few shifted to the other side of the room when Randy did, trying to keep up with the action.

Andrea was sitting behind the Black pieces at the first board on the other table. "Do you run this town?" Randy asked her.

"Go ahead, move," she said. She had the chain out of her blouse and was twisting it in her fingers; a tiny silver knight, with a finely sculpted mane, hung from it. Randy pushed his king pawn and winked at her. Andrea raised an eyebrow and made a note on her pad.

The rest of the players, all adults, looked like they could be holding down any kind of job. By the time Randy returned to Joe, the president of the club had thoroughly pondered the position and advanced his own king pawn two squares. Randy added his queen pawn to the pileup in the center; Joe started on a second fingernail. On the next board the young woman with the Eiffel Tower earring, not bothering with standard lines of play, had returned her knight to its starting point. Andrea was back behind her kids again, one of whom had made a solid positional move, posting her bishop on a good square. Ethan and the rest were making the ferocious moves typical of the very young, with no thought to defense. The cabbie and the man with the flamingo tie knew what they were doing.

The kid in the Muscle Beach shirt was still buried in *The Scarlet Letter*. Randy had planned to steer the game into one of the subvariations of the Sicilian he could play in his sleep, but Muscle Beach had his own plans. He had counterattacked, advancing his queen knight pawn two squares, offering it free to Black's pawn. Randy's outstretched hand fell back as he recognized the Wing Gambit to the Sicilian.

Another flash bulb exploded. "Wait till he makes a move, Frank," Andrea hissed.

In 1888, in Paris, the spit-in-the-wind Schiller had surprised the technician Steinitz with the Wing Gambit, this unexpected sacrifice of a pawn, and had gained an advantage sufficient to knock the champion off the board in nineteen moves. The gambit was the Master's main contribution to opening theory. A century of analysis had shown that the line failed against careful play; but in the Master's day, the game's age of exploration, knowledge had counted for less than nerve. The Wing Gambit had disappeared from the repertoire of the serious player by the Second World War. Several people edged closer, curious to see what had stalled the visiting hotshot in his march around the boards.

"Unsound," Randy blurted.

The kid looked at him.

Randy knew his face was red. "The Wing Gambit. I mean, it's been busted for decades."

The kid shrugged and flipped another four-color page in *The Scarlet Letter*. Randy shook his head and took White's pawn, the dark and light squares momentarily indistinguishable as Frank snapped another picture.

Andrea had also hit Randy with a gambit, attacking his king pawn with her queen pawn in the opening blast of the Center Counter Game. "This is a perfectly good opening," she warned him. "Don't you tell me any different." He took her pawn without a wink or a comment.

He went down the boards. He saw queens take the field too soon, knights sent forth on senseless charges, pawns pushed for no apparent reason, and the occasional good move. "Yes," he said, when he saw one of the latter. He saw beams of power leap from his pieces, the way the Master had taught him to see when he was still learning to talk: shooting from the squat, stubborn rooks vertically and horizontally, from the slim, sure-footed bishops diagonally, from the all-powerful queens in a combination of both.

Muscle Beach played his rook pawn up and Randy captured that one, too. The kid immediately recaptured with his knight—they played so quickly at that age—and then it was back to Hawthorne's sinful New England. Randy considered for a moment, then pushed his queen pawn ahead one square; better to consolidate rather than spread too far too fast. He remembered how it had been when he was in high school (he was sure he had been better-dressed), when combinations and positional moves, tactics and strategies simply popped to the surface of his brain without his having to dive in after them. When there was nothing else to dive in after; when chess was the only fish in the sea.

By his tenth circuit of the boards, Randy had most of the games going the way he wanted. He had scored one victory, against one of the grade-school boys, who kept his neighbors amused by tipping his "horses" to "give them a drink" from the rooks. He knew whom he had to watch: the cabbie, who was determined to bog them down in trench warfare; Flamingo Tie, who was playing inspired defense; and Andrea, who was not afraid to push him. This is *my* board she declared through her sniping bishops and impatient knights; no, *mine*, he told her with his expanding perimeter of pawns.

And Muscle Beach, who had read his chess books. When they both castled their kings to safety on the ninth move, they had duplicated the first nine moves of Schiller-Steinitz 1888. However buoyant he felt after leaving Andrea, he felt heavy and oppressed by the time he returned to the kid. Their game, out here in the limboland of amateur chess, meant nothing; no master would ever ponder these moves; it would have no effect on his international rating. But he was playing against his grandfather's opening, and even as he pushed pieces on other boards, in one clear corner of his mind he was picking at this game, wondering if he should have stayed "in the book" for this many moves, if he shouldn't have done something startling a move or two ago, as startling as the Wing Gambit itself had been when the Master unveiled it. He imagined the Master and Steinitz at their board in the main gaming room of the Café de la Regence, the air equal parts tobacco and excitement, "check" and "checkmate" the only words the rivals would surrender to each other.

By his fifteenth circuit—and the one-hour mark—he had won three more games: one against the little girl in the dress, who clapped before each move; one against a man in an expensive suit cut too tight at the waist, who asked Randy to autograph his score sheet and then waved it to a roomful of good-natured hurrahs; and one against Joe, who, unnerved when Randy's rook broke through his lines, countered by blundering away his queen.

Flamingo Tie had not been able to stop Randy from posting a knight on the fifth rank, an unblinking lighthouse that exposed and restricted movement. The cabbie had as yet shown no weakness. He was like a turtle; Randy would have to flip him over. On Andrea's board, Randy had let his queen waltz across the board, drawing his opponent's attention, while behind the lines his rooks waited for the call to deliver the real checkmate.

Muscle Beach was only on page three of his comic book. Either Hawthorne was more difficult than Randy remembered or his opponent was a bit more distracted than he cared to show. Behind the kid, the Master took from his pocket a cigar like a pipe bomb. A White knight had leapfrogged onto Randy's half of the board; its power washed Randy's queen in a hungry glow. This was the pivotal move in "Schiller's Gold," the fiery game in which Schiller, the disciple of the old school, the romantic who attacked and never looked back, had beaten Steinitz, the founder of the modern school, the precision man who weighed every plus and minus. Steinitz, with his receding hair and his shiny forehead like the Dome of the Rock, stood at Randy's side. Steinitz had lost only once to Rudolph Schiller, but whenever he referred to the game in his chess magazine, it was always as "Schiller's Cheat." Neither man would have won points for personality.

Analysts had shown that the Master's knight sacrifice was daring, elegant, and wrong, wrong, wrong. In 1888 Steinitz had done the obvious thing, capturing the knight with his pawn; that had cleared the king file and given the Master too much leverage for his attack. Randy knew he had only to retreat the queen and all would be well. He stared at the board, but the chessmen, oddly turned bits of plastic scattered across a field of squares, made no sense to him. The Master, arms crossed, took the first puff of his cigar.

"Excuse me," Randy said.

The men's room was unheated and smelled of disinfectant. The faucets dribbled a little water into the chipped porcelain of the basin; the water was cold, calming. "Why must you live like this," Lena had asked him. "Always trying to beat a dead man!" Randy wiped his face with some paper towels. He was never going to finish first at the Paris Chess Congress of 1888. He was never going to match the Master's status. Who could? There were two hundred masters then, there were thousands now. Chess players would remember his name only because it was his grandfather's. Live like this? What else was he supposed to do? When he wouldn't even consider alternatives, Lena said goodbye.

As he stepped from the men's room he saw Steinitz back at the phone. Steinitz held the receiver in his hand. He was holding it out to Randy. Randy suddenly knew that being afraid to move this piece or not move that one was nothing; trying to get a word out of his demon grandfather was nothing; now he could just get on that phone and ask, "Are you watching this game? How am I doing?" Steinitz walked toward him, the phone cord stretching to infinity.

And then someone grabbed his hand and asked him, "What do I do?" It was Ethan. "How do I get out of check?"

Andrea put her hands on Ethan's shoulders; he squirmed out from under her but still held Randy's hand. "At the chess club in school," she explained, "when they have a problem, they're supposed to ask an adult for help."

"Let's get back to the exhibition," Joe scolded. "Ethan can't ask for help—they're in the middle of a game!"

"That's okay," Randy said, Ethan's hand in his a connection with the things of this world. An exploding flash bulb froze them, Andrea, Ethan, Joe, Randy, the telephone. "*Frank*," Andrea said. People laughed. "Let's see the position," Randy said.

On Ethan's board, Randy's rook was closing in on the boy's king. King and rook versus king—the simplest checkmate, the one you learned when an adult or an older kid in the neighborhood trapped your unprotected king on the back rank. After the game they explained it to you, or maybe they didn't. Maybe you had a grandfather who expected you to do your own thinking, who mowed down your armies and ignored your tears. Your grandfather was a bastard, but he taught you to think. Randy addressed the children. He knew the people gathered around would enjoy this and remember it. "There are three ways to defend your king from check," he began. "Who can tell me one way?"

"Take the piece!" one of the girls said.

"Take the piece that has you in check. Correct. Who can tell me another?"

"Well," said the boy who had made sure his horses had had

enough to drink, "you could put one of your guys between you and the other guy."

"Block the check. Good. And the third way?"

"Move the king!" the children said. "Get out of there!"

"Oh, okay," Ethan said. He waved at Randy. "Go away, I've got it now."

Muscle Beach was waiting for Randy to move. His knight still sat in the middle of Randy's camp. The Master stood in an atmosphere of cigar smoke, an elongated tobacco planet. Retreat the queen. The gambit was just a curio now; retreat, and Randy could keep the advantage of the gambit pawn. Retreat, and they'd be out of "Schiller's Gold," making their own moves. Retreat.

And with nothing to go on except sudden, encompassing anger, Randy ignored the attack on his queen and swooped down the long diagonal with his queen bishop. He removed the pawn that sat before the White king and banged his bishop down on that square. The crowd had been quiet; now those with more knowledge of chess started whispering. Muscle Beach closed his book and let it flutter to the floor. The Master was nodding his head. He had dropped his cigar, ground it into the linoleum floor, and *he was nodding his head*. Randy fled to Andrea.

By the end of an hour and a half Randy had won seventeen games. He had beaten all of Andrea's kids. He had beaten everyone at Andrea's table except Andrea. He had beaten Eiffel Tower, who had moved her knights around until he took them; she had then begun moving her bishops. The cabbie, reckless in a balanced position, had launched his queenside pawns in a premature attack. When he realized the consequences of his mistake, he had resigned, shaken hands quickly, and left the building with no words for anyone. Flamingo Tie, despite the knight at his throat, was holding on. Andrea was slipping, but slowly; she had a talent for creating complicated positions. This one looked as if the pieces had been dropped on the board from a height of two feet.

Muscle Beach was at last playing some original chess. He didn't panic when the bishop crashed into the line of pawns guarding his king; he proceeded with his plan and captured Randy's queen. Even Bobby Fischer would have had doubts in this position, but Randy was riding high on the euphoria that had burst upon him when he saw the bishop's light pour down the board. He moved his knight forward.

Andrea tipped her king two moves later. Her kids, gathered around her, protested: "Does that mean you lost?" "Move the pawn, Mrs. Leveque!" "Look, Mom, can't you just move your rook over?" "Quiet," Randy said. "Good game, Andrea." He shook her hand, holding it a bit longer than was customary after most chess games.

At his game with Muscle Beach, he saw, not the Master, not Steinitz, just the sweet soft glow of victory. Even in this age of information, even though his solution had been an accident, it was still possible to discover something new. Randy almost laughed. A new way to crush the Wing Gambit—a gambit no one played for fear of being crushed. He brought up his rook. The kid could either throw his queen in the rook's path or submit to a barrage of checks on his king. Muscle Beach, playing it very straight, picked his comic book off the floor, smoothed the pages, and slipped it carefully into his back-pack. He stood, swung the pack onto his back, and, as if he had almost forgotten, reached over and tipped his king.

"Do you want to go over the game?" Randy asked.

The kid looked at the pieces on the board, then at Randy. "Nah," he said, and left.

"Punk," Randy said.

Randy had begun a series of exchanges in the last game, the one with Flamingo Tie, hoping to deplete the available forces while maintaining the better position. His opponent had played a hell of a game. They each had a knight and five pawns, but Randy's pawns could support each other in any advance; his opponent's could not. He could see his rook pawn eventually breaking free, heading like a comet for the outer limits. Easy win. The Master patted the pockets of his long black coat, looking for another cigar. *He* wouldn't let a win like this get away. "Would you like a draw?" Randy asked.

Flamingo Tie beamed and extended his hand. "Yes!"

The spectators around Flamingo Tie applauded, and a white-haired man in electric-blue pants and a hat pinned with fishing lures slapped him on the back. "Quiet, quiet," Joe said, waving his arms. Randy took his opponent's score sheet and read the man's name. "Good game, Mr. Weinberg," he said. "That was courageous chess."

"Years ago," Weinberg said, "when I lived in New Haven, your grandfather gave an exhibition there. I played White against him. The English Opening."

"How'd you do?" Randy asked, signing his name.

Weinberg shrugged. "Oh, he beat me good."

Randy laughed and returned the score sheet. "Grandpa was a good player," he said. "I often think of him."

"You sure don't play like him," Weinberg said.

"No," Randy said, "I sure don't."

"Nineteen wins, one draw," Andrea said, shaking his hand, not letting it go. "What a headline this is going to make!"

"Thanks," he said. Andrea signaled Frank, and as the photographer raised his camera she raised Randy's hand. Randy stood serene in his arena, the winner and still champion.

The Contributors

CHRISTINA ADAM lives on a ranch on the west side of the Teton Mountain Range. Her story, "The Flying Red Horse," was co-winner of the *Crazyhorse* Prize in 1990. In 1991 she was awarded an Idaho Commission on the Arts Fellowship in literature and a residency at Centrum, in Port Townsend, Washington. She is currently finishing a novel.

LAURIE ALBERTS, who grew up in New England, received an MFA from the Iowa Writers' Workshop and now teaches at the University of New Mexico. She has traveled extensively in the Soviet Union as an exchange teacher, tour guide, and journalist. Her novel, *Tempting Fate*, was published by Houghton Mifflin in 1987. She has published stories in *Fiction International* and *Nimrod*, and won the 1988 Katherine Anne Porter Prize for Fiction.

JOHN ALSPAUGH's book of poetry *Everything Dark Is a Doorway* (Palimpsest Press) was nominated for the Pulitzer Prize. He has received endowments from the National Endowment for the Arts and the Virginia Commission for the Arts. Recently, he was awarded the *New Virginia Review* Prize for short fiction.

LESLEE BECKER has had stories in *The Atlantic, Iowa Review, New Letters, Nimrod*, and elsewhere. A former Wallace Stegner Writing Fellow and Jones Lecturer in Fiction at Stanford University, she is currently teaching at Colorado State University. This is her third appearance in *AF*.

STEVEN BRYAN BIELER's stories have appeared in *Asimov's*, *Clinton Street Quarterly*, and *Seattle Review*, and in the anthologies *Full Spectrum* and *New Dimensions*. A native of Massachusetts, he lives in Seattle where he is the copy editor for *Seattle Weekly*.

CAROLE L. GLICKFELD's collection, *Useful Gifts*, won the Flannery O'Connor Award for Short Fiction. A native New Yorker, she has won the Governor's Arts Award in Washington state where she is a free-lance writer and teaches at the University of Washington. She has been Writer-in-Residence at Interlochen Arts Academy and the University of Alaska and a Fellow of both the MacDowell Colony and the Bread Loaf Writers' Conference. Recipient of a 1991 NEA Fellowship, she is at work on a novel, *The Salt of Riches*.

EMILY HAMMOND has had work appear in *Crazyhorse*, *Fiction*, *Colorado Review*, and other magazines, as well as in the anthology *Henfield Prize Stories*. She has received awards from *Prism International* and the Henfield Foundation, and has won the Katherine Anne Porter Prize from *Nimrod*.

JOANNA HIGGINS' fiction has appeared in *MSS*, *Passages North*, *Prairie Schooner*, the *1985 PEN Short Fiction Collection*, and *The Best American Short Stories 1982*. She has recently had a collection accepted by Milkweed Editions (*Voyageur: A Novella and Stories*). A recipient of a Pennsylvania Council on the Arts Award as well as an NEA, she is currently at work on a new novel. She lives in the Endless Mountains of northeastern Pennsylvania with her husband.

VALERIE HOBBS teaches writing at the University of California, Santa Barbara. Her short fiction has appeared in literary and commercial magazines, and one story was selected for syndication by the PEN 1990 Fiction Project.

PERSIS KNOBBE is working on a collection called *The Morris Stories*, of which "Gathering" is one. She has studied violin and voice, and has written a play called *Enter Elijah*. She lives in Kentfield, California.

RAY DEAN MIZE was born and raised in the rural counties along the Illinois and Mississippi rivers. He studied literature at Oxford as a Rhodes Scholar and worked as a reporter in Colorado, Mississippi, and Washington, D.C. before settling down in Chicago. Though he has had a number of nonfiction works appear in national publications, "The Blooding" is his first published work of fiction.

BRIAN MOONEY was born in Massachusetts and currently resides in Seattle. He is at work on his fourth play and is collaborating on a series of books for young adults, *The Amazing School Days of Barrimore Brimble*.

JESSICA NEELY's fiction has appeared in *The Best American Stories 1986*, *New England Review and Bread Loaf Quarterly*, *Tendril*, and other magazines. She lives and teaches in Washington, D.C., where, with the assistance of a W. K. Rose Fellowship from Vassar College, she is completing a first novel.

CATHERINE SCHERER has published extensively since her first story appeared in *Chicago Review* in 1983. One of her stories, which appeared in *Ascent*, won an Illinois Arts Council Award in 1988. She lives in Chicago.

THALIA SELZ has won 24 grants and awards for her fiction. Her short stories have appeared in *Partisan Review*, *Antaeus*, *Chicago*, and in both *The Best American Short Stories* and *The O. Henry Awards* anthologies. She is Writer-in-Residence at Trinity College in Hartford, Connecticut.

NOELLE SICKELS has written a historical novel, *Walking West*, and a memoir about her mother, *What Was Hers*. Through a grant from the Cultural Affairs Department of the City of Los Angeles, she is editing *The Memory of All That: L.A.'s Backyard History*. She lives in Los Angeles with her husband and 12-year-old son.

JUDITH TEMPLE's stories have appeared in the *Sonora Review* and *Redbook*, and one will soon be published by *New England Review*. She lives in Tucson with her husband and two daughters, and teaches at Pima Community College and at the University of Arizona.

MARY TROY has published fiction in *Ascent*, *San José Studies*, and the *Ball State Forum*. She was a recipient of the John Gould Fletcher Award and currently teaches creative writing at Webster University and at Washington University. She lives in St. Louis.

The Editors

TOBIAS WOLFF, Guest Judge, has published a number of books, including the award-winning *The Barracks Thief, In the Garden of the North American Martyrs, Back in the World,* and *This Boy's Life: A Memoir.* He teaches at Syracuse University.

MICHAEL C. WHITE, Editor, has had work appear in *New Letters, Four Quarters, Mid-American Review, Redbook,* and other magazines, and has work forthcoming from *The Nebraska Review* and *Beloit Fiction Journal.* He teaches at Springfield College in Springfield, Massachusetts.

ALAN R. DAVIS, Associate Editor, grew up in Louisiana. His stories and articles have appeared in *The New York Times, The Quarterly,* and many other notable publications. A collection of his stories will be published by New Rivers Press. He teaches at Moorhead State University in Moorhead, Minnesota, where he lives with his wife Catherine and his children Sara and Dillon.